MR. WOLF'S CLASS

ARON NELS STEINKE

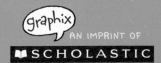
graphix
AN IMPRINT OF
SCHOLASTIC

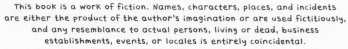

For Don and Alona

Library of Congress Control Number: 2017945601

ISBN 978-1-338-04769-1 (hardcover)
ISBN 978-1-338-04768-4 (paperback)

22 21 20 19 18 17   23 24 25

Printed in China   62
First edition, July 2018

Edited by Cassandra Pelham Fulton
Book design by Phil Falco
Creative Director: David Saylor

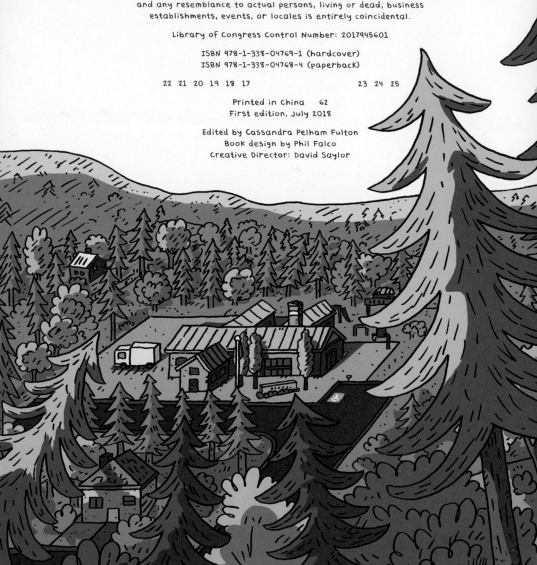

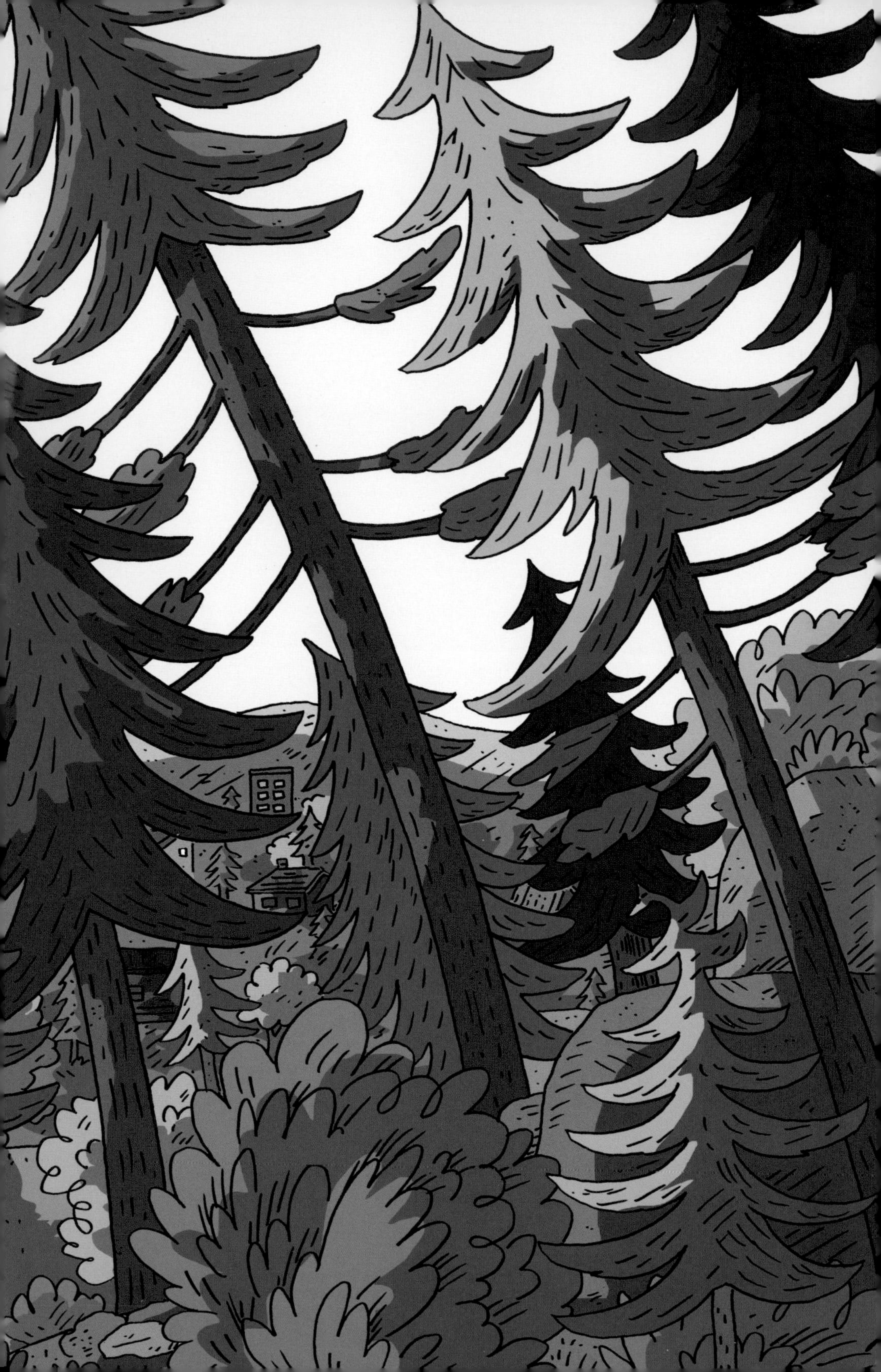

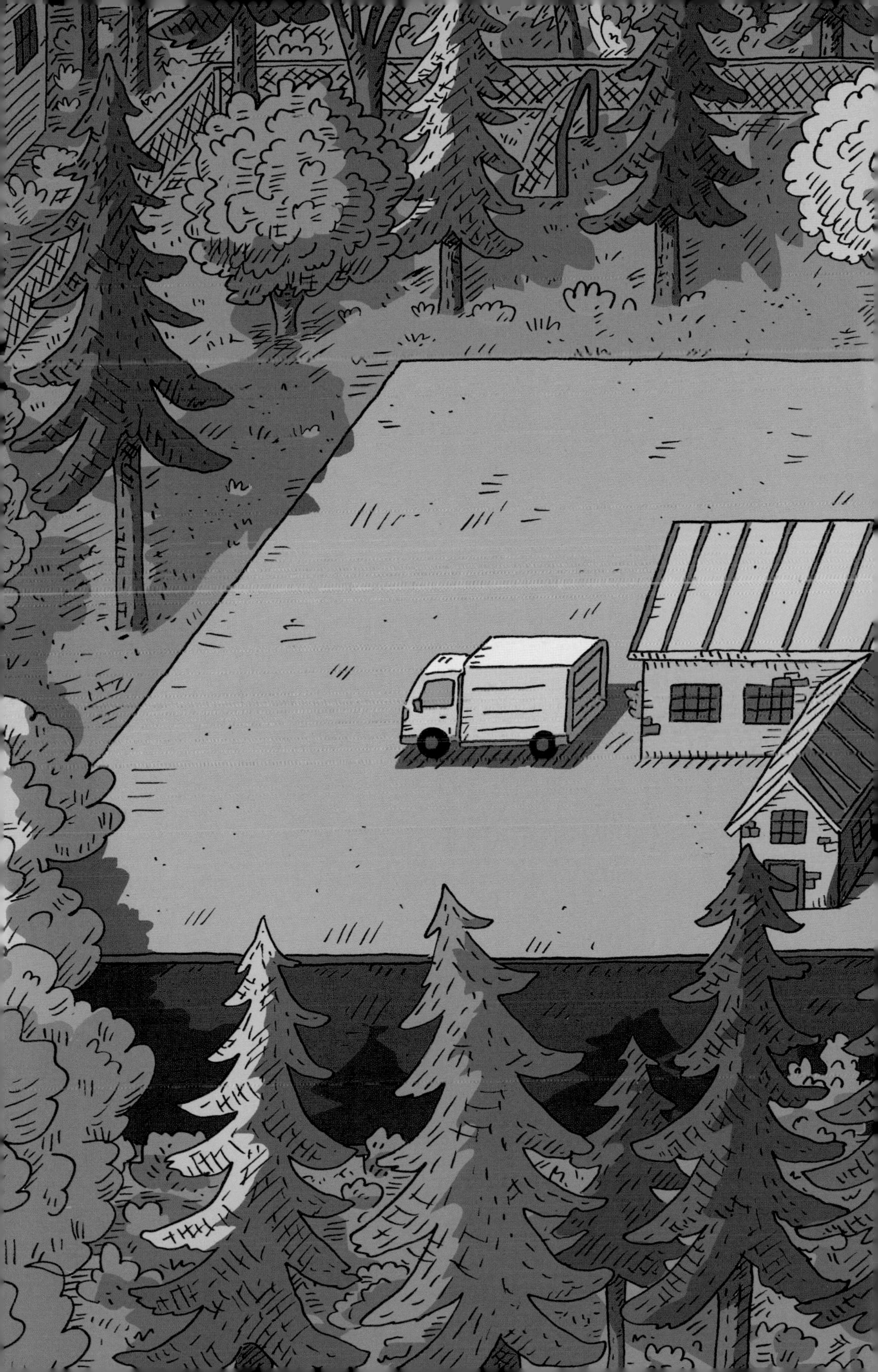

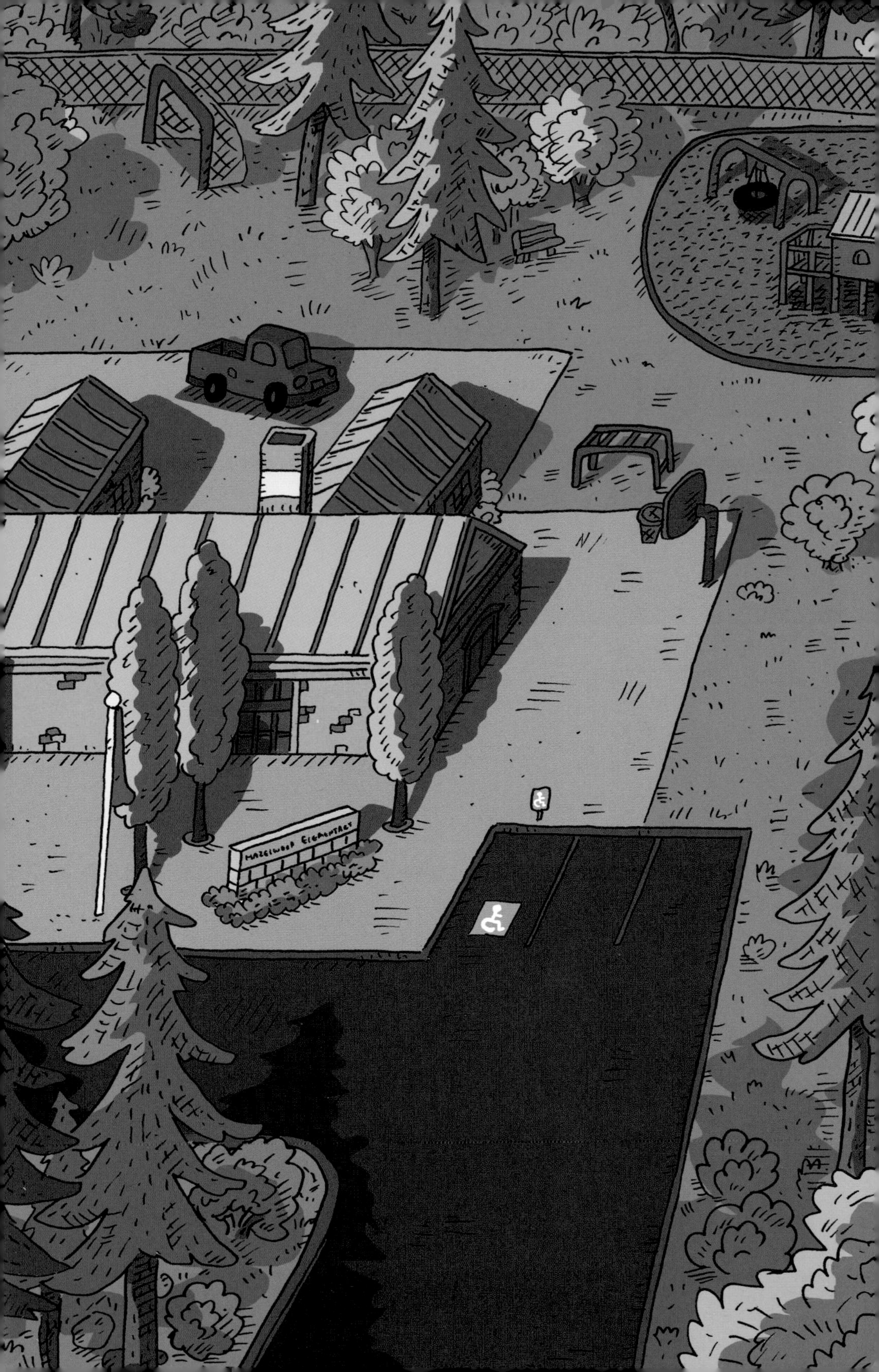
HAZELWOOD ELEMENTARY

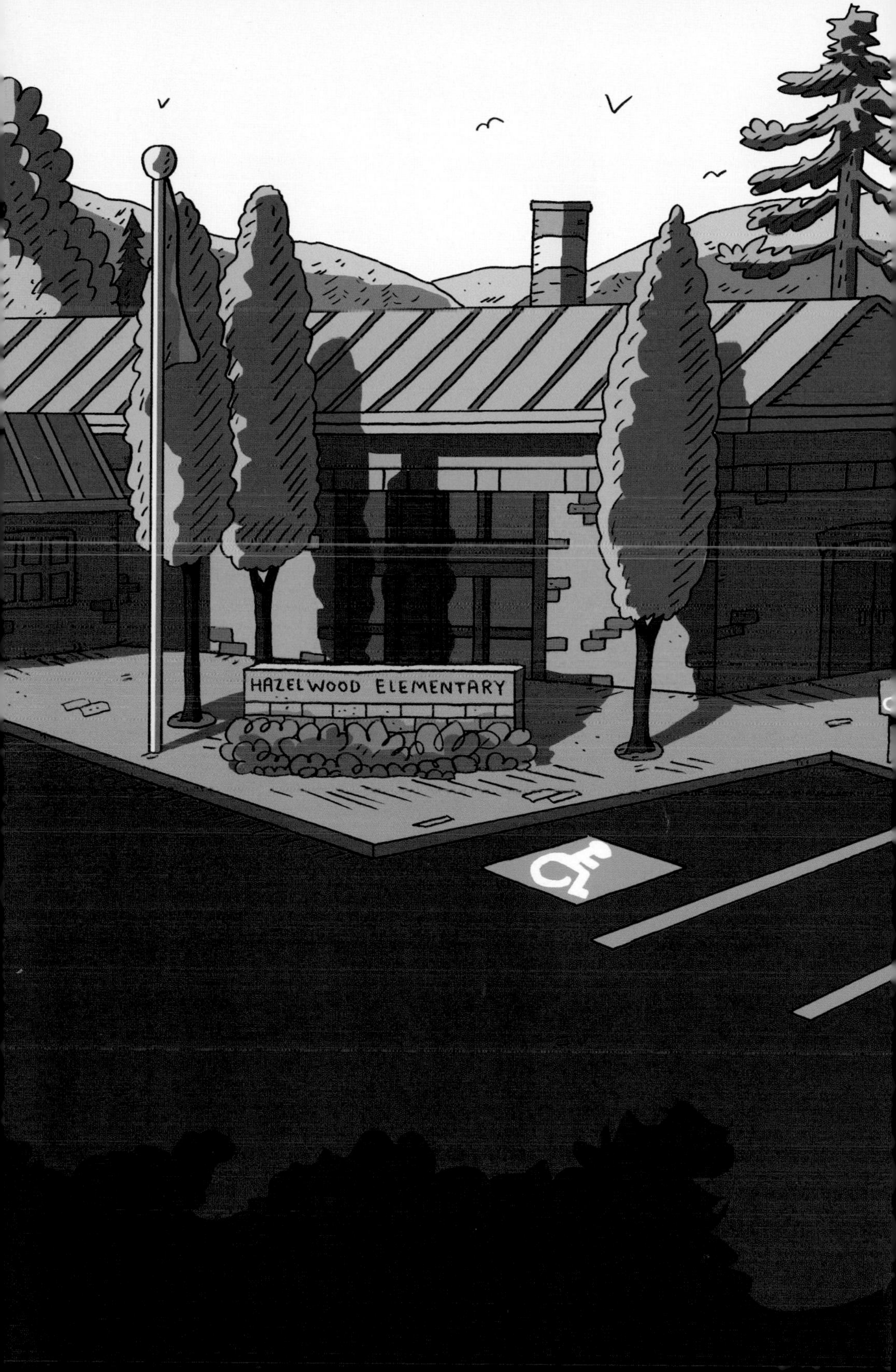
HAZELWOOD ELEMENTARY

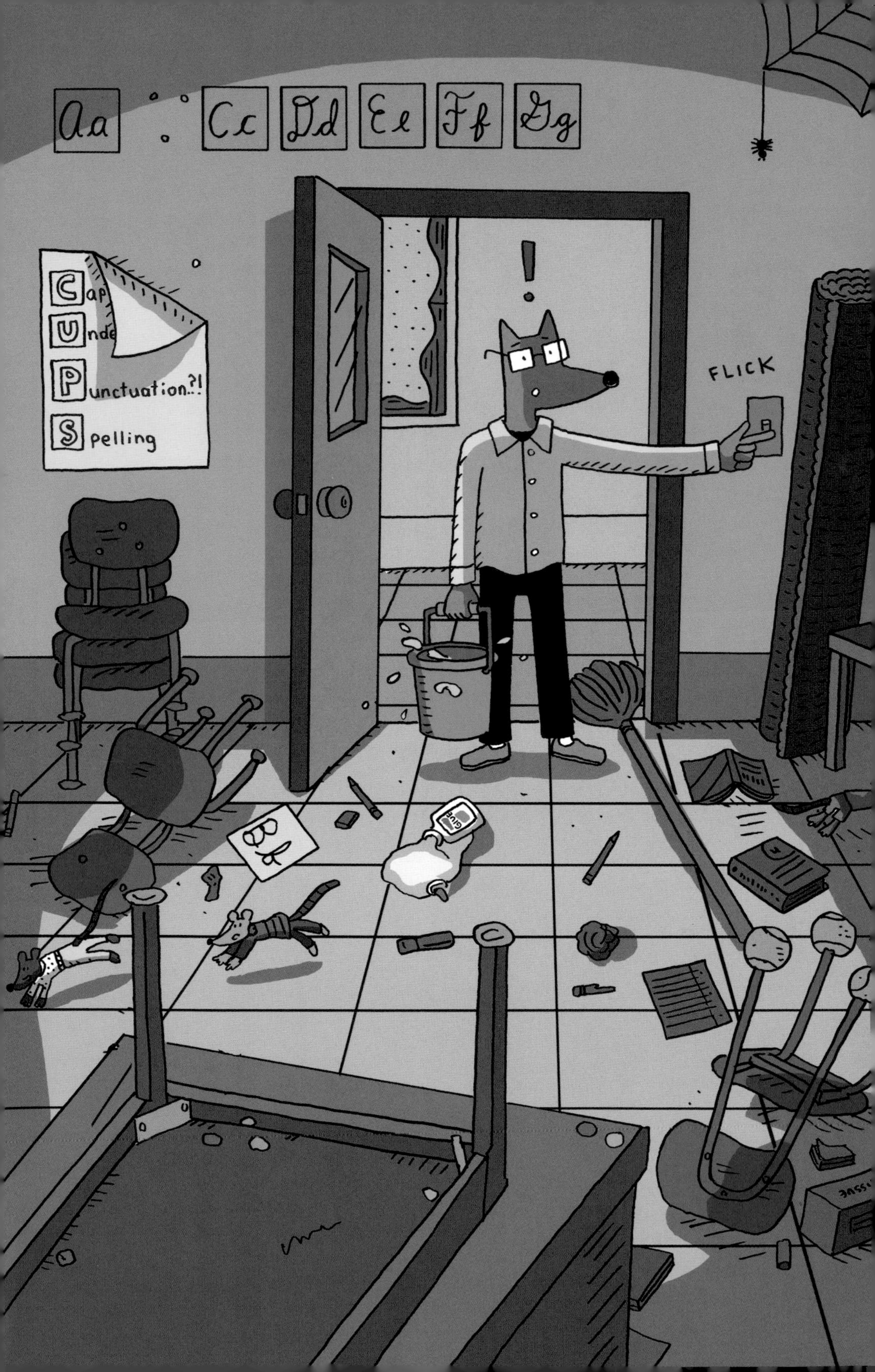
Aa Cc Dd Ee Ff Gg
Cap
Unde
Punctuation?!
Spelling
!
FLICK

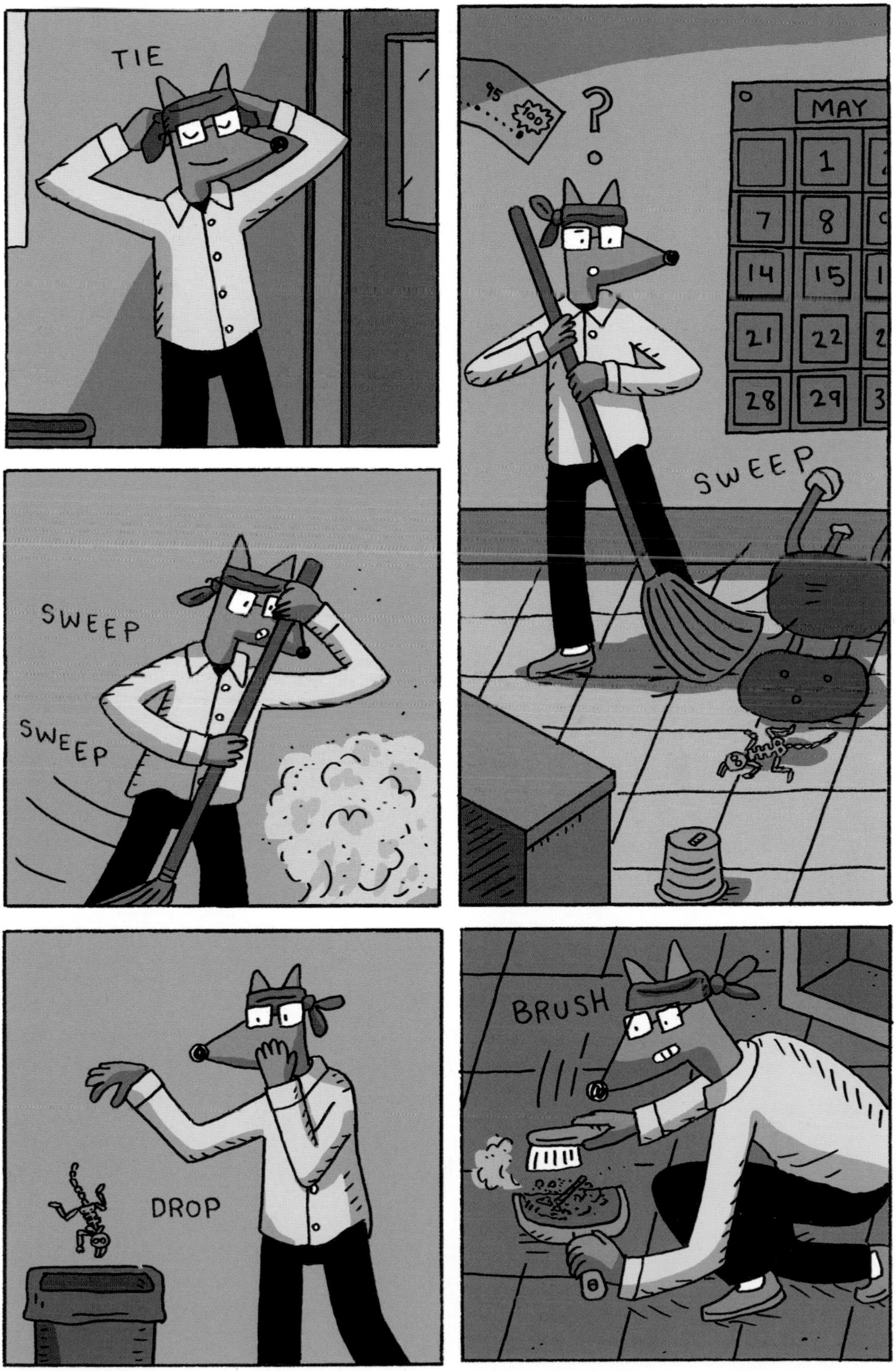
TIE
SWEEP
SWEEP
95
100
?
MAY
SWEEP
DROP
BRUSH

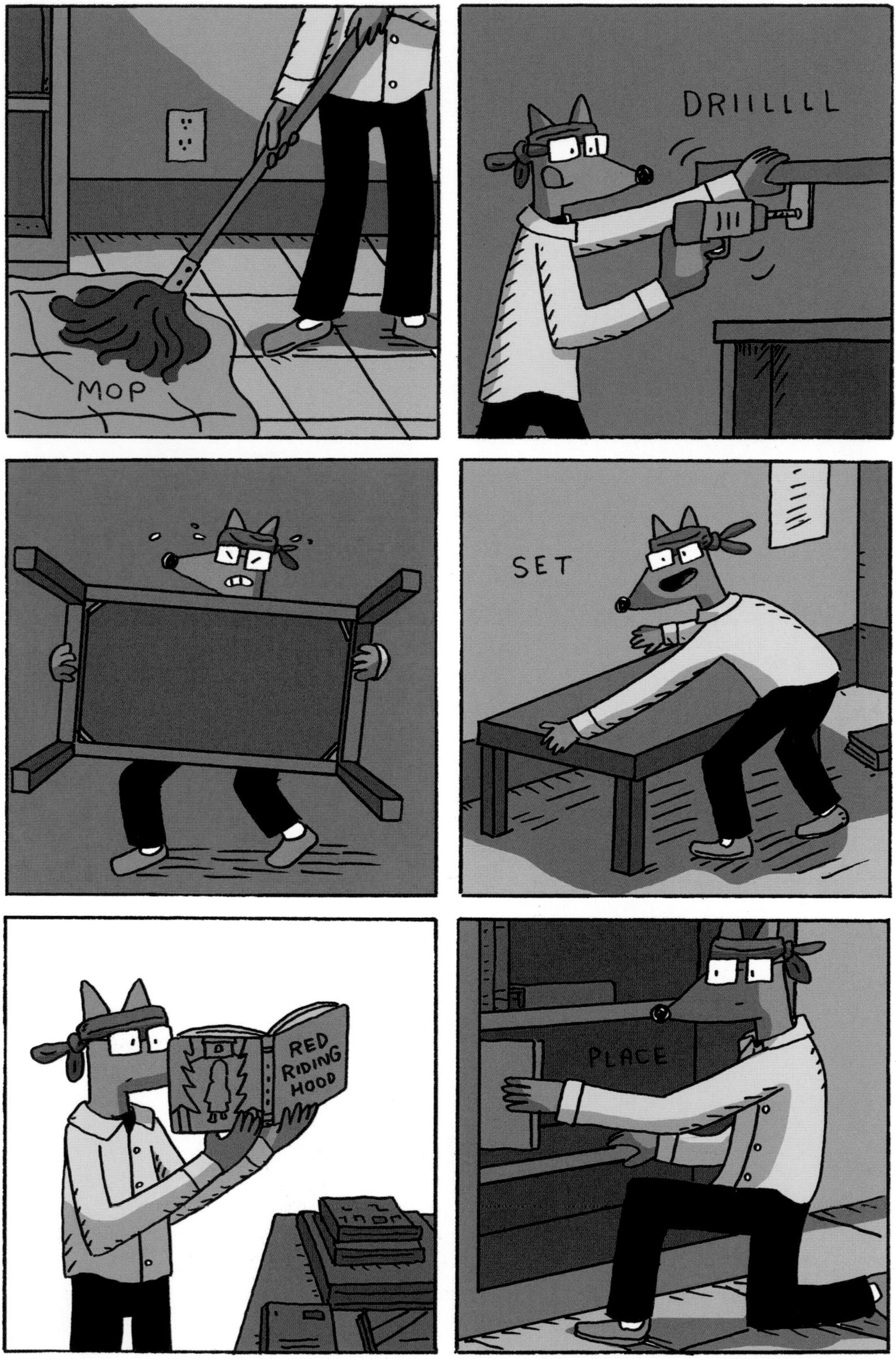
MOP
DRIIILLLL
SET
RED RIDING HOOD
PLACE

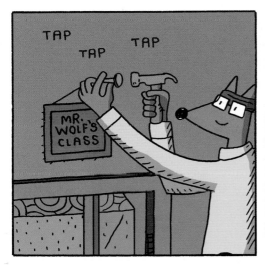

TAP TAP TAP

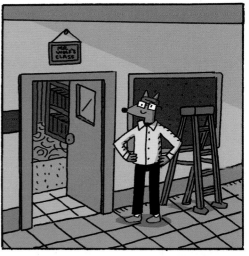

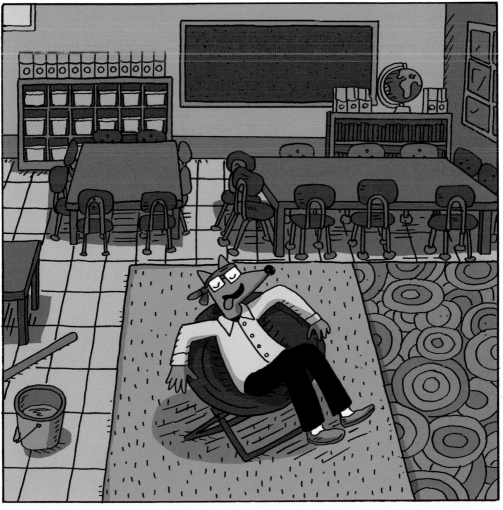

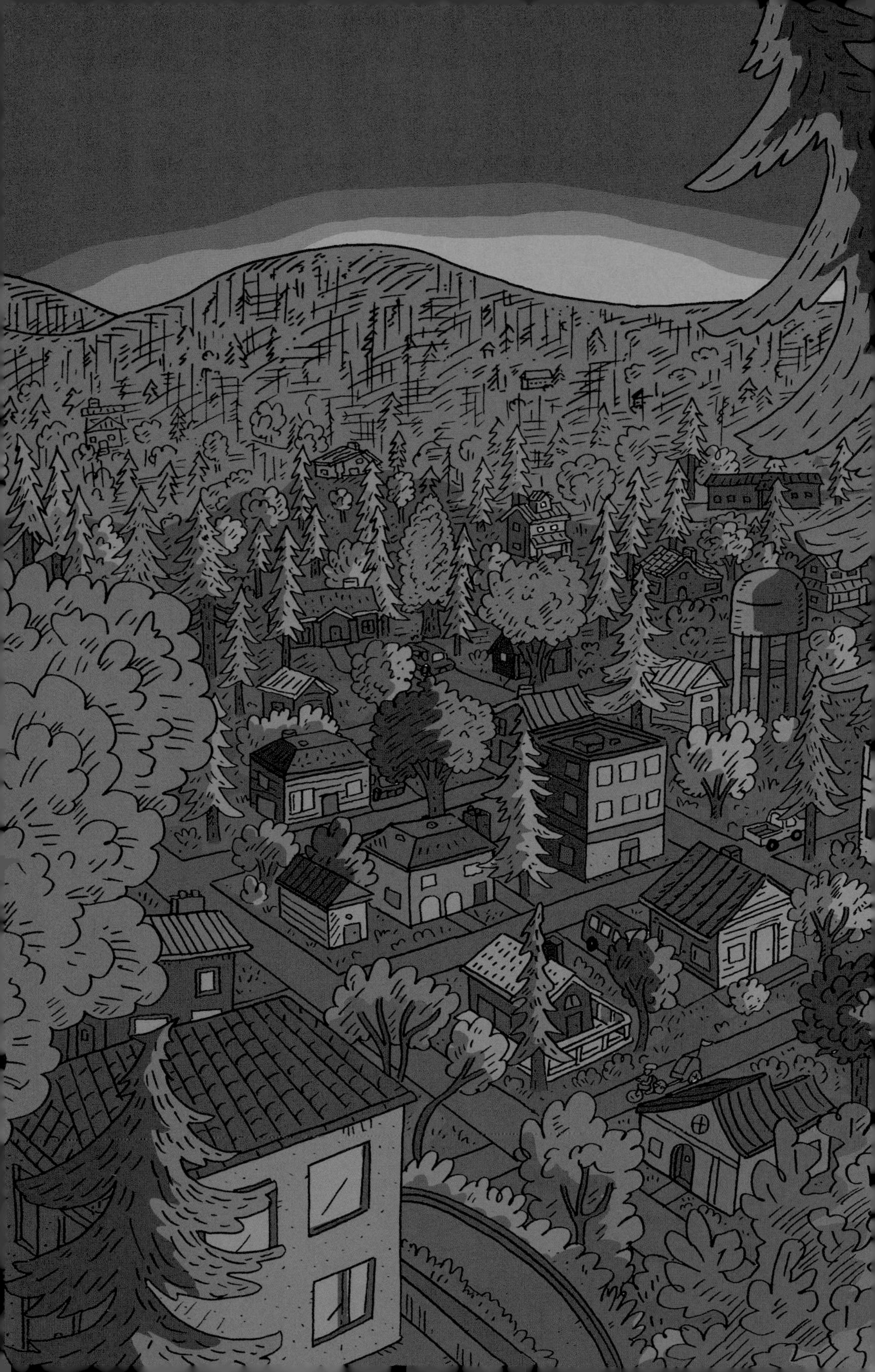

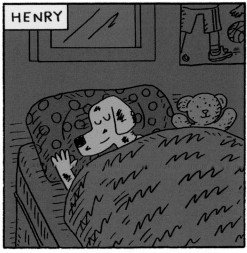

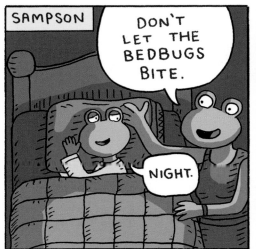

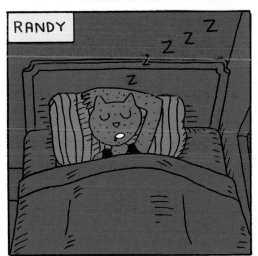

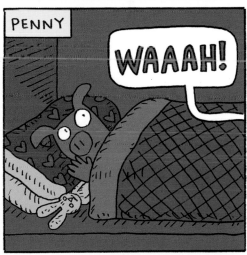

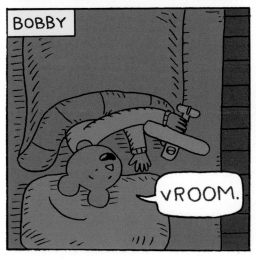

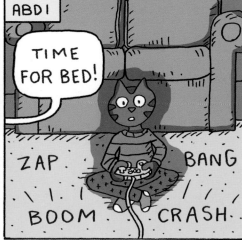

8

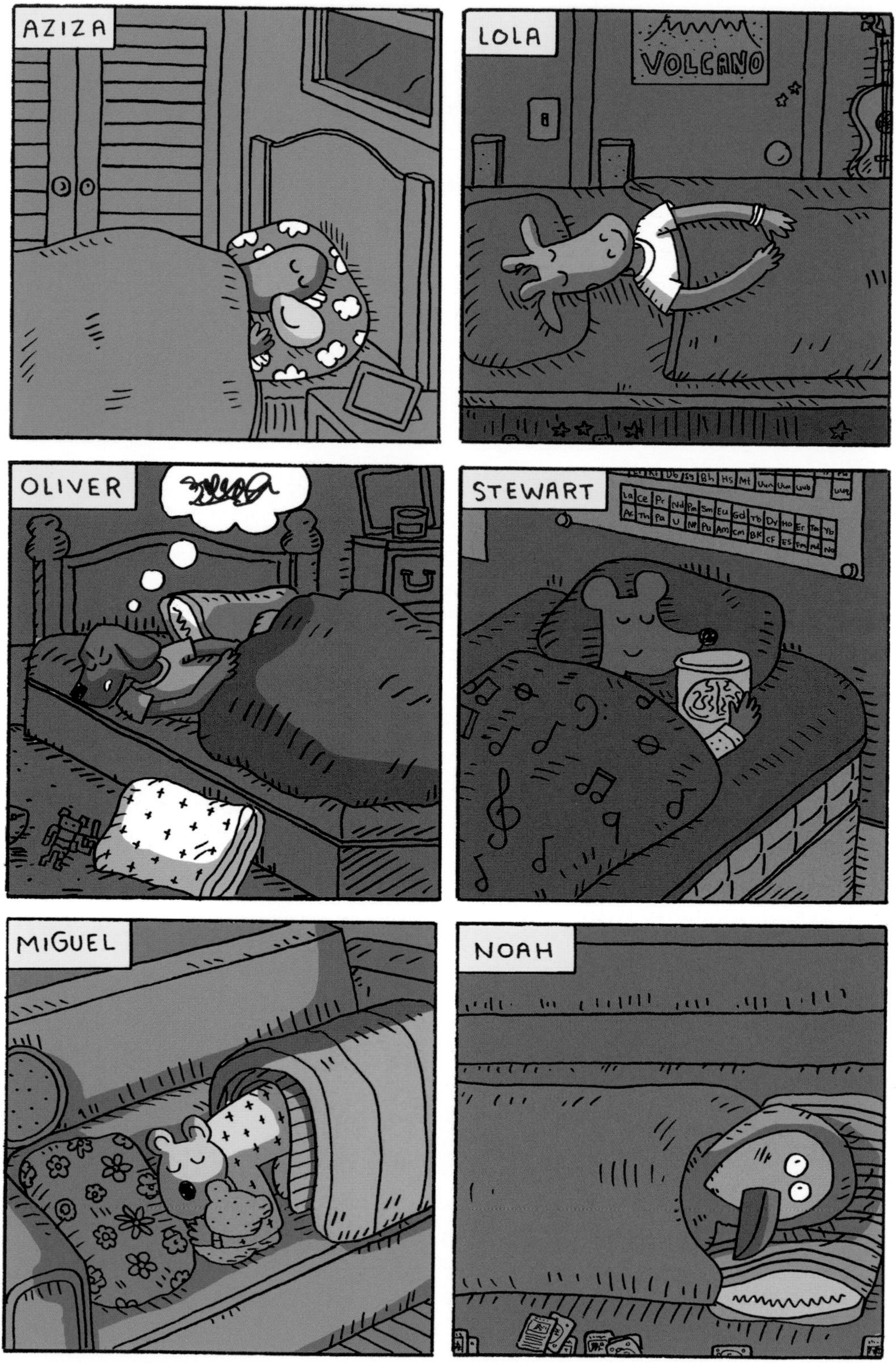
AZIZA
LOLA
VOLCANO
OLIVER
STEWART
MIGUEL
NOAH

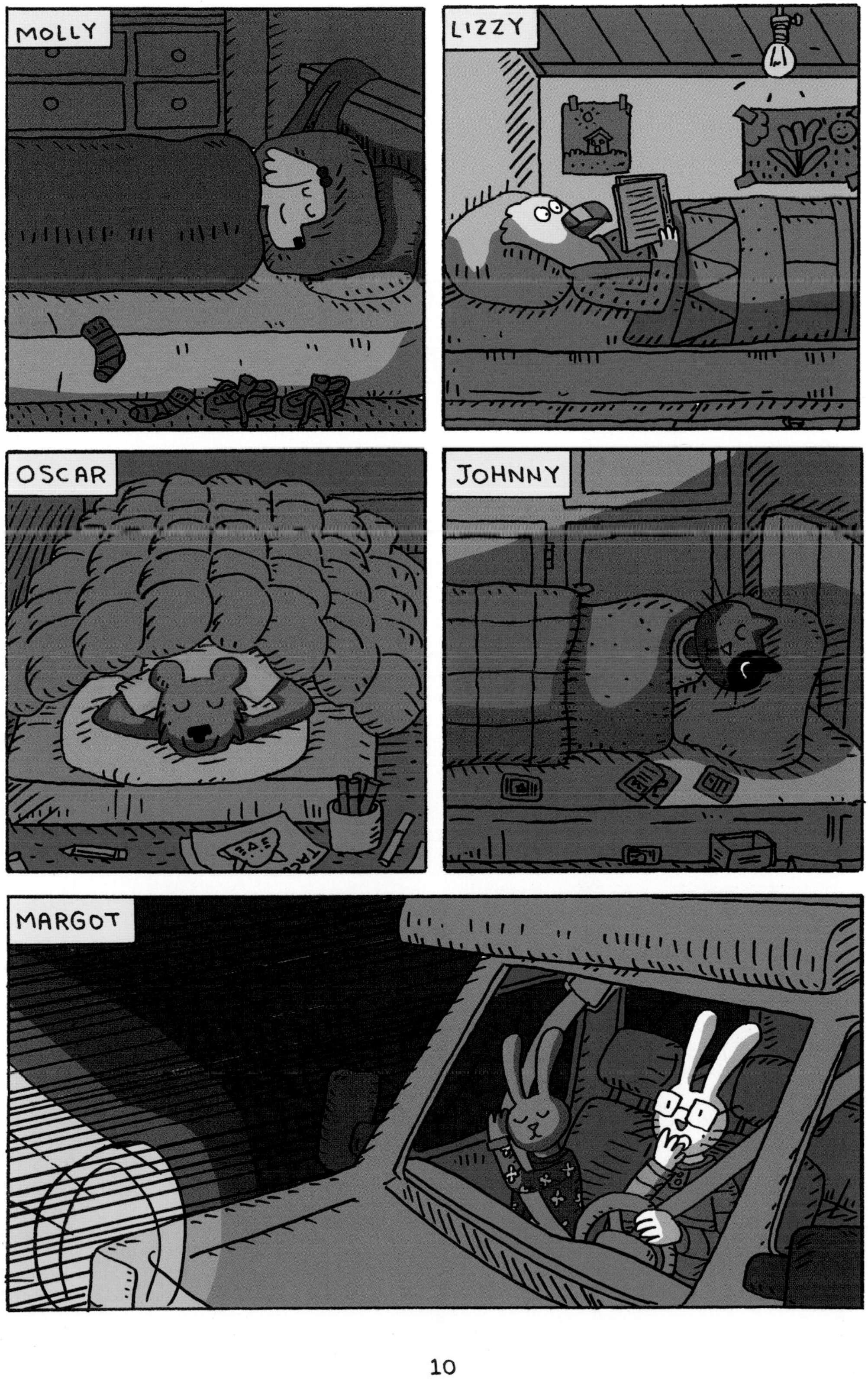
MOLLY
LIZZY
OSCAR
JOHNNY
MARGOT

CHAPTER ONE
Wake Up

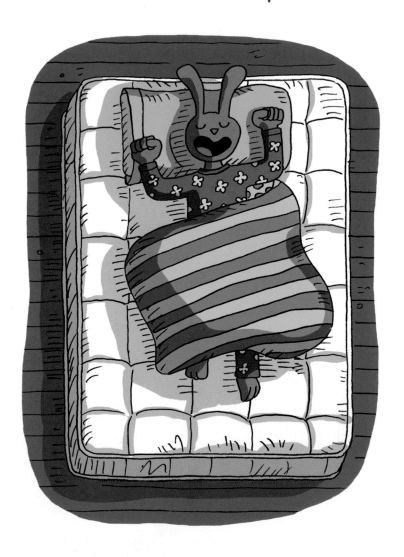

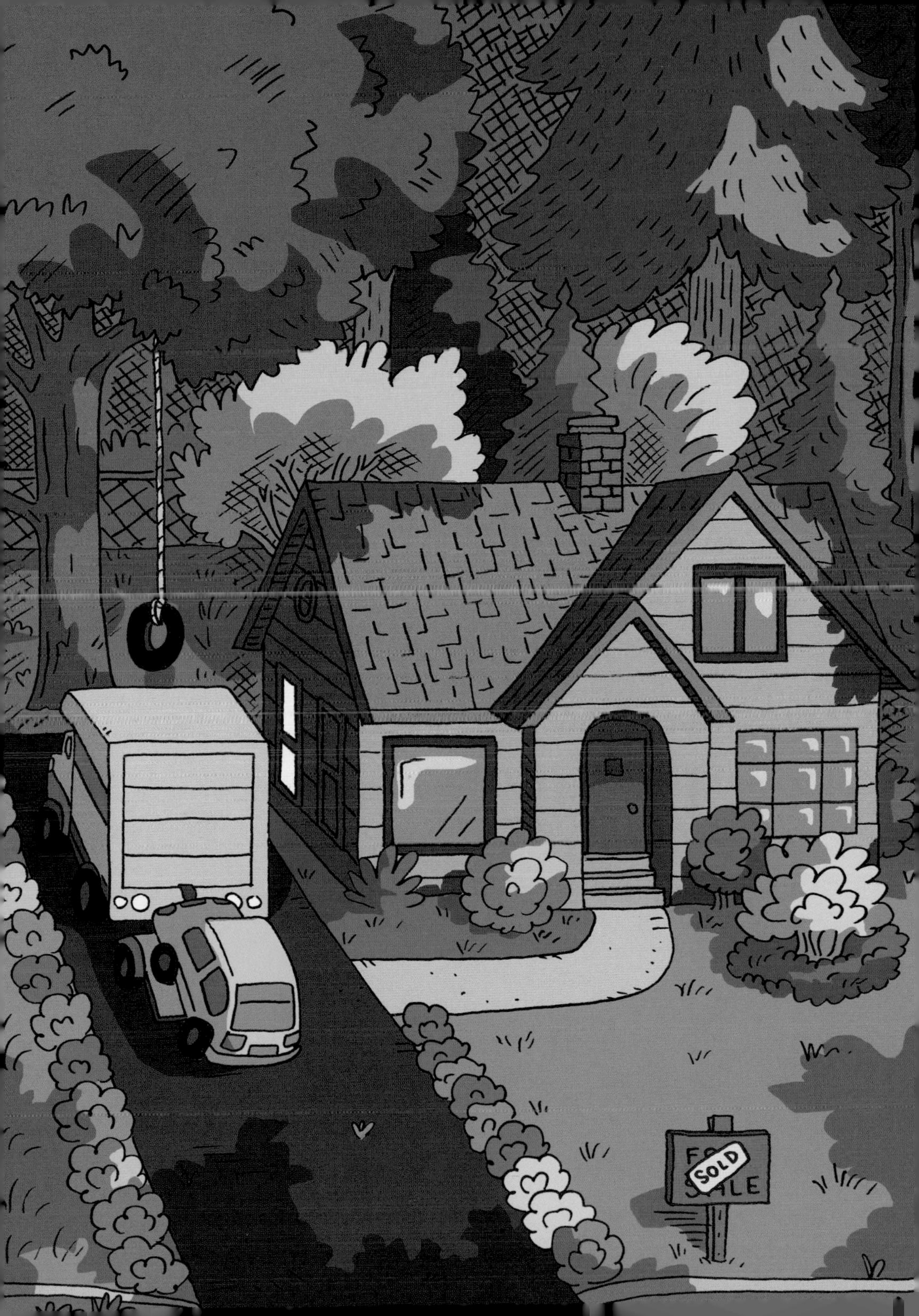
SOLD

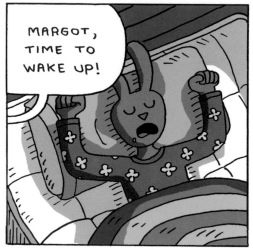

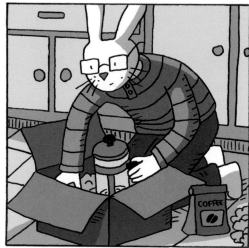

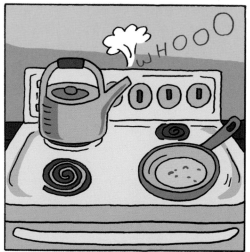

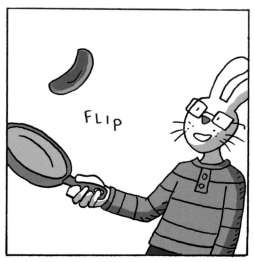

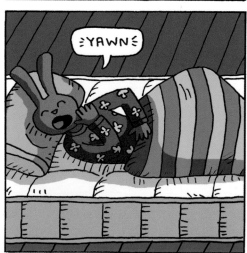

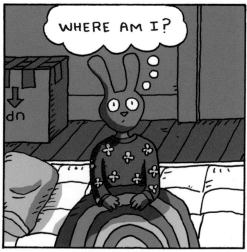

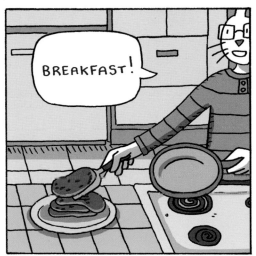

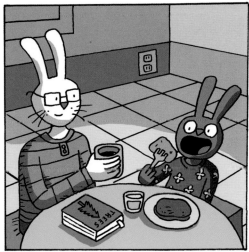

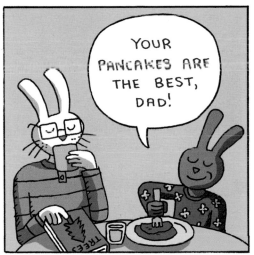

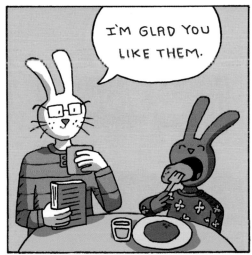

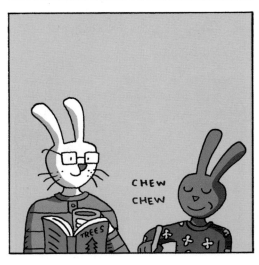

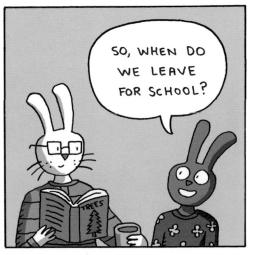

14

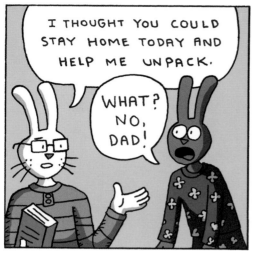

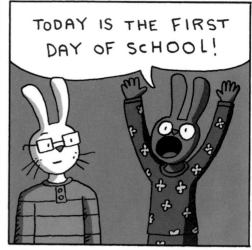

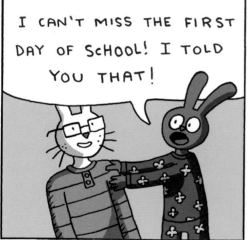

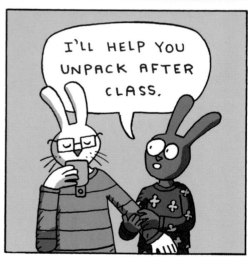

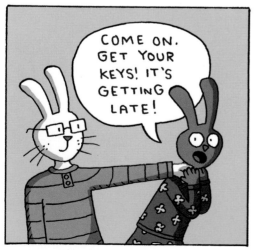

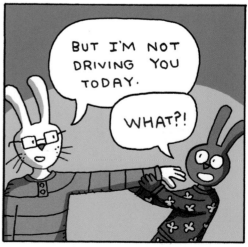

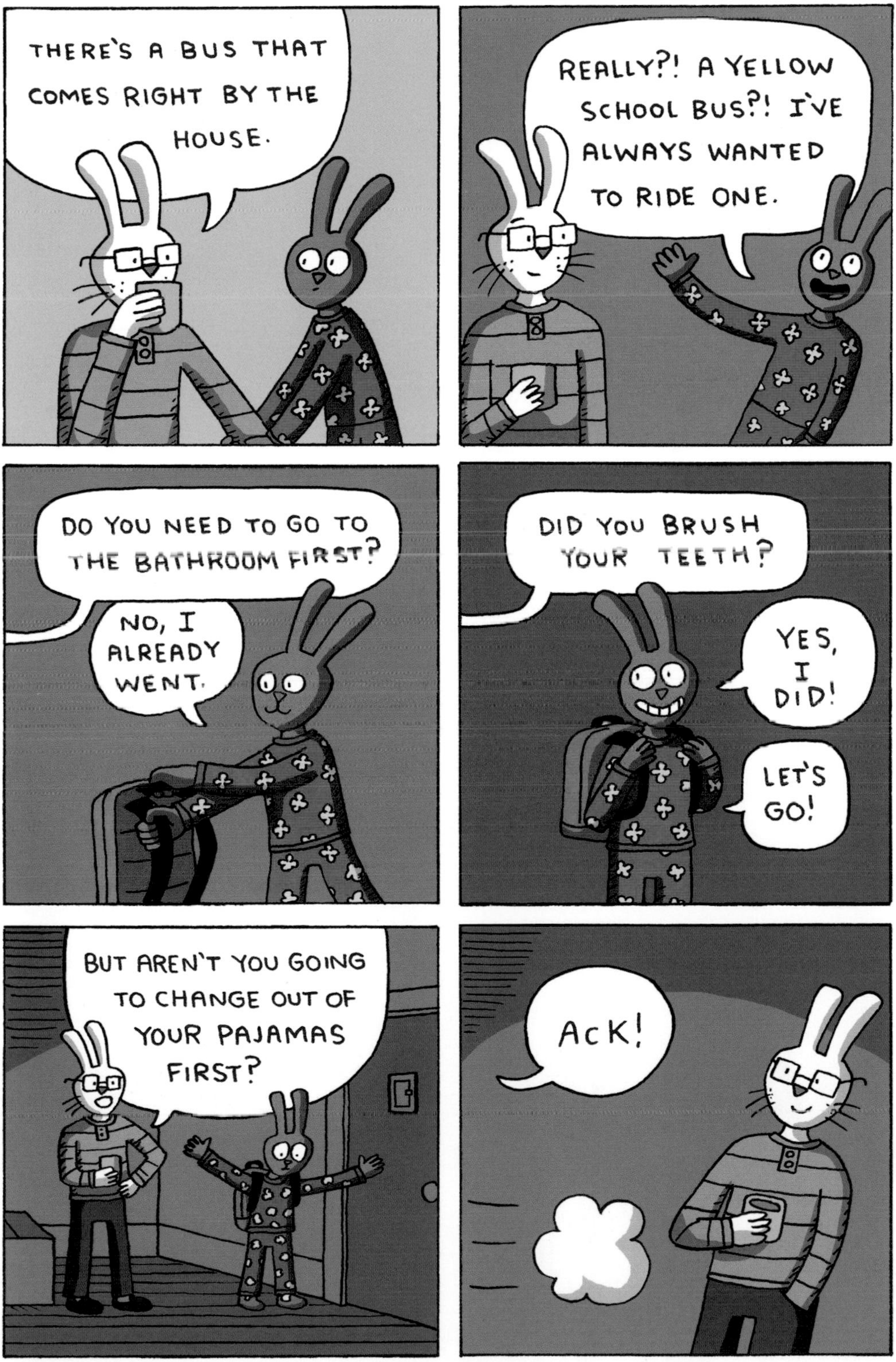
THERE'S A BUS THAT COMES RIGHT BY THE HOUSE.
REALLY?! A YELLOW SCHOOL BUS?! I'VE ALWAYS WANTED TO RIDE ONE.
DO YOU NEED TO GO TO THE BATHROOM FIRST?
NO, I ALREADY WENT.
DID YOU BRUSH YOUR TEETH?
YES, I DID!
LET'S GO!
BUT AREN'T YOU GOING TO CHANGE OUT OF YOUR PAJAMAS FIRST?
ACK!

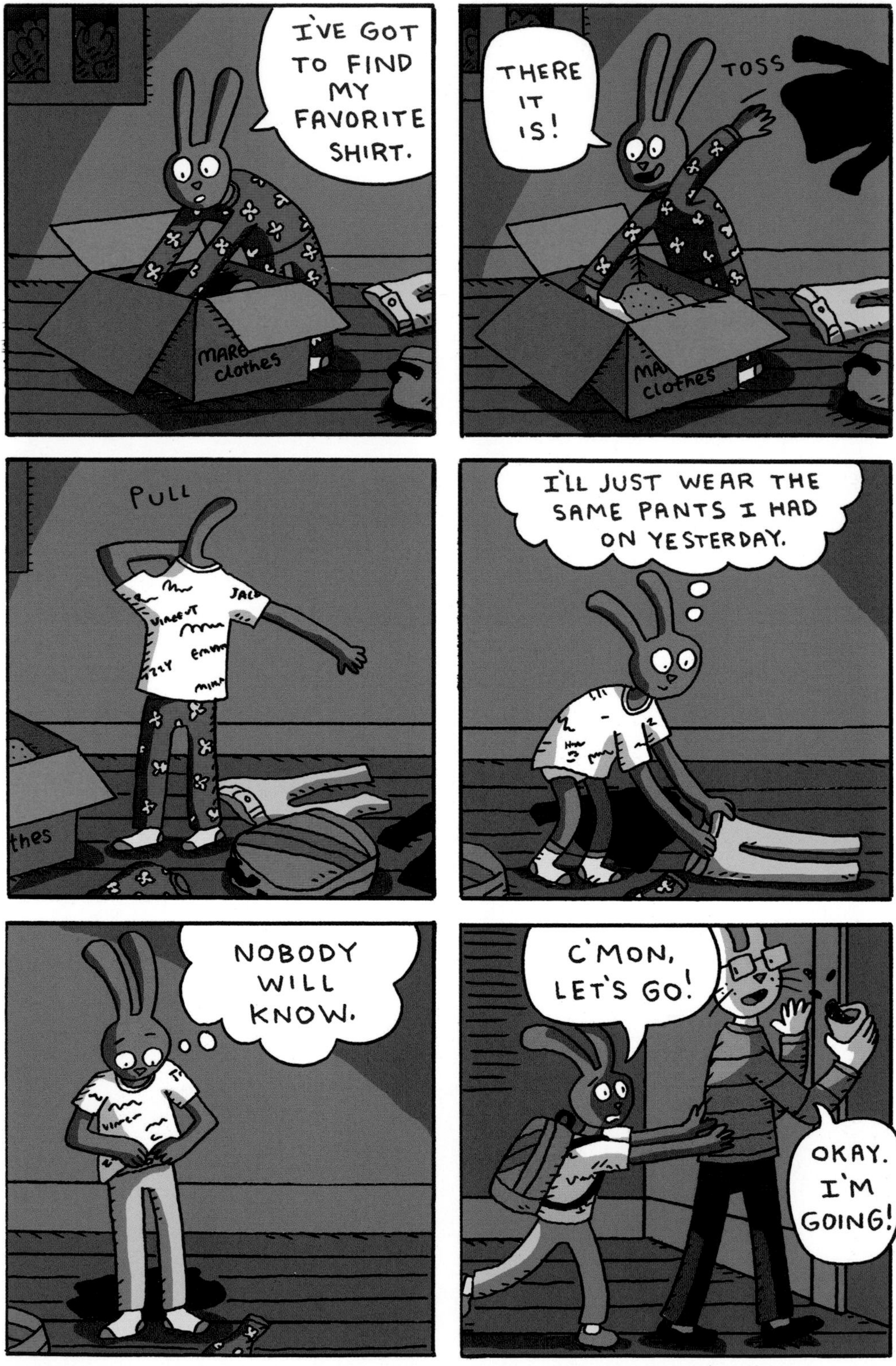
I'VE GOT TO FIND MY FAVORITE SHIRT.
THERE IT IS!
TOSS
PULL
I'LL JUST WEAR THE SAME PANTS I HAD ON YESTERDAY.
NOBODY WILL KNOW.
C'MON, LET'S GO!
OKAY. I'M GOING!

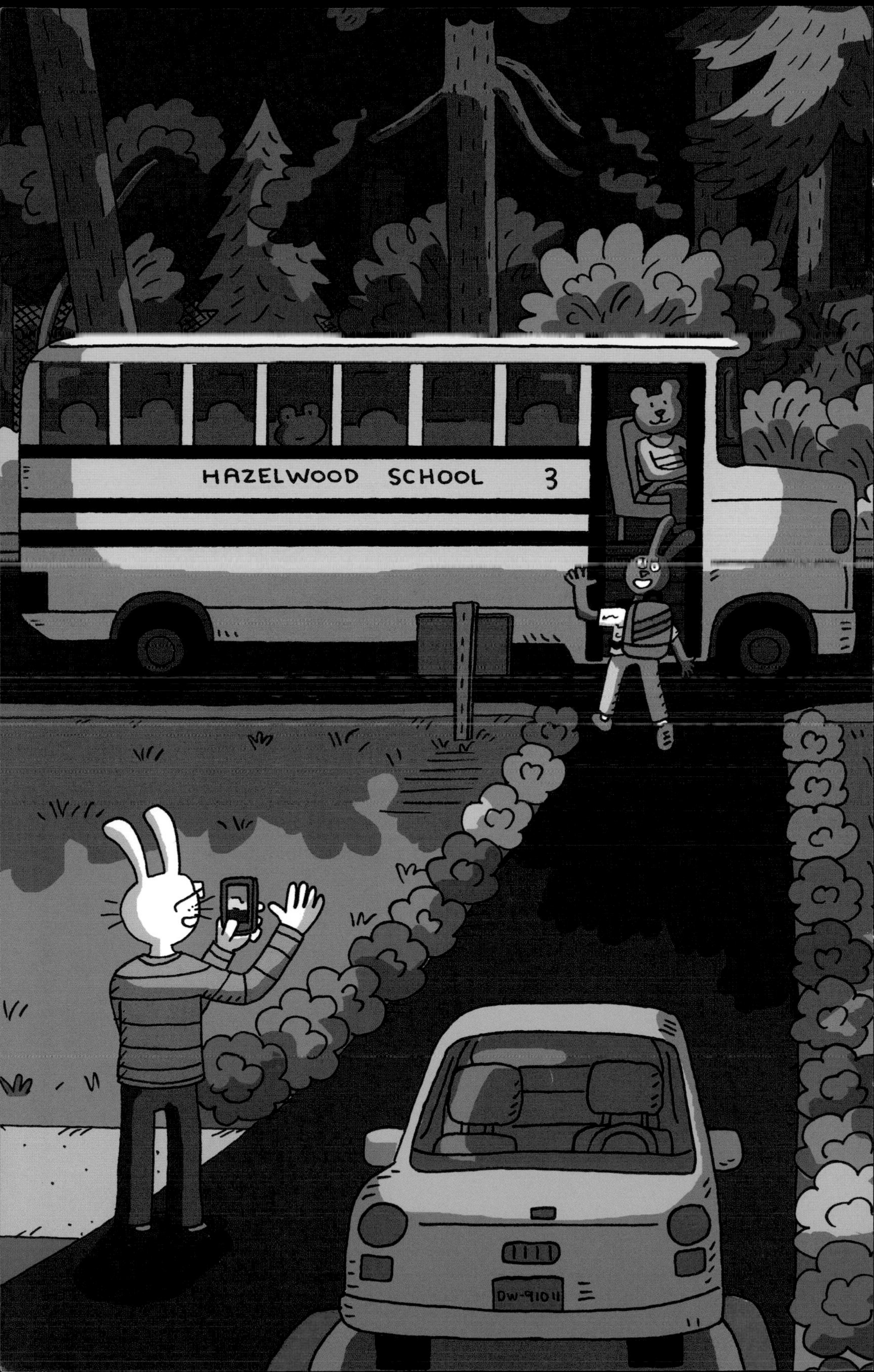
HAZELWOOD SCHOOL 3
DW-91011

CHAPTER TWO
Hold It!

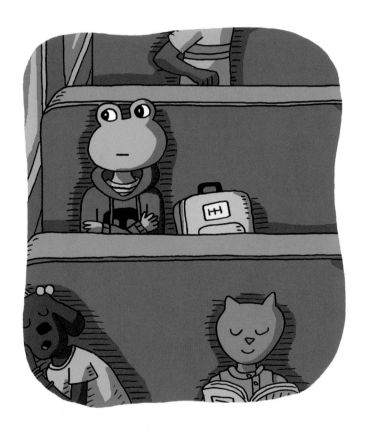

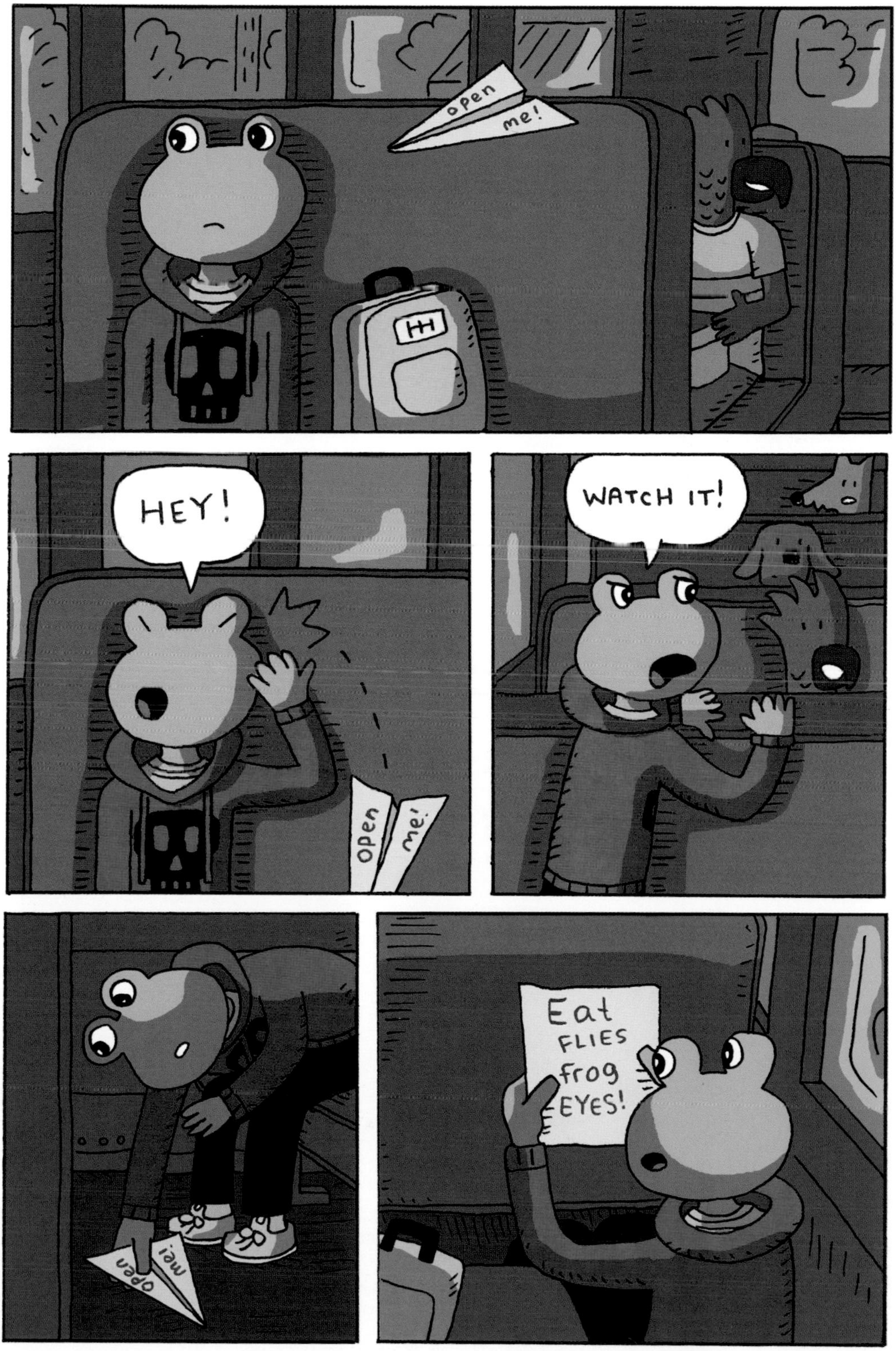
open
me!
HEY!
open
me!
WATCH IT!
open
me!
Eat
FLIES
frog
EYES!

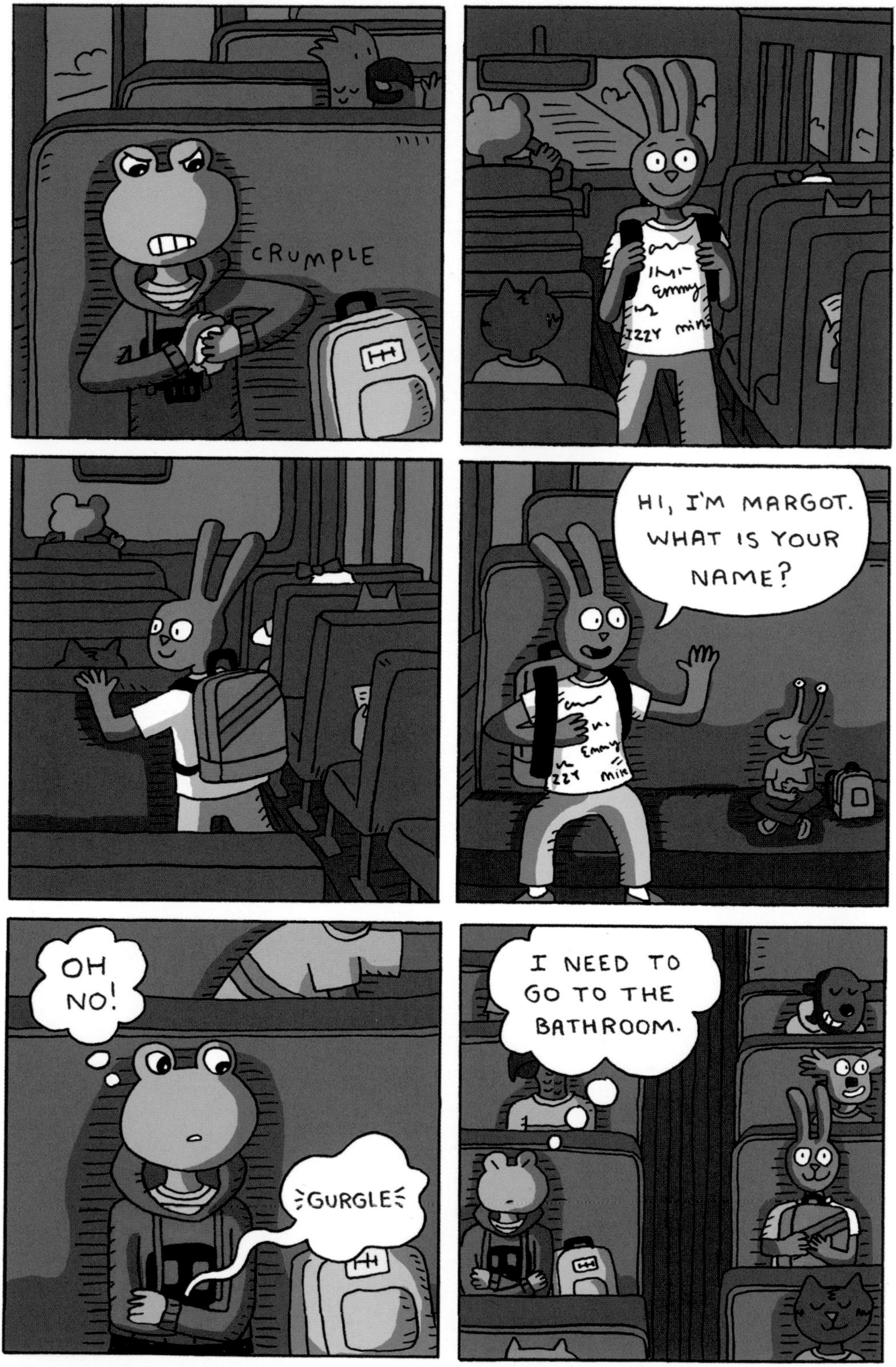
CRUMPLE
HI, I'M MARGOT. WHAT IS YOUR NAME?
OH NO!
GURGLE
I NEED TO GO TO THE BATHROOM.

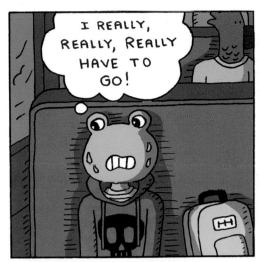
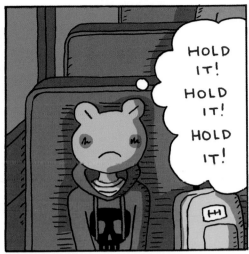
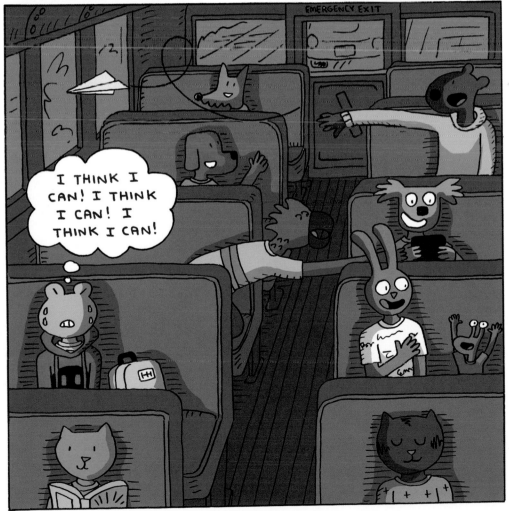

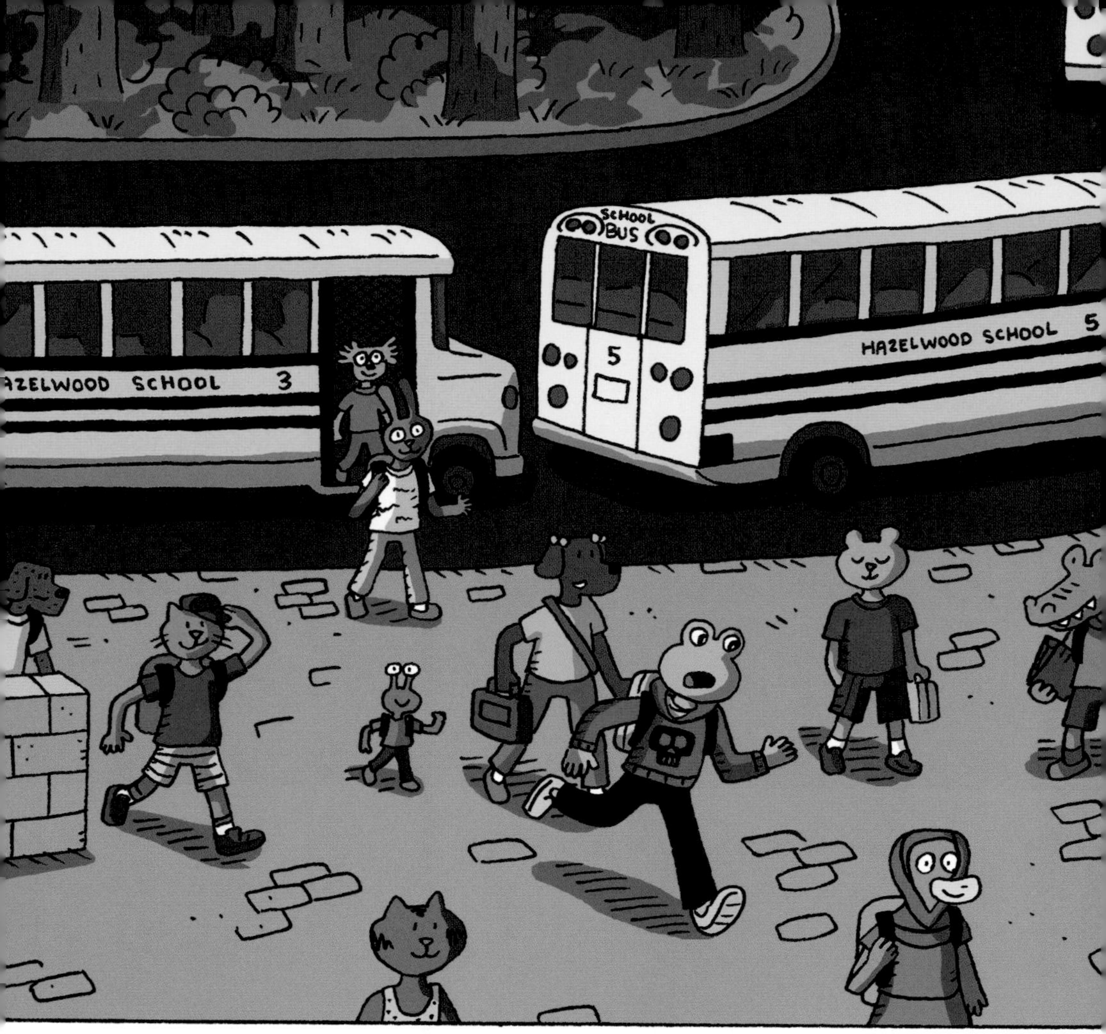
SCHOOL BUS
AZELWOOD SCHOOL 3
5
HAZELWOOD SCHOOL 5

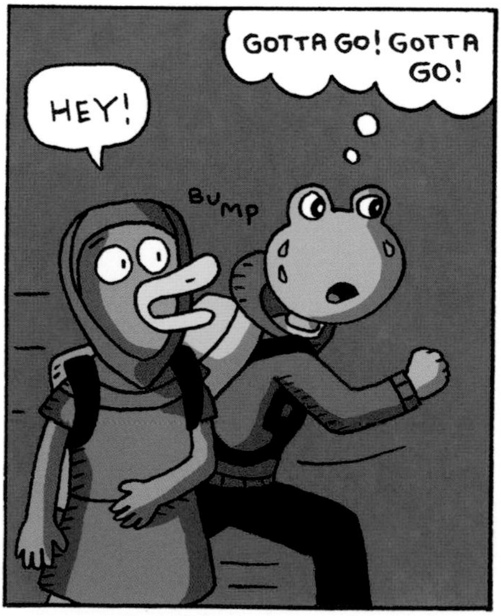
HEY!
GOTTA GO! GOTTA GO!
BUMP

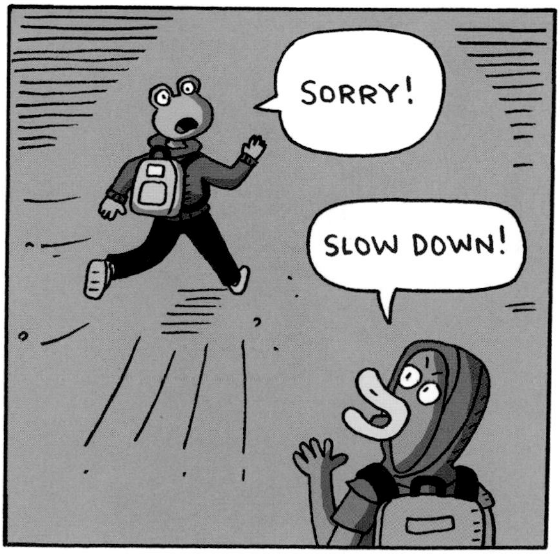
SORRY!
SLOW DOWN!

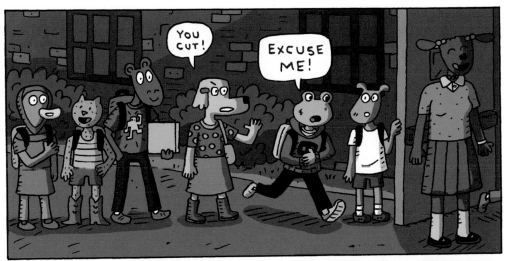

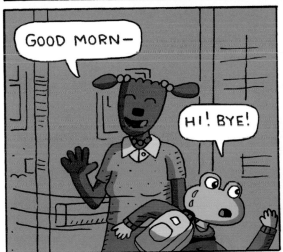

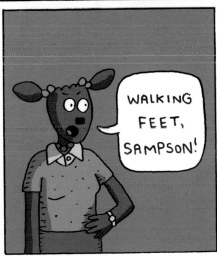

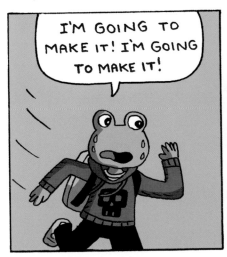

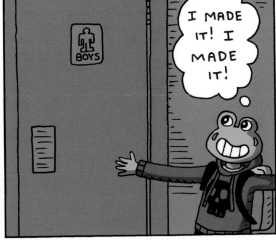

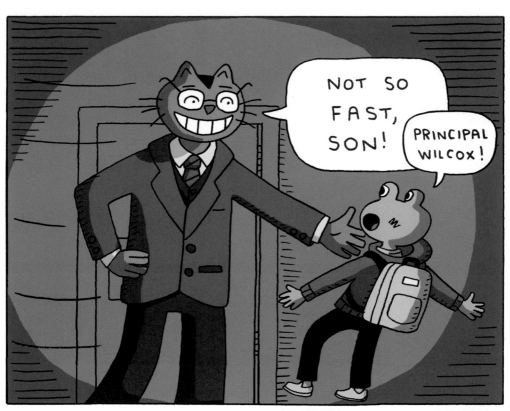

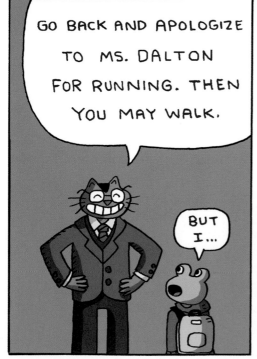

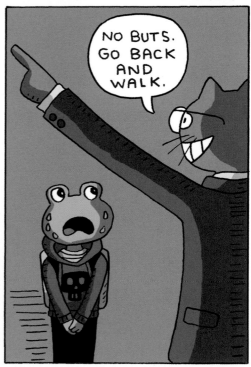

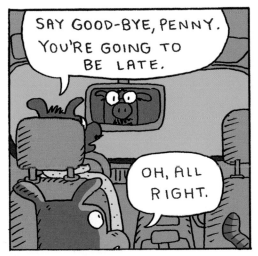

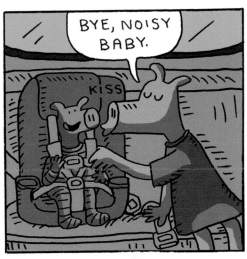

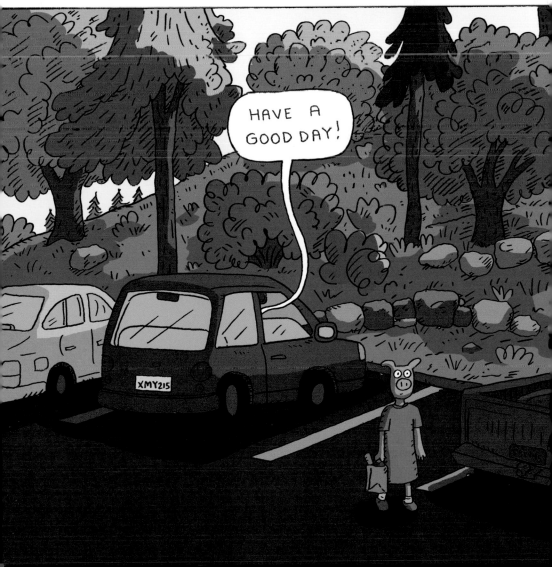

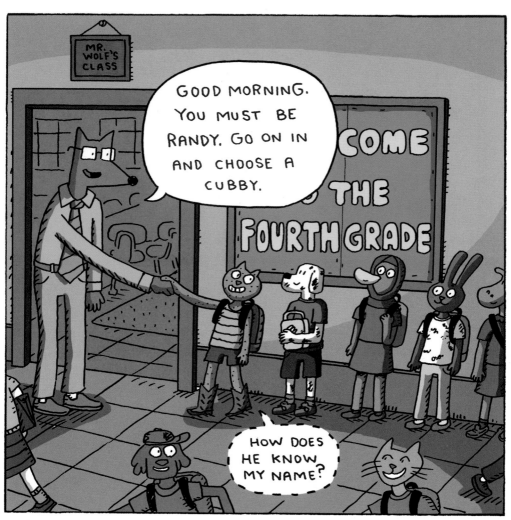

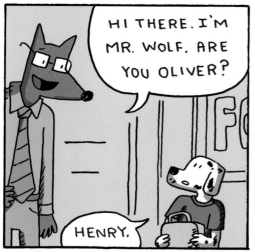

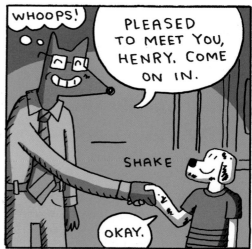

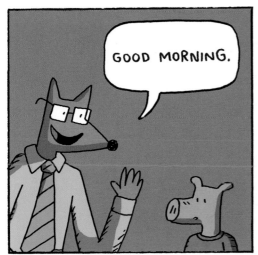

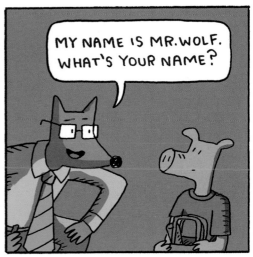

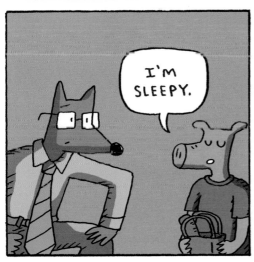

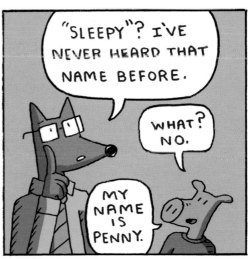

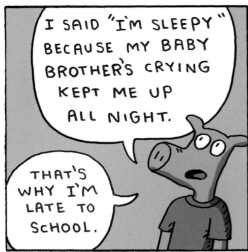

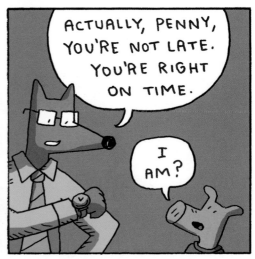

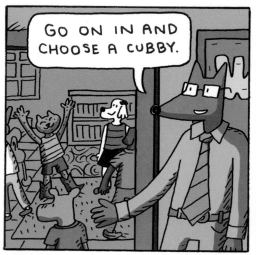

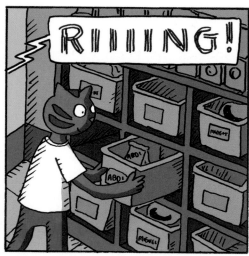

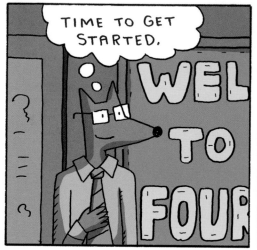

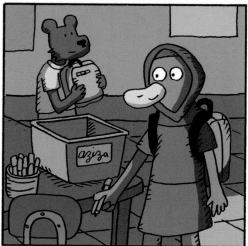

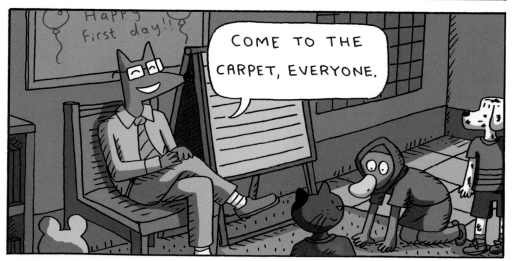

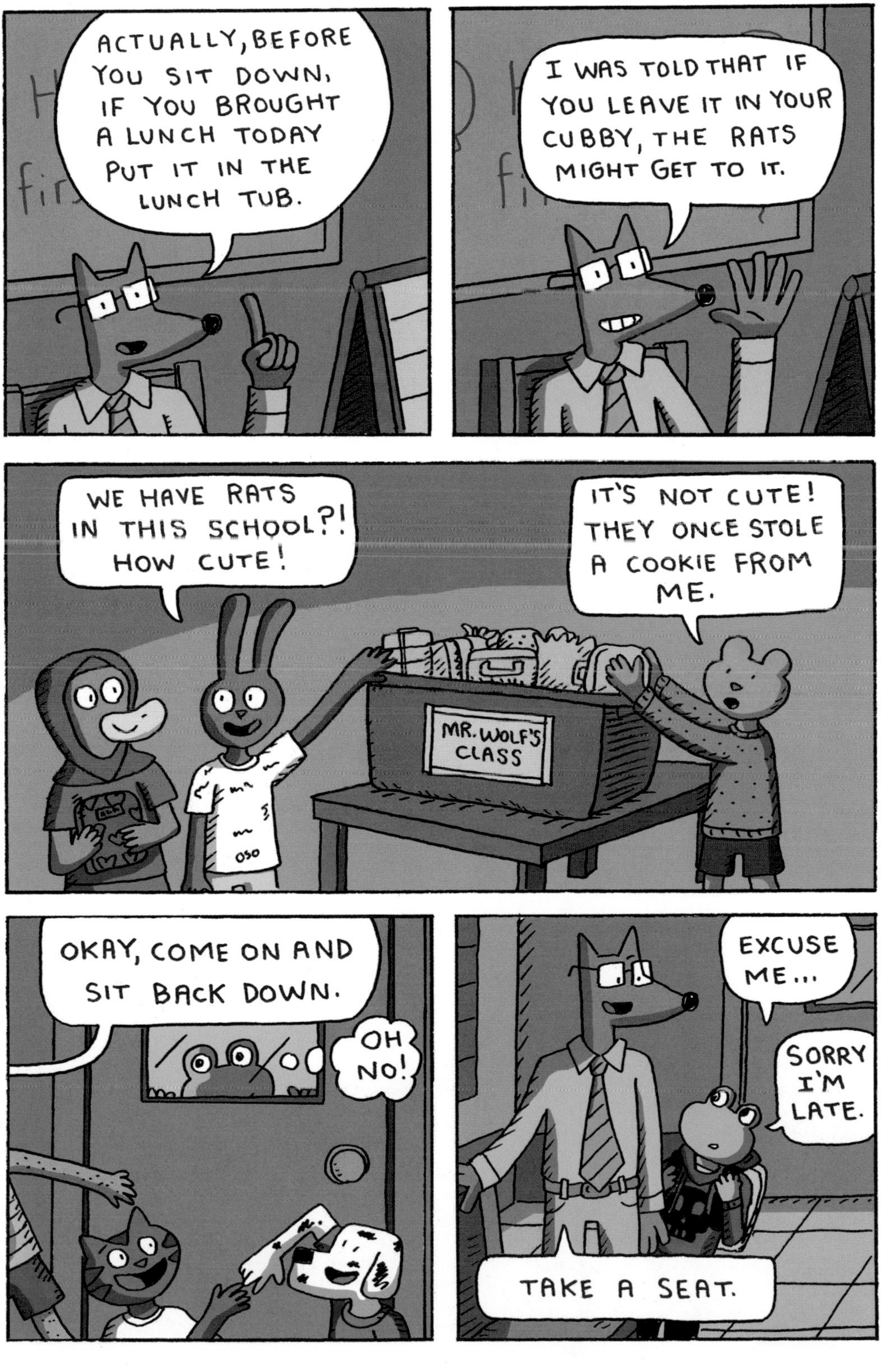
ACTUALLY, BEFORE YOU SIT DOWN, IF YOU BROUGHT A LUNCH TODAY PUT IT IN THE LUNCH TUB.
I WAS TOLD THAT IF YOU LEAVE IT IN YOUR CUBBY, THE RATS MIGHT GET TO IT.
WE HAVE RATS IN THIS SCHOOL?! HOW CUTE!
MR. WOLF'S CLASS
IT'S NOT CUTE! THEY ONCE STOLE A COOKIE FROM ME.
OKAY, COME ON AND SIT BACK DOWN.
OH NO!
EXCUSE ME...
SORRY I'M LATE.
TAKE A SEAT.

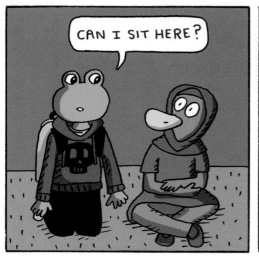

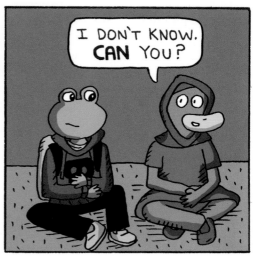

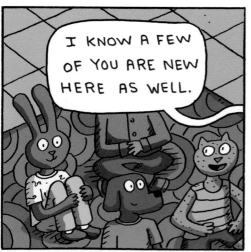

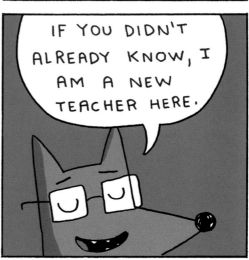

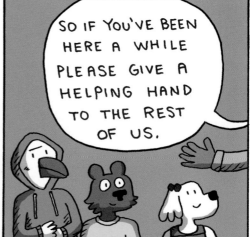

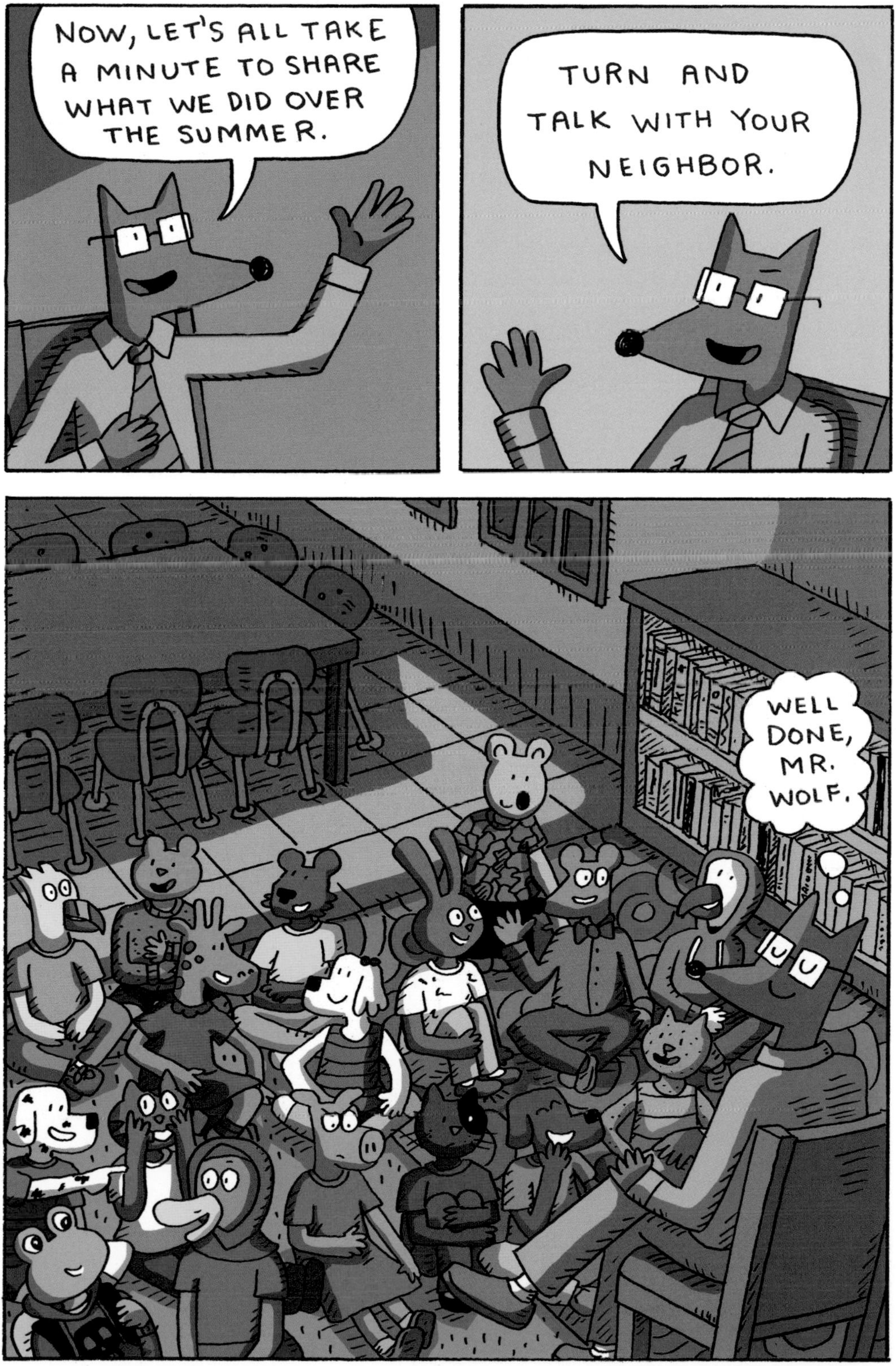
NOW, LET'S ALL TAKE A MINUTE TO SHARE WHAT WE DID OVER THE SUMMER.
TURN AND TALK WITH YOUR NEIGHBOR.
WELL DONE, MR. WOLF.

CHAPTER THREE
Palindromes

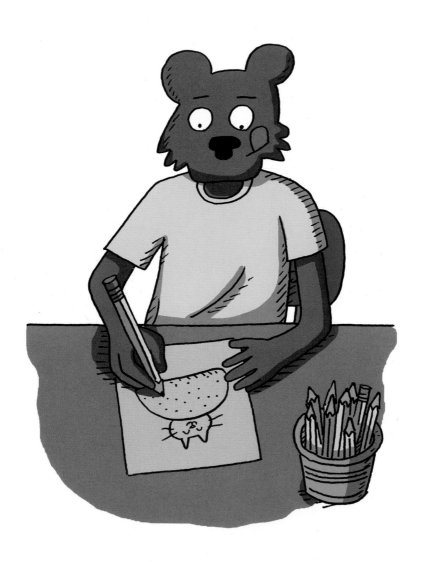

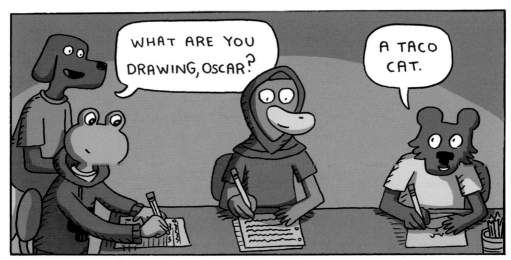

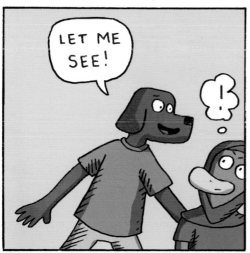

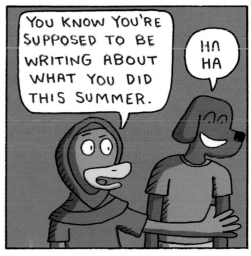

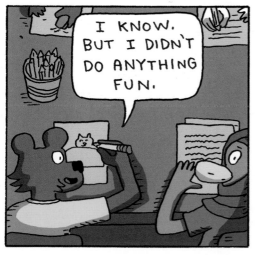

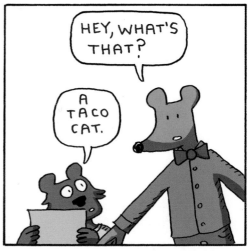

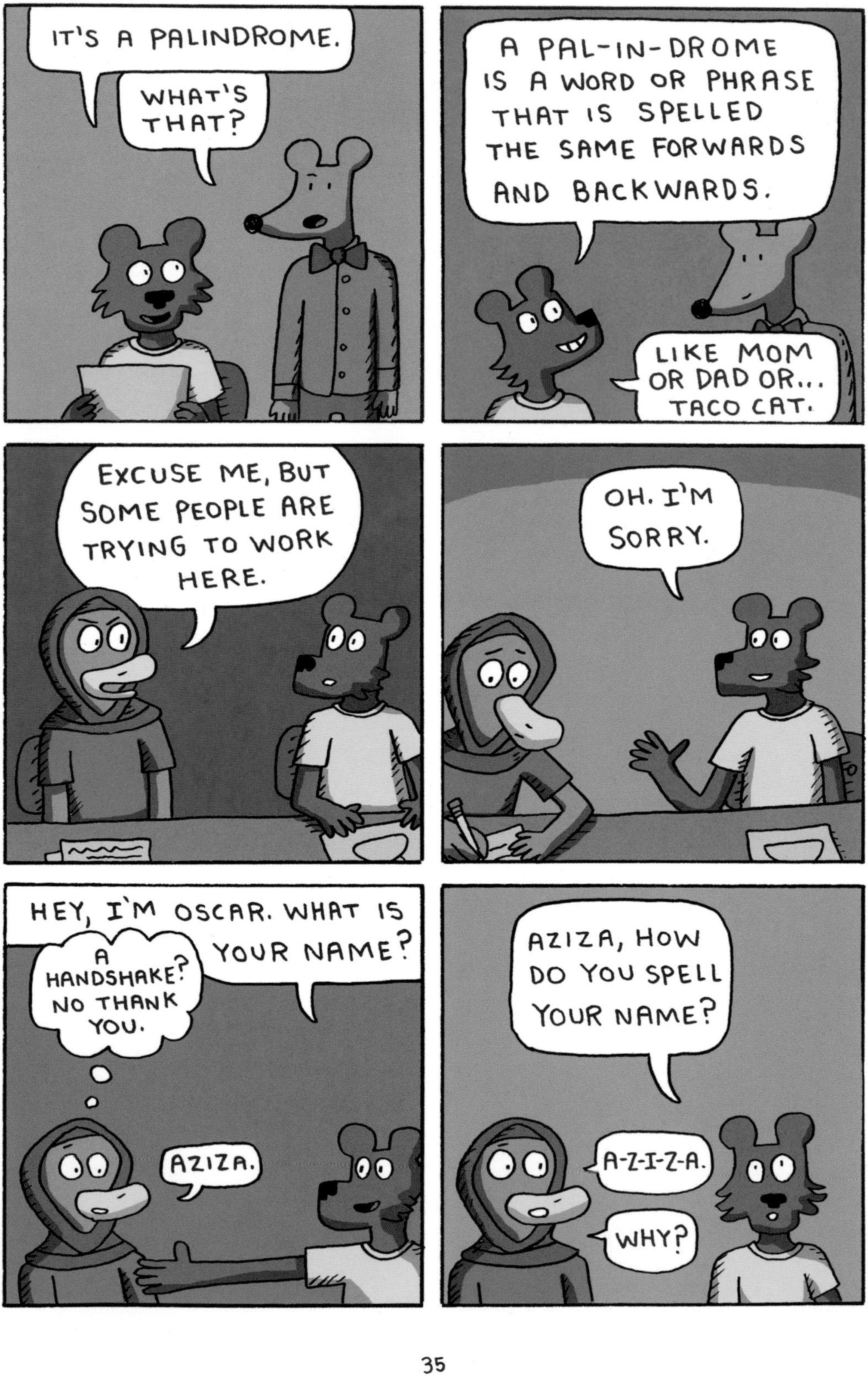
IT'S A PALINDROME.
WHAT'S THAT?
A PAL-IN-DROME IS A WORD OR PHRASE THAT IS SPELLED THE SAME FORWARDS AND BACKWARDS.
LIKE MOM OR DAD OR... TACO CAT.
EXCUSE ME, BUT SOME PEOPLE ARE TRYING TO WORK HERE.
OH. I'M SORRY.
HEY, I'M OSCAR. WHAT IS YOUR NAME?
A HANDSHAKE? NO THANK YOU.
AZIZA.
AZIZA, HOW DO YOU SPELL YOUR NAME?
A-Z-I-Z-A.
WHY?

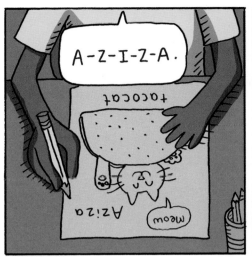

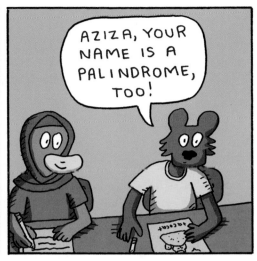

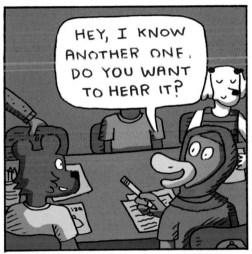

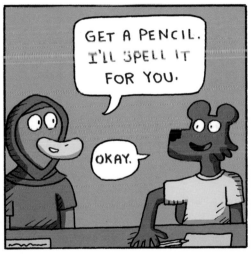

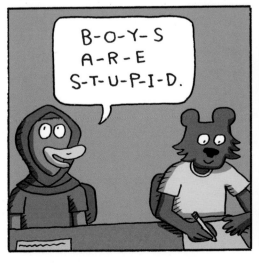

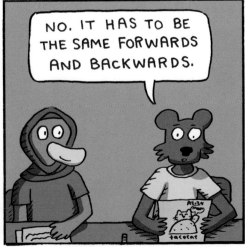

36

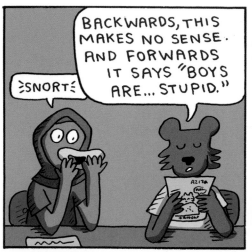

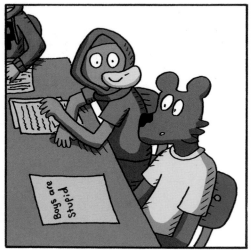

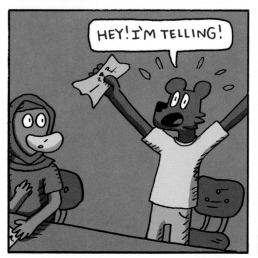

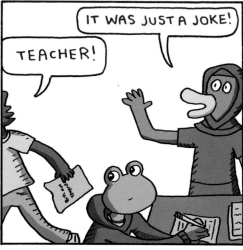

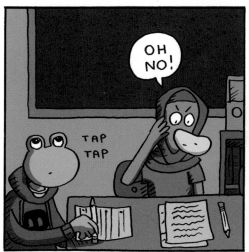

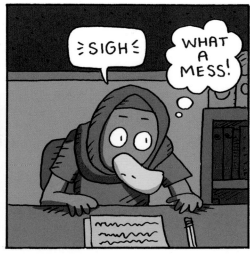

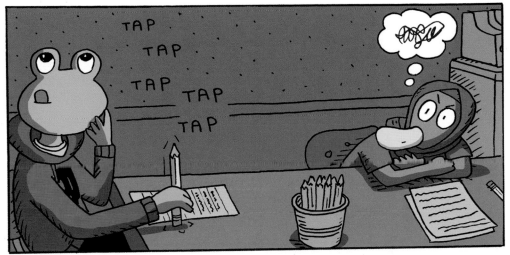

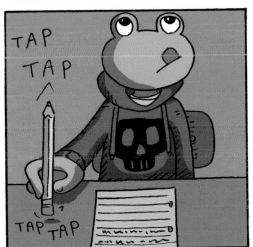

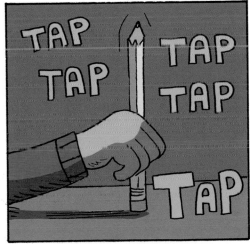

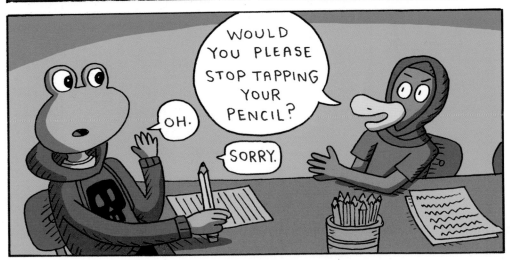

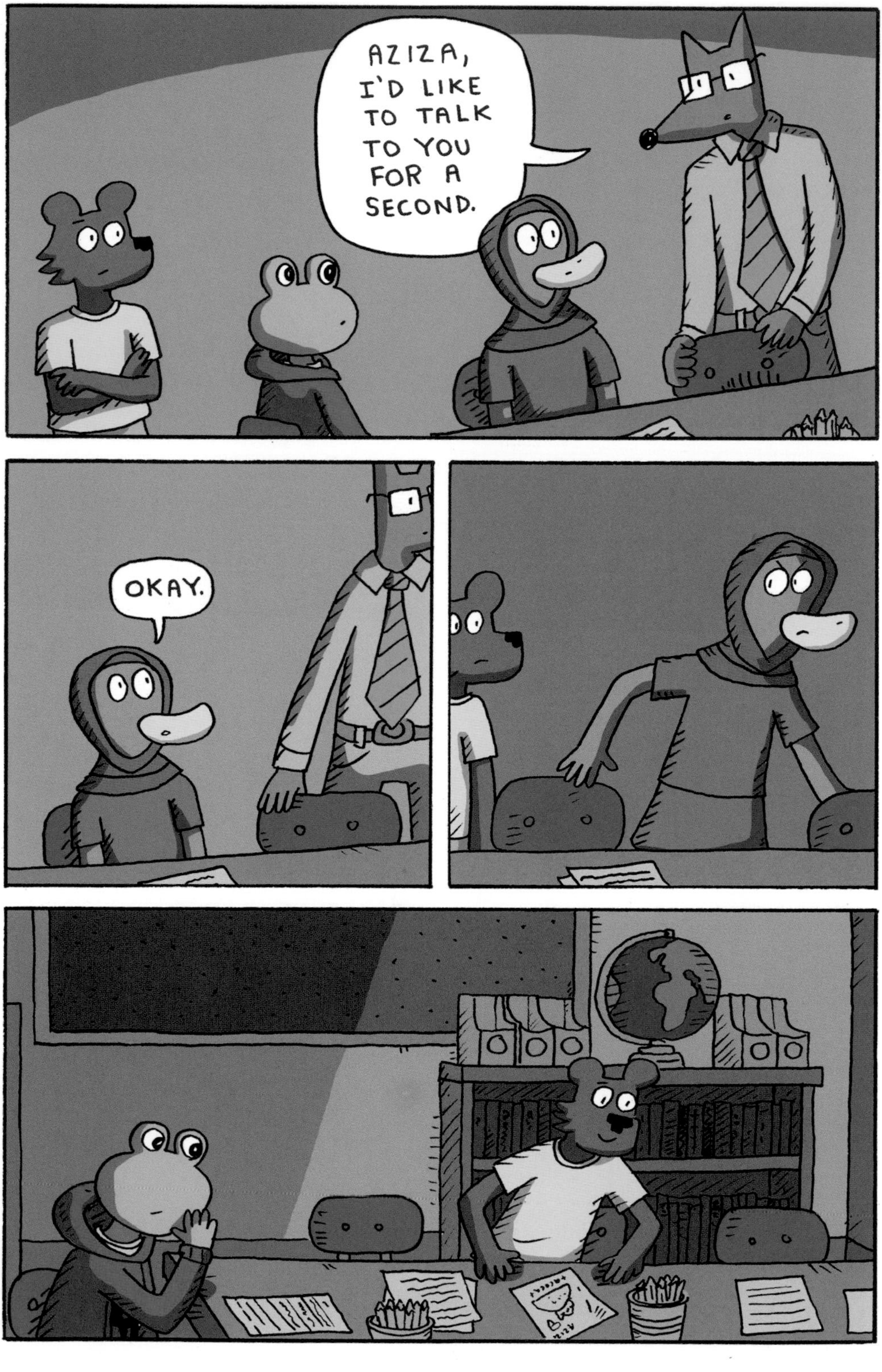
AZIZA, I'D LIKE TO TALK TO YOU FOR A SECOND.
OKAY.

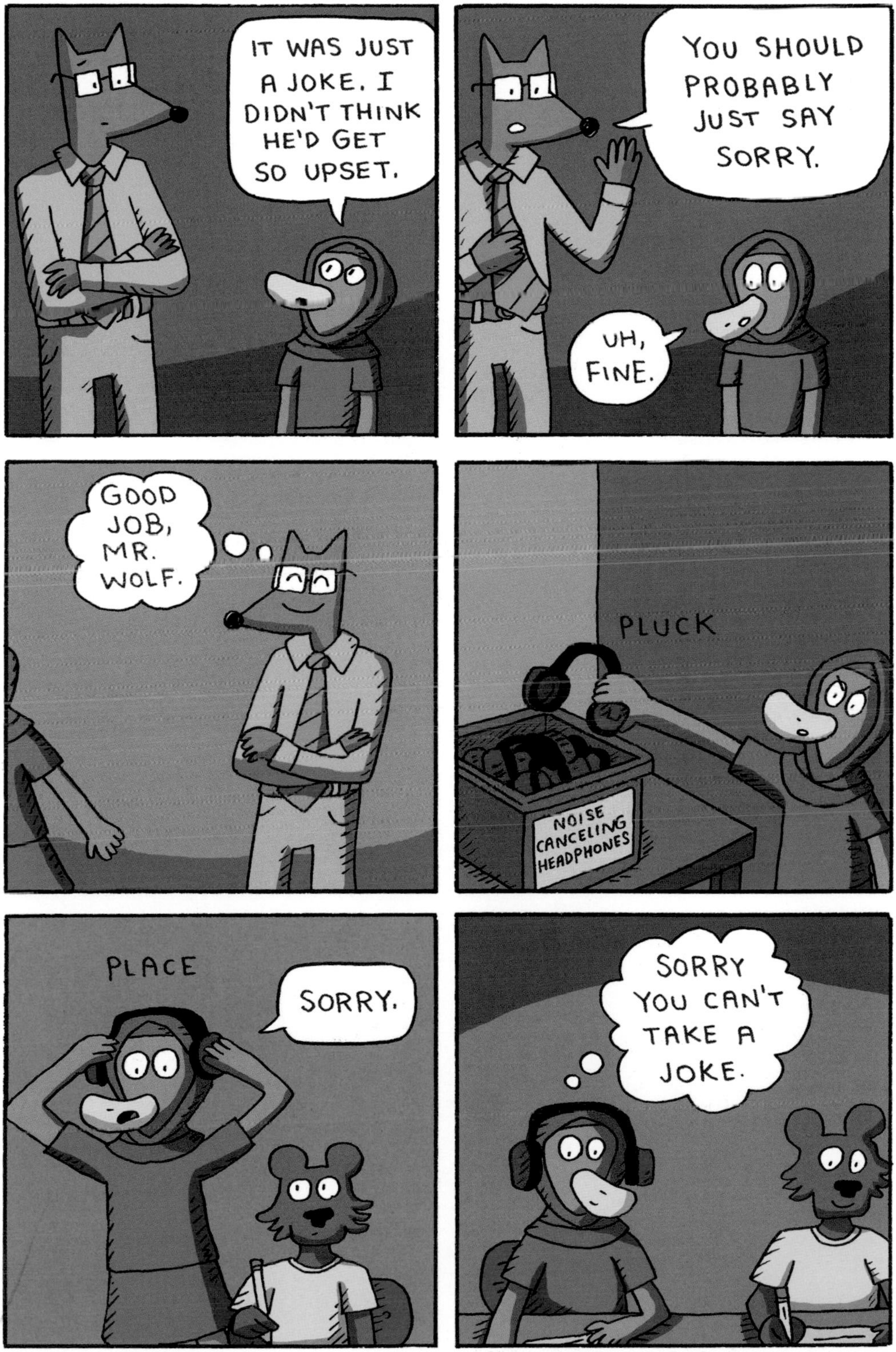
IT WAS JUST A JOKE. I DIDN'T THINK HE'D GET SO UPSET.
YOU SHOULD PROBABLY JUST SAY SORRY.
UH, FINE.
GOOD JOB, MR. WOLF.
PLUCK
NOISE CANCELING HEADPHONES
PLACE
SORRY.
SORRY YOU CAN'T TAKE A JOKE.

CHAPTER FOUR
Peace and Quiet

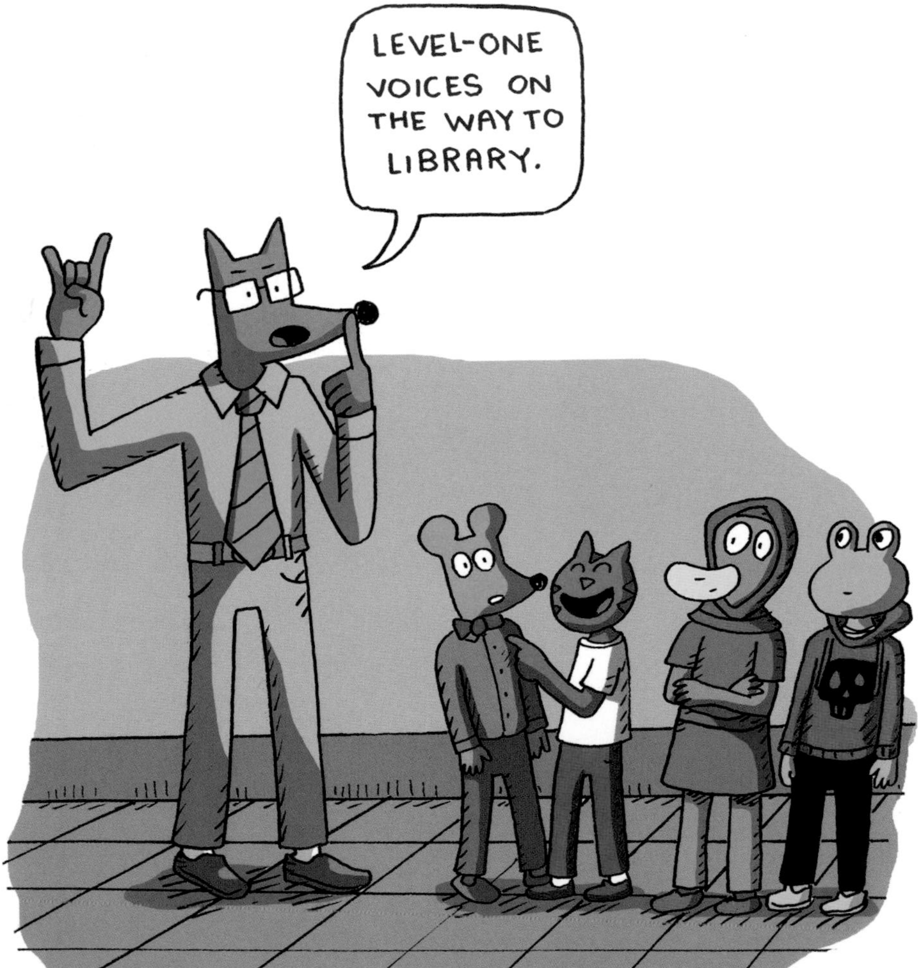

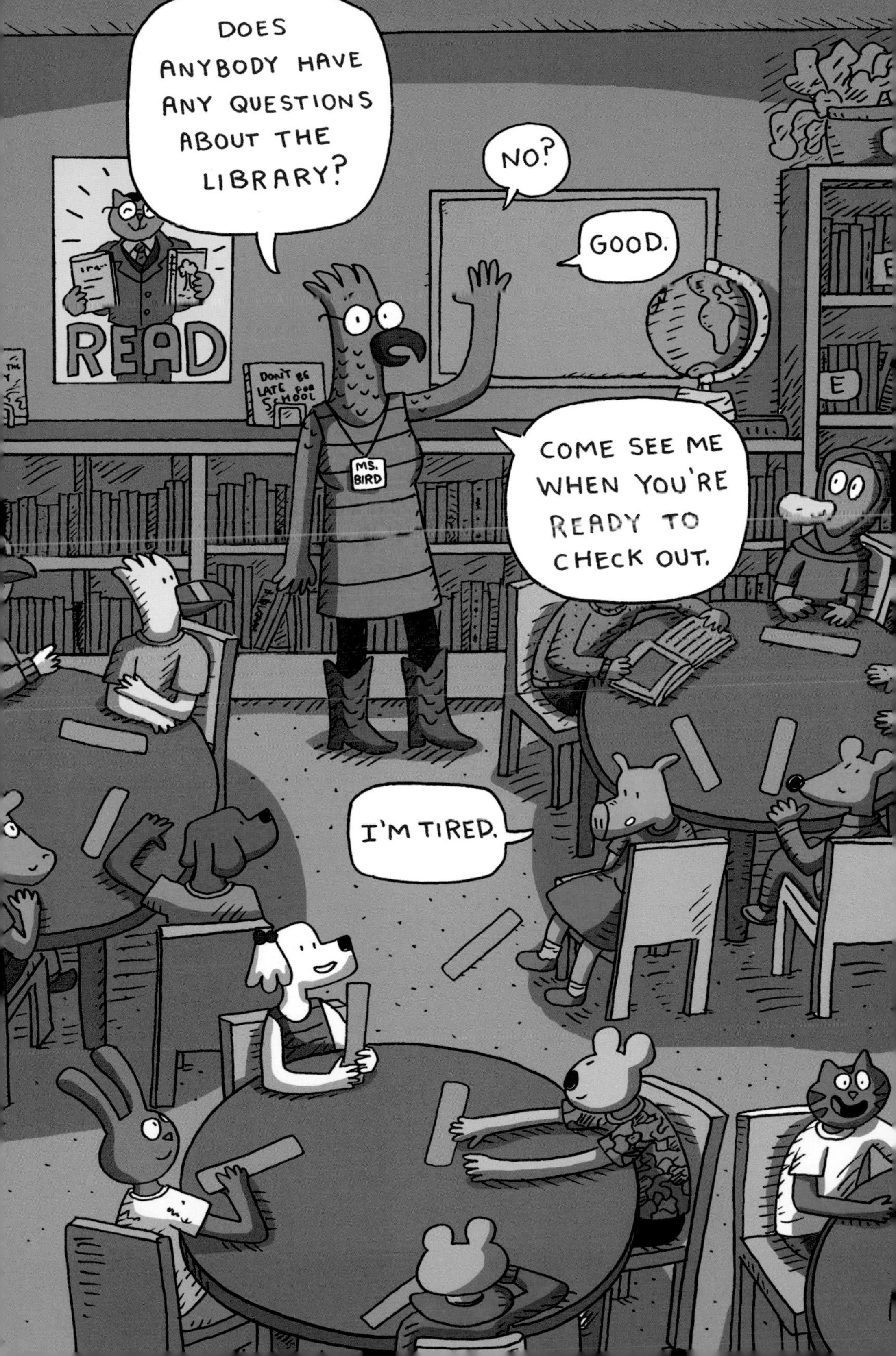
DOES ANYBODY HAVE ANY QUESTIONS ABOUT THE LIBRARY?
NO?
GOOD.
READ
DON'T BE LATE FOR SCHOOL
MS. BIRD
COME SEE ME WHEN YOU'RE READY TO CHECK OUT.
I'M TIRED.

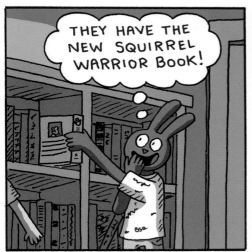

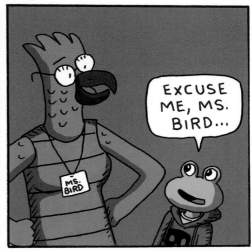

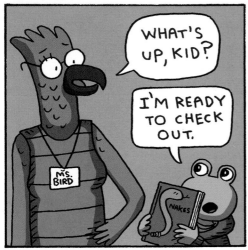

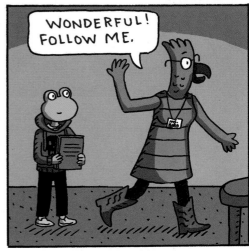

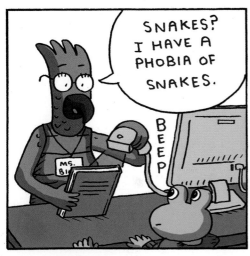

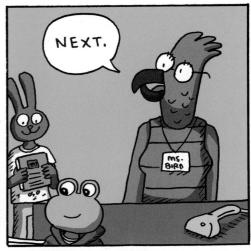

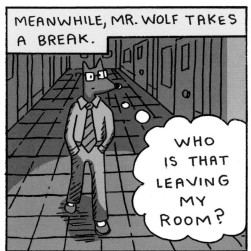

MEANWHILE, MR. WOLF TAKES A BREAK.

WHO IS THAT LEAVING MY ROOM?

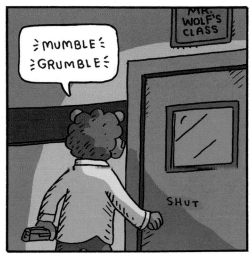

≥MUMBLE≤
≥GRUMBLE≤

SHUT

MR. WOLF'S CLASS

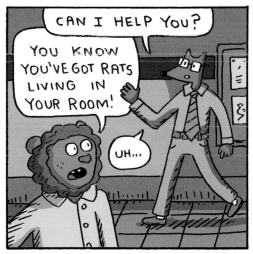

CAN I HELP YOU?

YOU KNOW YOU'VE GOT RATS LIVING IN YOUR ROOM!

UH...

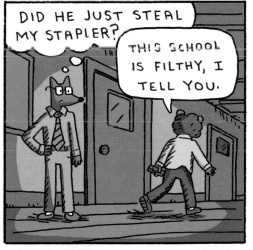

DID HE JUST STEAL MY STAPLER?

THIS SCHOOL IS FILTHY, I TELL YOU.

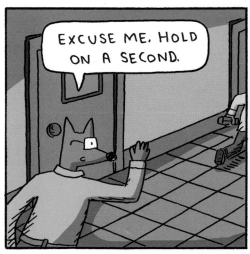

EXCUSE ME. HOLD ON A SECOND.

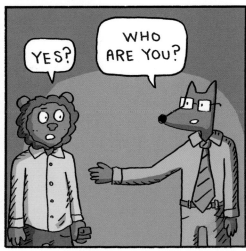

YES?

WHO ARE YOU?

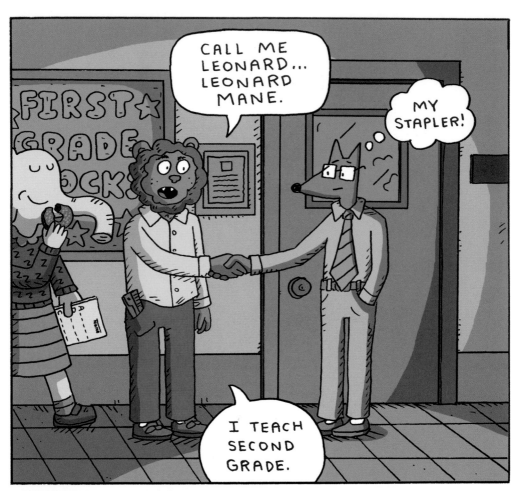

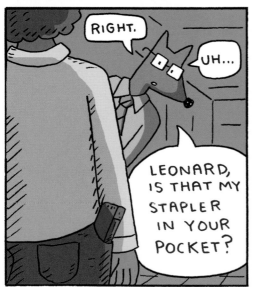

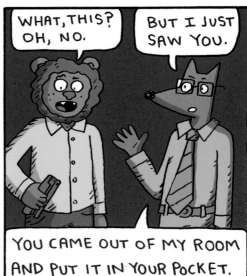

45

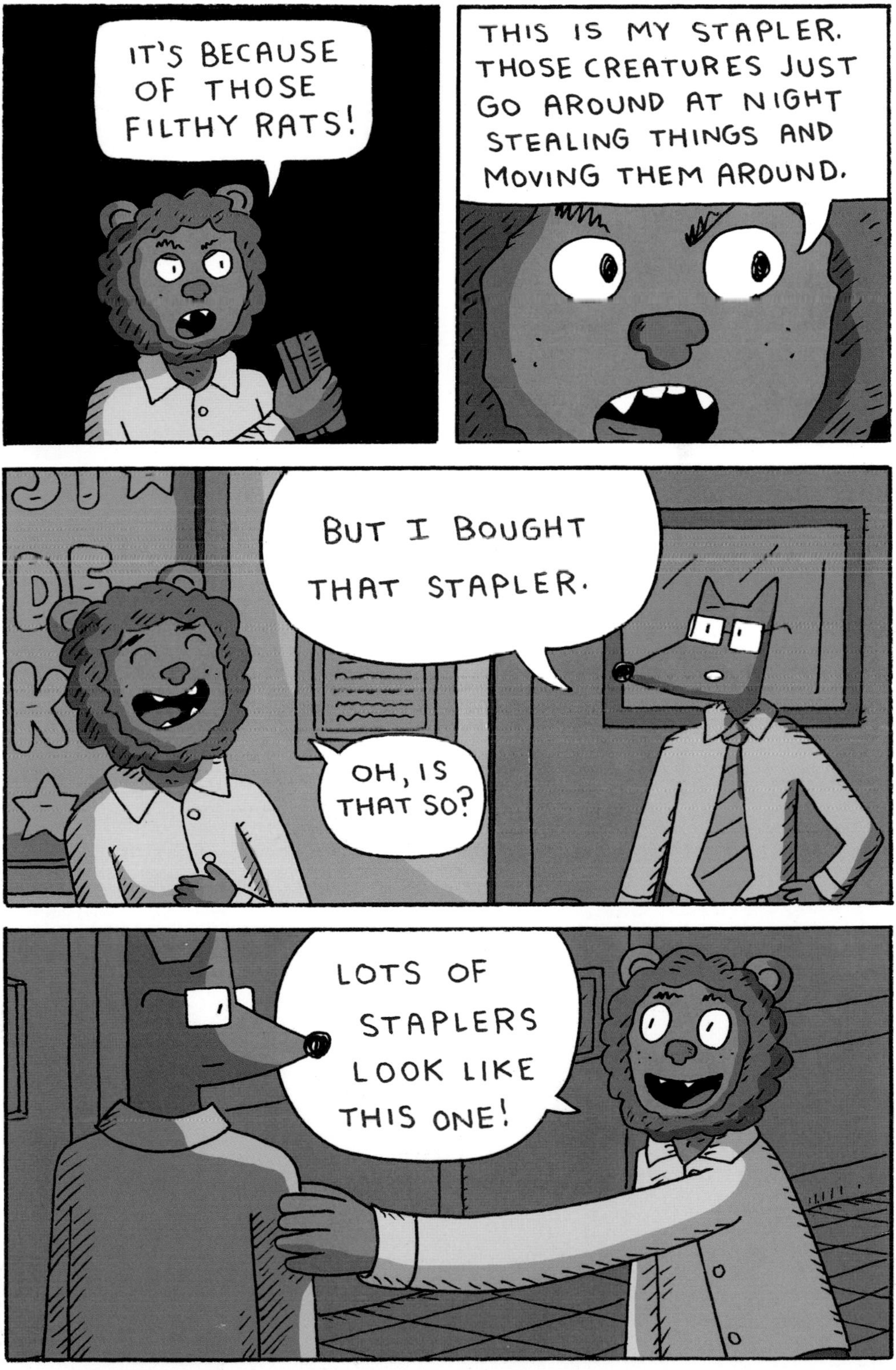
IT'S BECAUSE OF THOSE FILTHY RATS!
THIS IS MY STAPLER. THOSE CREATURES JUST GO AROUND AT NIGHT STEALING THINGS AND MOVING THEM AROUND.
BUT I BOUGHT THAT STAPLER.
OH, IS THAT SO?
LOTS OF STAPLERS LOOK LIKE THIS ONE!

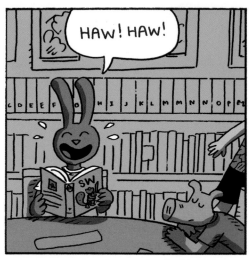

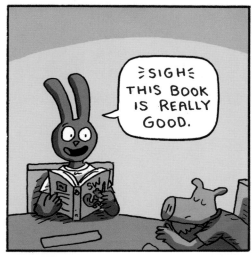

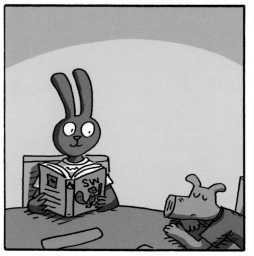

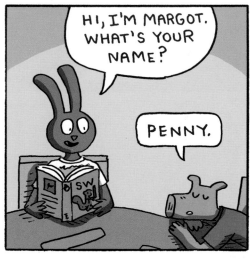

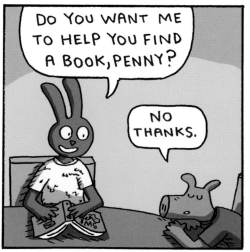

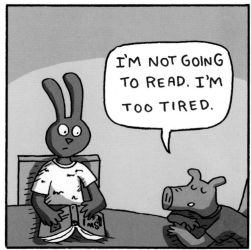

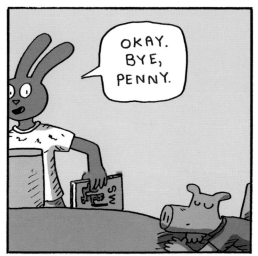

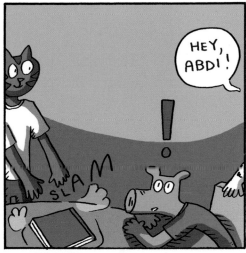

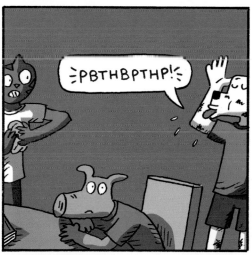

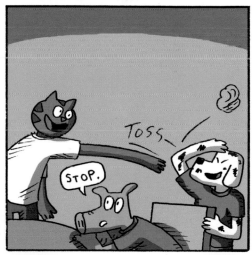

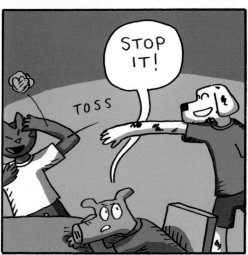

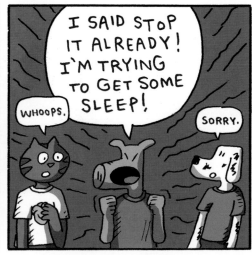

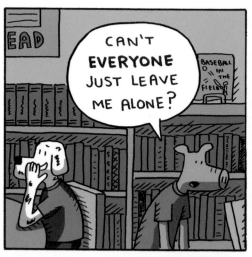

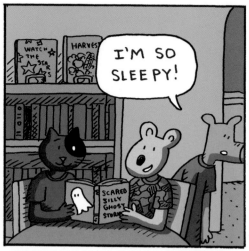

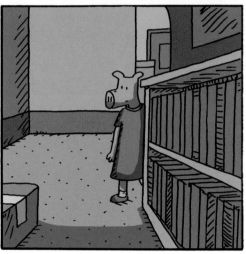

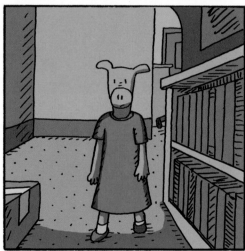

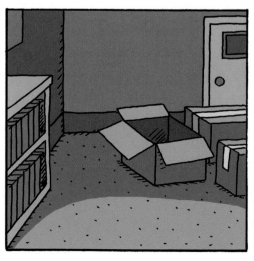

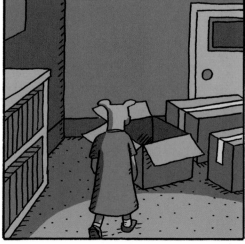

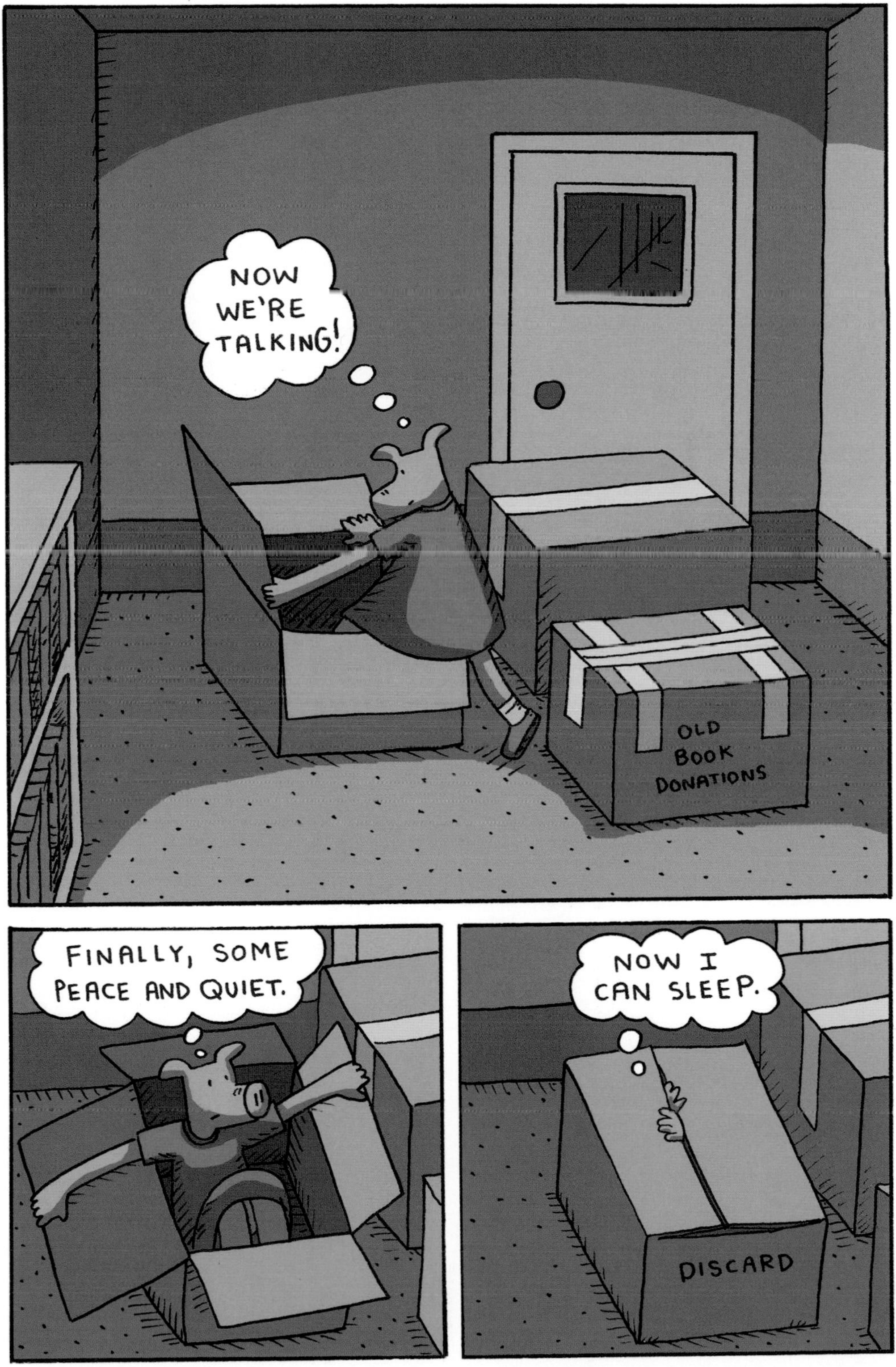
NOW WE'RE TALKING!
OLD BOOK DONATIONS
FINALLY, SOME PEACE AND QUIET.
NOW I CAN SLEEP.
DISCARD

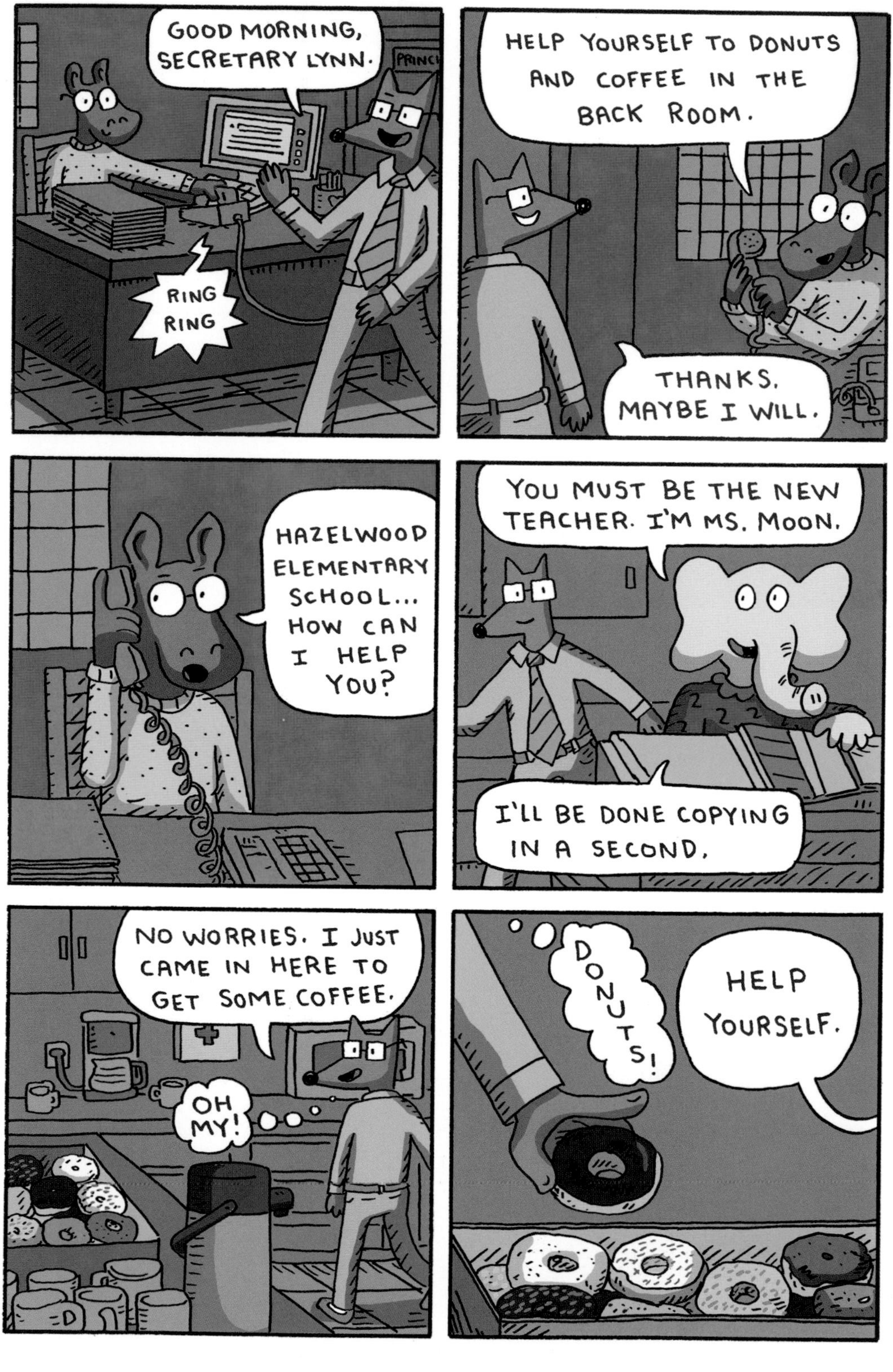
GOOD MORNING, SECRETARY LYNN.
RING RING
HELP YOURSELF TO DONUTS AND COFFEE IN THE BACK ROOM.
THANKS. MAYBE I WILL.
HAZELWOOD ELEMENTARY SCHOOL... HOW CAN I HELP YOU?
YOU MUST BE THE NEW TEACHER. I'M MS. MOON.
I'LL BE DONE COPYING IN A SECOND.
NO WORRIES. I JUST CAME IN HERE TO GET SOME COFFEE.
OH MY!
DONUTS!
HELP YOURSELF.

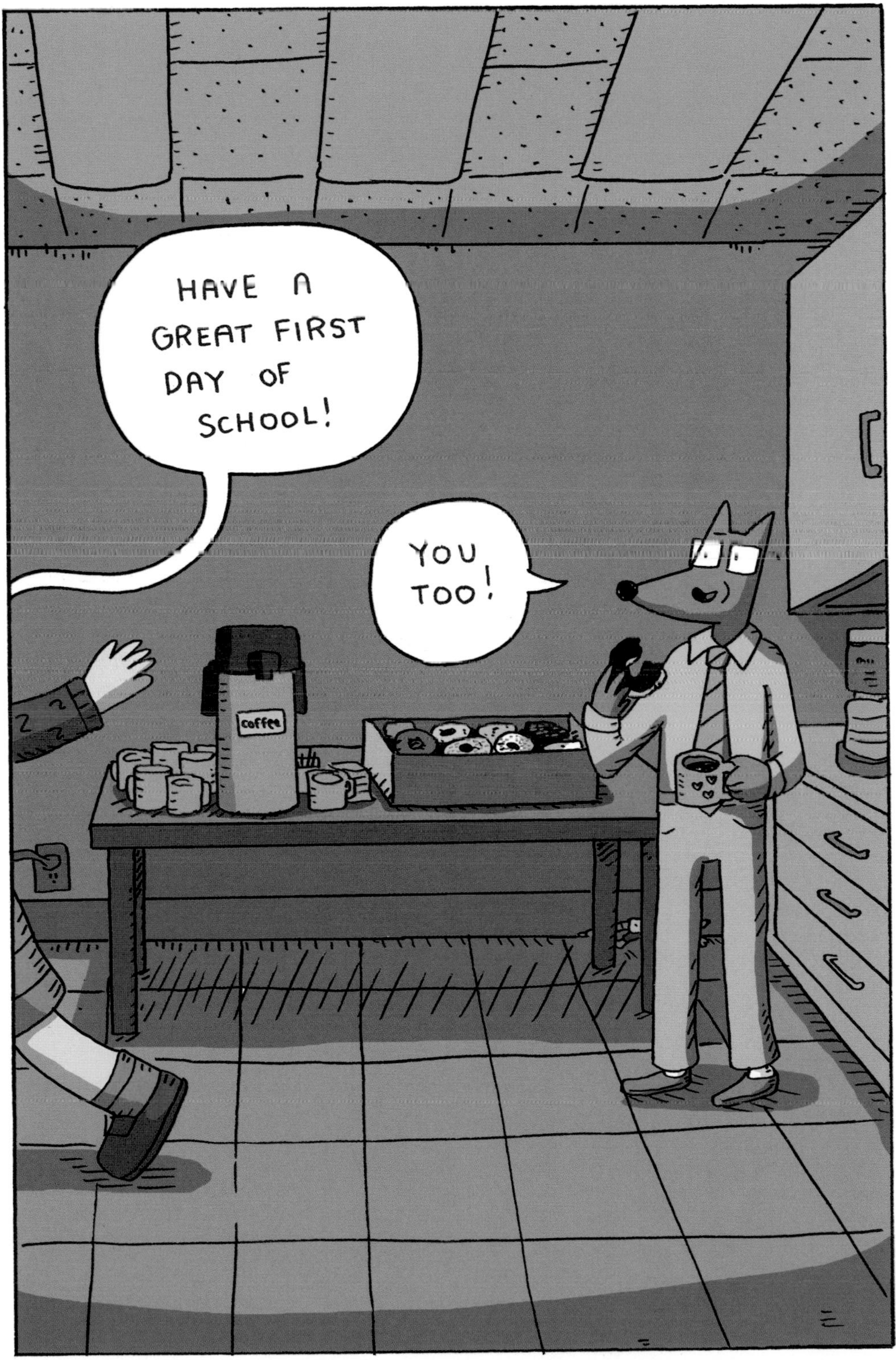
HAVE A GREAT FIRST DAY OF SCHOOL!
YOU TOO!
coffee

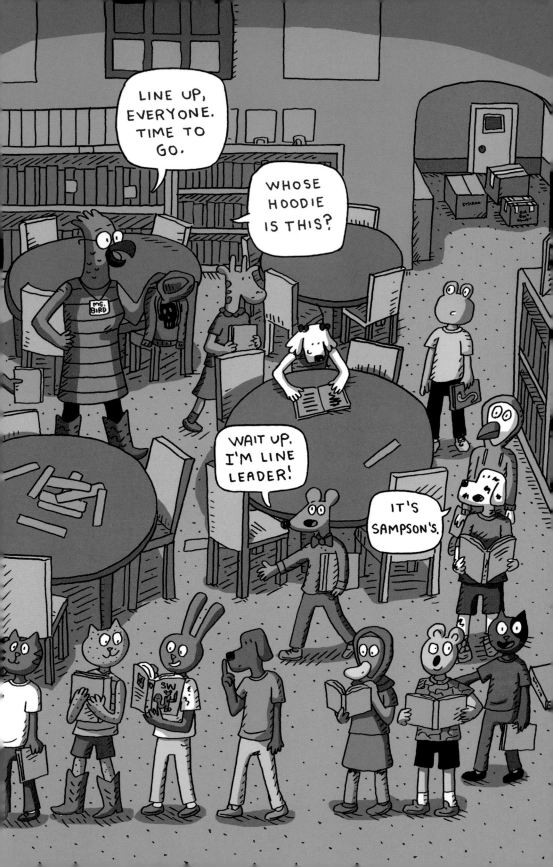

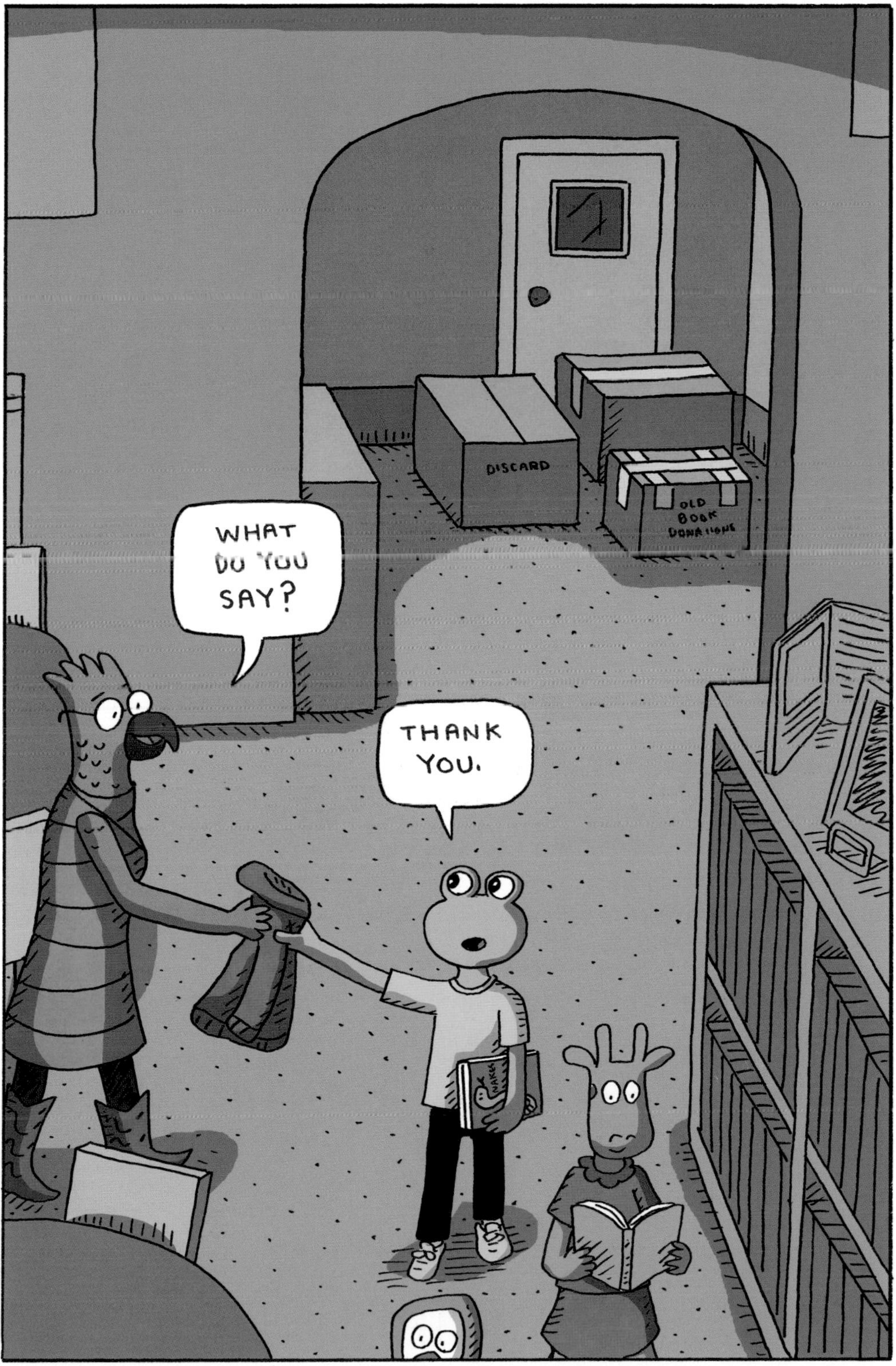
DISCARD
OLD BOOK DONATIONS
WHAT DO YOU SAY?
THANK YOU.

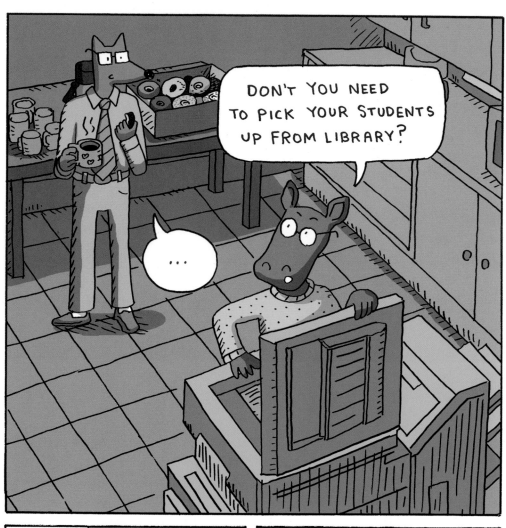

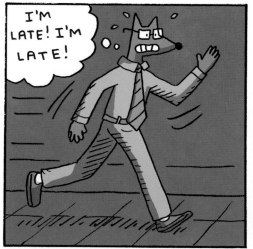

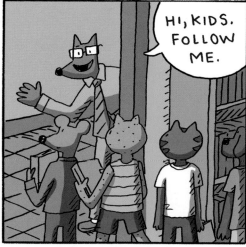

55

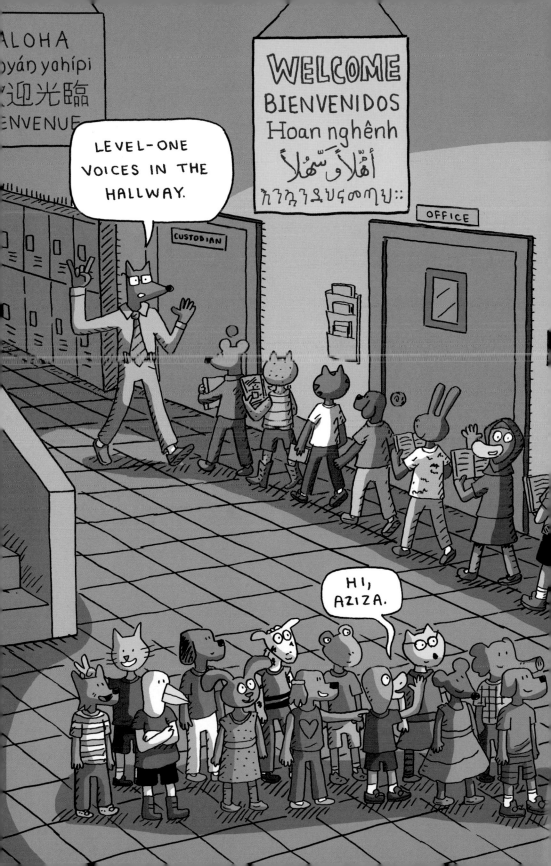

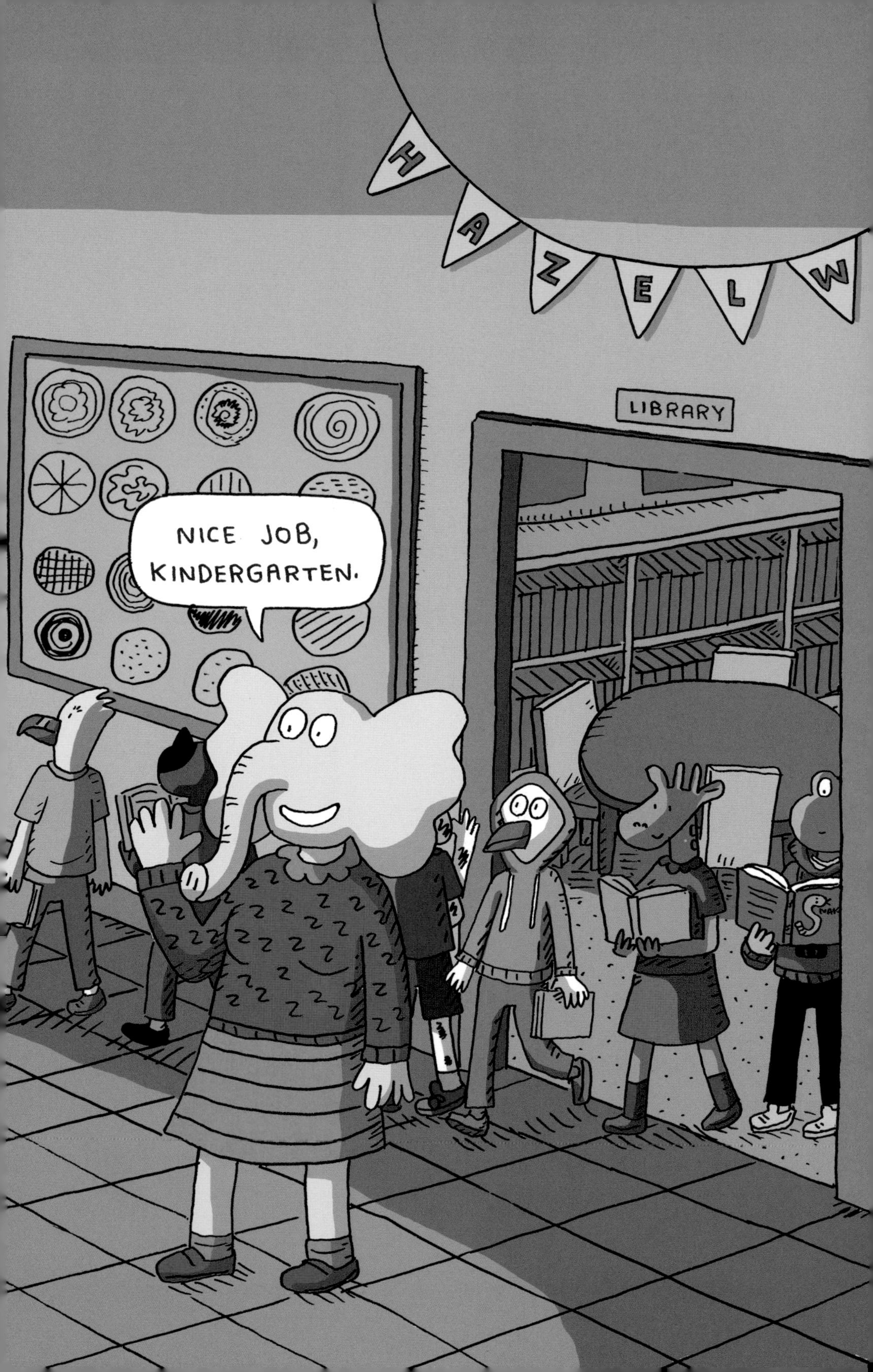
H A Z E L W
LIBRARY
NICE JOB, KINDERGARTEN.

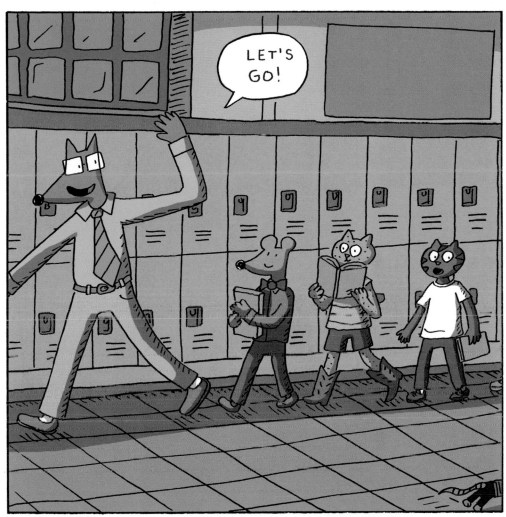

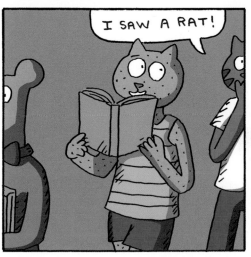

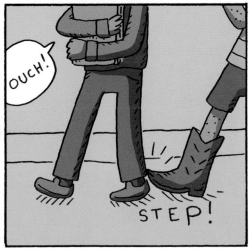

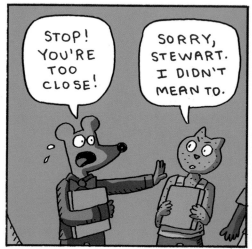

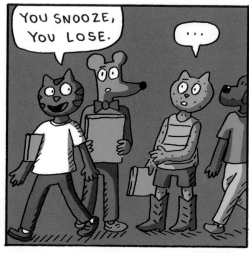

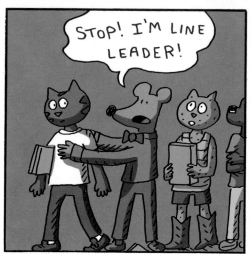

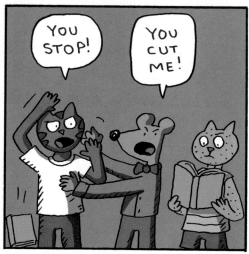

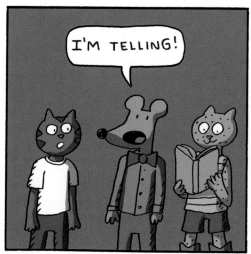

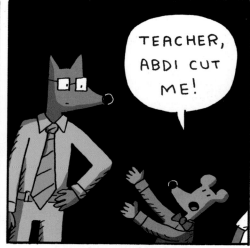

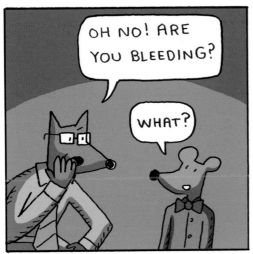

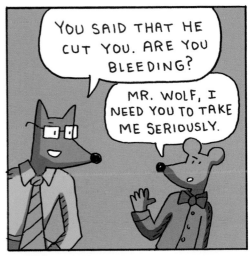

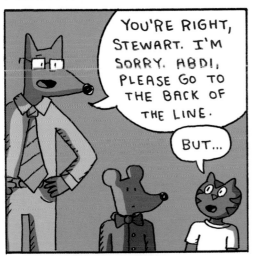

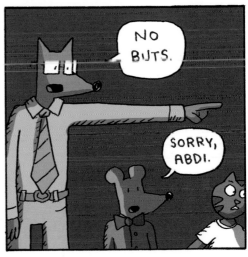

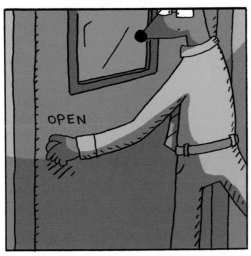

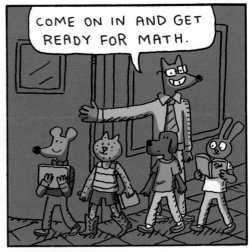

CHAPTER FIVE

Survey Says

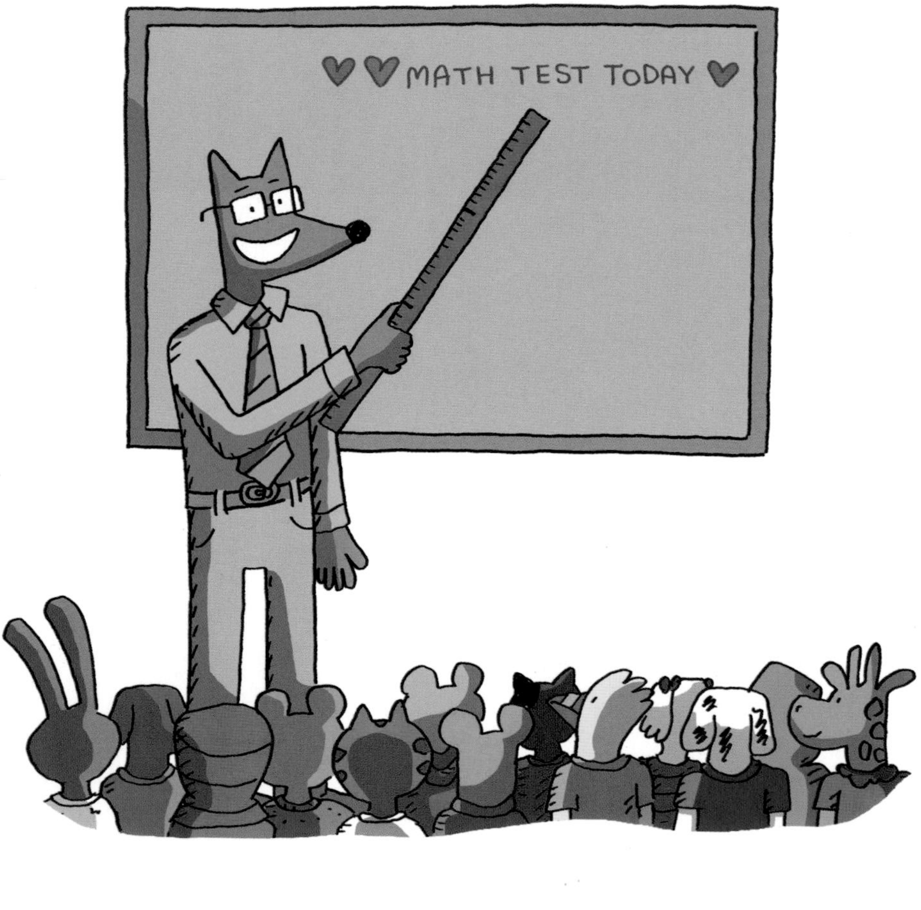
MATH TEST TODAY

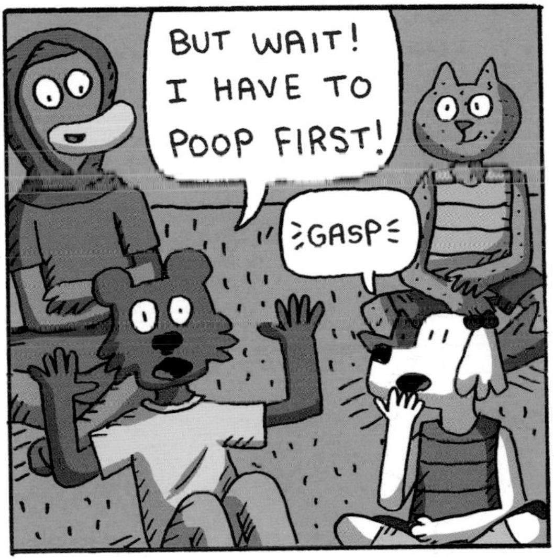
BUT WAIT! I HAVE TO POOP FIRST!
GASP

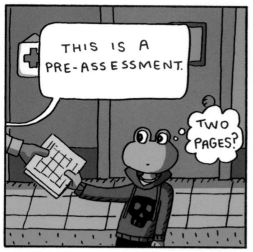

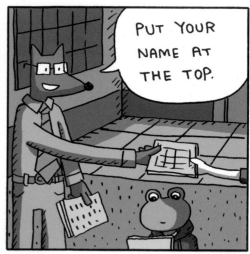

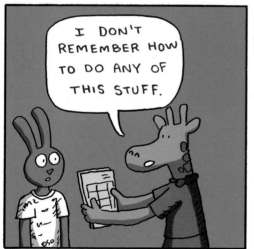

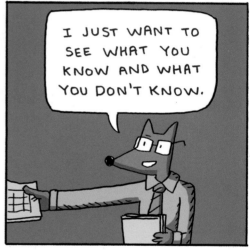

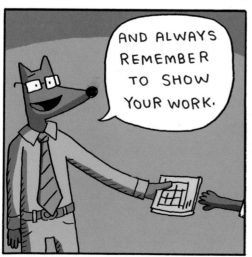

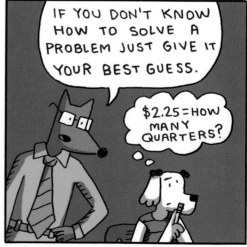

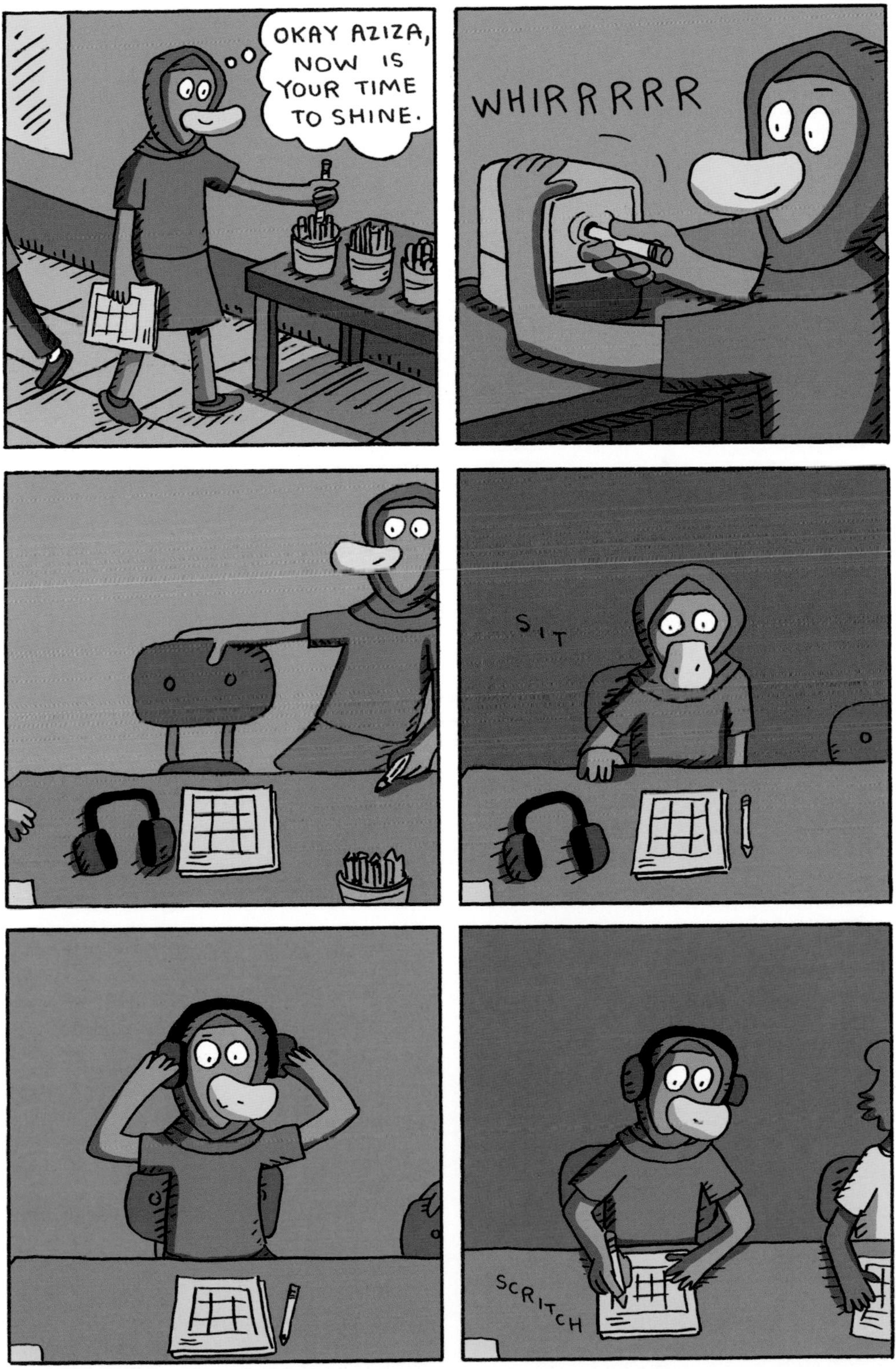
OKAY AZIZA, NOW IS YOUR TIME TO SHINE.
WHIRRRRR
SIT
SCRITCH

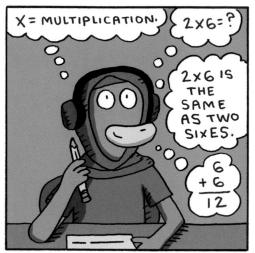

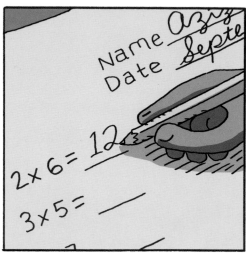

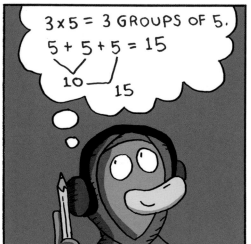

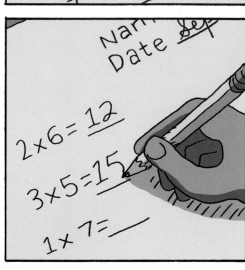

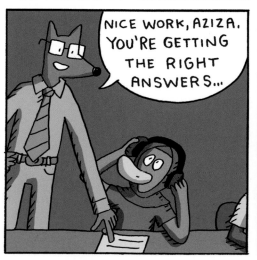

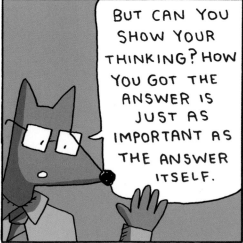

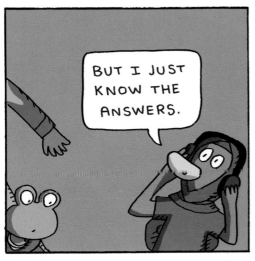

BUT I JUST KNOW THE ANSWERS.

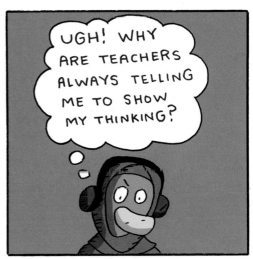

UGH! WHY ARE TEACHERS ALWAYS TELLING ME TO SHOW MY THINKING?

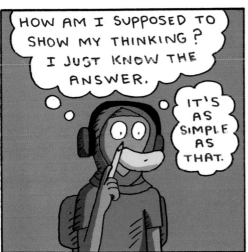

HOW AM I SUPPOSED TO SHOW MY THINKING? I JUST KNOW THE ANSWER.

IT'S AS SIMPLE AS THAT.

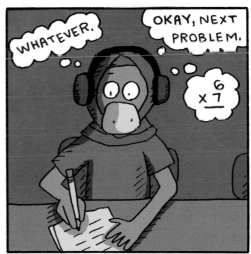

WHATEVER.

OKAY, NEXT PROBLEM.

$\begin{array}{r} 6 \\ \times 7 \\ \hline \end{array}$

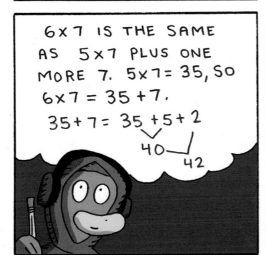

6 × 7 IS THE SAME AS 5 × 7 PLUS ONE MORE 7. 5 × 7 = 35, SO 6 × 7 = 35 + 7.

35 + 7 = 35 + 5 + 2

40

42

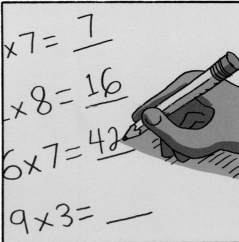

×7 = 7

×8 = 16

6 × 7 = 42

9 × 3 = ___

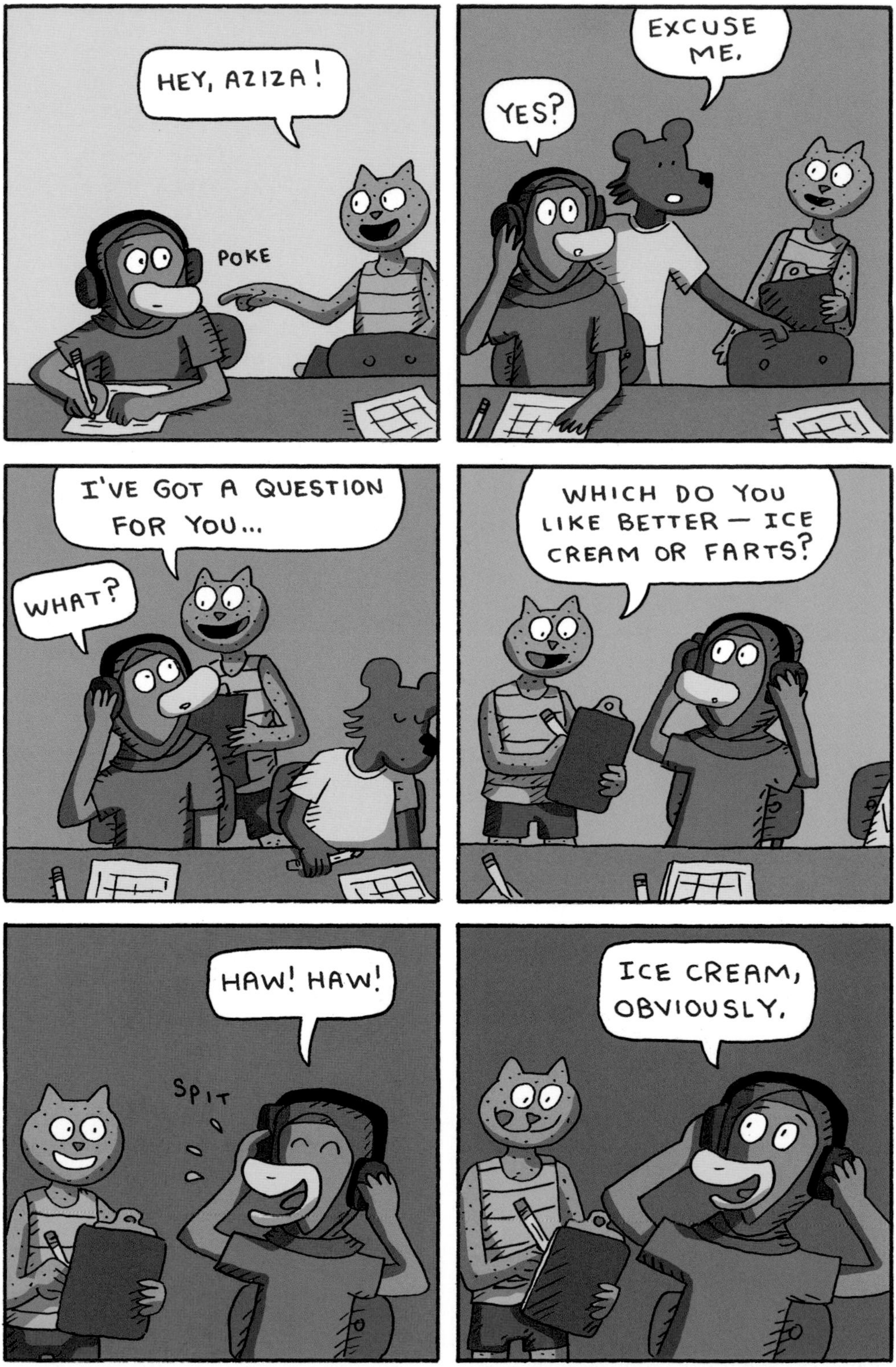
HEY, AZIZA!
POKE
EXCUSE ME.
YES?
I'VE GOT A QUESTION FOR YOU...
WHAT?
WHICH DO YOU LIKE BETTER — ICE CREAM OR FARTS?
HAW! HAW!
SPIT
ICE CREAM, OBVIOUSLY.

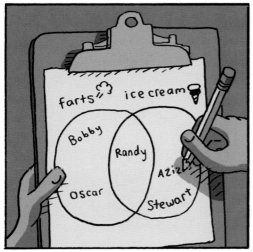

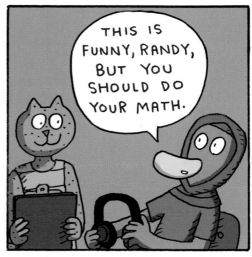

THIS IS FUNNY, RANDY, BUT YOU SHOULD DO YOUR MATH.

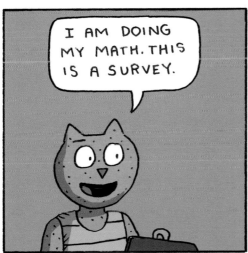

I AM DOING MY MATH. THIS IS A SURVEY.

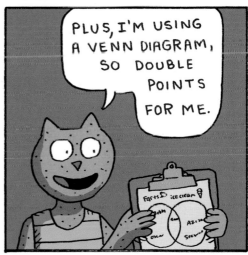

PLUS, I'M USING A VENN DIAGRAM, SO DOUBLE POINTS FOR ME.

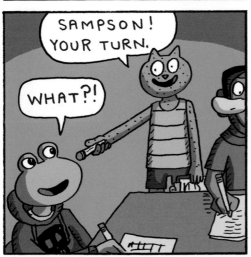

SAMPSON! YOUR TURN.

WHAT?!

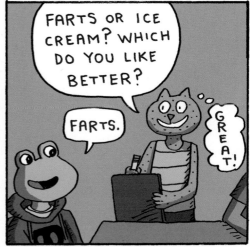

FARTS OR ICE CREAM? WHICH DO YOU LIKE BETTER?

FARTS.

GREAT!

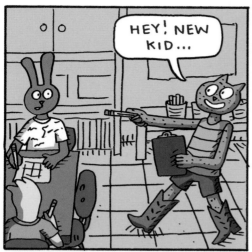

HEY! NEW KID...

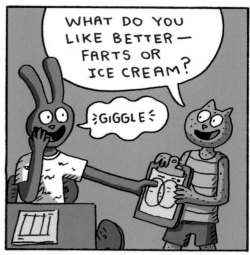

WHAT DO YOU LIKE BETTER — FARTS OR ICE CREAM?

GIGGLE

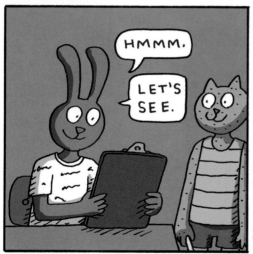

HMMM.

LET'S SEE.

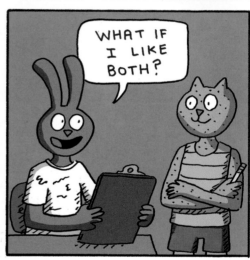

WHAT IF I LIKE BOTH?

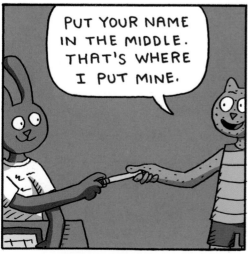

PUT YOUR NAME IN THE MIDDLE. THAT'S WHERE I PUT MINE.

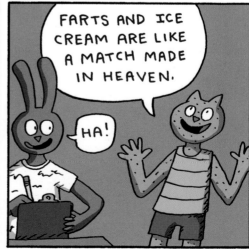

FARTS AND ICE CREAM ARE LIKE A MATCH MADE IN HEAVEN.

HA!

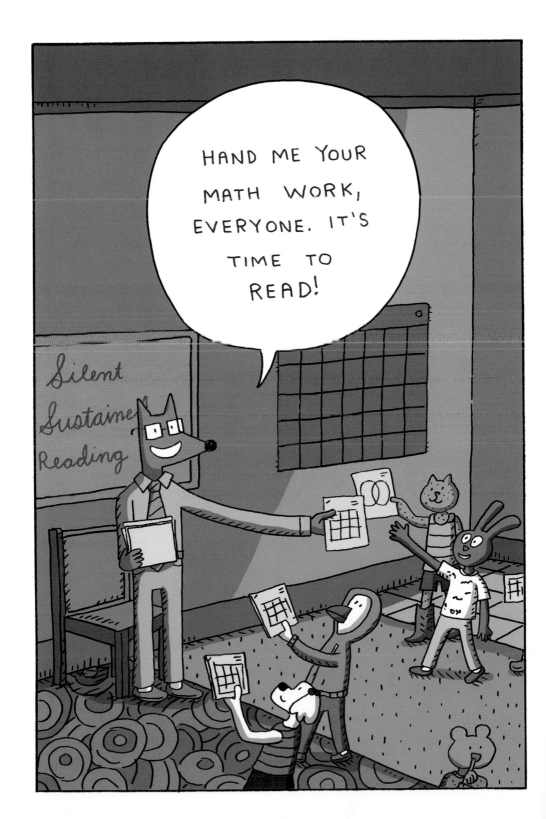

CHAPTER SIX
Someone Is Missing

DISCARD
OLD
BOOK
DONATIONS

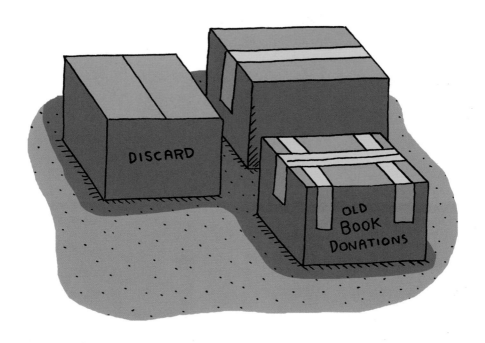

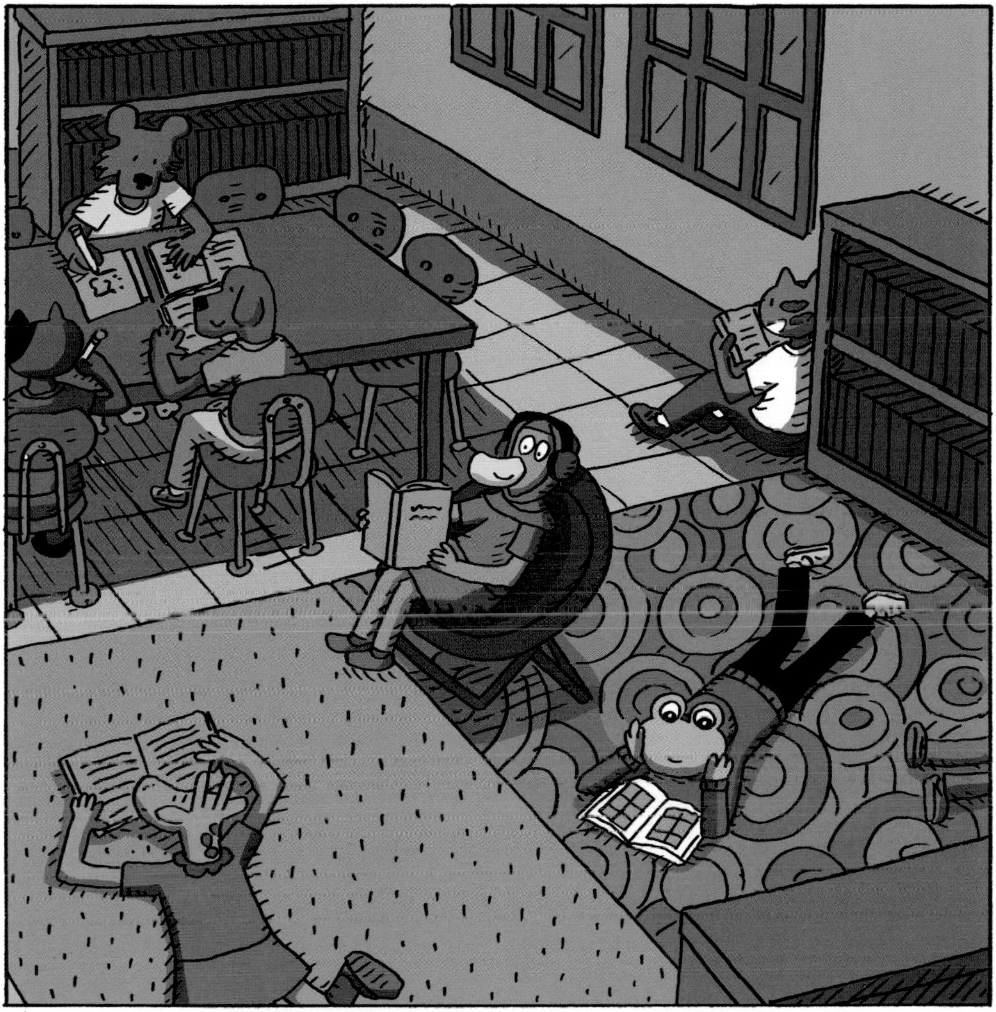

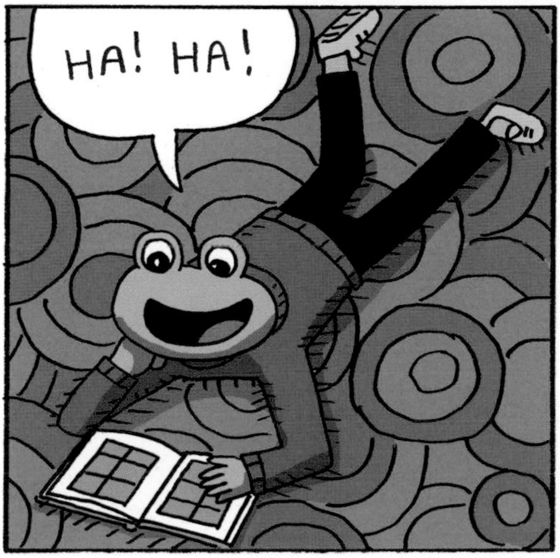
HA! HA!

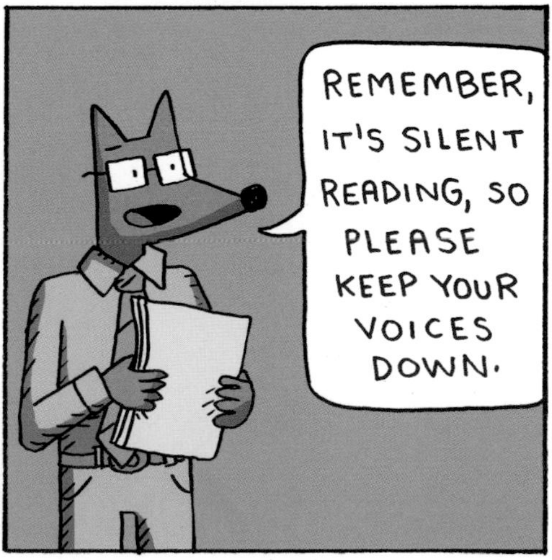
REMEMBER, IT'S SILENT READING, SO PLEASE KEEP YOUR VOICES DOWN.

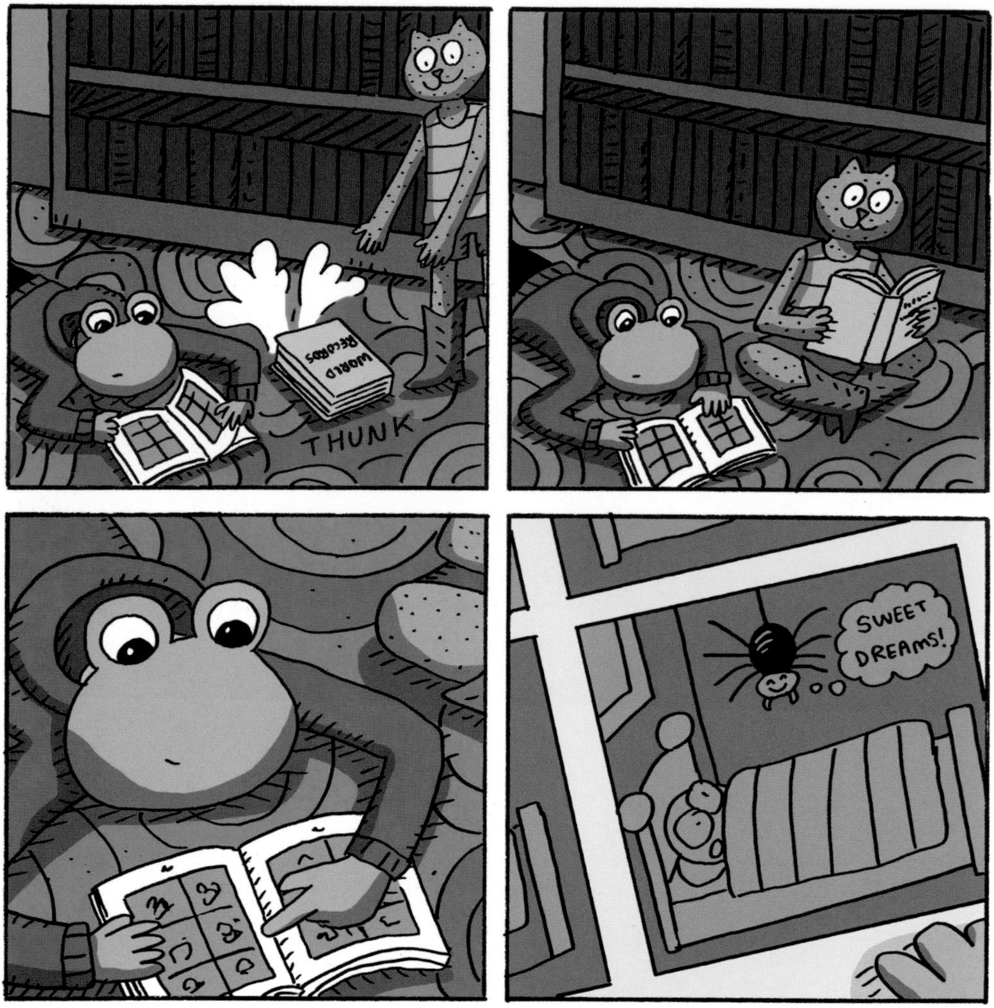
WORLD RECORDS
THUNK
SWEET DREAMS!
HAW HAW HAW
OOPS!

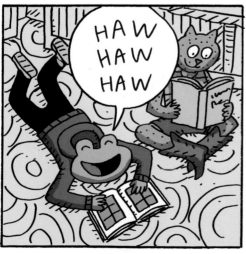

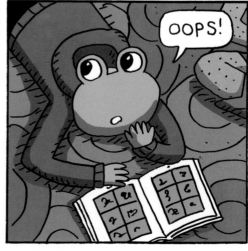

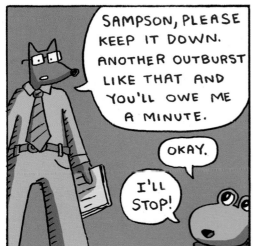

SAMPSON, PLEASE KEEP IT DOWN. ANOTHER OUTBURST LIKE THAT AND YOU'LL OWE ME A MINUTE.

OKAY.

I'LL STOP!

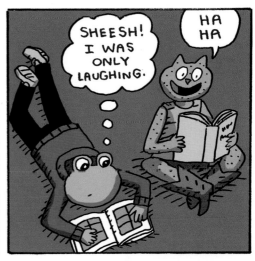

SHEESH! I WAS ONLY LAUGHING.

HA HA

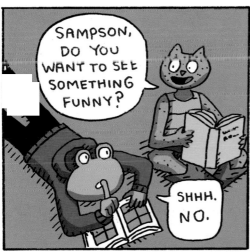

SAMPSON, DO YOU WANT TO SEE SOMETHING FUNNY?

SHHH. NO.

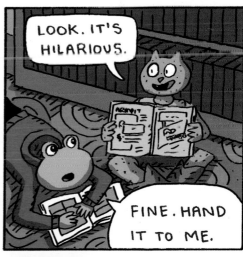

LOOK. IT'S HILARIOUS.

FINE. HAND IT TO ME.

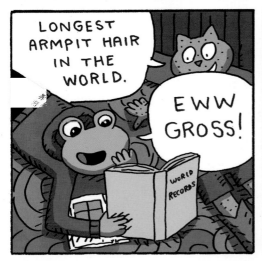

LONGEST ARMPIT HAIR IN THE WORLD.

EWW GROSS!

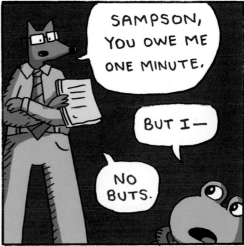

SAMPSON, YOU OWE ME ONE MINUTE.

BUT I—

NO BUTS.

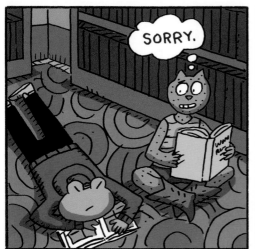

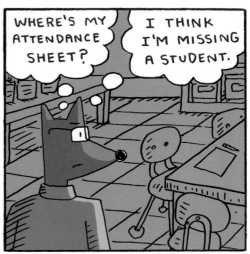

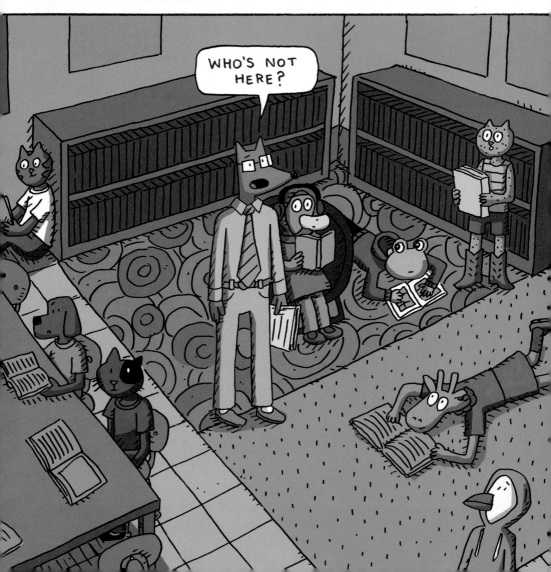

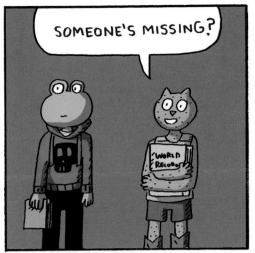

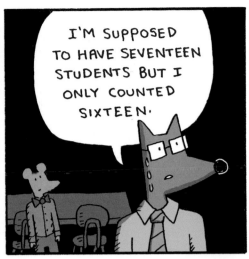

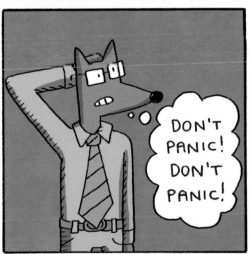

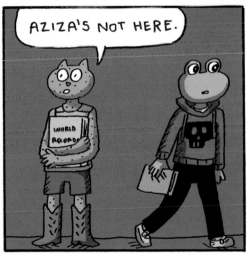

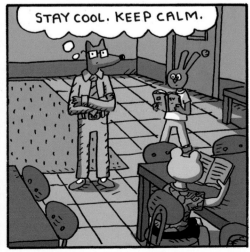

76

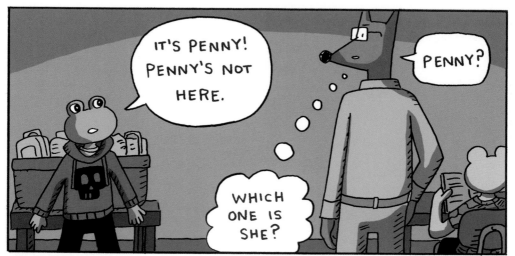

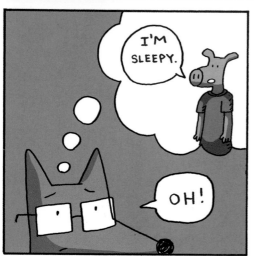

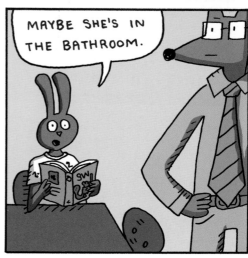

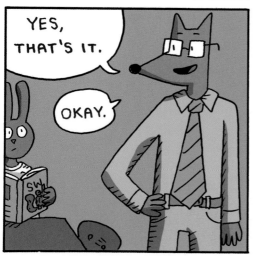

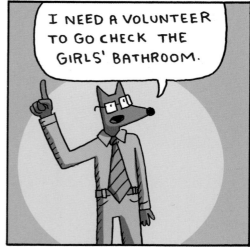

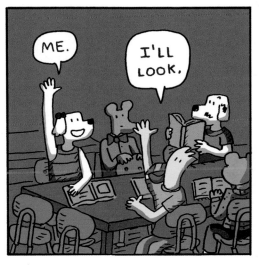

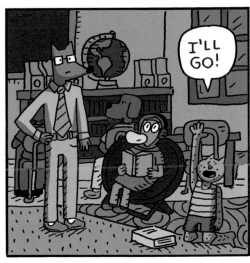

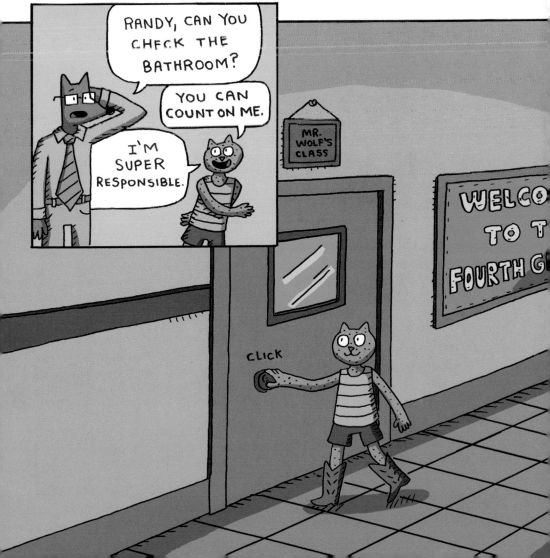

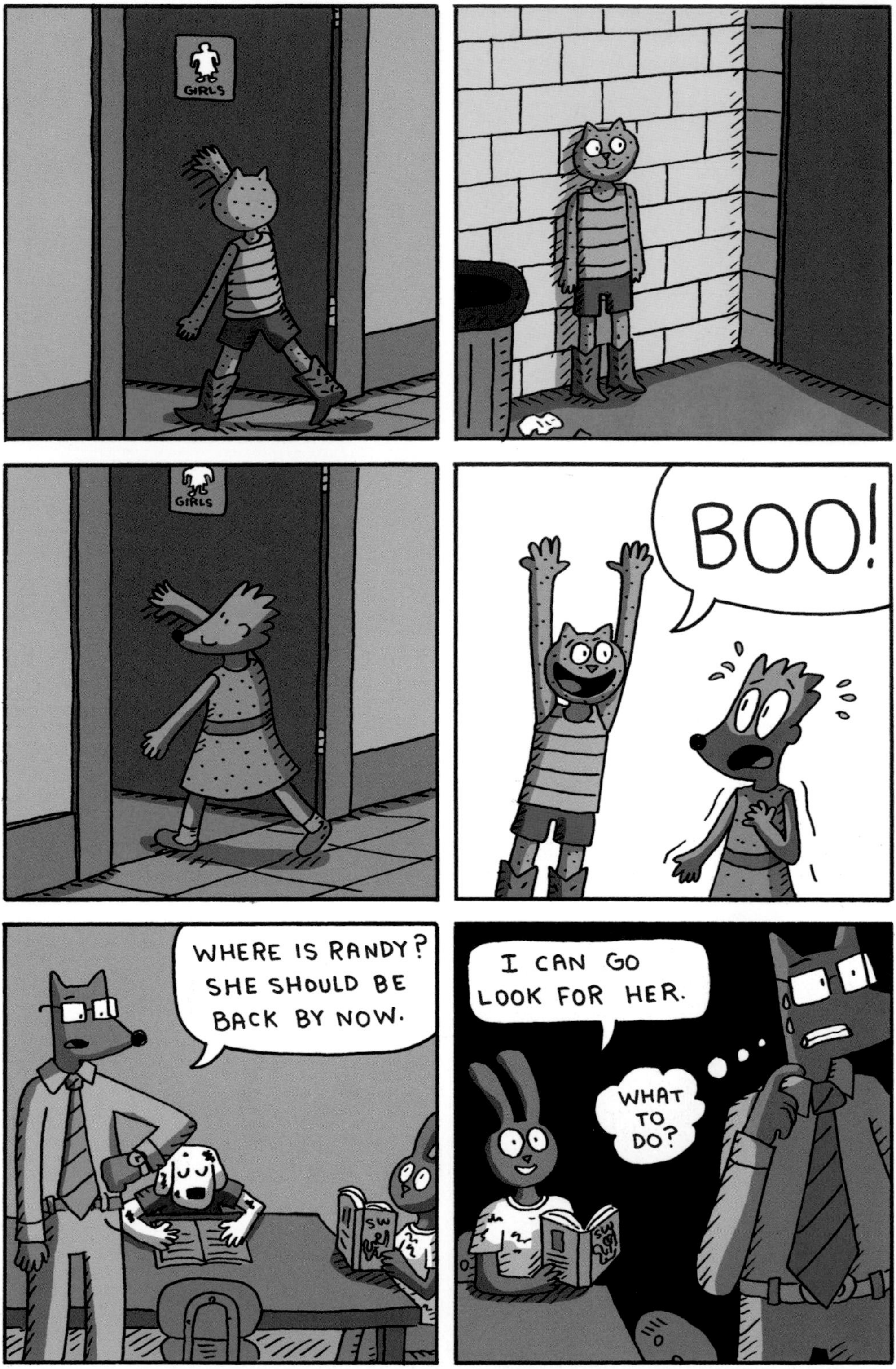
GIRLS
GIRLS
BOO!
WHERE IS RANDY? SHE SHOULD BE BACK BY NOW.
I CAN GO LOOK FOR HER.
WHAT TO DO?

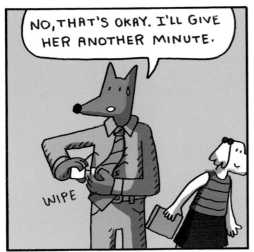

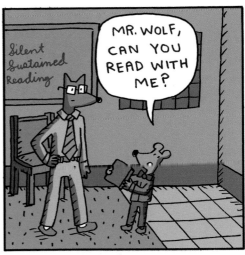

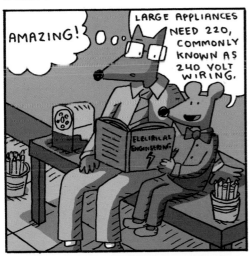

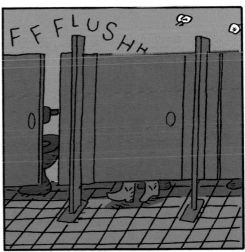

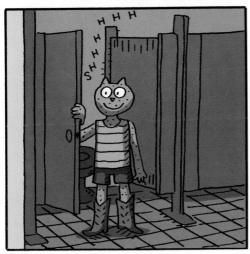

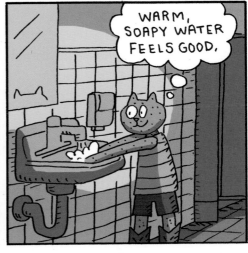

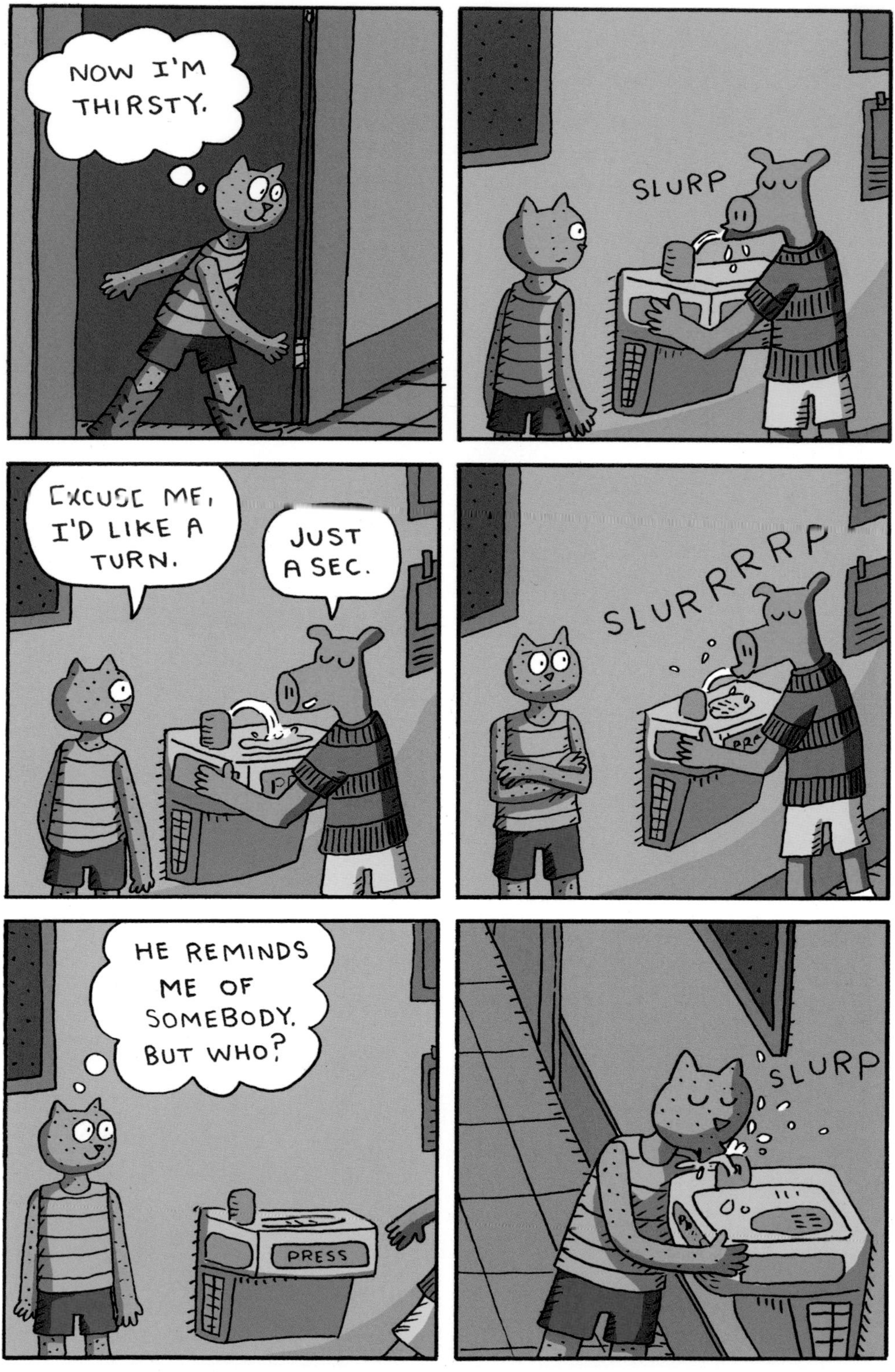
NOW I'M THIRSTY.
SLURP
EXCUSE ME, I'D LIKE A TURN.
JUST A SEC.
SLURRRRP
HE REMINDS ME OF SOMEBODY. BUT WHO?
PRESS
SLURP

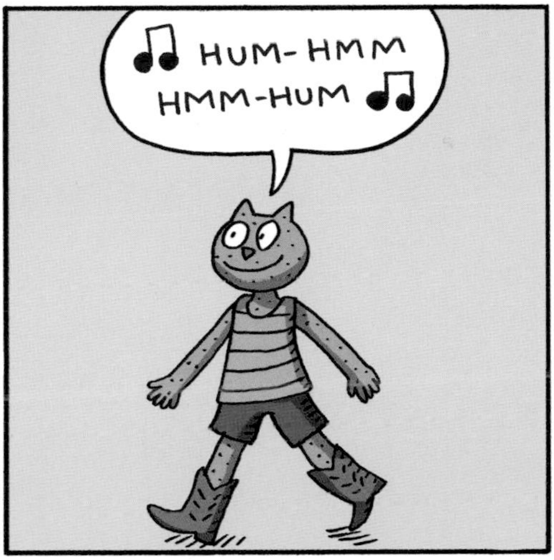
HUM-HMM HMM-HUM

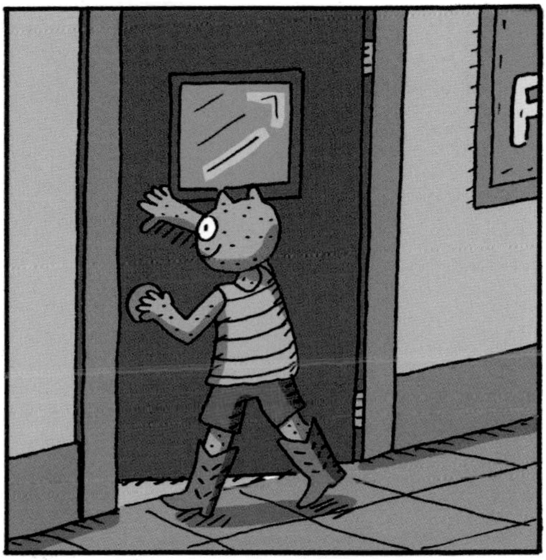

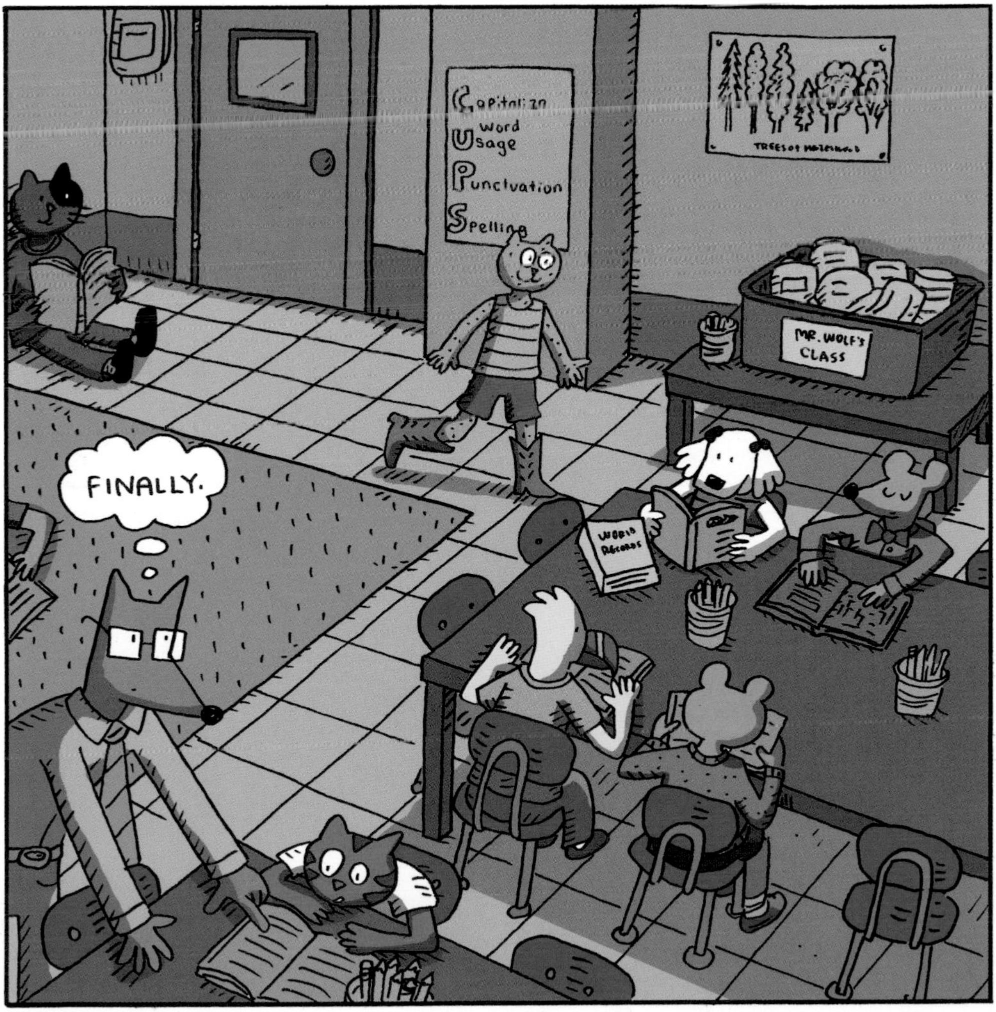
Capitalizn
Word Usage
Punctuation
Spelling
MR. WOLF'S CLASS
FINALLY.

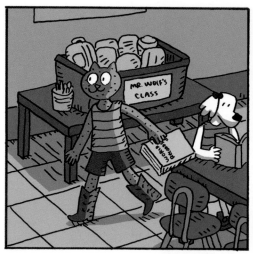

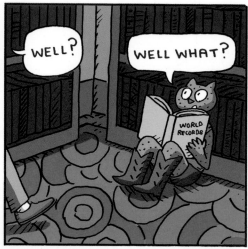

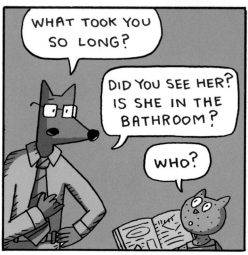

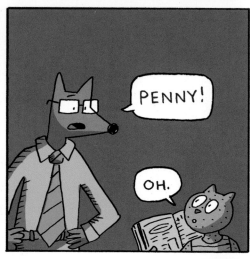

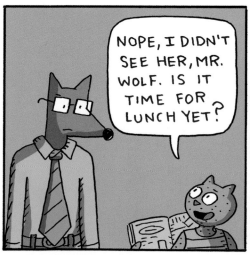

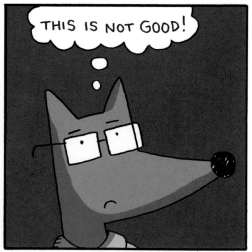

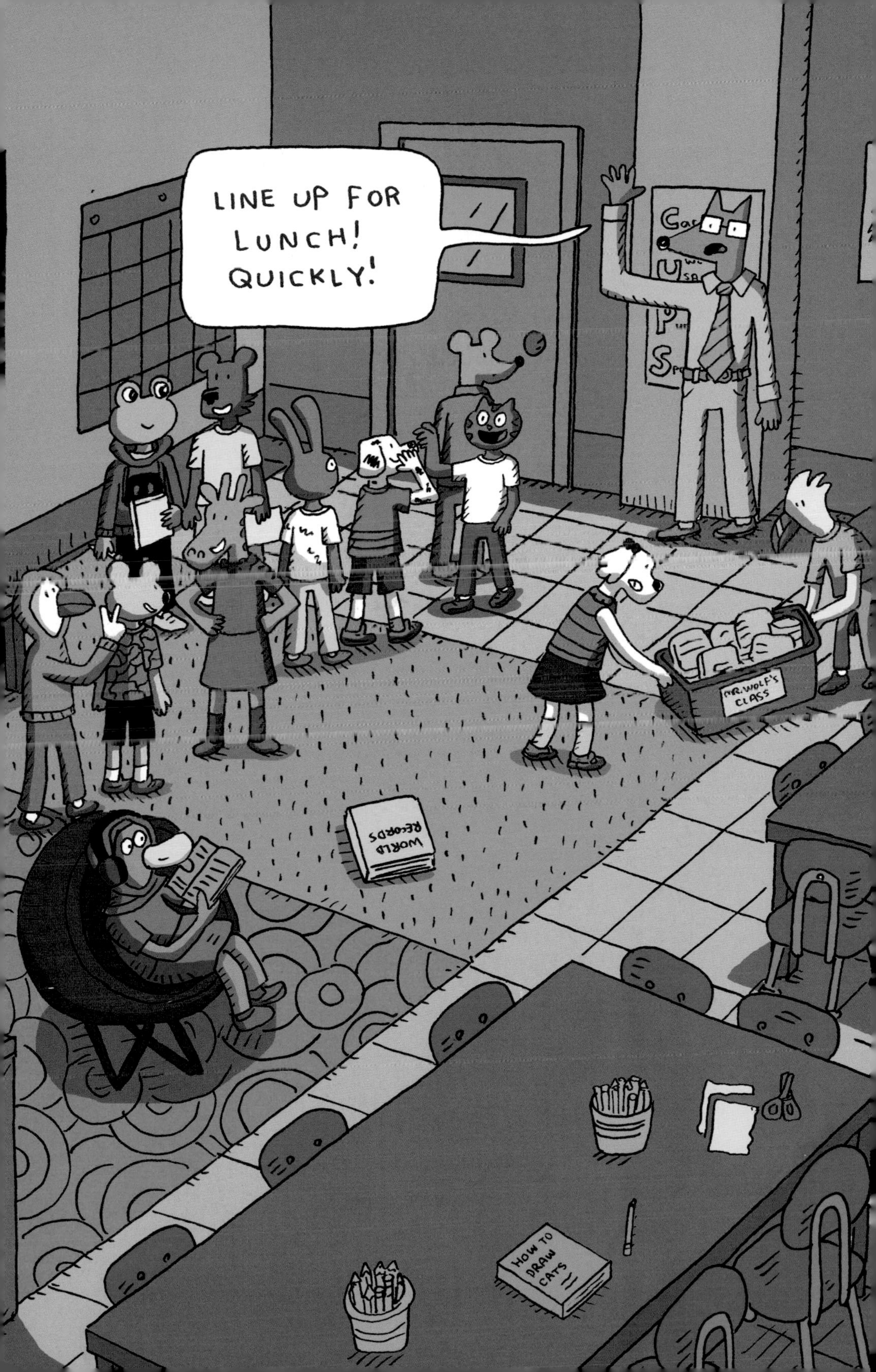
LINE UP FOR LUNCH! QUICKLY!
MR. WOLF'S CLASS
WORLD RECORDS
HOW TO DRAW CATS

CHAPTER SEVEN
Rats!

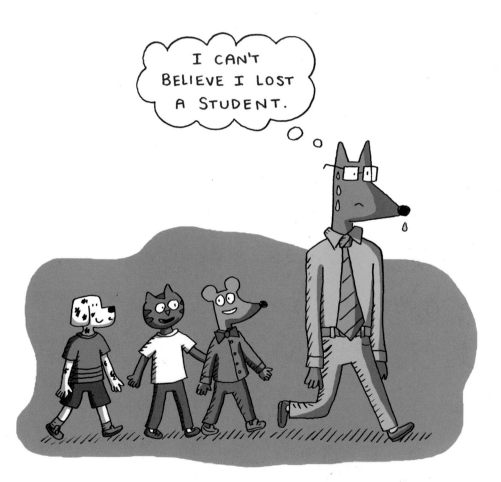

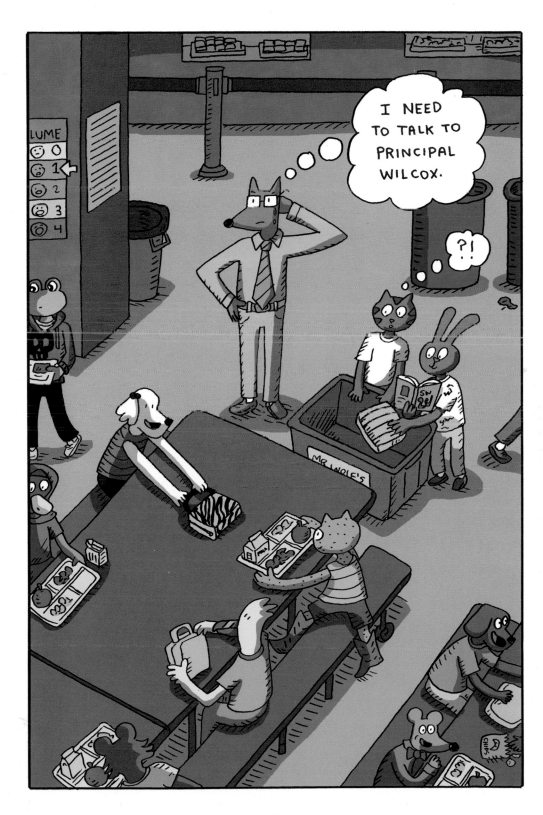

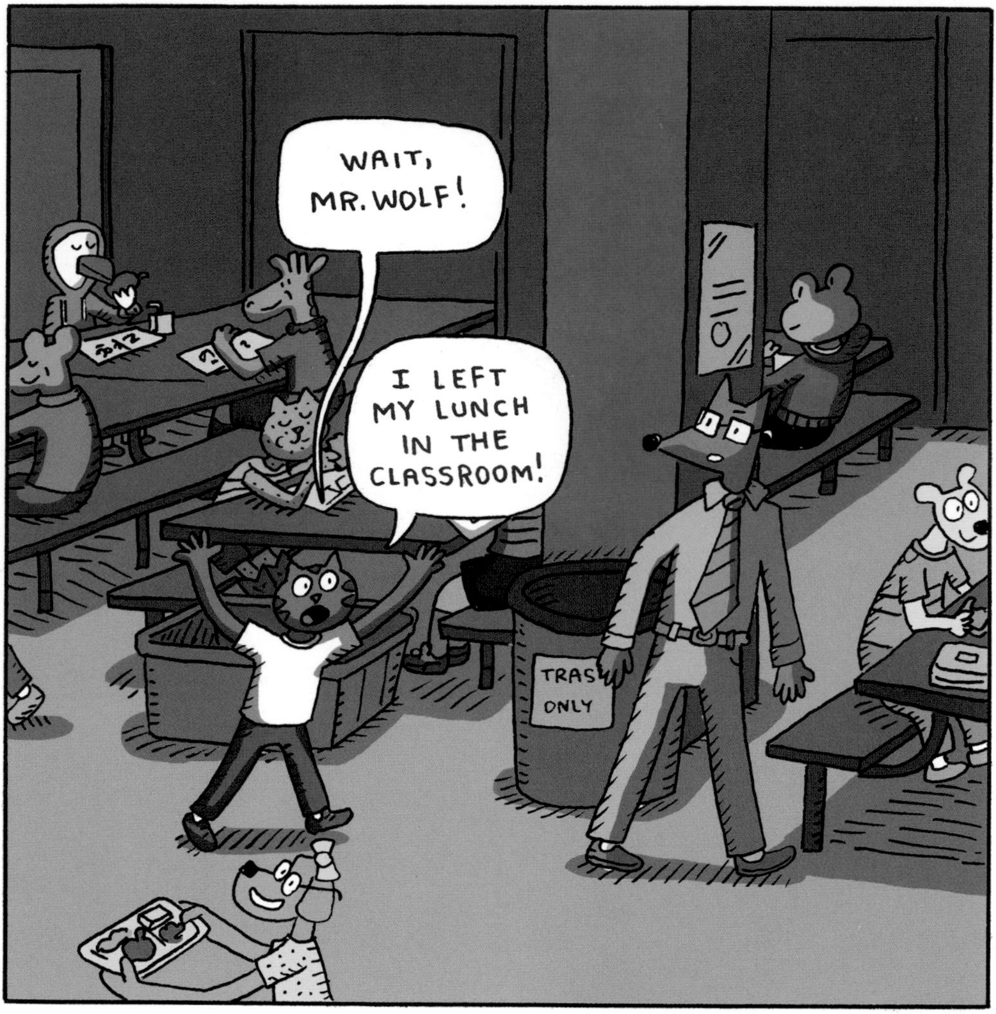
WAIT, MR. WOLF!
I LEFT MY LUNCH IN THE CLASSROOM!
TRAS ONLY

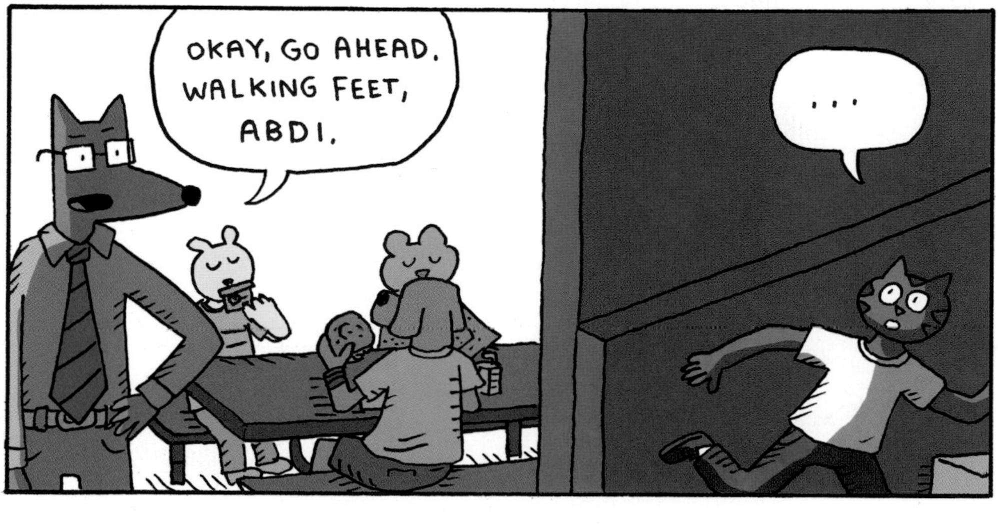
OKAY, GO AHEAD. WALKING FEET, ABDI.
...

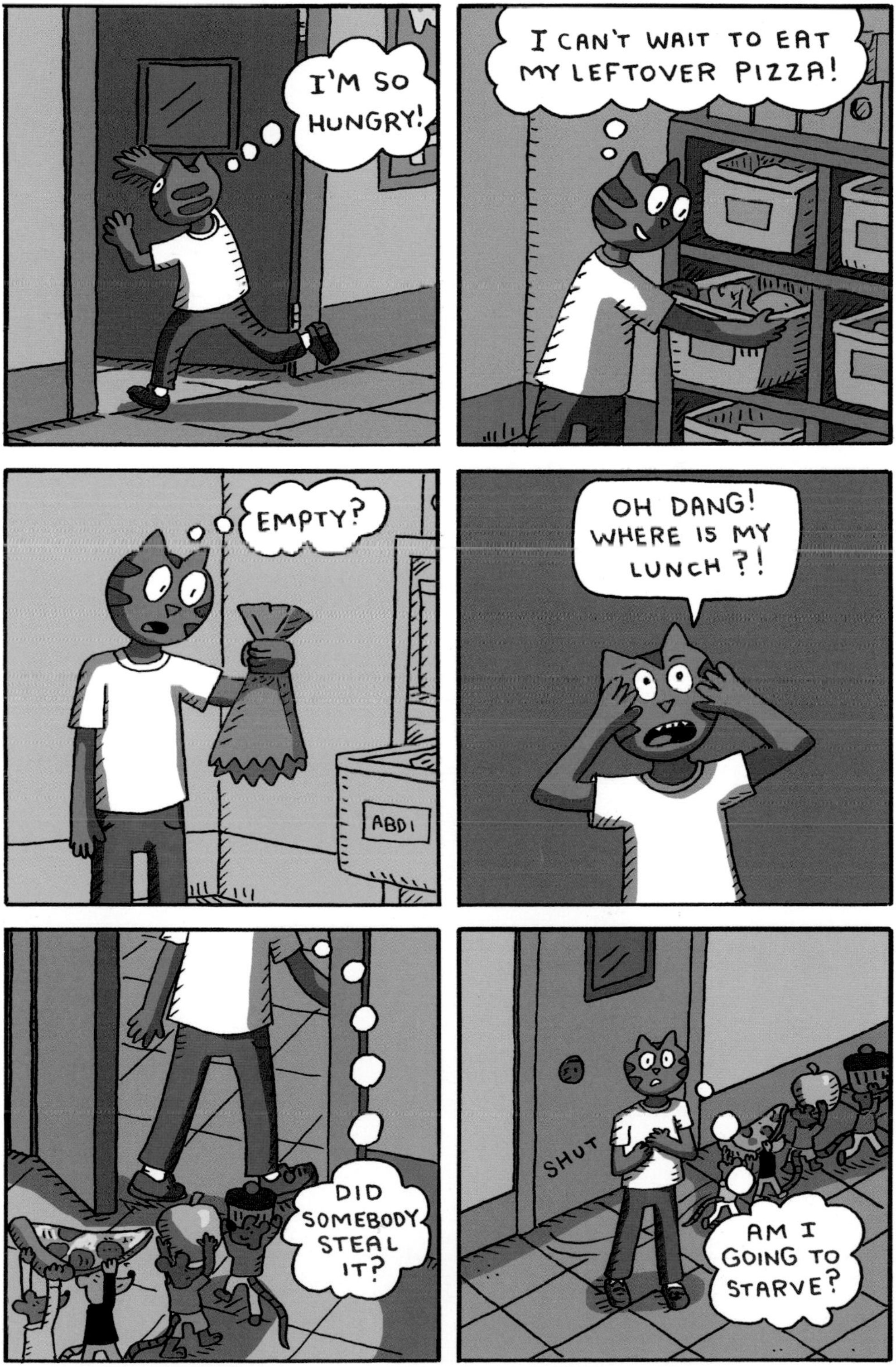
I'M SO HUNGRY!
I CAN'T WAIT TO EAT MY LEFTOVER PIZZA!
EMPTY?
ABDI
OH DANG! WHERE IS MY LUNCH ?!
DID SOMEBODY STEAL IT?
SHUT
AM I GOING TO STARVE?

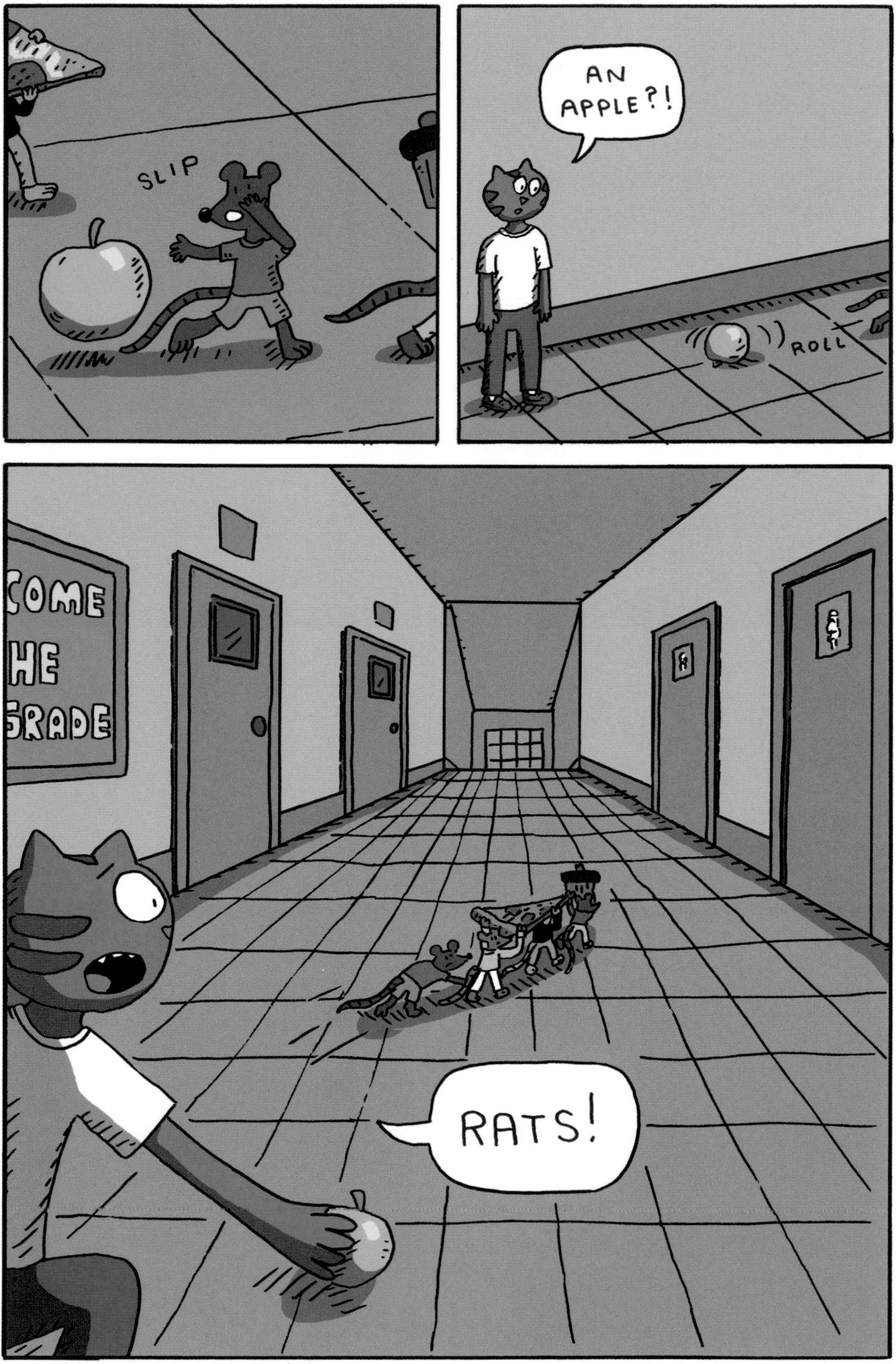
SLIP
AN APPLE?!
ROLL
RATS!

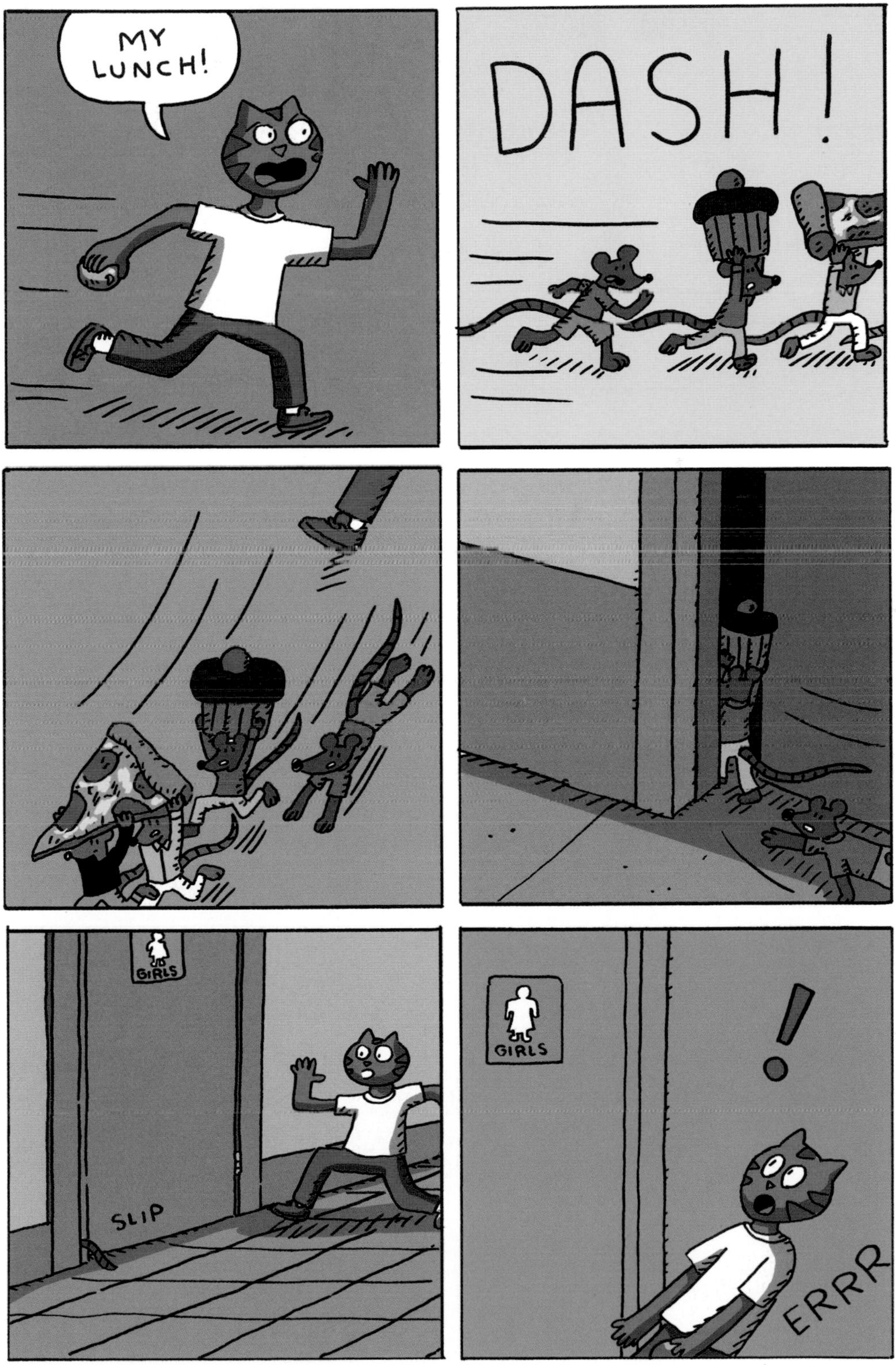
MY LUNCH!
DASH!
GIRLS
SLIP
GIRLS
!
ERRR

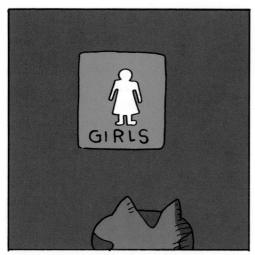

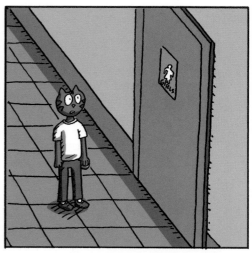

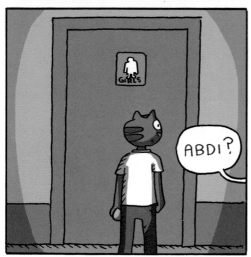

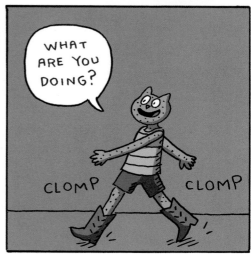

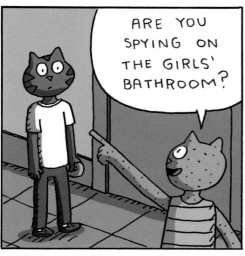

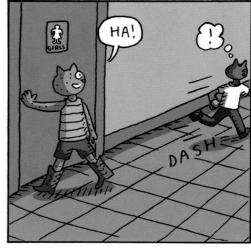

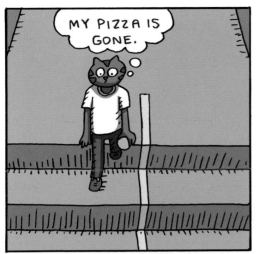

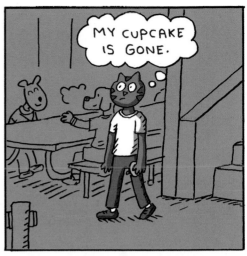

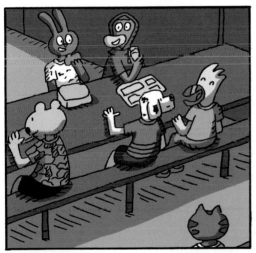

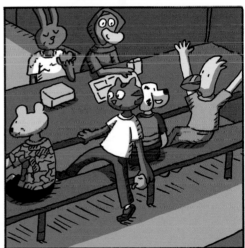

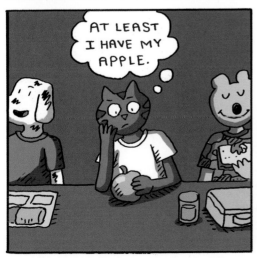

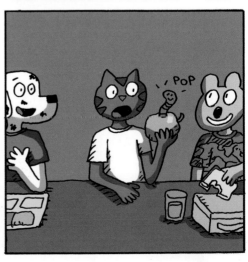

CHAPTER EIGHT
A Close Call

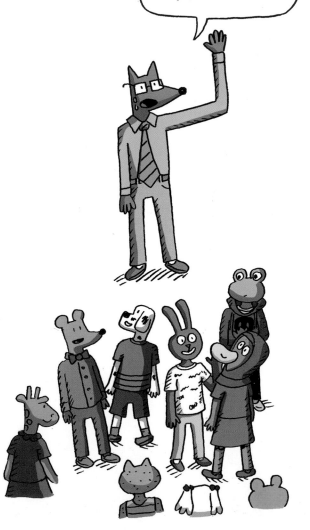

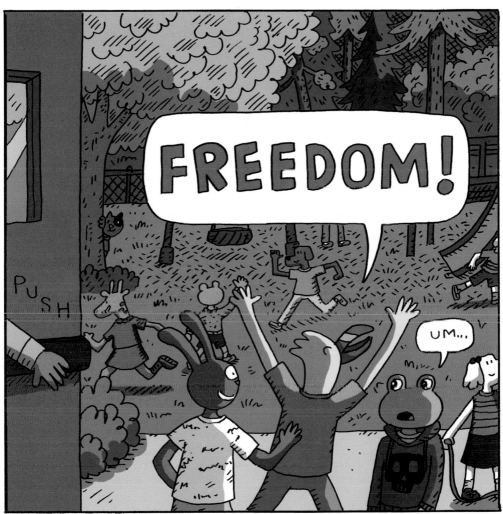

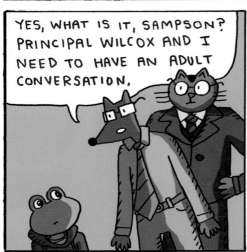

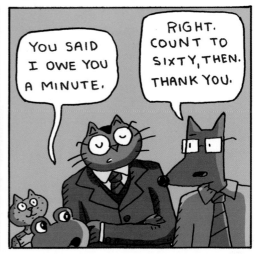

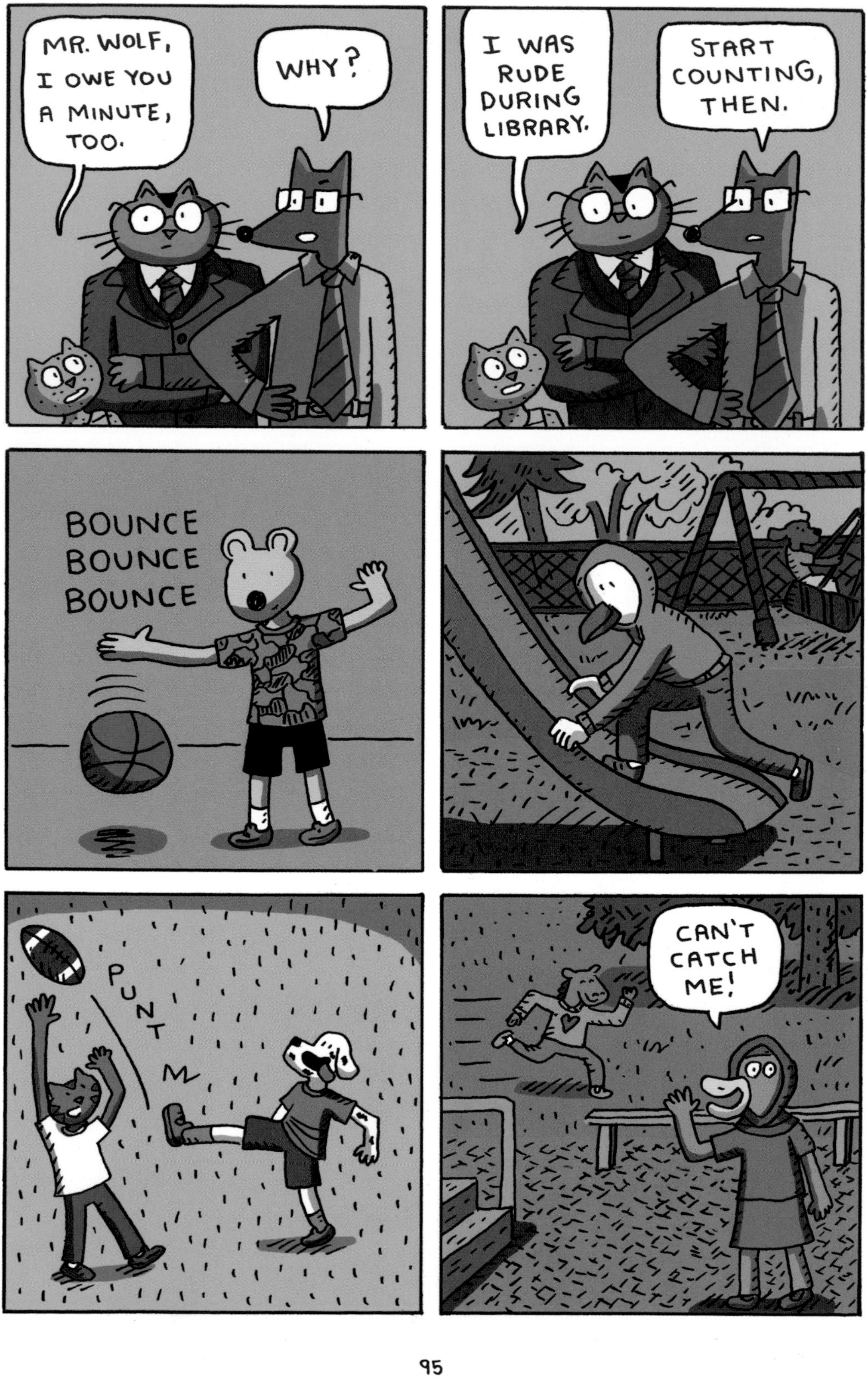
MR. WOLF, I OWE YOU A MINUTE, TOO.
WHY?
I WAS RUDE DURING LIBRARY.
START COUNTING, THEN.
BOUNCE BOUNCE BOUNCE
PUNT
CAN'T CATCH ME!

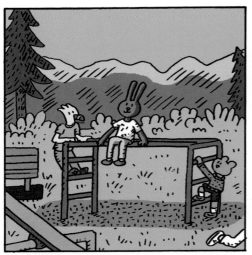
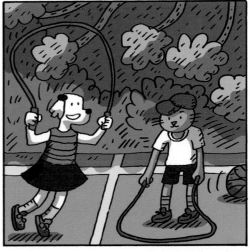
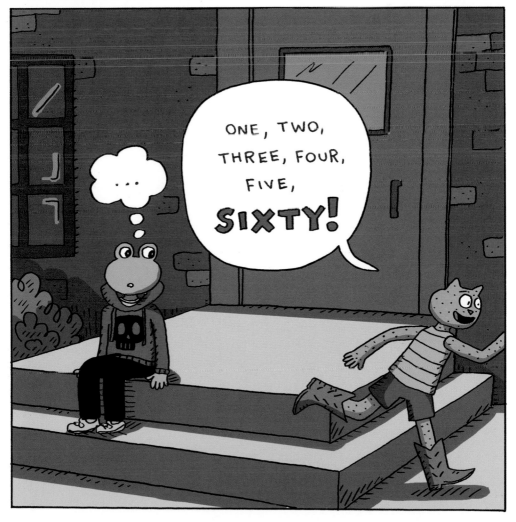

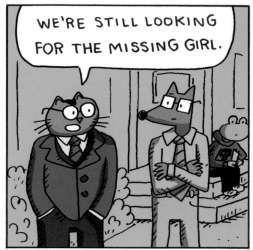

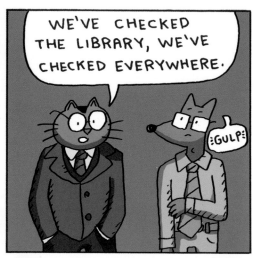

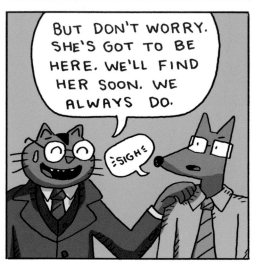

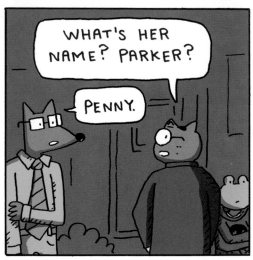

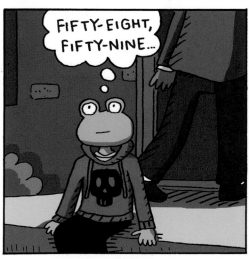

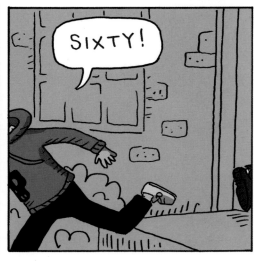

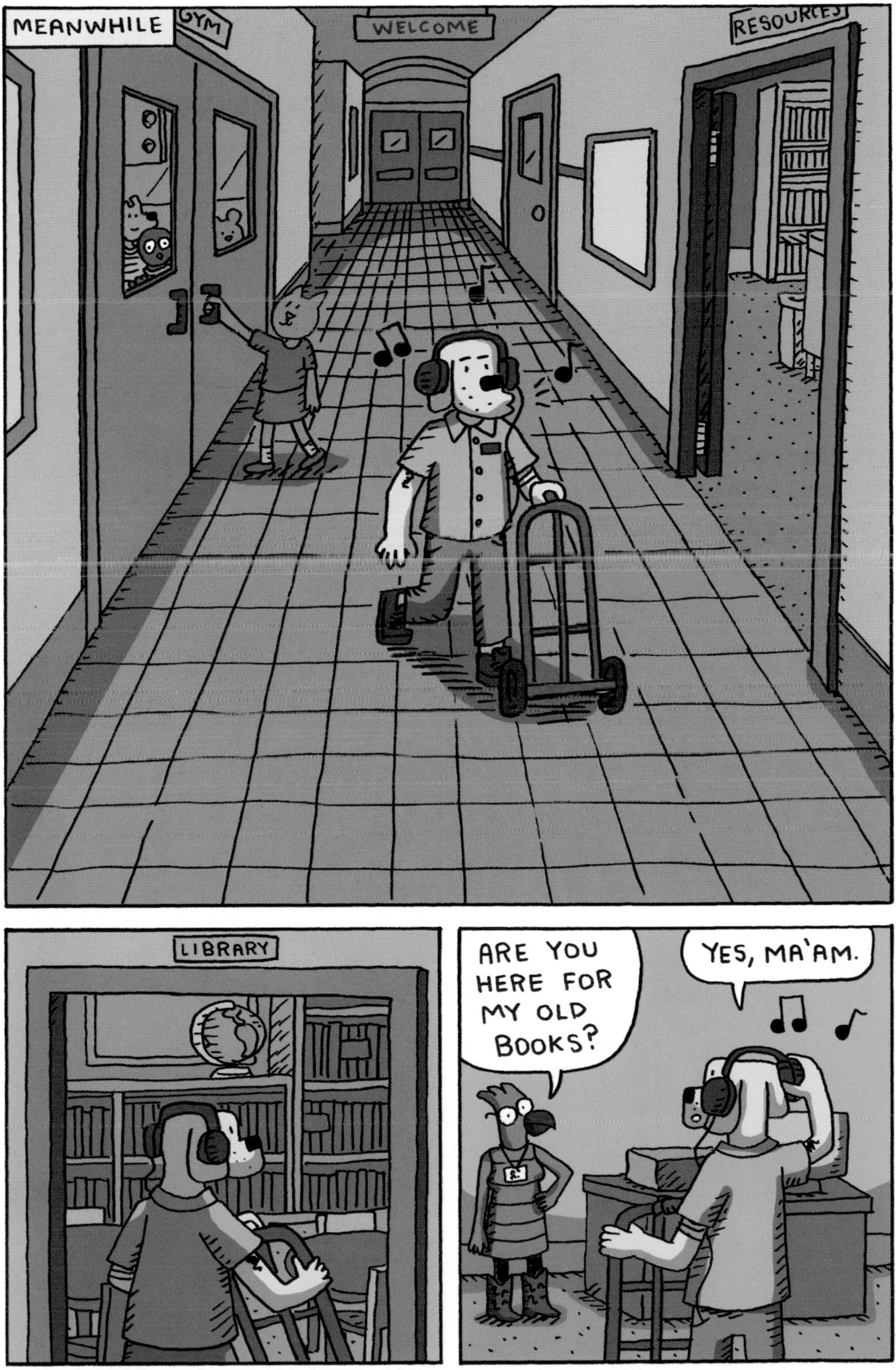
MEANWHILE
GYM
WELCOME
RESOURCES
LIBRARY
ARE YOU HERE FOR MY OLD BOOKS?
YES, MA'AM.

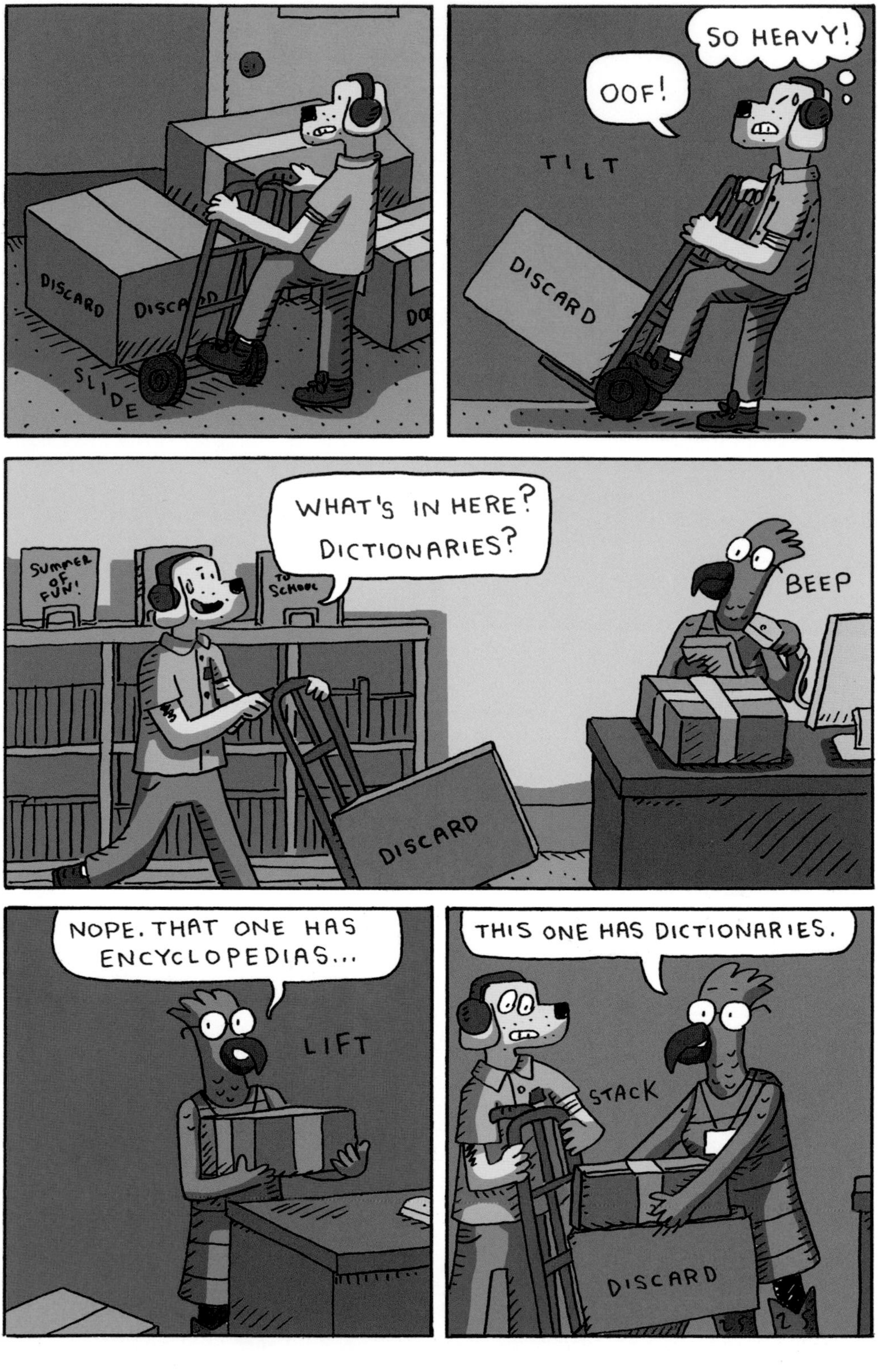
DISCARD
SLIDE
OOF!
SO HEAVY!
TILT
DISCARD
SUMMER OF FUN!
WHAT'S IN HERE? DICTIONARIES?
BEEP
DISCARD
NOPE. THAT ONE HAS ENCYCLOPEDIAS...
LIFT
THIS ONE HAS DICTIONARIES.
STACK
DISCARD

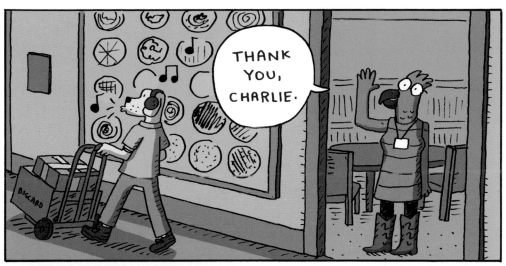

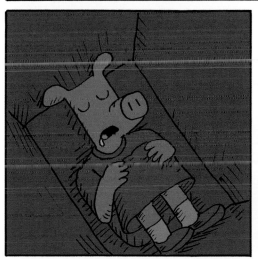

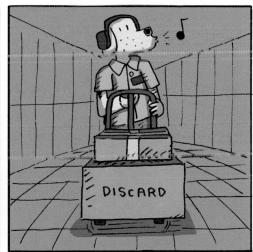

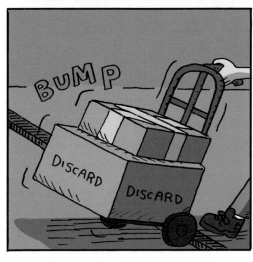

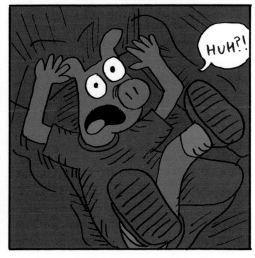

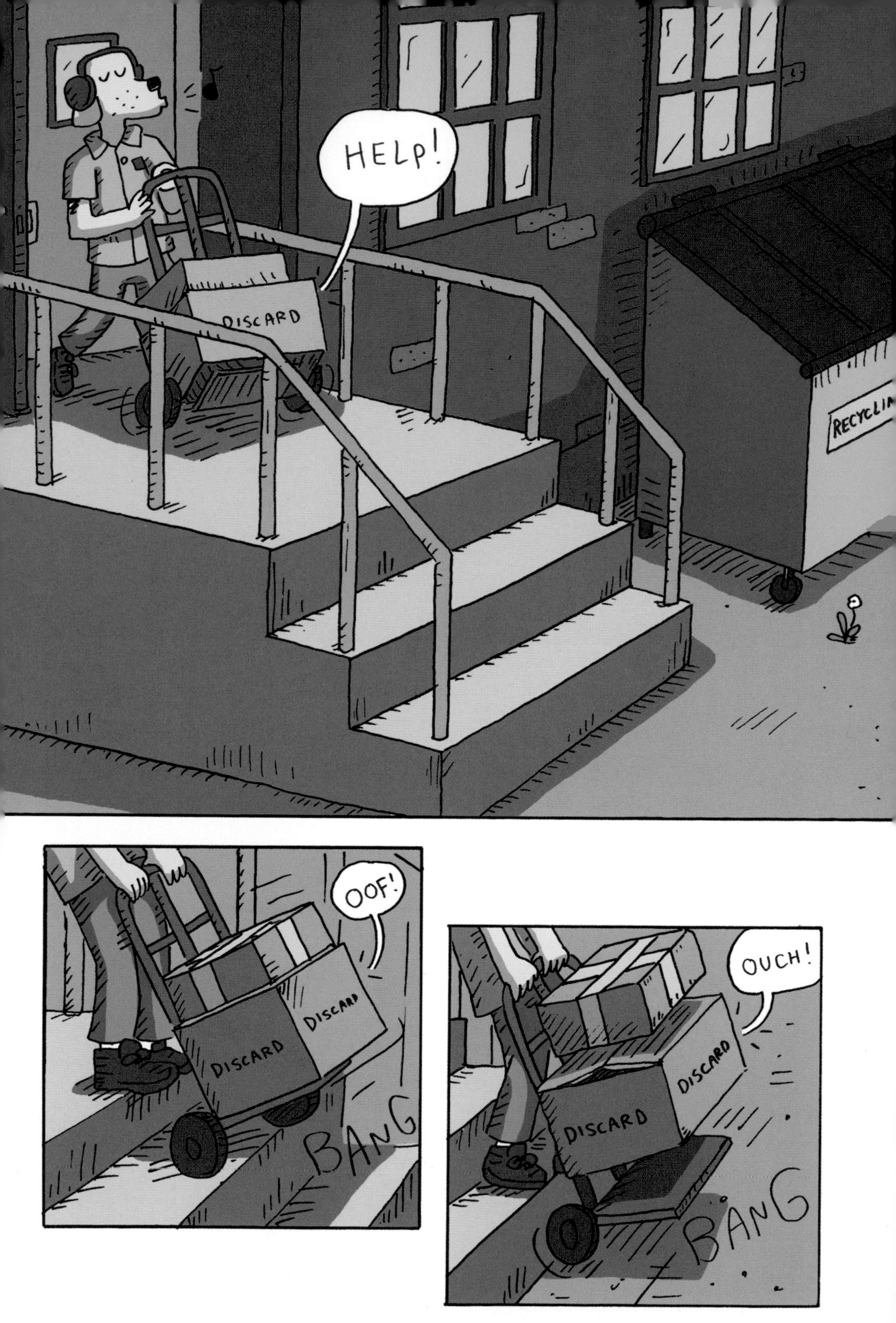
HELP!
DISCARD
RECYCLIN
OOF!
DISCARD
DISCARD
BANG
OUCH!
DISCARD
DISCARD
BANG

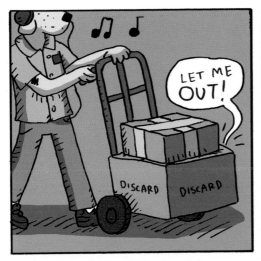

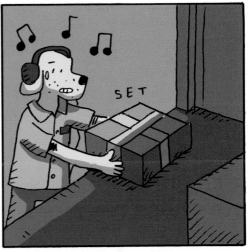

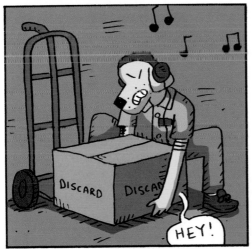

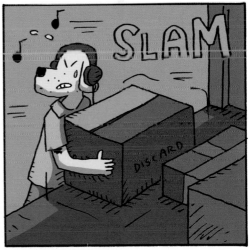

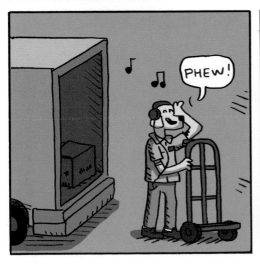

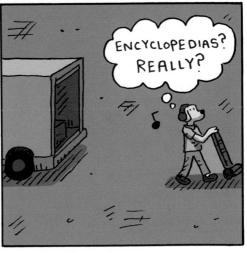

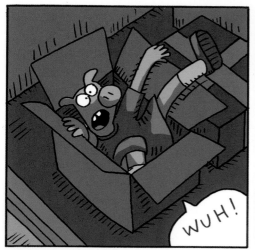

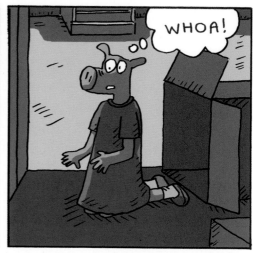

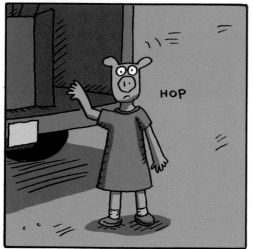

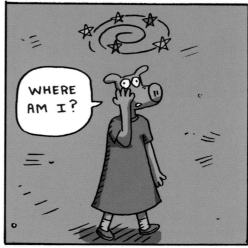

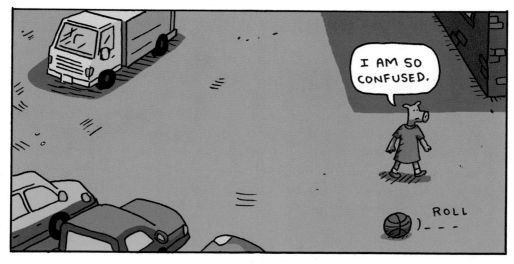

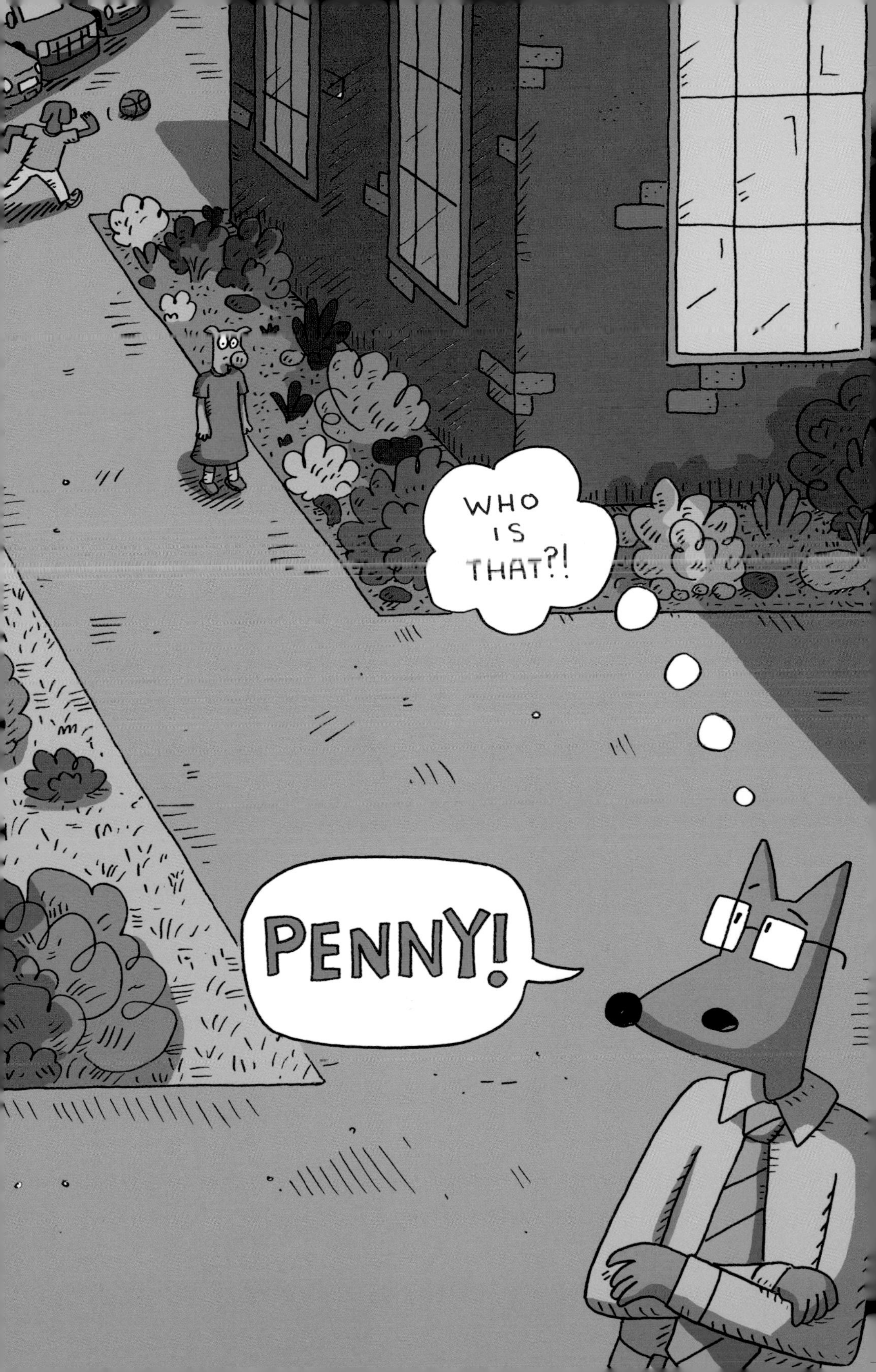
WHO IS THAT?!
PENNY!

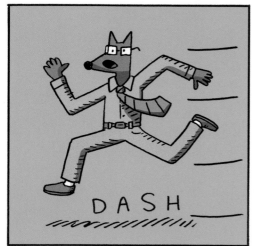

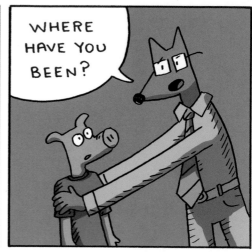

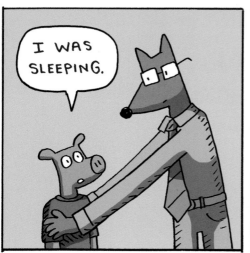

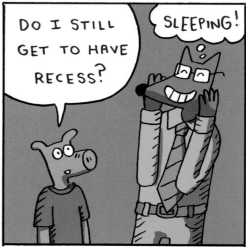

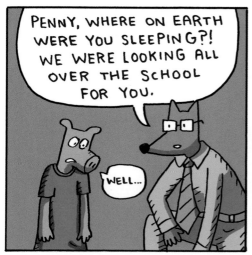

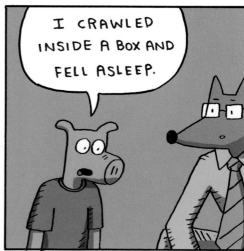

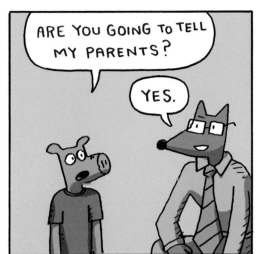

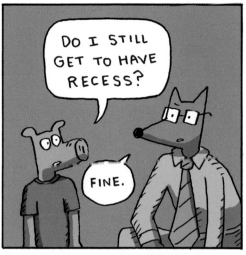

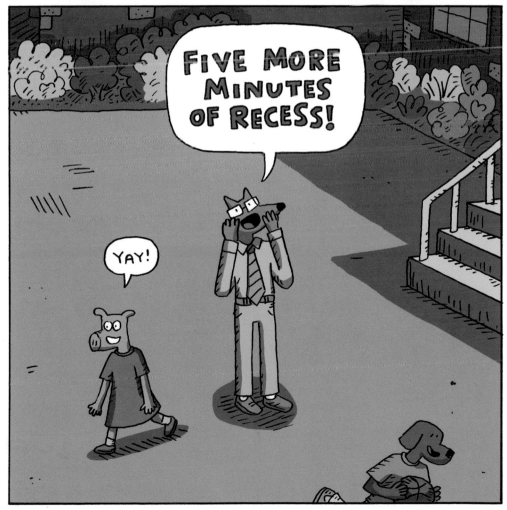

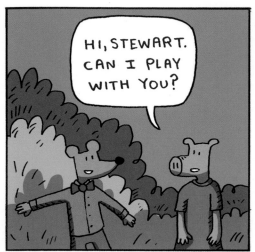

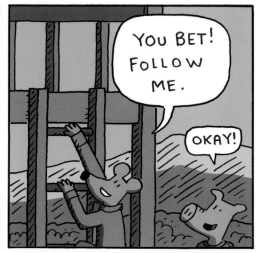

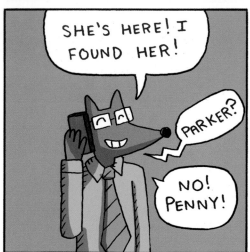

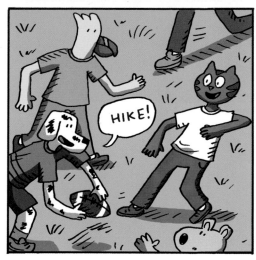

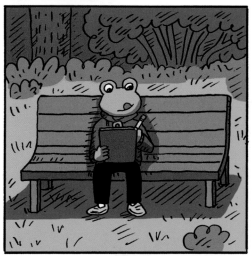

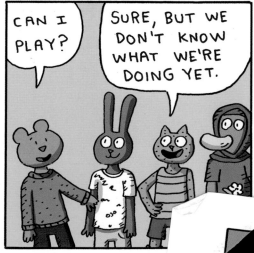

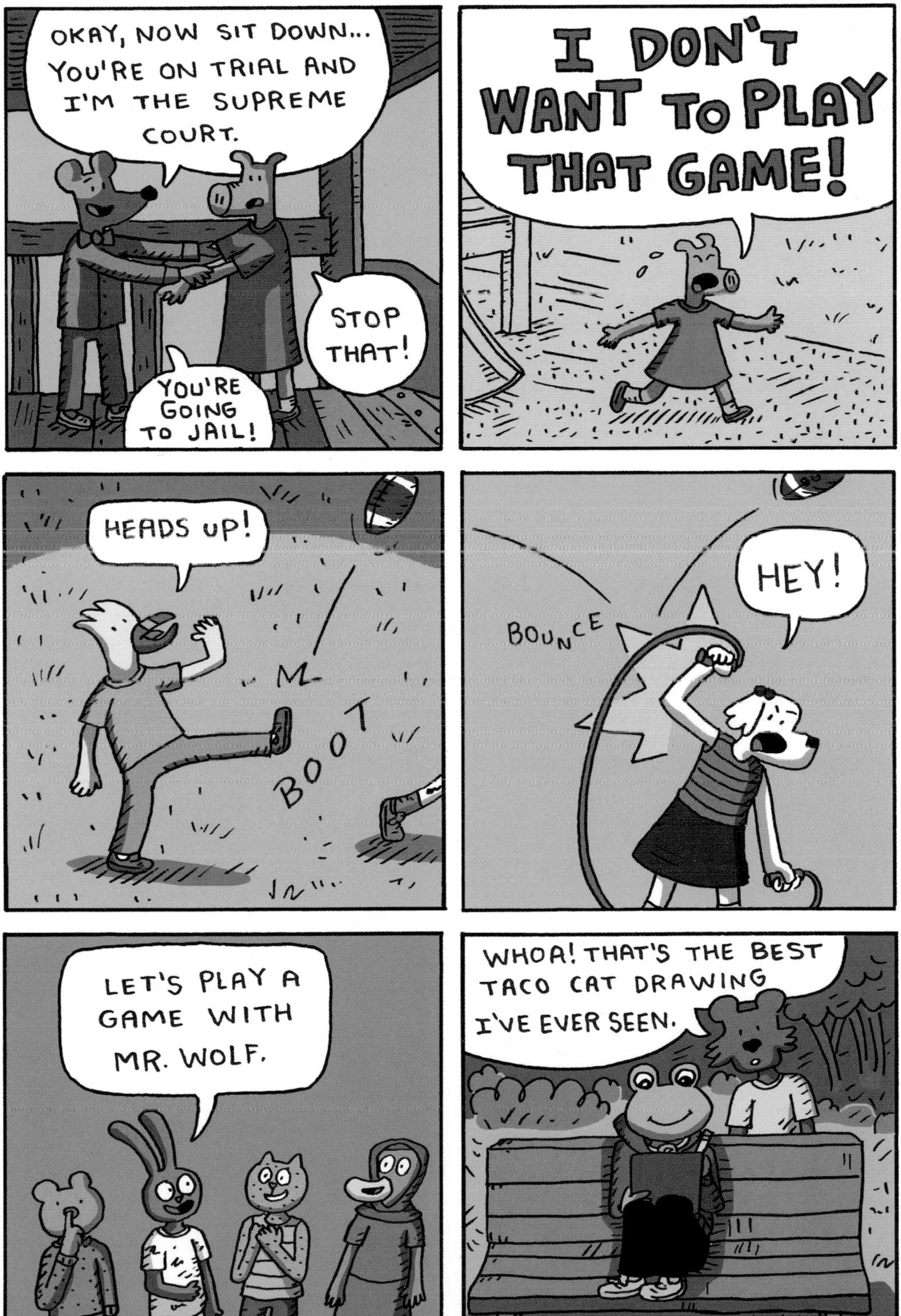
OKAY, NOW SIT DOWN... YOU'RE ON TRIAL AND I'M THE SUPREME COURT.
STOP THAT!
YOU'RE GOING TO JAIL!
I DON'T WANT TO PLAY THAT GAME!
HEADS UP!
BOOT
HEY!
BOUNCE
LET'S PLAY A GAME WITH MR. WOLF.
WHOA! THAT'S THE BEST TACO CAT DRAWING I'VE EVER SEEN.

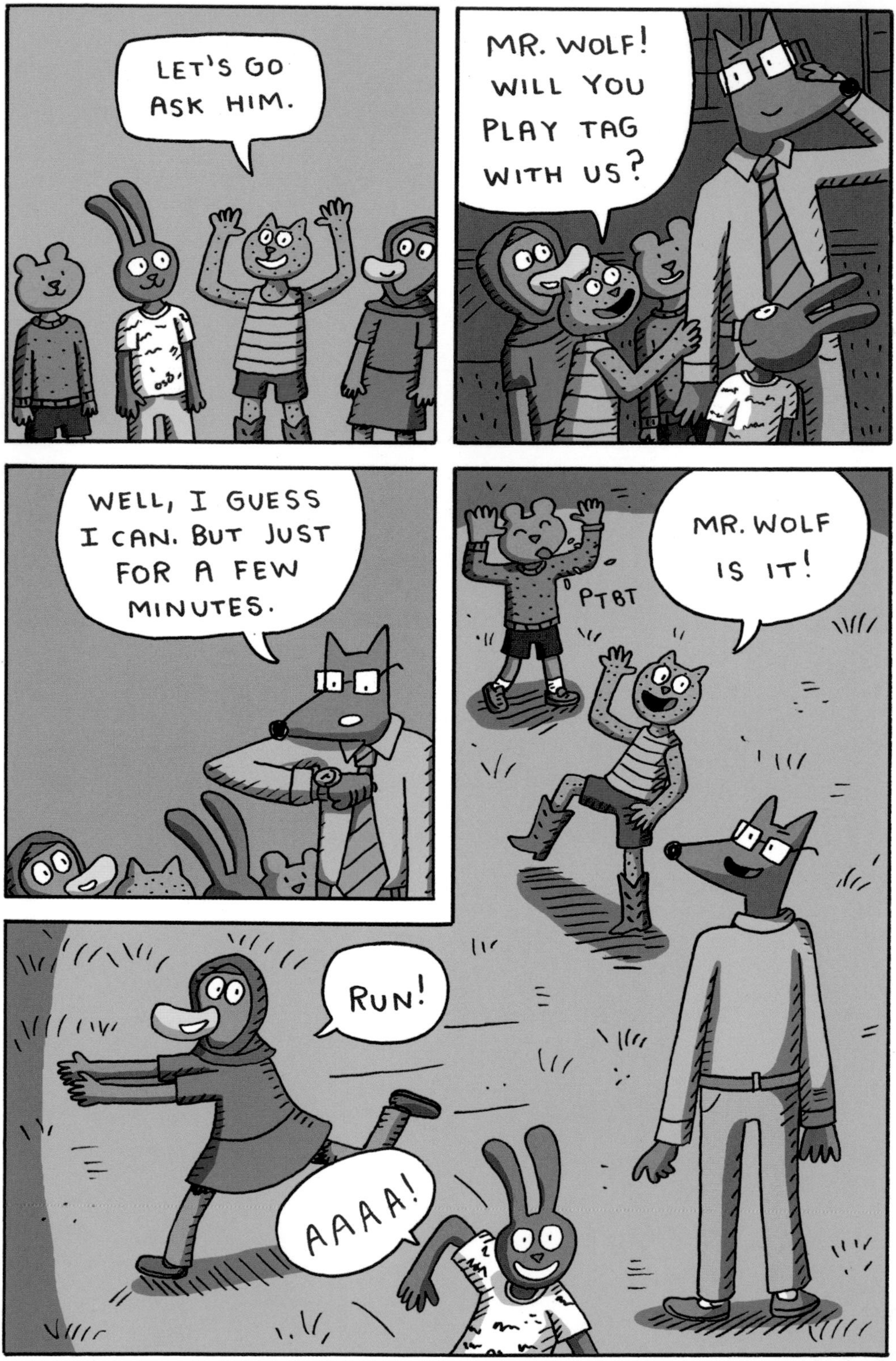
LET'S GO ASK HIM.
MR. WOLF! WILL YOU PLAY TAG WITH US?
WELL, I GUESS I CAN. BUT JUST FOR A FEW MINUTES.
MR. WOLF IS IT!
PTBT
RUN!
AAAA!

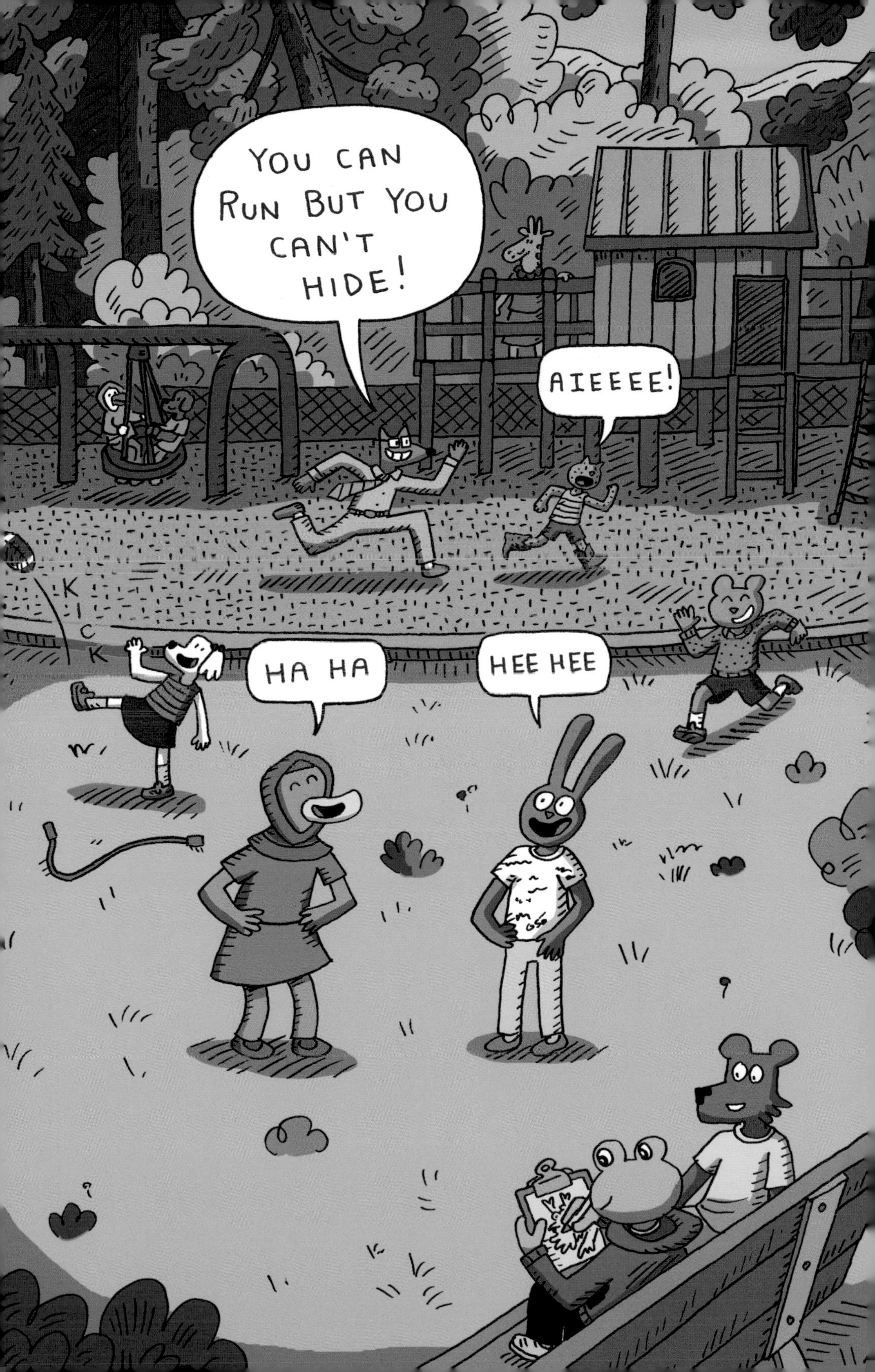
YOU CAN RUN BUT YOU CAN'T HIDE!
AIEEEE!
KICK
HA HA
HEE HEE

CHAPTER NINE

Show and Scare

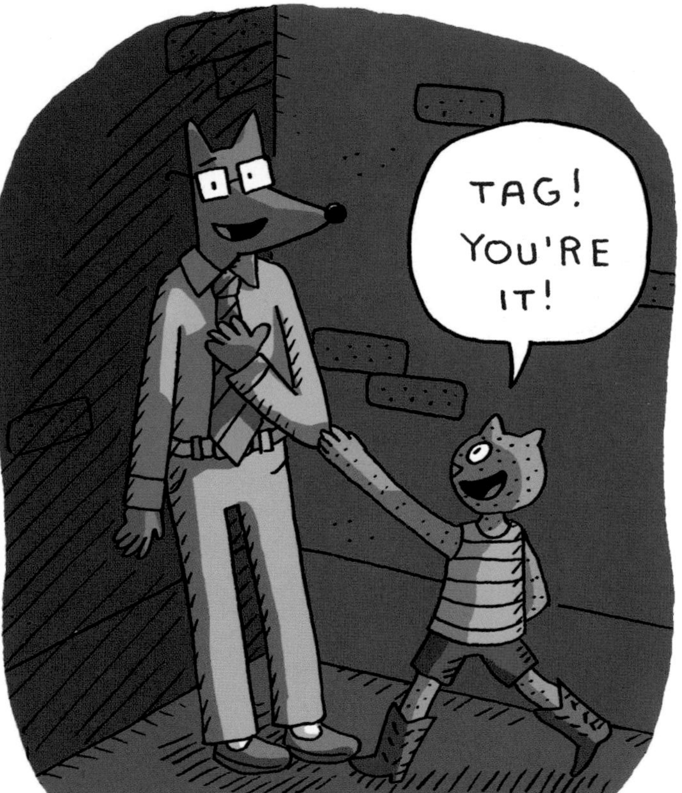
TAG! YOU'RE IT!

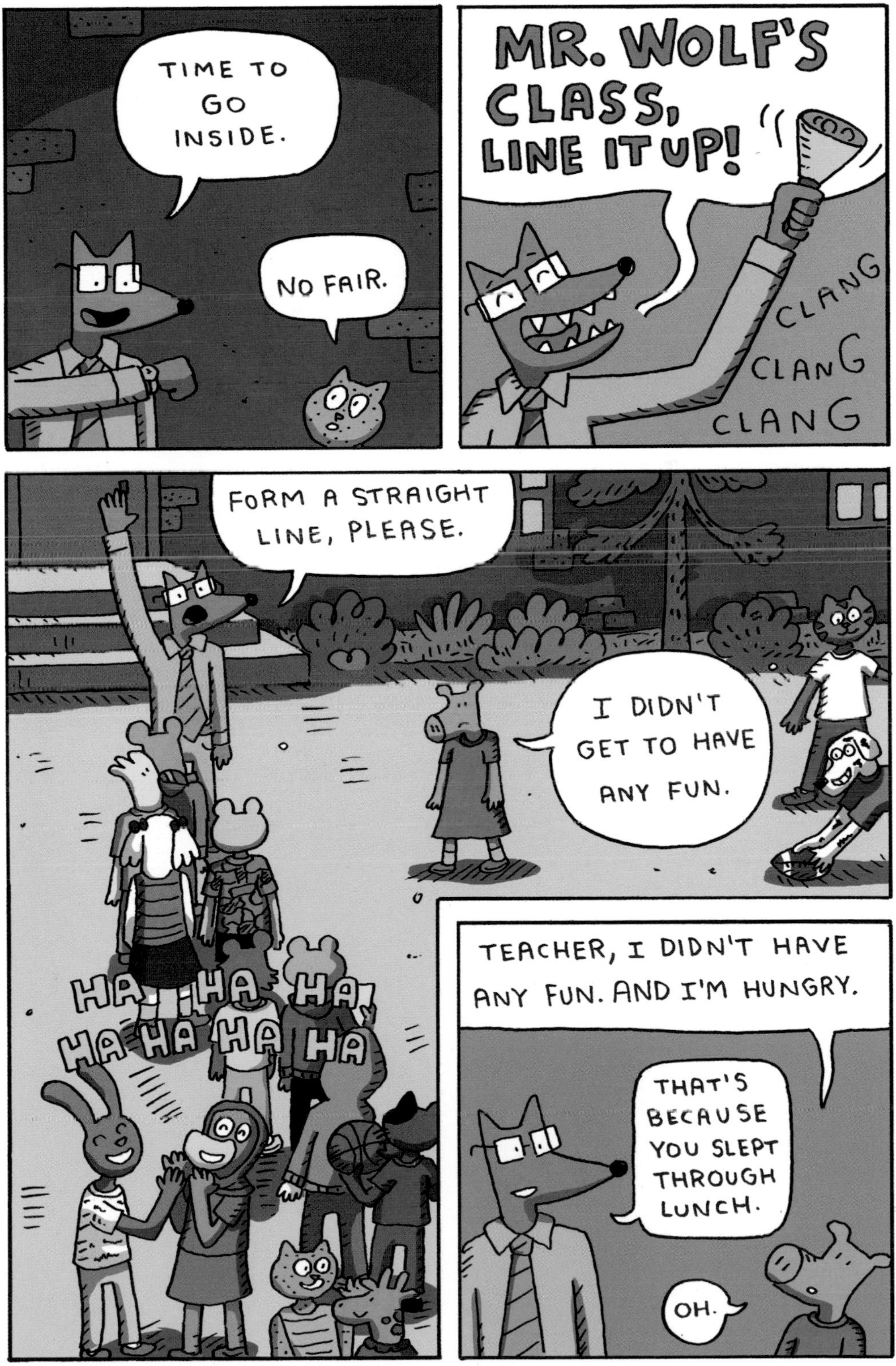
TIME TO GO INSIDE.
NO FAIR.
MR. WOLF'S CLASS, LINE IT UP!
CLANG
CLANG
CLANG
FORM A STRAIGHT LINE, PLEASE.
HA HA HA
HA HA HA HA
I DIDN'T GET TO HAVE ANY FUN.
TEACHER, I DIDN'T HAVE ANY FUN. AND I'M HUNGRY.
THAT'S BECAUSE YOU SLEPT THROUGH LUNCH.
OH.

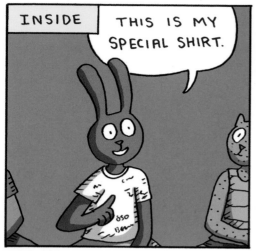

INSIDE

THIS IS MY SPECIAL SHIRT.

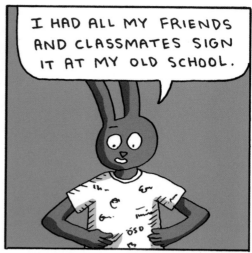

I HAD ALL MY FRIENDS AND CLASSMATES SIGN IT AT MY OLD SCHOOL.

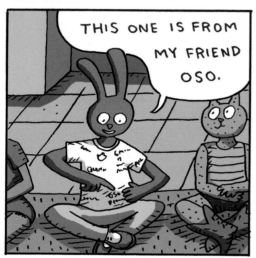

THIS ONE IS FROM MY FRIEND OSO.

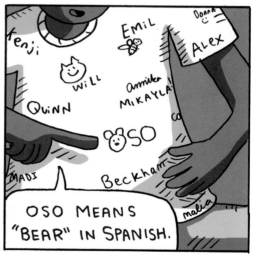

OSO MEANS "BEAR" IN SPANISH.

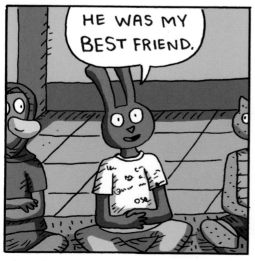

HE WAS MY BEST FRIEND.

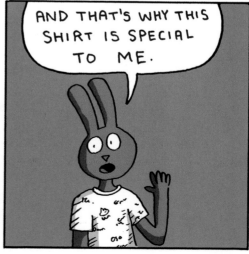

AND THAT'S WHY THIS SHIRT IS SPECIAL TO ME.

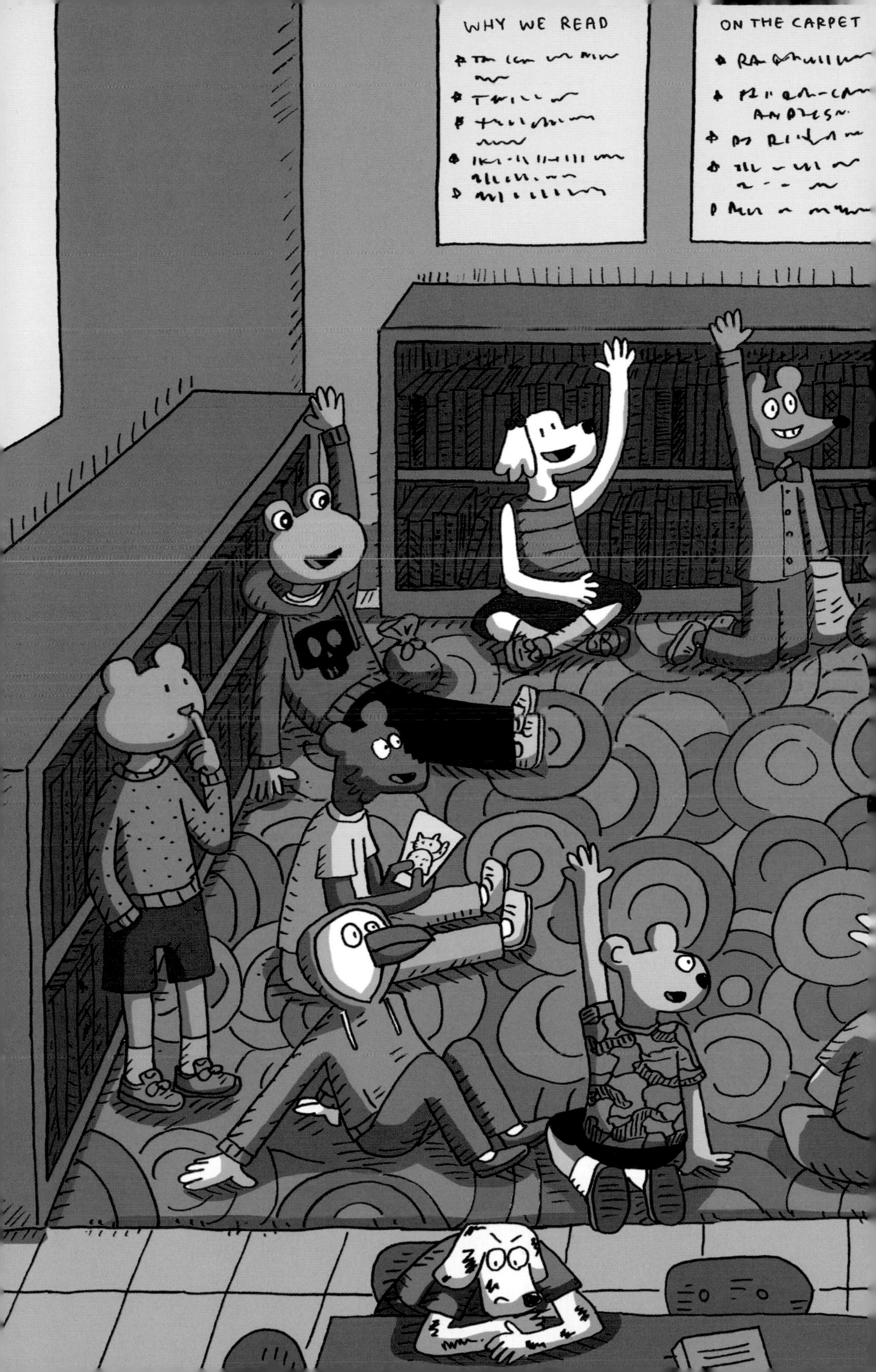
WHY WE READ
ON THE CARPET

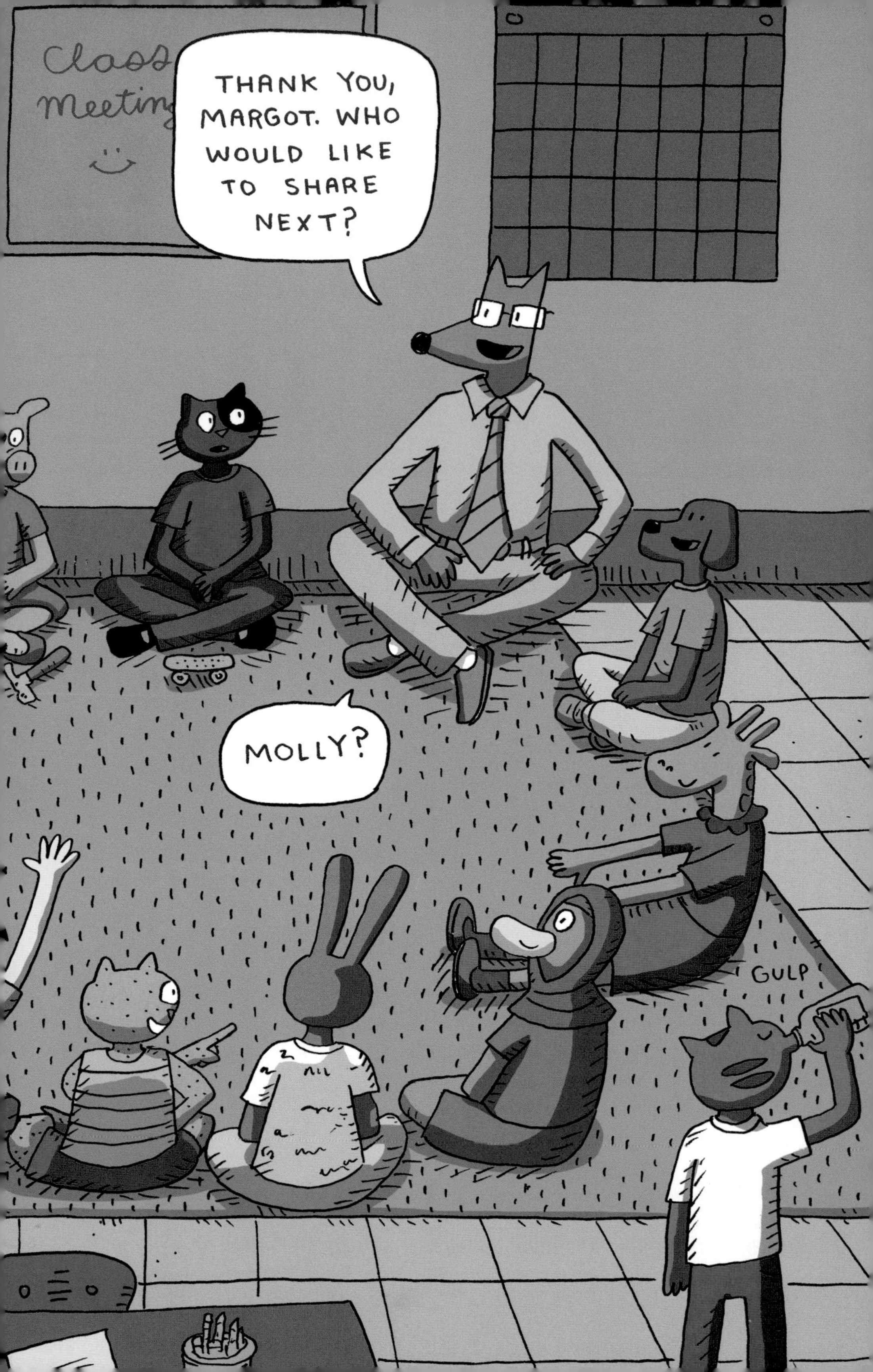
Class Meeting
THANK YOU, MARGOT. WHO WOULD LIKE TO SHARE NEXT?
MOLLY?
GULP

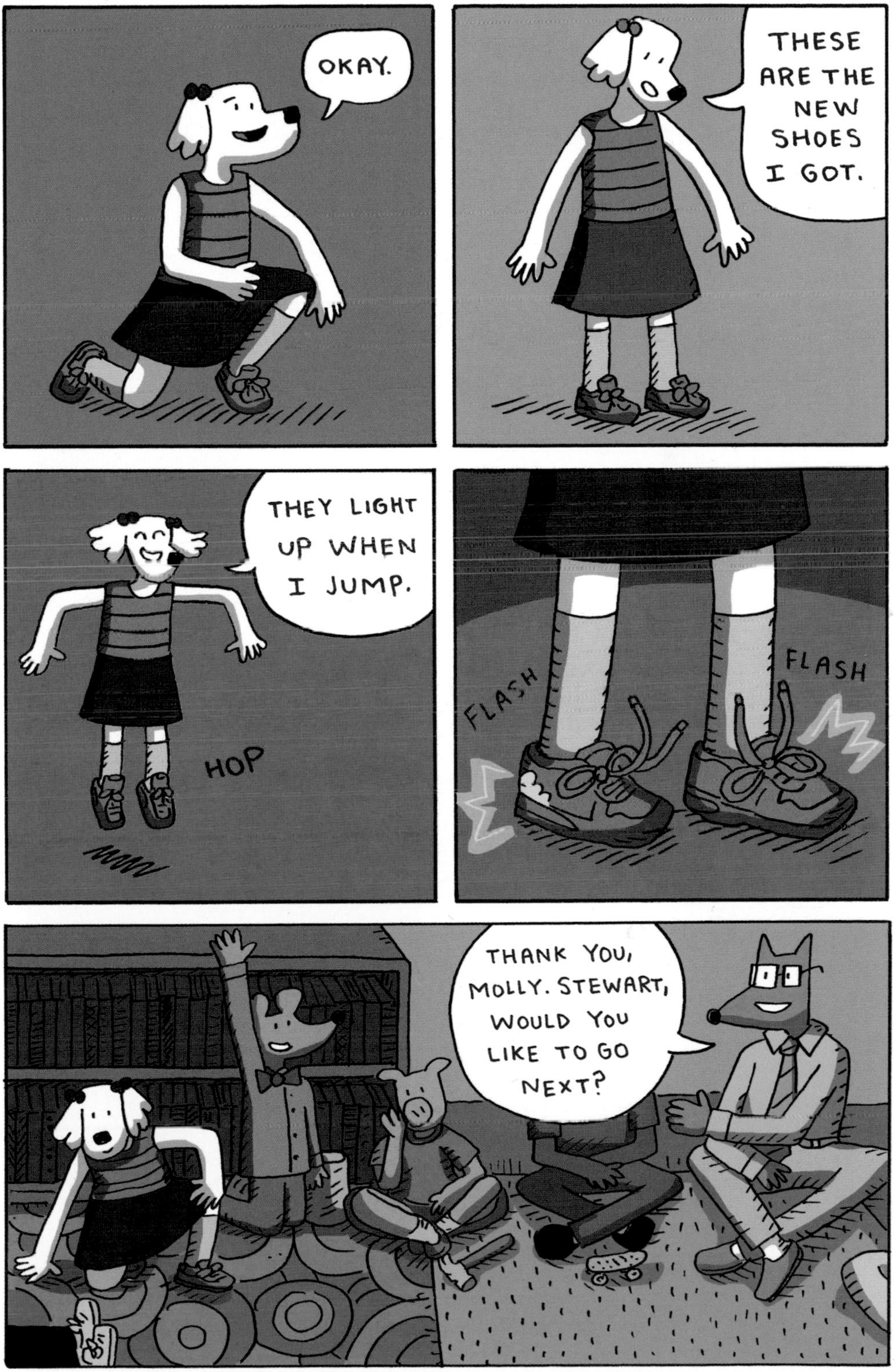
OKAY.
THESE ARE THE NEW SHOES I GOT.
THEY LIGHT UP WHEN I JUMP.
HOP
FLASH
FLASH
THANK YOU, MOLLY. STEWART, WOULD YOU LIKE TO GO NEXT?

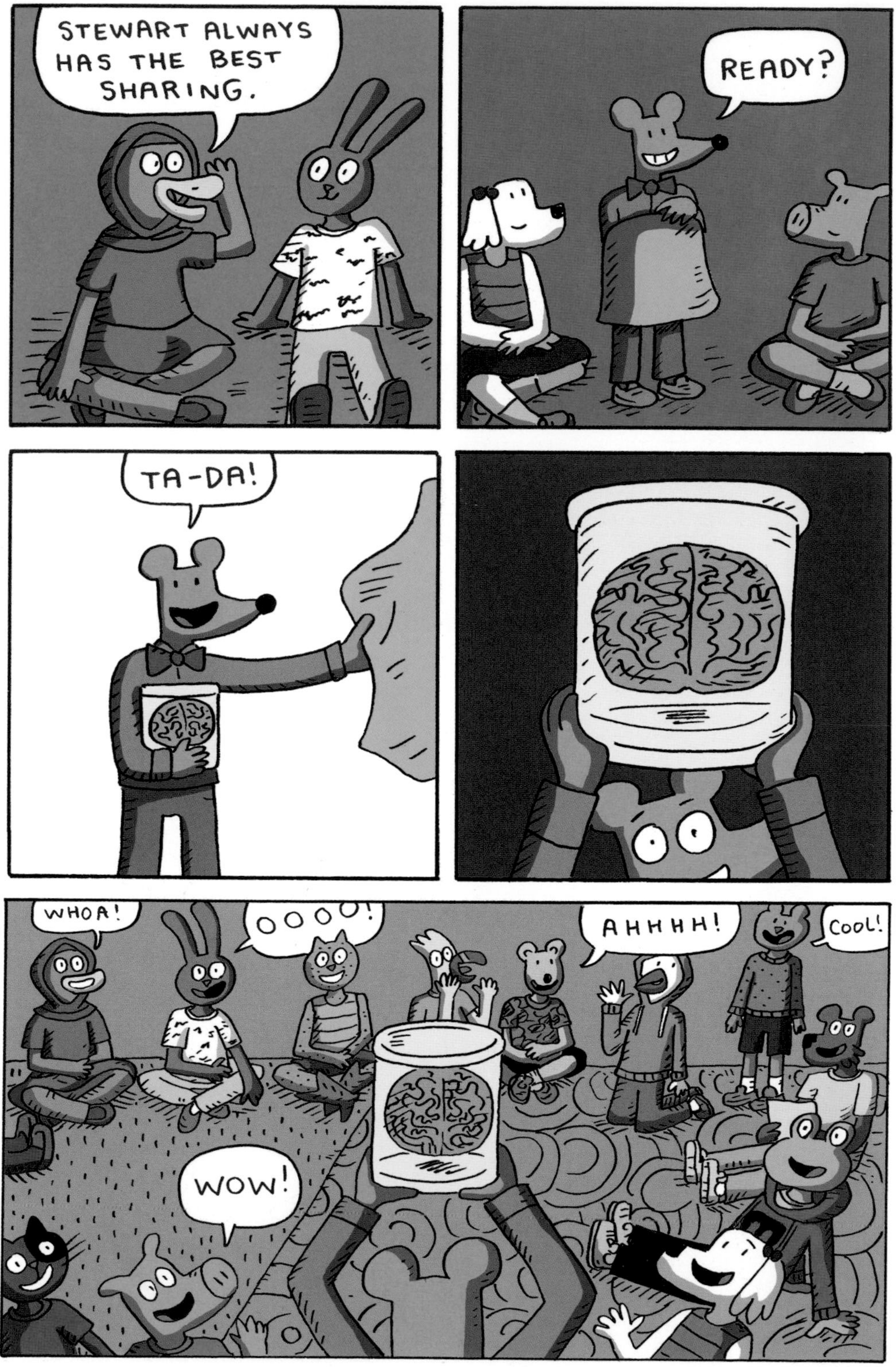
STEWART ALWAYS HAS THE BEST SHARING.
READY?
TA-DA!
WHOA!
OOOO!
AHHHH!
COOL!
WOW!

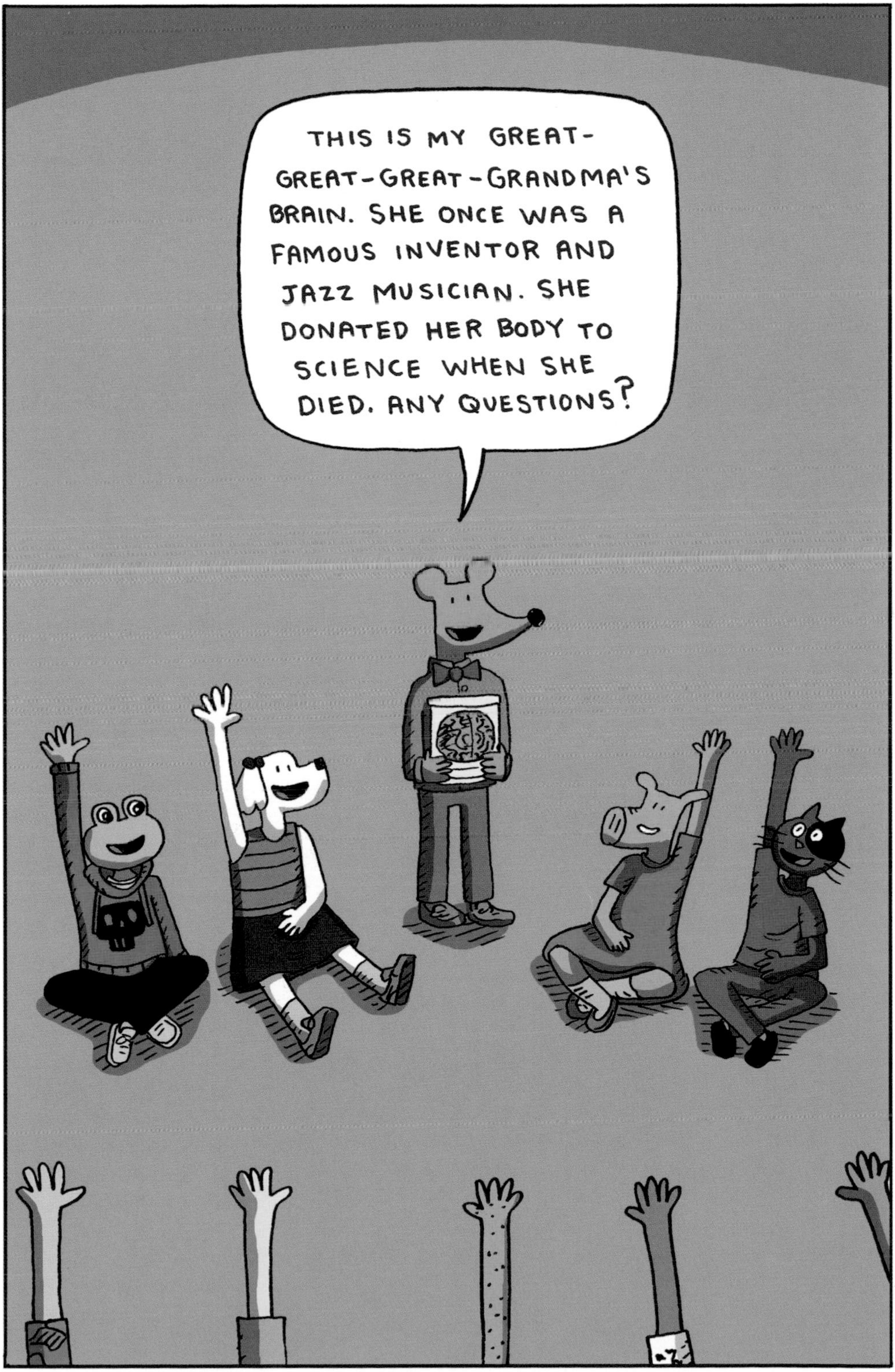
THIS IS MY GREAT-GREAT-GREAT-GREAT-GRANDMA'S BRAIN. SHE ONCE WAS A FAMOUS INVENTOR AND JAZZ MUSICIAN. SHE DONATED HER BODY TO SCIENCE WHEN SHE DIED. ANY QUESTIONS?

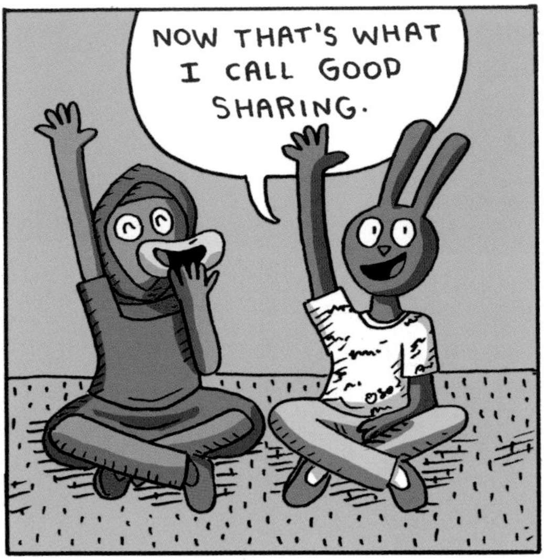
NOW THAT'S WHAT I CALL GOOD SHARING.

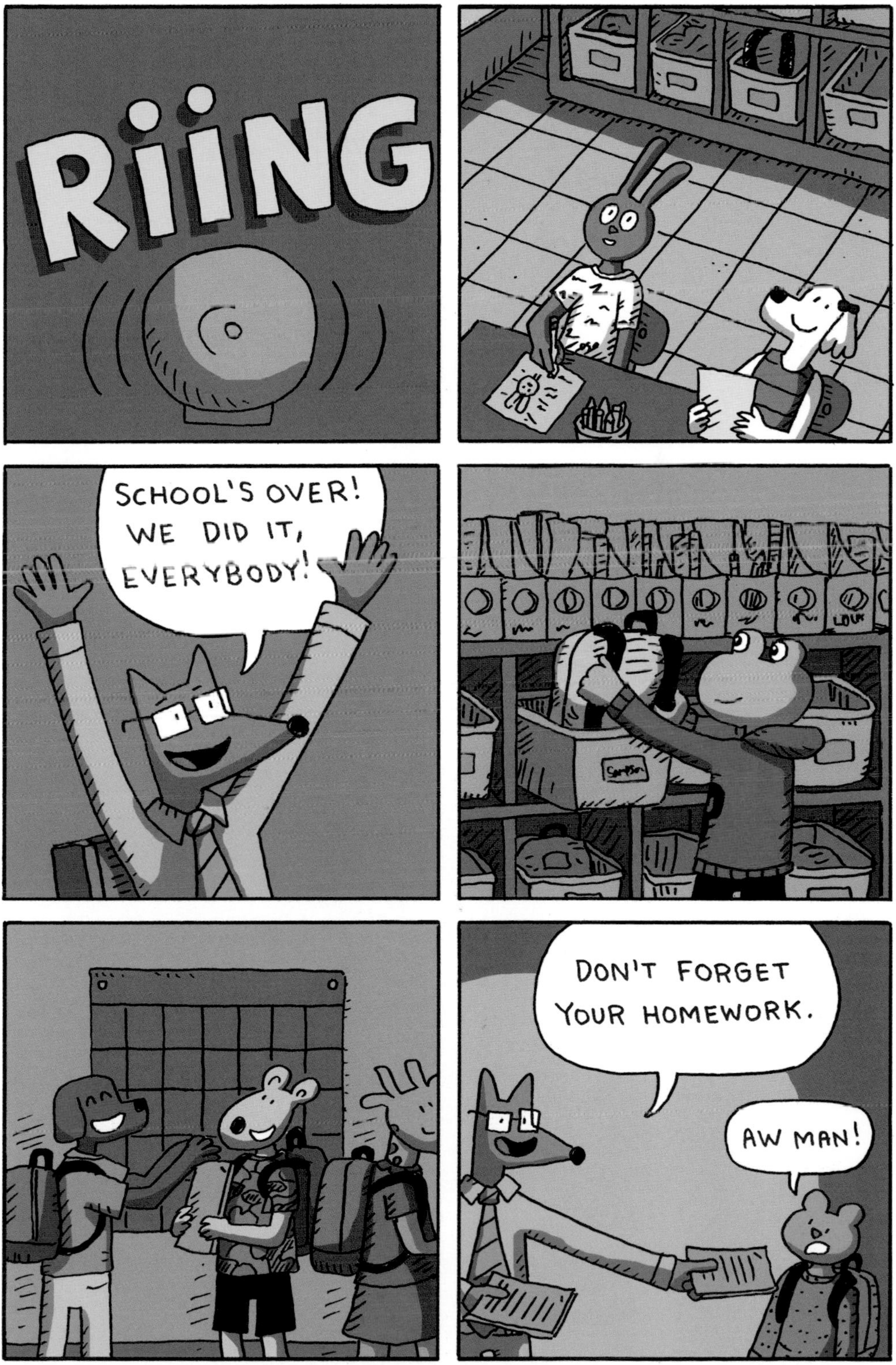
RIING
SCHOOL'S OVER! WE DID IT, EVERYBODY!
DON'T FORGET YOUR HOMEWORK.
AW MAN!

CHAPTER TEN
An Empty Seat

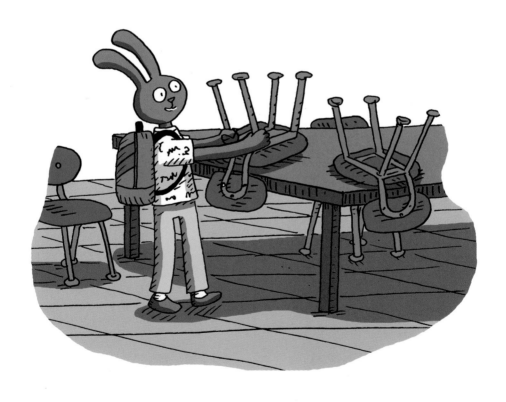

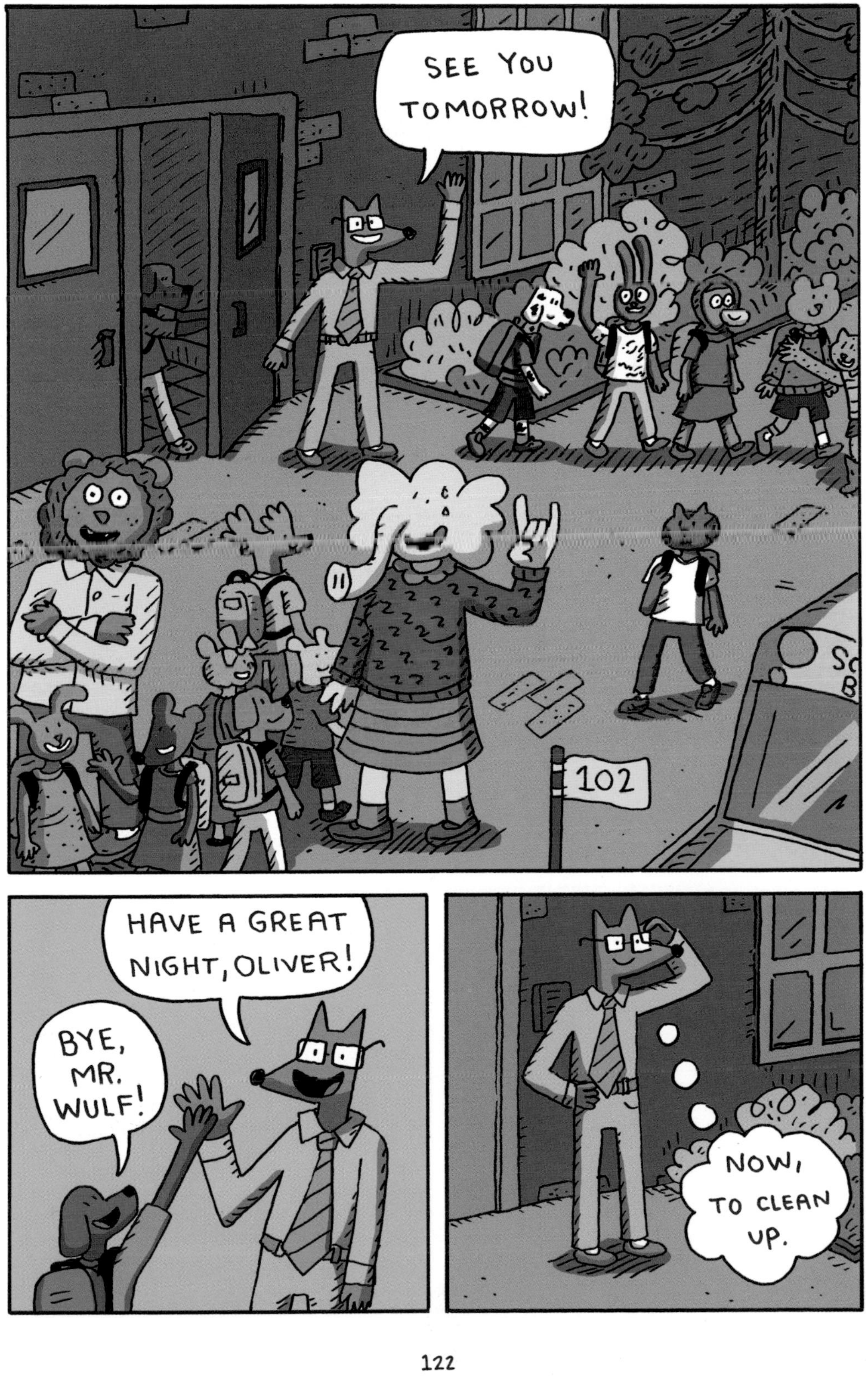
SEE YOU TOMORROW!
102
HAVE A GREAT NIGHT, OLIVER!
BYE, MR. WULF!
NOW, TO CLEAN UP.

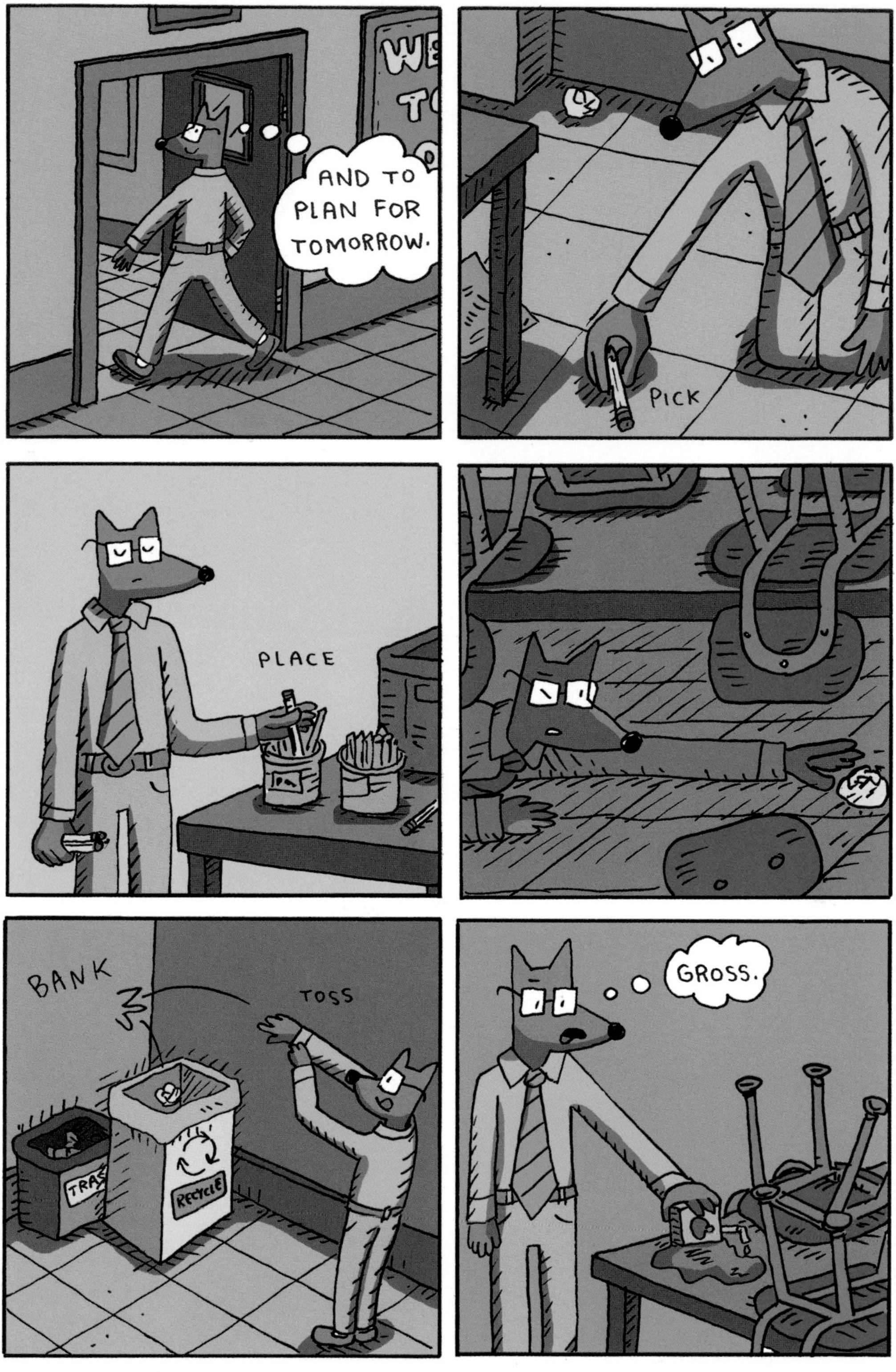
AND TO PLAN FOR TOMORROW.
PICK
PLACE
BANK
TOSS
RECYCLE
GROSS.

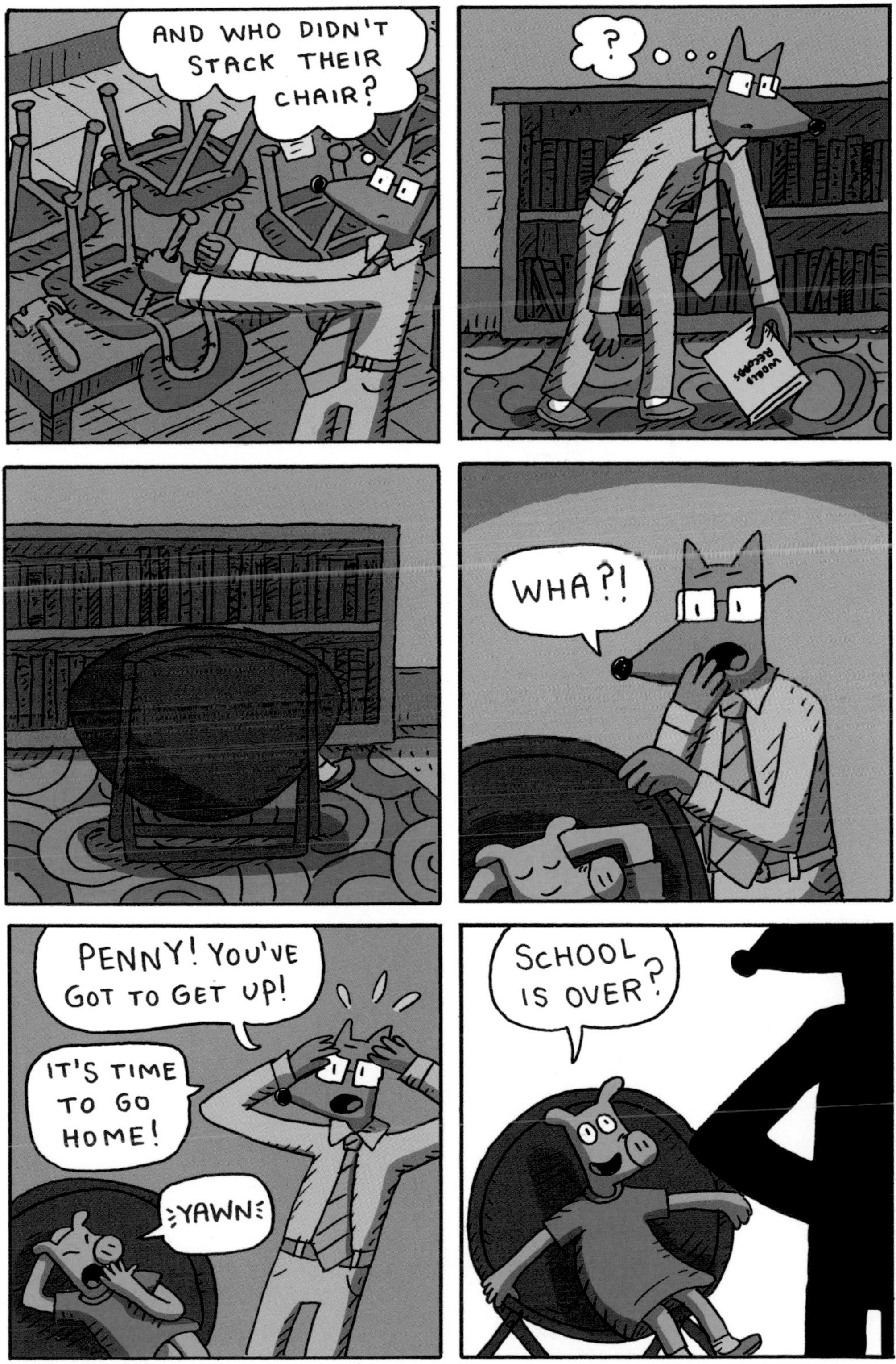
AND WHO DIDN'T STACK THEIR CHAIR?
?
WHA?!
PENNY! YOU'VE GOT TO GET UP!
IT'S TIME TO GO HOME!
YAWN
SCHOOL IS OVER?

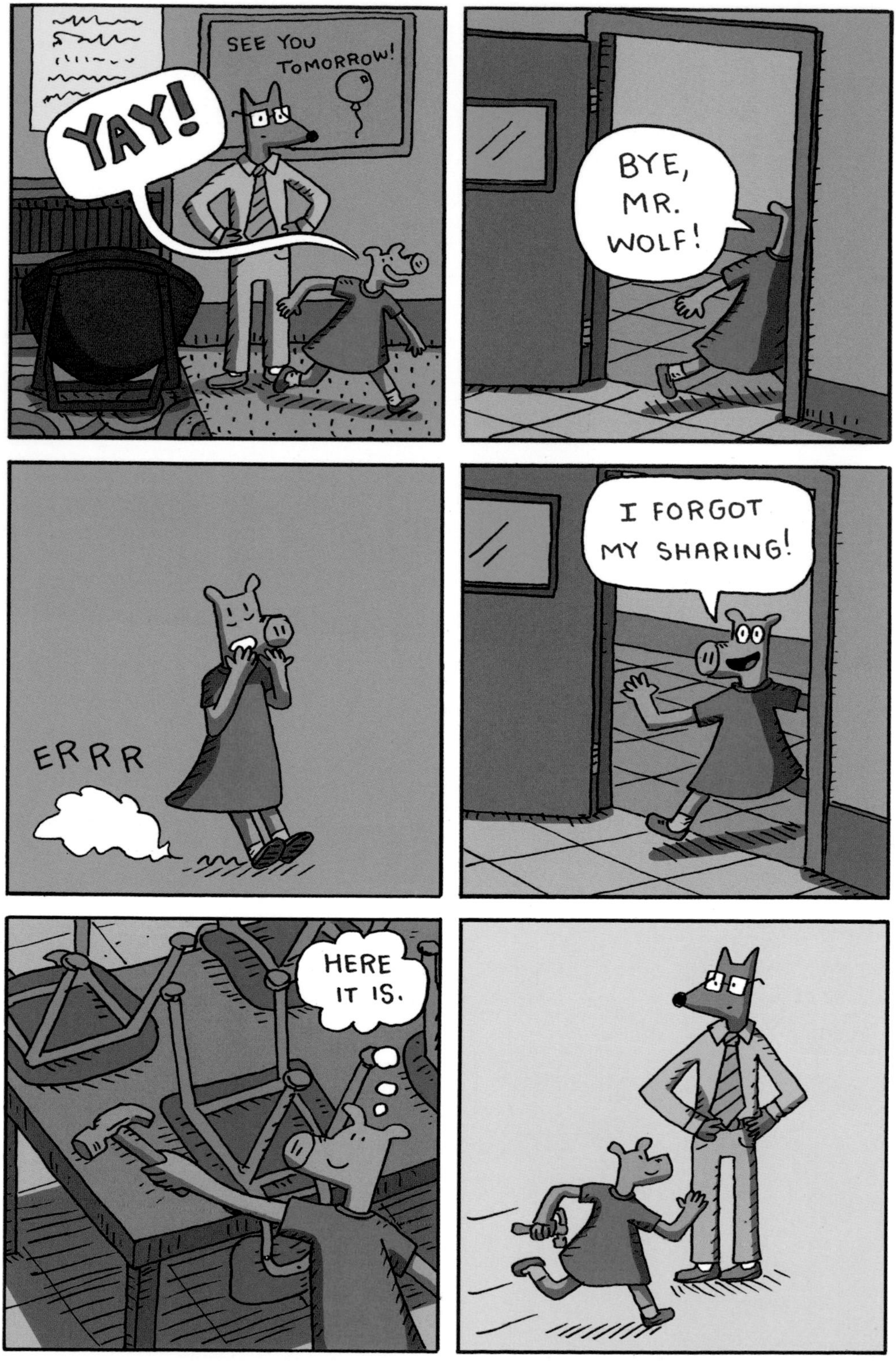
SEE YOU TOMORROW!
YAY!
BYE, MR. WOLF!
ERRR
I FORGOT MY SHARING!
HERE IT IS.

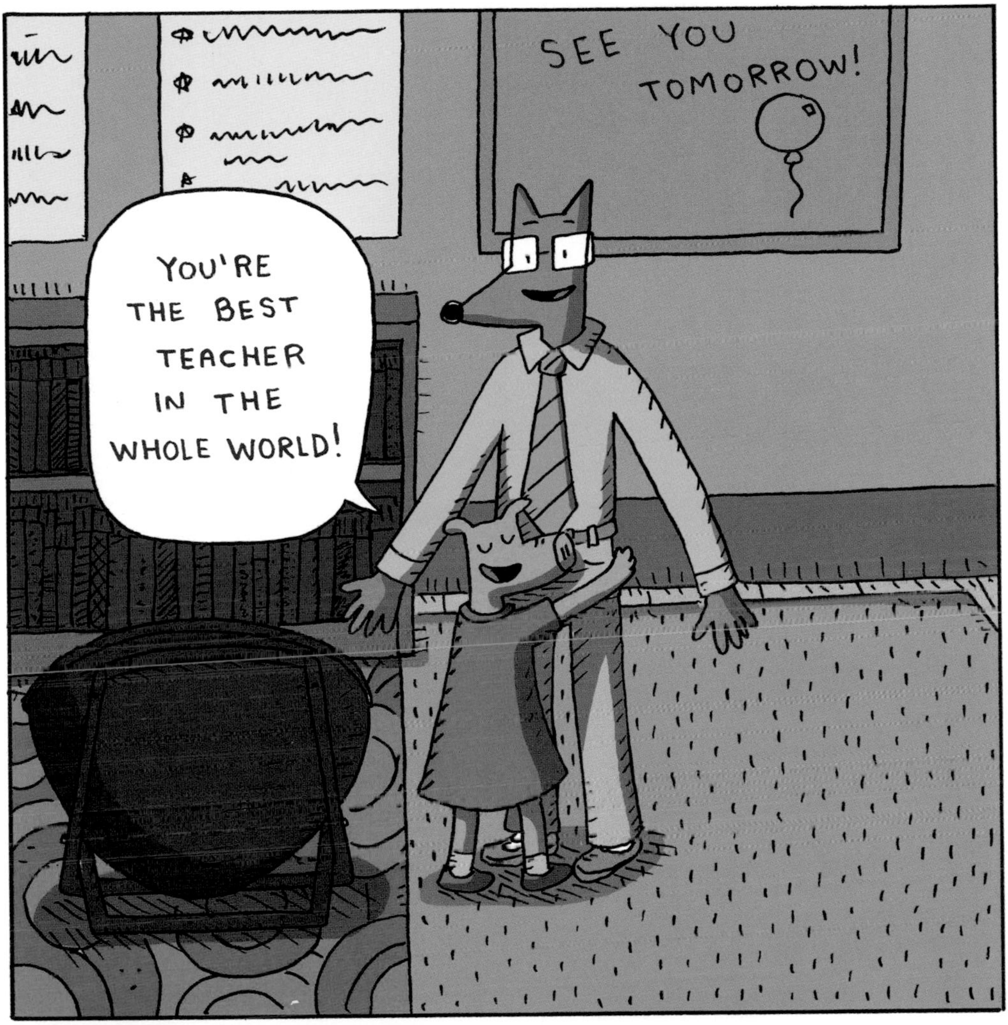
SEE YOU TOMORROW!
YOU'RE THE BEST TEACHER IN THE WHOLE WORLD!

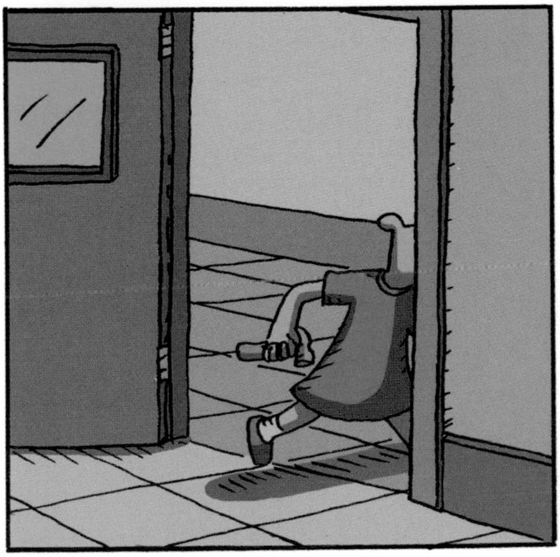

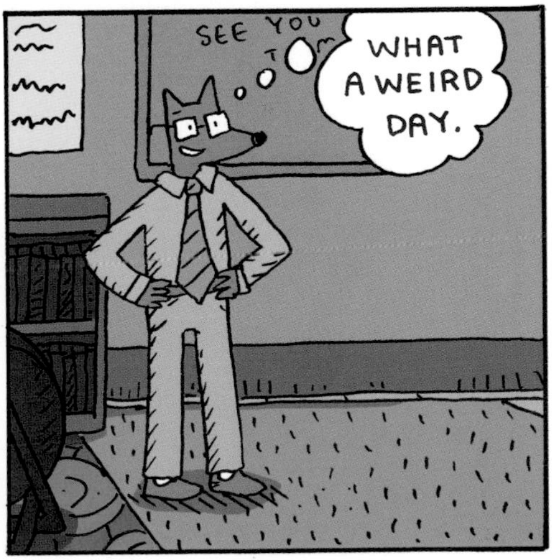
WHAT A WEIRD DAY.

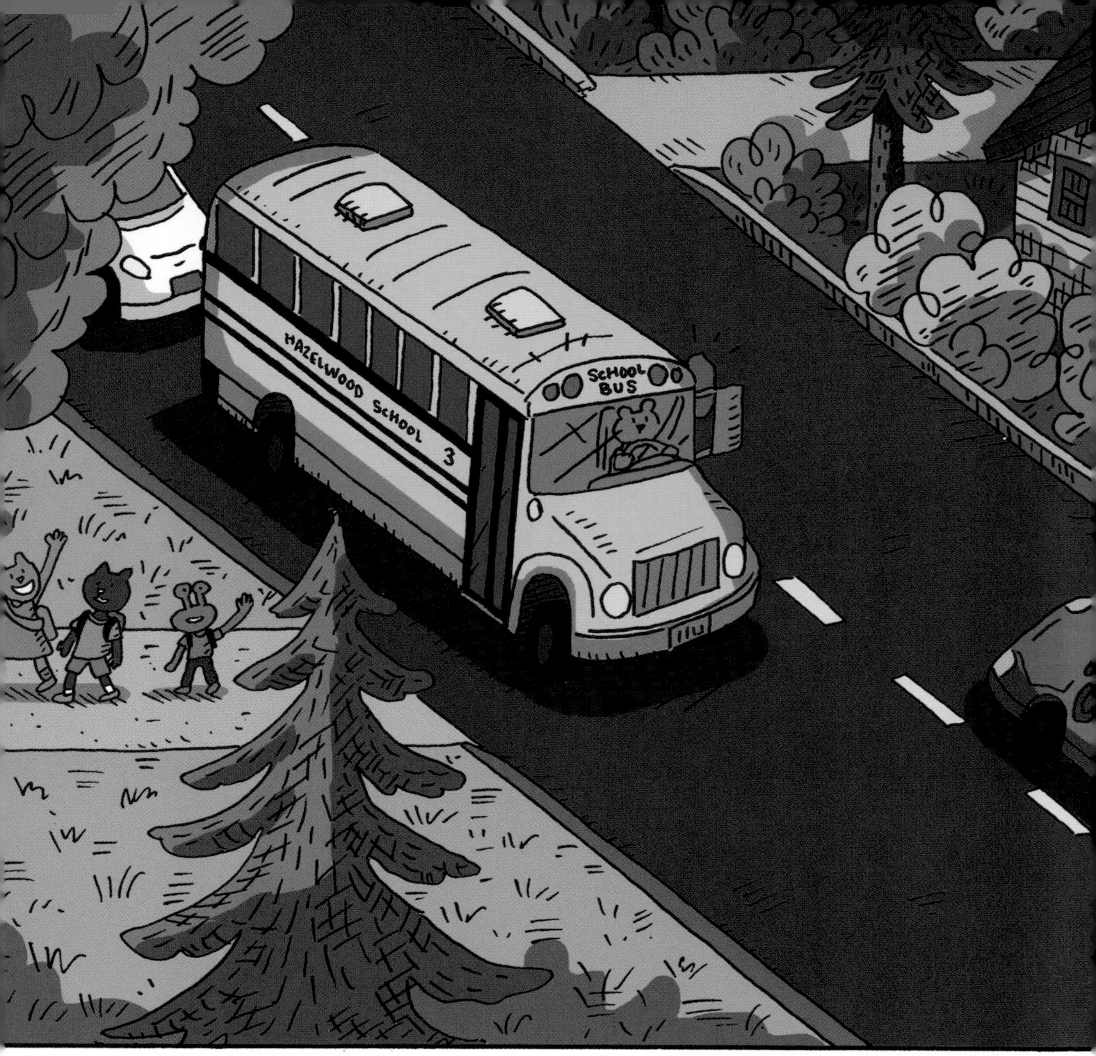
HAZELWOOD SCHOOL 3
SCHOOL BUS

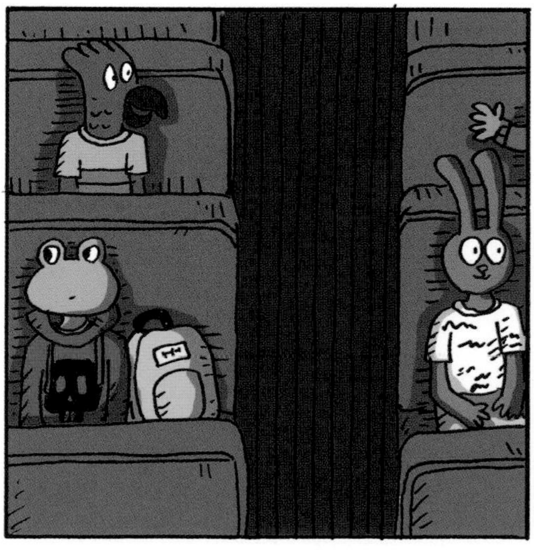

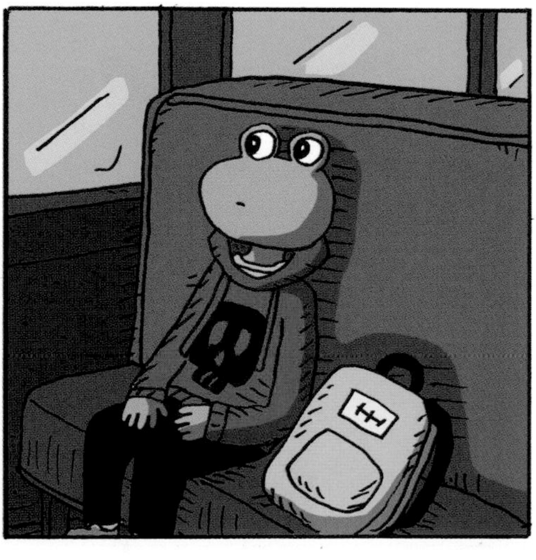

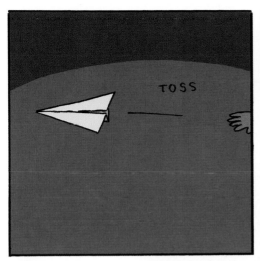

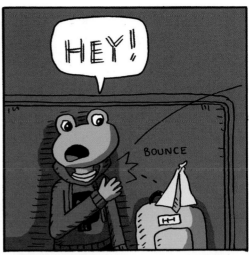

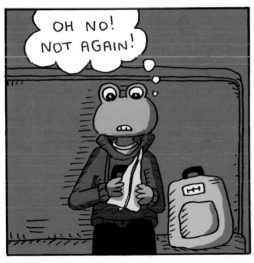

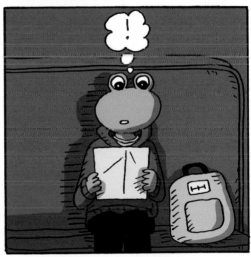

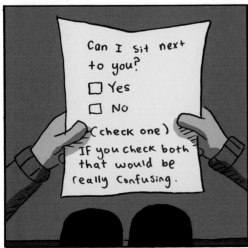

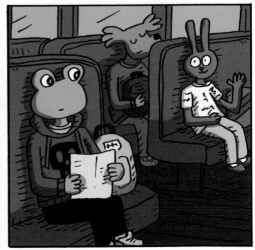

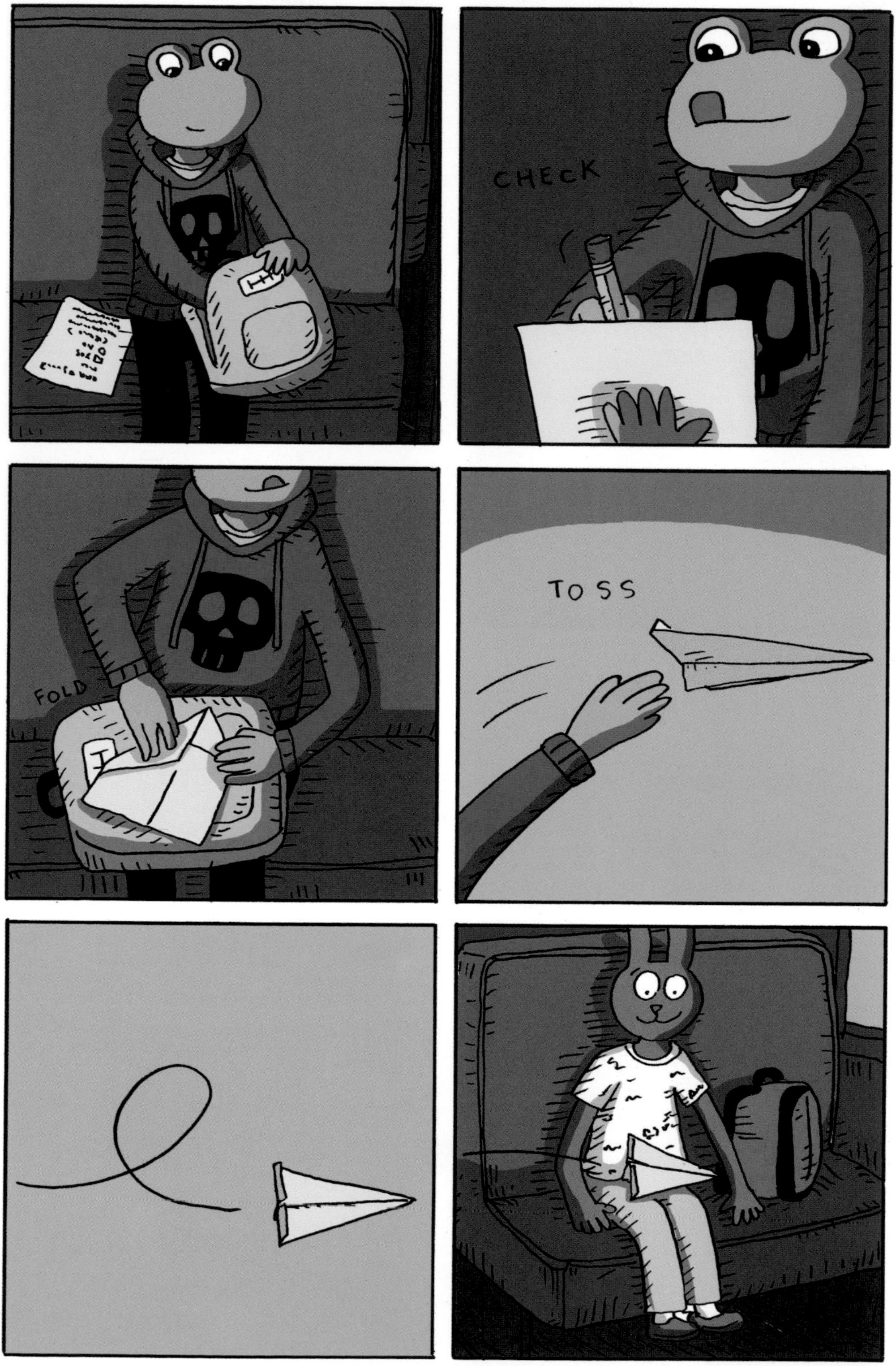
CHECK
FOLD
TOSS

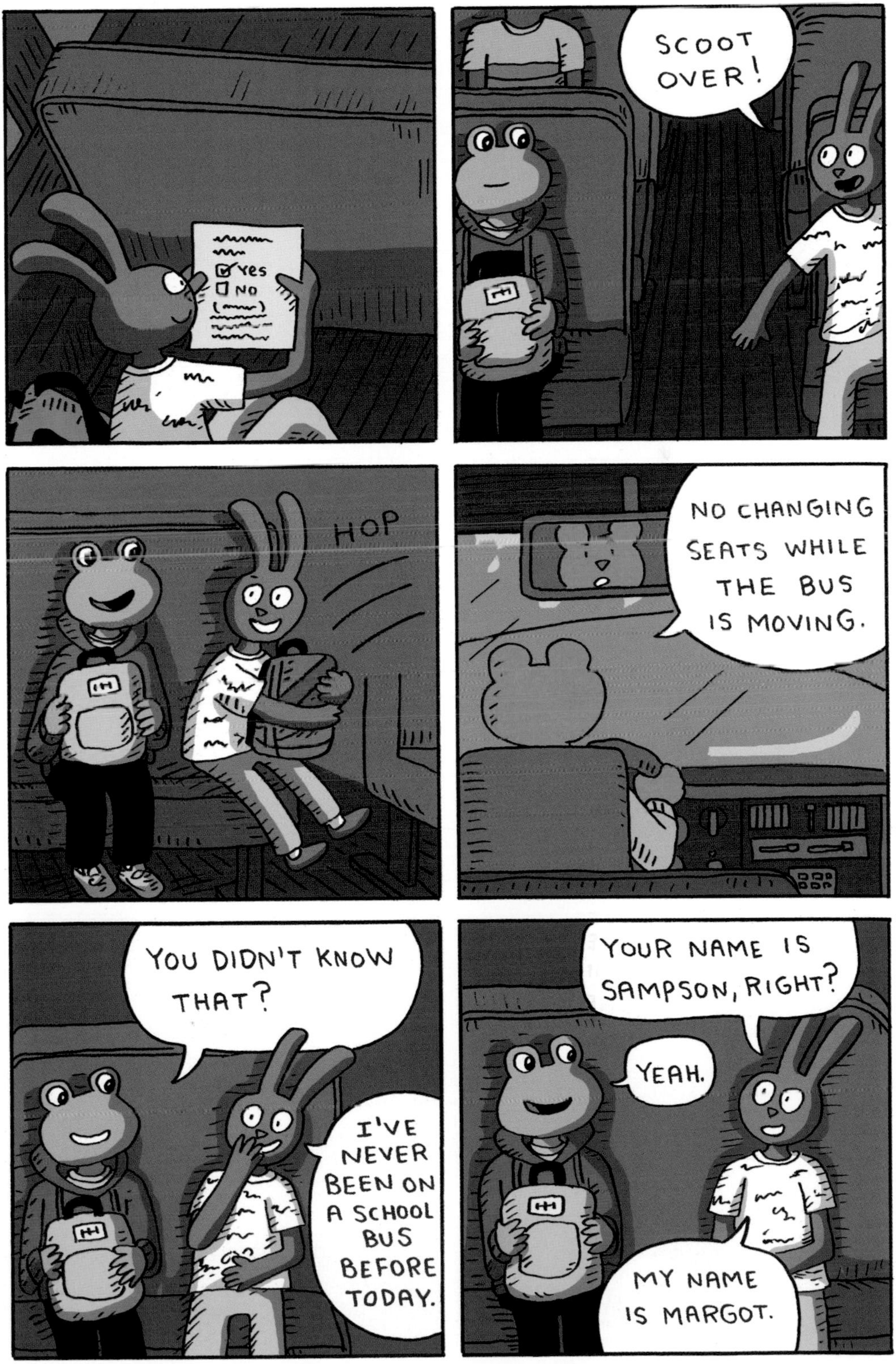
YES
NO
SCOOT OVER!
HOP
NO CHANGING SEATS WHILE THE BUS IS MOVING.
YOU DIDN'T KNOW THAT?
I'VE NEVER BEEN ON A SCHOOL BUS BEFORE TODAY.
YOUR NAME IS SAMPSON, RIGHT?
YEAH.
MY NAME IS MARGOT.

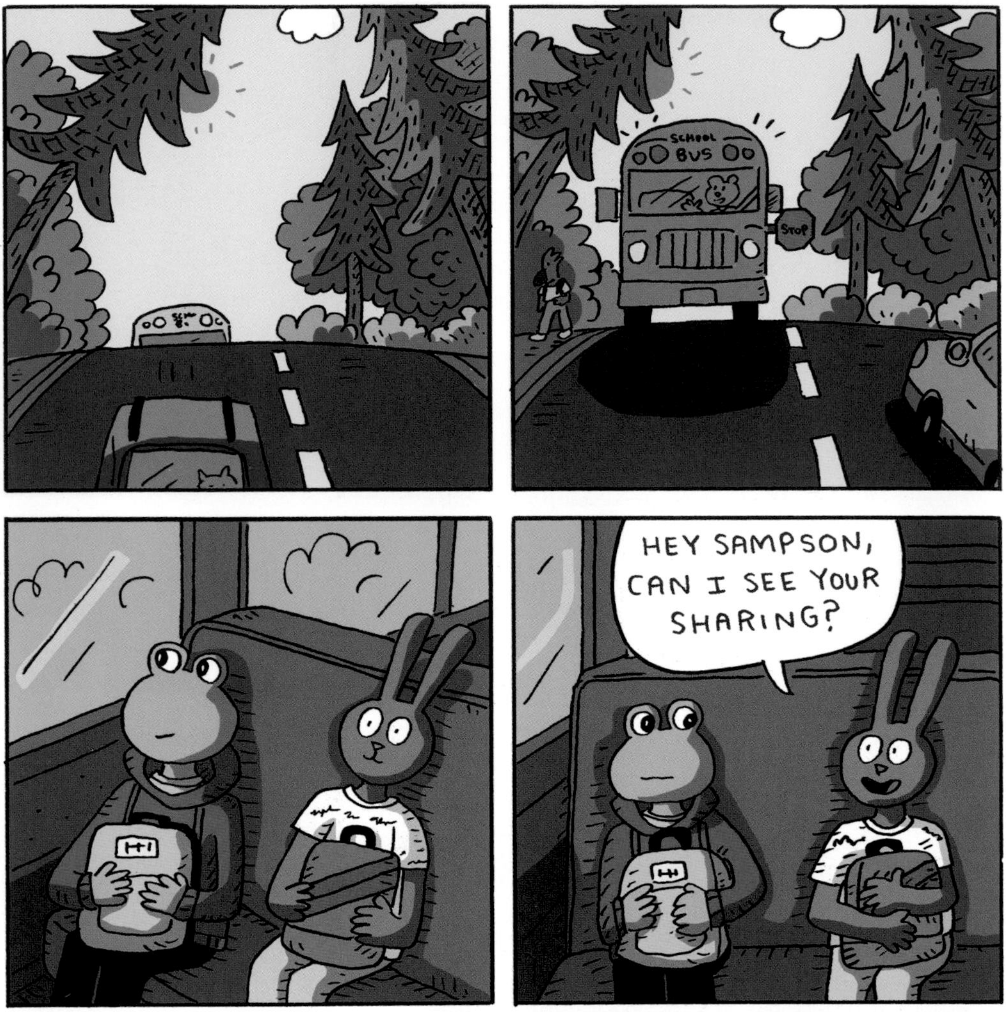
SCHOOL BUS
STOP
HEY SAMPSON, CAN I SEE YOUR SHARING?
I DIDN'T REALLY GET A CHANCE TO SEE THEM IN CLASS.
MY SHELLS?
OKAY.
UNZIP

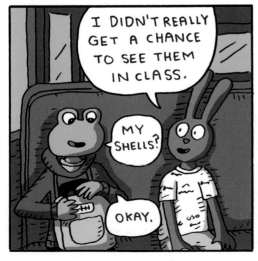

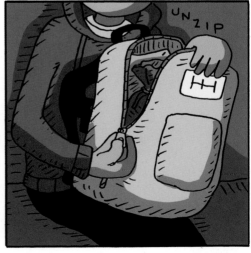

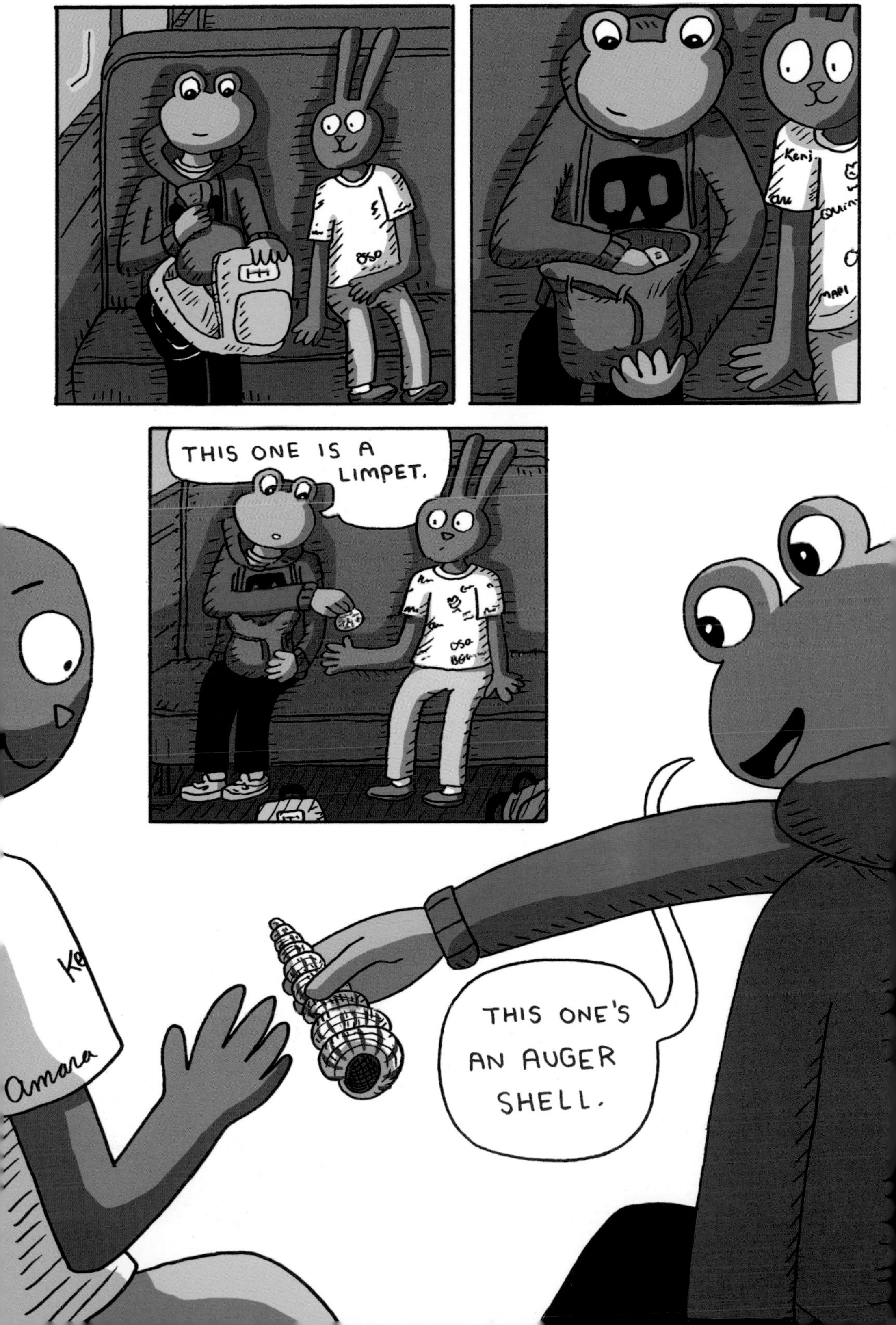
THIS ONE IS A LIMPET.
THIS ONE'S AN AUGER SHELL.

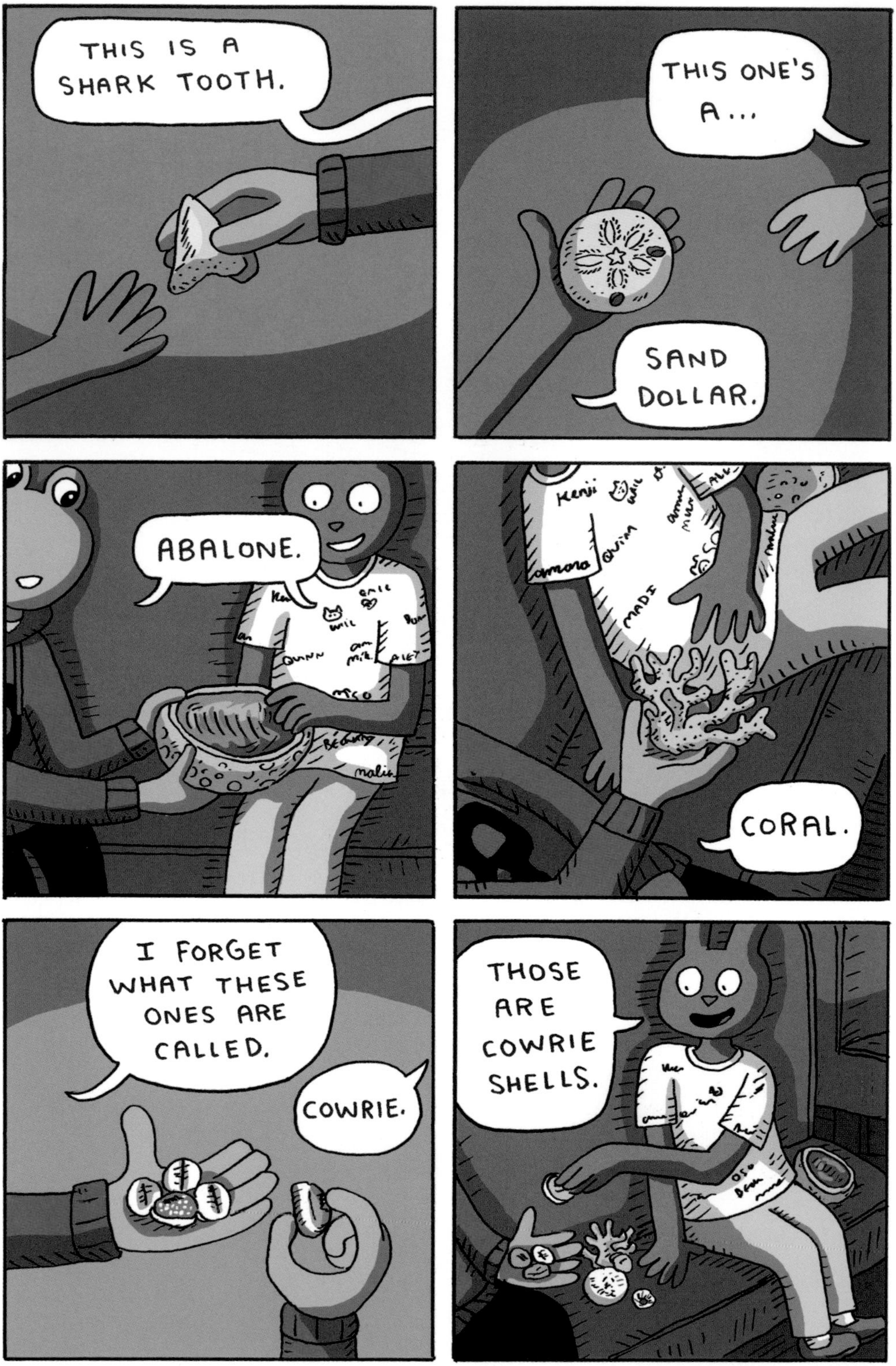
THIS IS A SHARK TOOTH.
THIS ONE'S A...
SAND DOLLAR.
ABALONE.
CORAL.
I FORGET WHAT THESE ONES ARE CALLED.
COWRIE.
THOSE ARE COWRIE SHELLS.

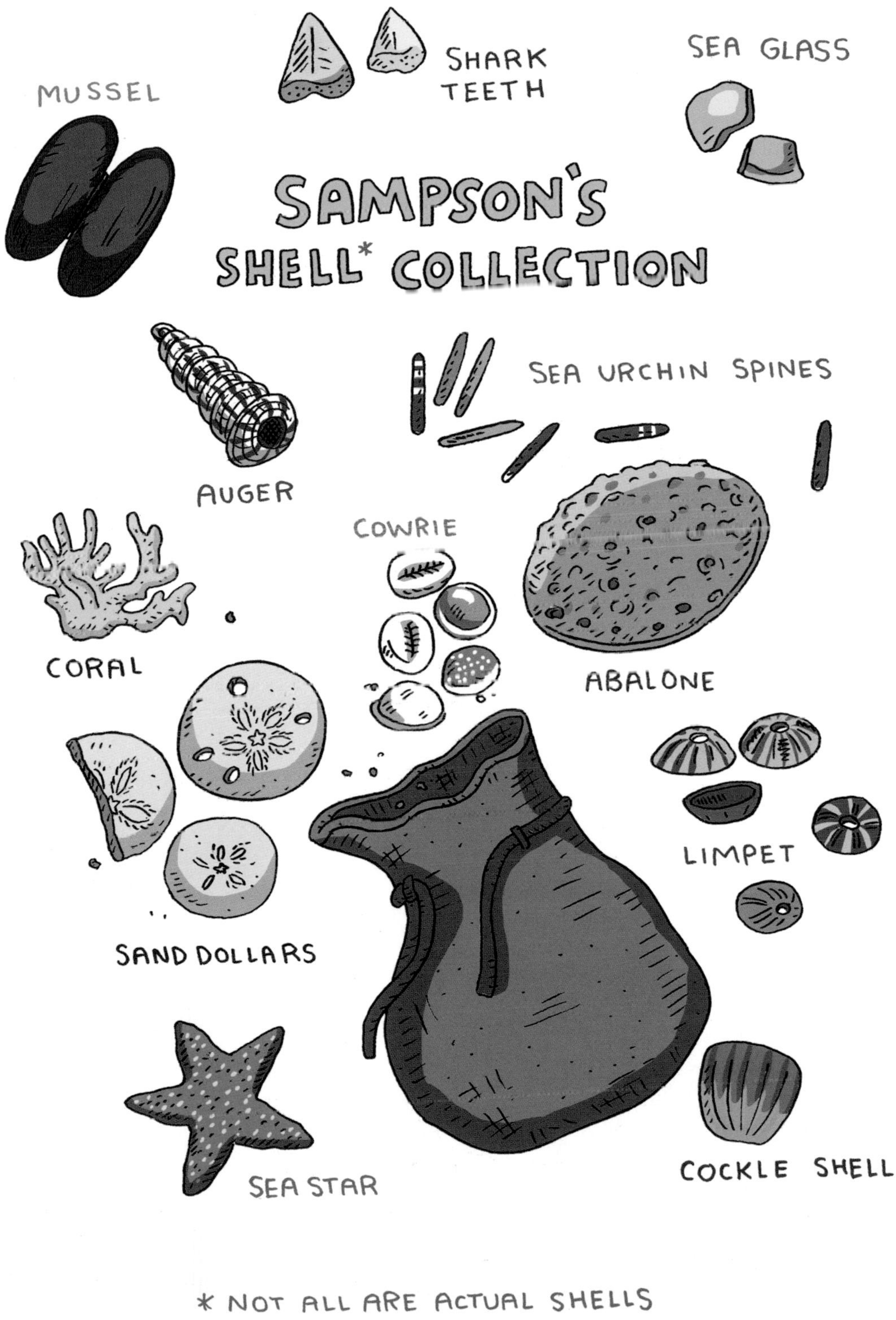
SAMPSON'S SHELL* COLLECTION
MUSSEL
SHARK TEETH
SEA GLASS
AUGER
SEA URCHIN SPINES
CORAL
COWRIE
ABALONE
SAND DOLLARS
LIMPET
SEA STAR
COCKLE SHELL
* NOT ALL ARE ACTUAL SHELLS

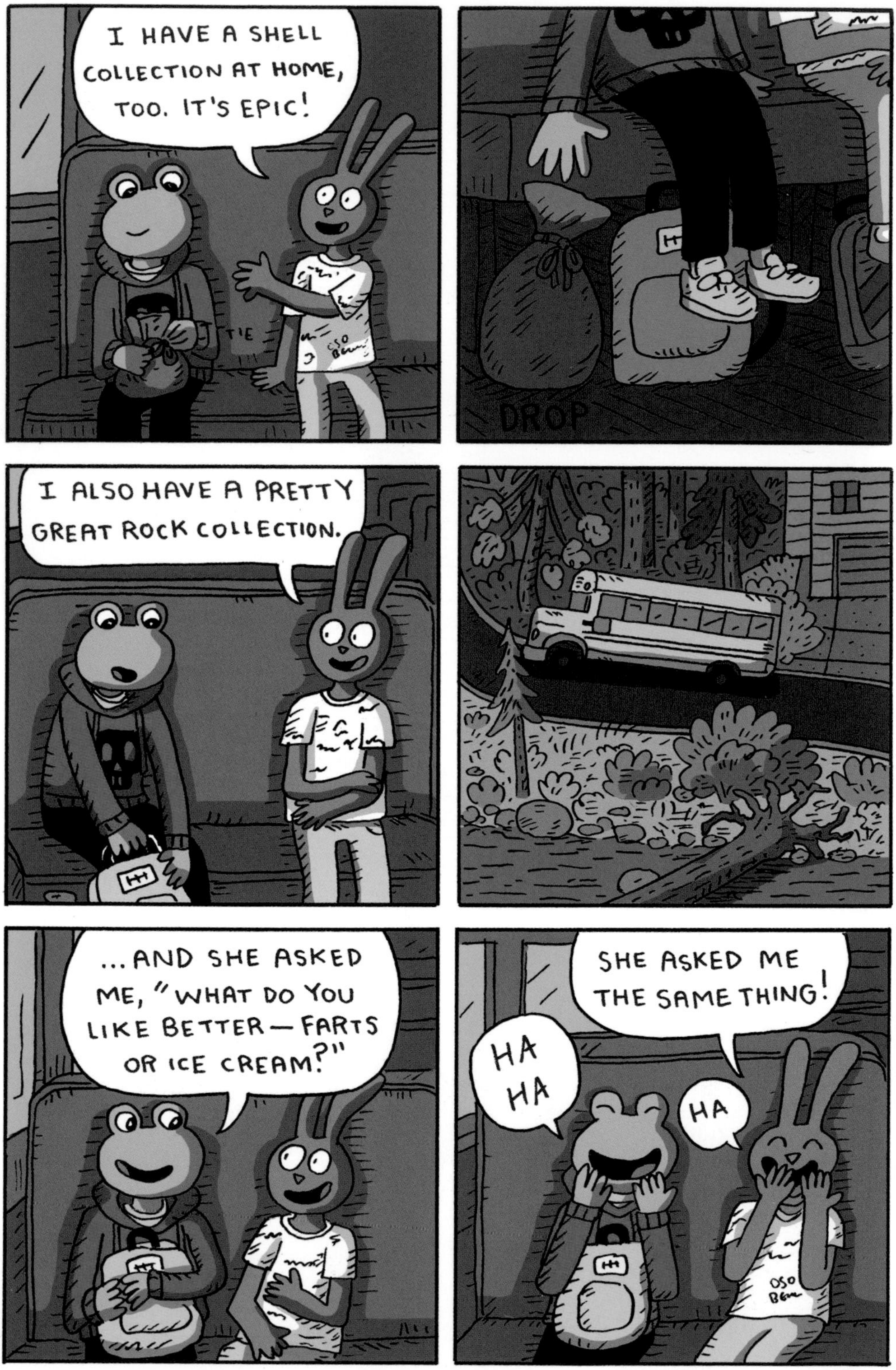
I HAVE A SHELL COLLECTION AT HOME, TOO. IT'S EPIC!
DROP
I ALSO HAVE A PRETTY GREAT ROCK COLLECTION.
...AND SHE ASKED ME, "WHAT DO YOU LIKE BETTER—FARTS OR ICE CREAM?"
SHE ASKED ME THE SAME THING!
HA HA
HA

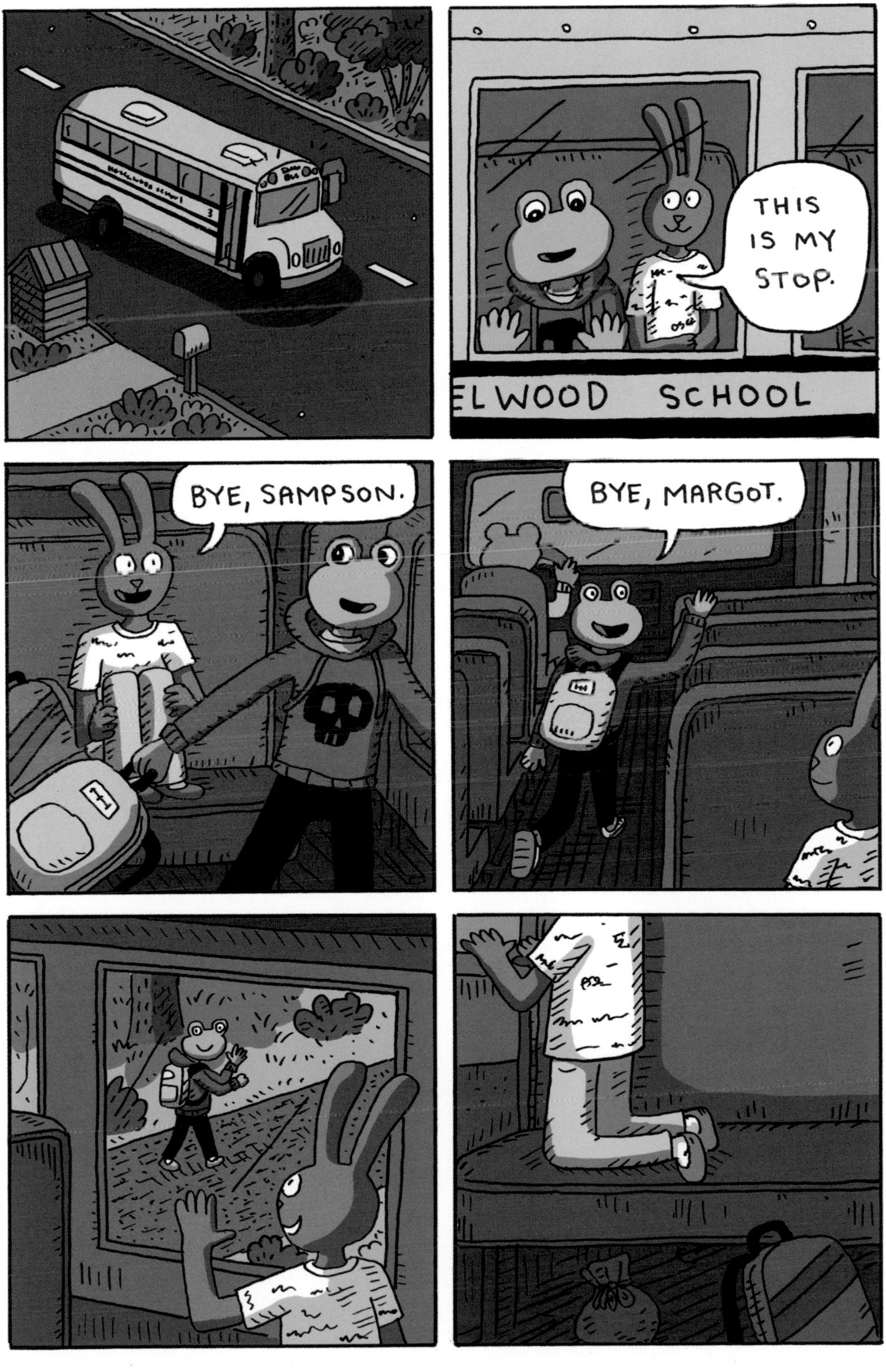
THIS IS MY STOP.
ELWOOD SCHOOL
BYE, SAMPSON.
BYE, MARGOT.

CHAPTER ELEVEN
Knock! Knock!

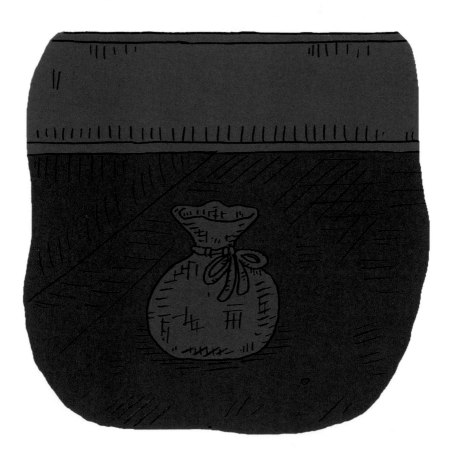

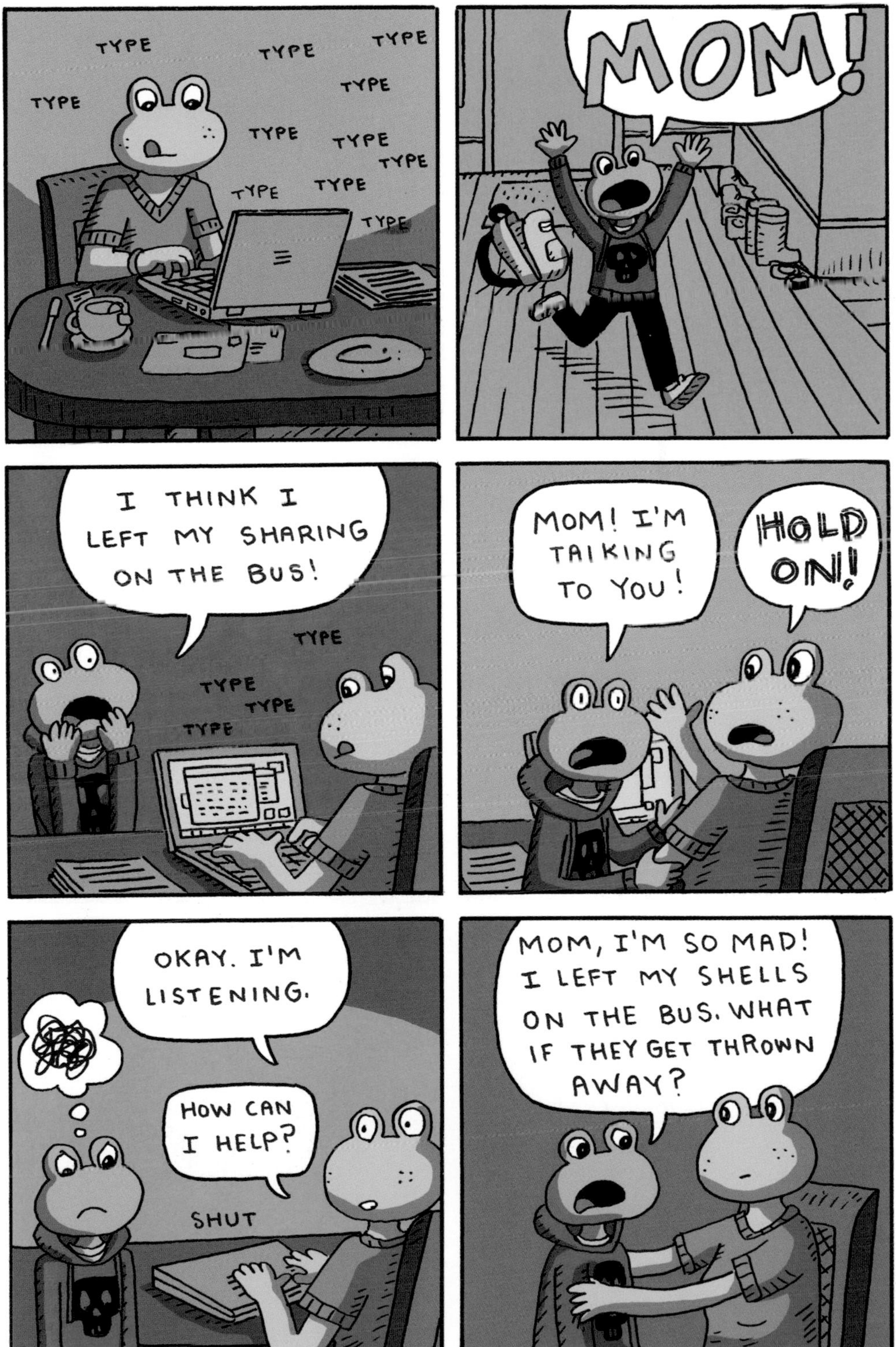
TYPE
TYPE
TYPE
TYPE
TYPE
TYPE
TYPE
TYPE
TYPE
TYPE
TYPE
MOM!
I THINK I LEFT MY SHARING ON THE BUS!
TYPE
TYPE
TYPE
TYPE
MOM! I'M TALKING TO YOU!
HOLD ON!
OKAY. I'M LISTENING.
HOW CAN I HELP?
SHUT
MOM, I'M SO MAD! I LEFT MY SHELLS ON THE BUS. WHAT IF THEY GET THROWN AWAY?

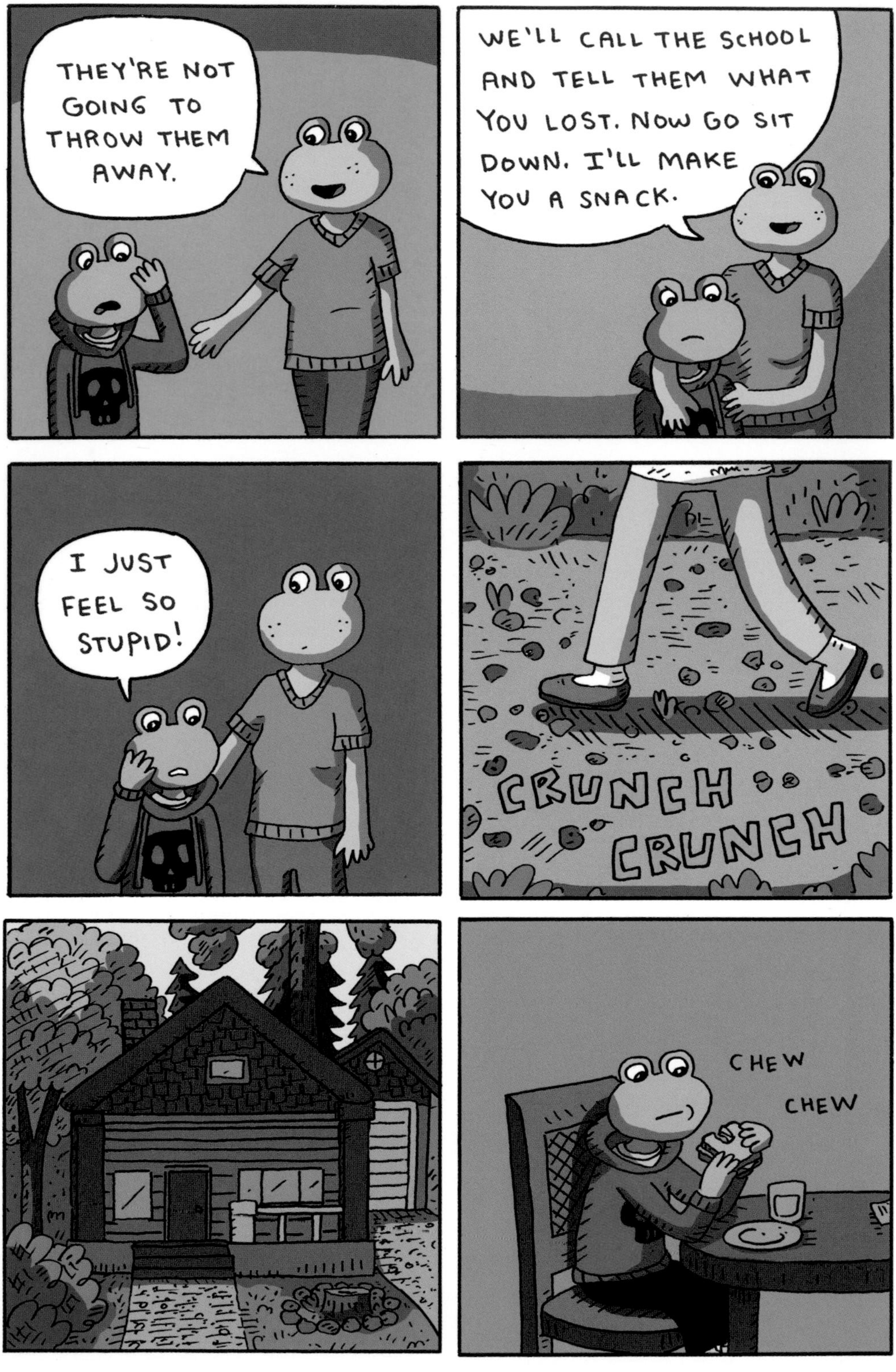
THEY'RE NOT GOING TO THROW THEM AWAY.
WE'LL CALL THE SCHOOL AND TELL THEM WHAT YOU LOST. NOW GO SIT DOWN. I'LL MAKE YOU A SNACK.
I JUST FEEL SO STUPID!
CRUNCH
CRUNCH
CHEW
CHEW

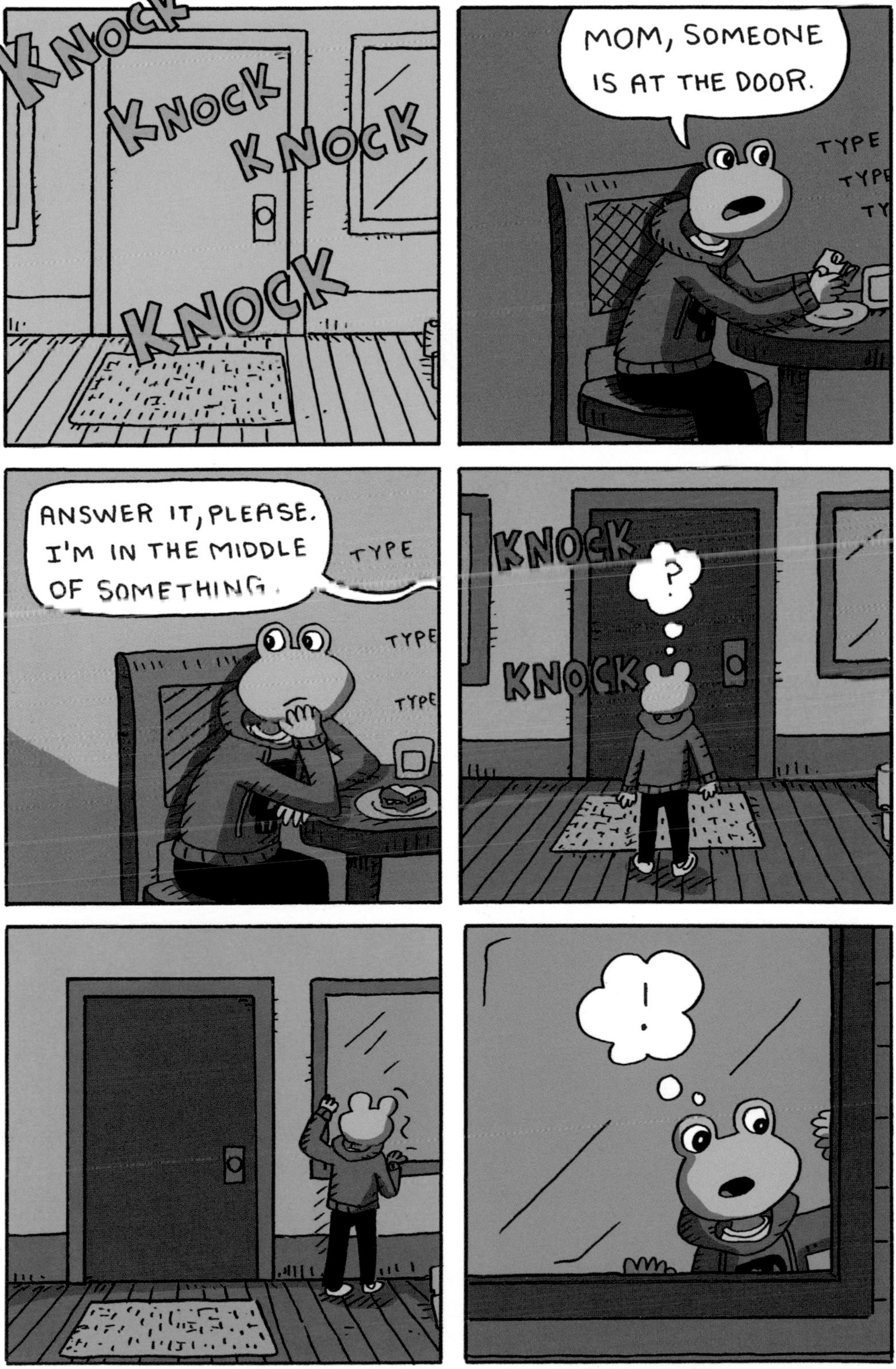
KNOCK
KNOCK
KNOCK
KNOCK
MOM, SOMEONE IS AT THE DOOR.
TYPE
TYPE
ANSWER IT, PLEASE. I'M IN THE MIDDLE OF SOMETHING.
TYPE
TYPE
TYPE
KNOCK
KNOCK
?
!

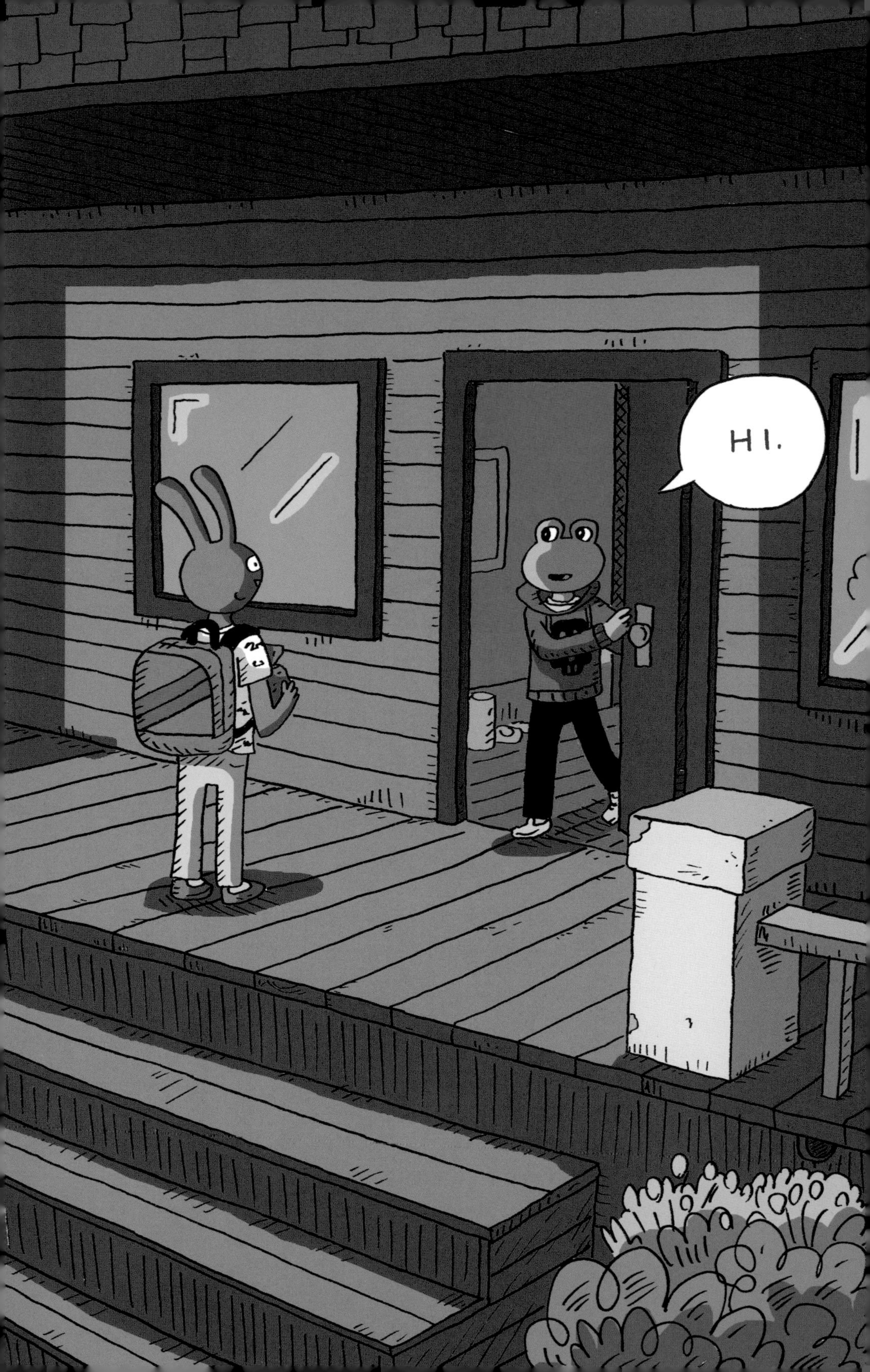
HI.

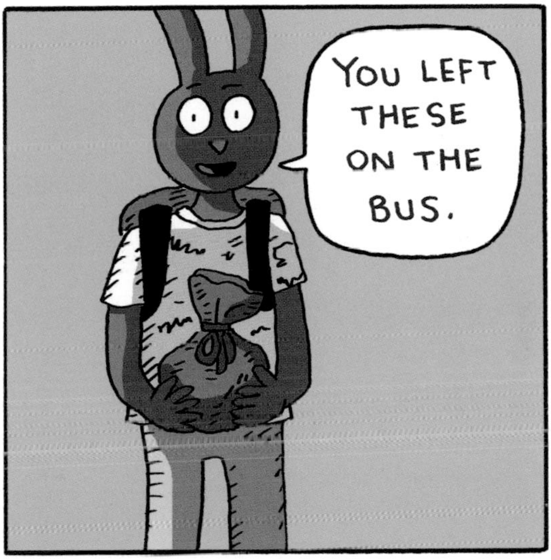
YOU LEFT THESE ON THE BUS.

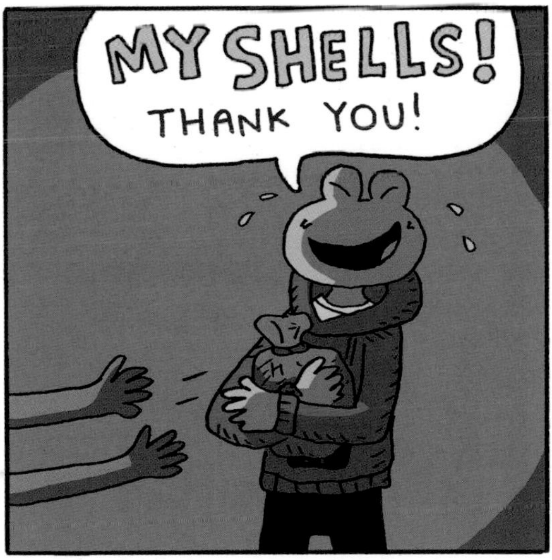
MY SHELLS! THANK YOU!

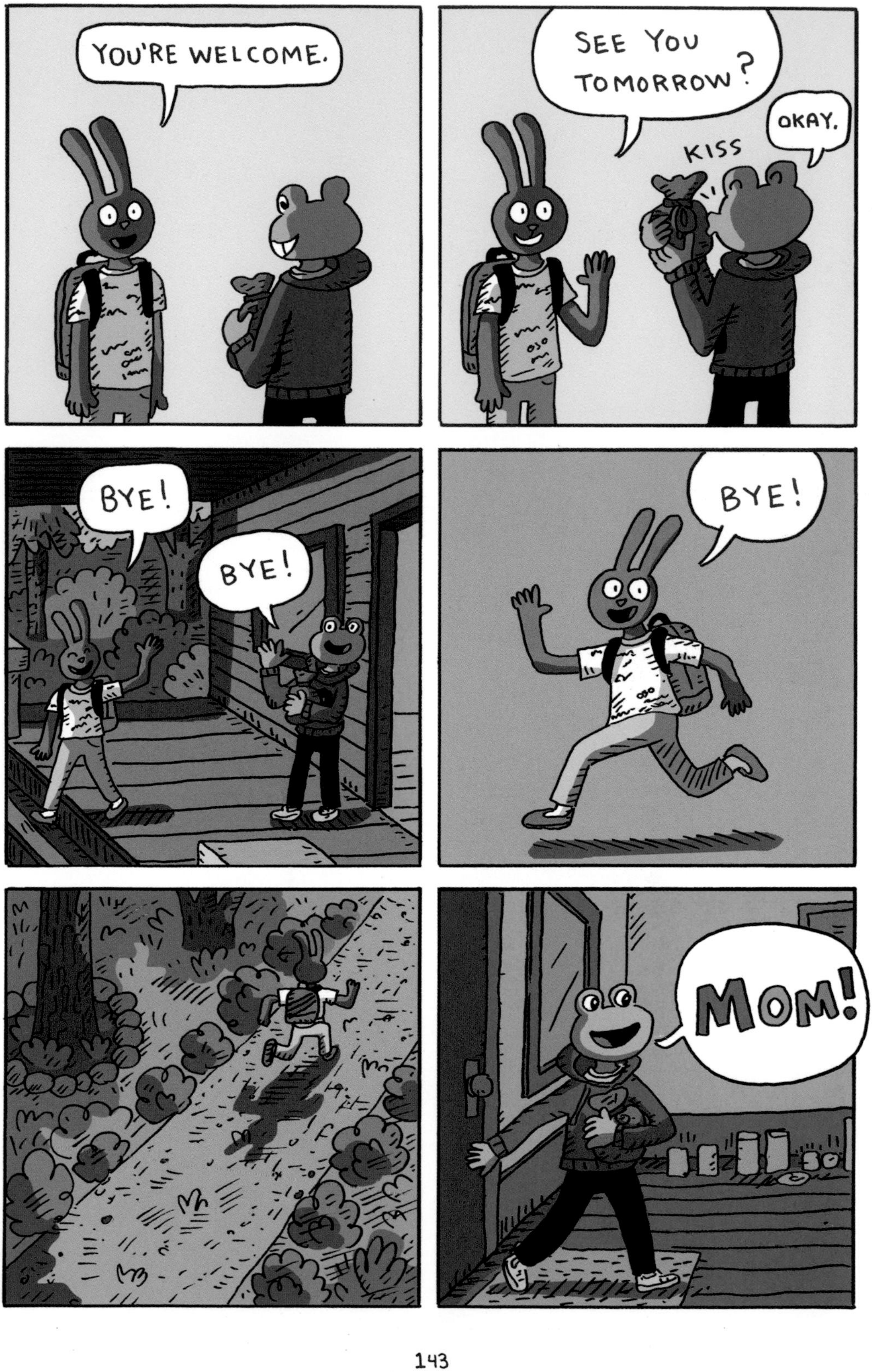

YOU'RE WELCOME.
SEE YOU TOMORROW?
KISS
OKAY.
BYE!
BYE!
BYE!
MOM!

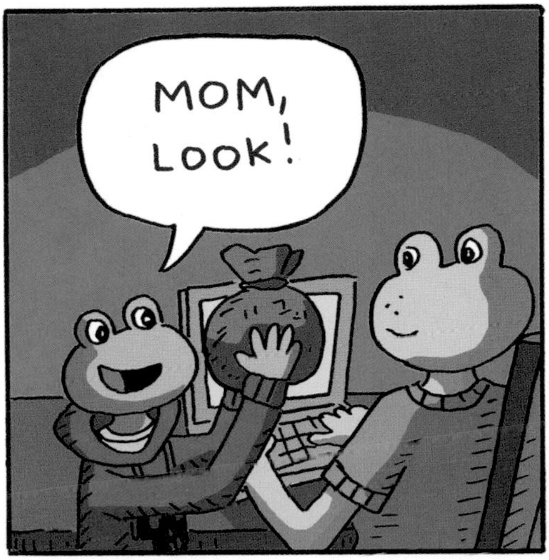
MOM, LOOK!
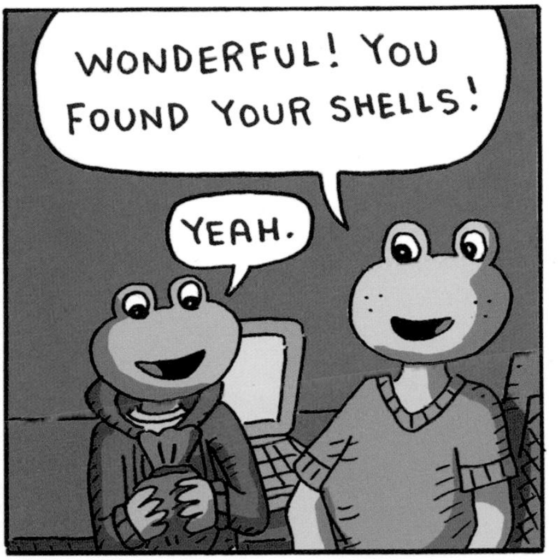
WONDERFUL! YOU FOUND YOUR SHELLS!
YEAH.
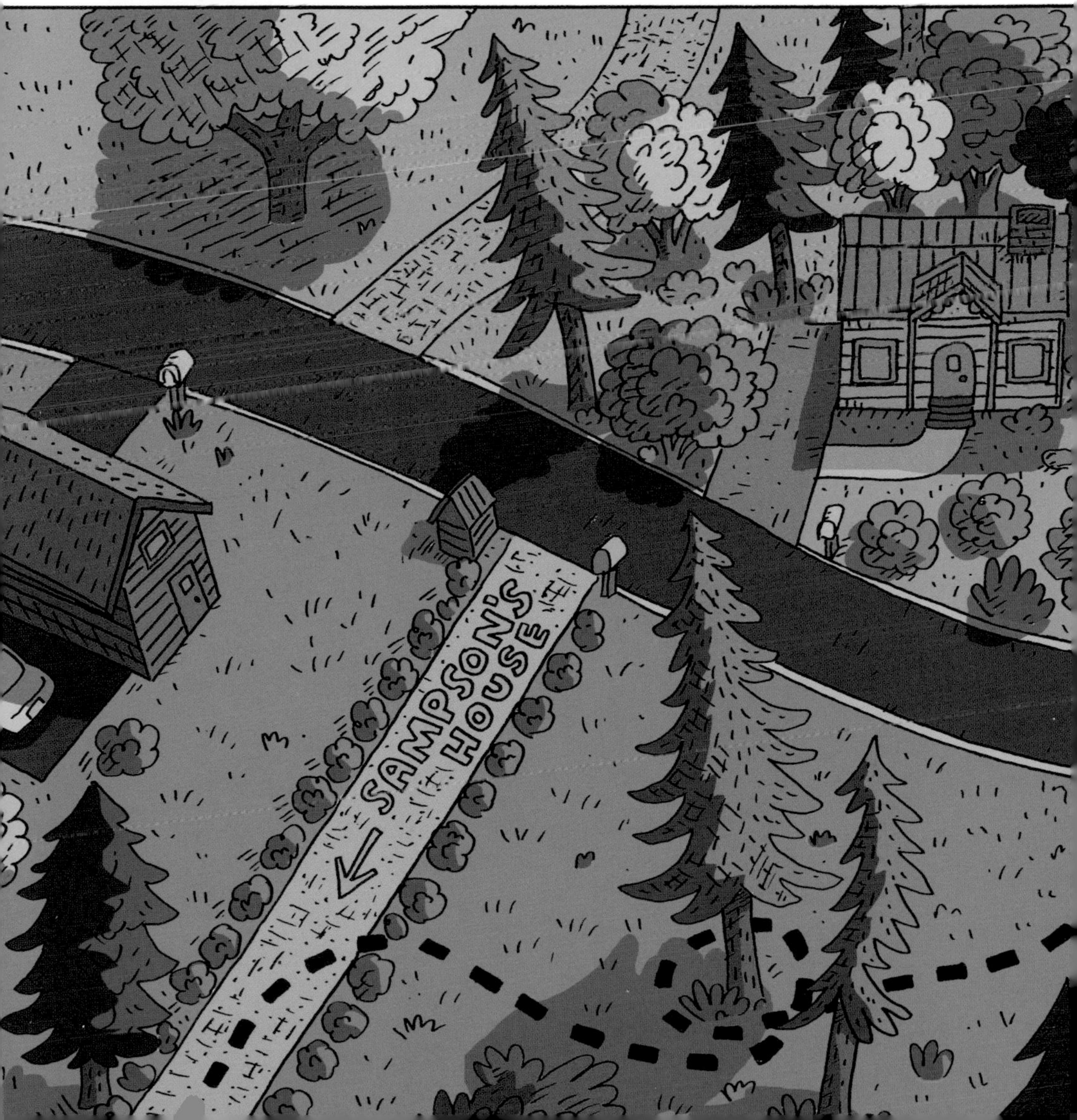
SAMPSON'S HOUSE

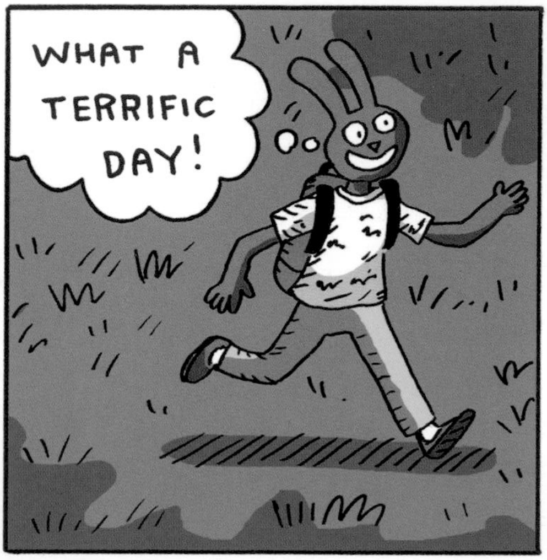
WHAT A TERRIFIC DAY!

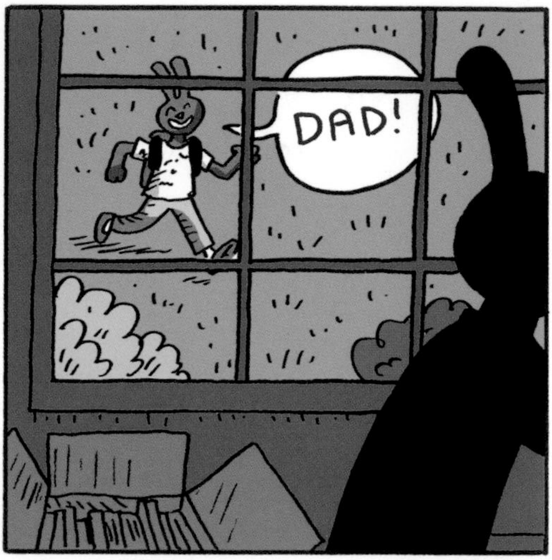
DAD!

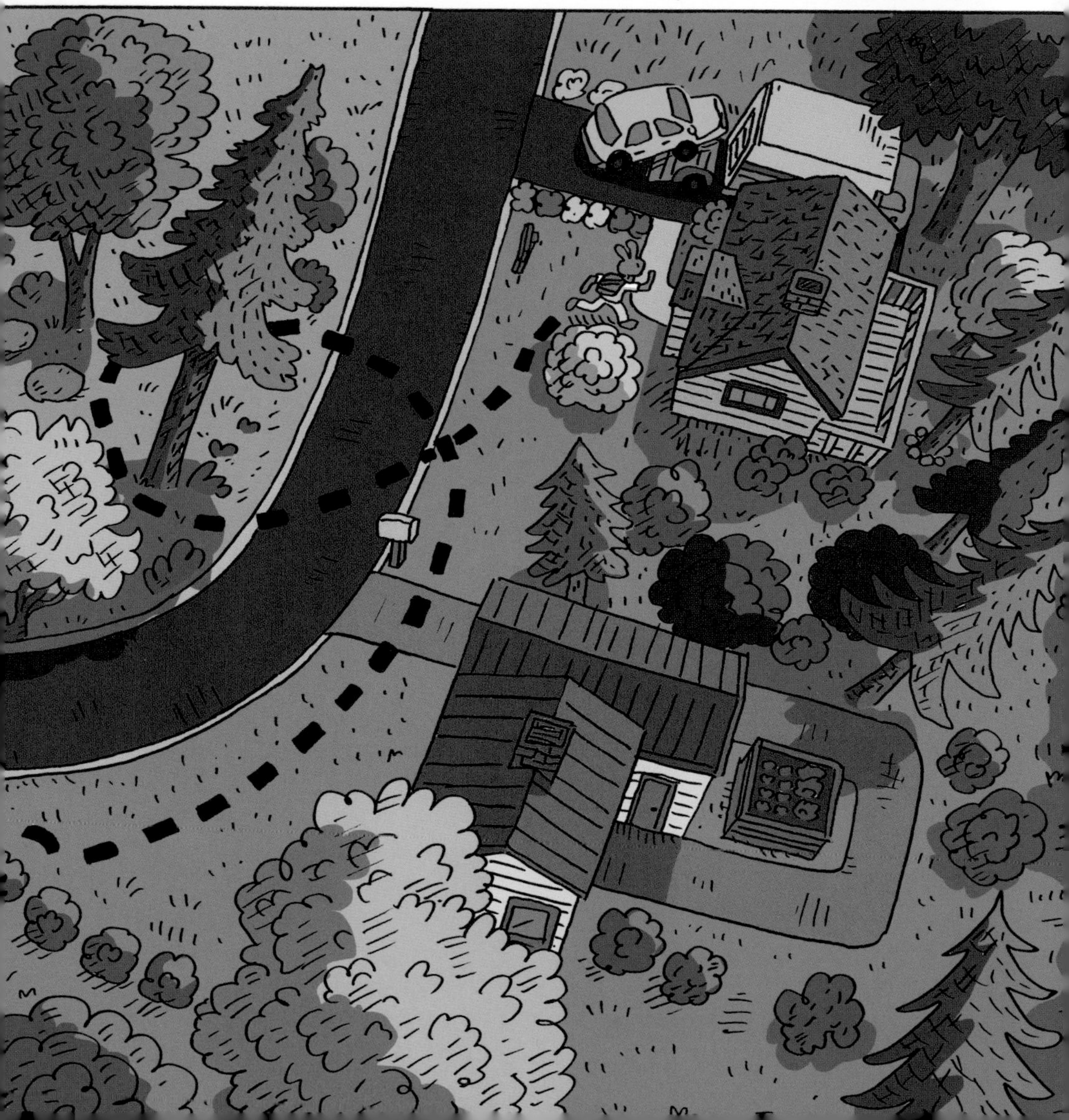

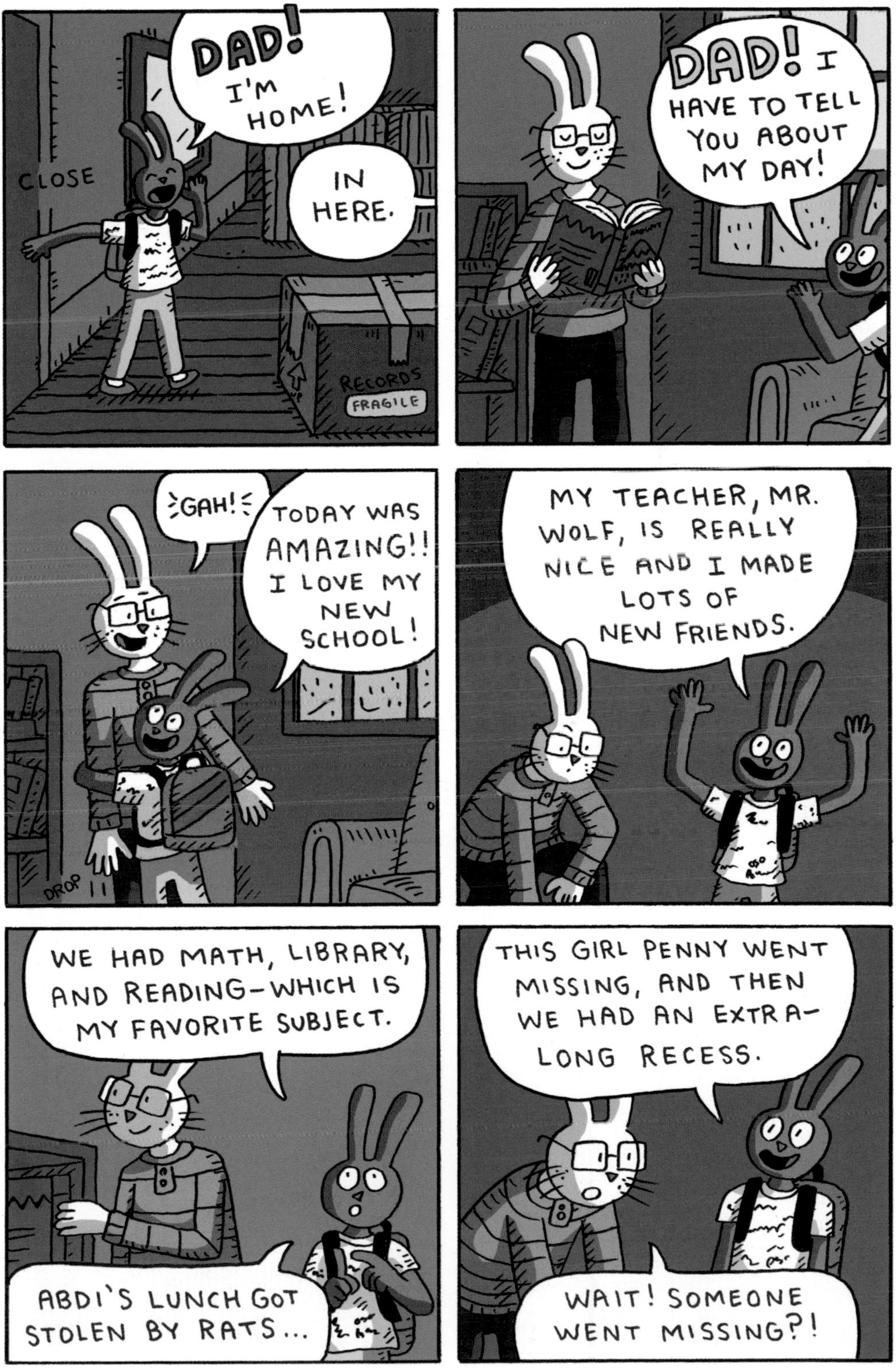
DAD! I'M HOME!
CLOSE
IN HERE.
RECORDS
FRAGILE
DAD! I HAVE TO TELL YOU ABOUT MY DAY!
GAH!
TODAY WAS AMAZING!! I LOVE MY NEW SCHOOL!
DROP
MY TEACHER, MR. WOLF, IS REALLY NICE AND I MADE LOTS OF NEW FRIENDS.
WE HAD MATH, LIBRARY, AND READING—WHICH IS MY FAVORITE SUBJECT.
ABDI'S LUNCH GOT STOLEN BY RATS...
THIS GIRL PENNY WENT MISSING, AND THEN WE HAD AN EXTRA-LONG RECESS.
WAIT! SOMEONE WENT MISSING?!

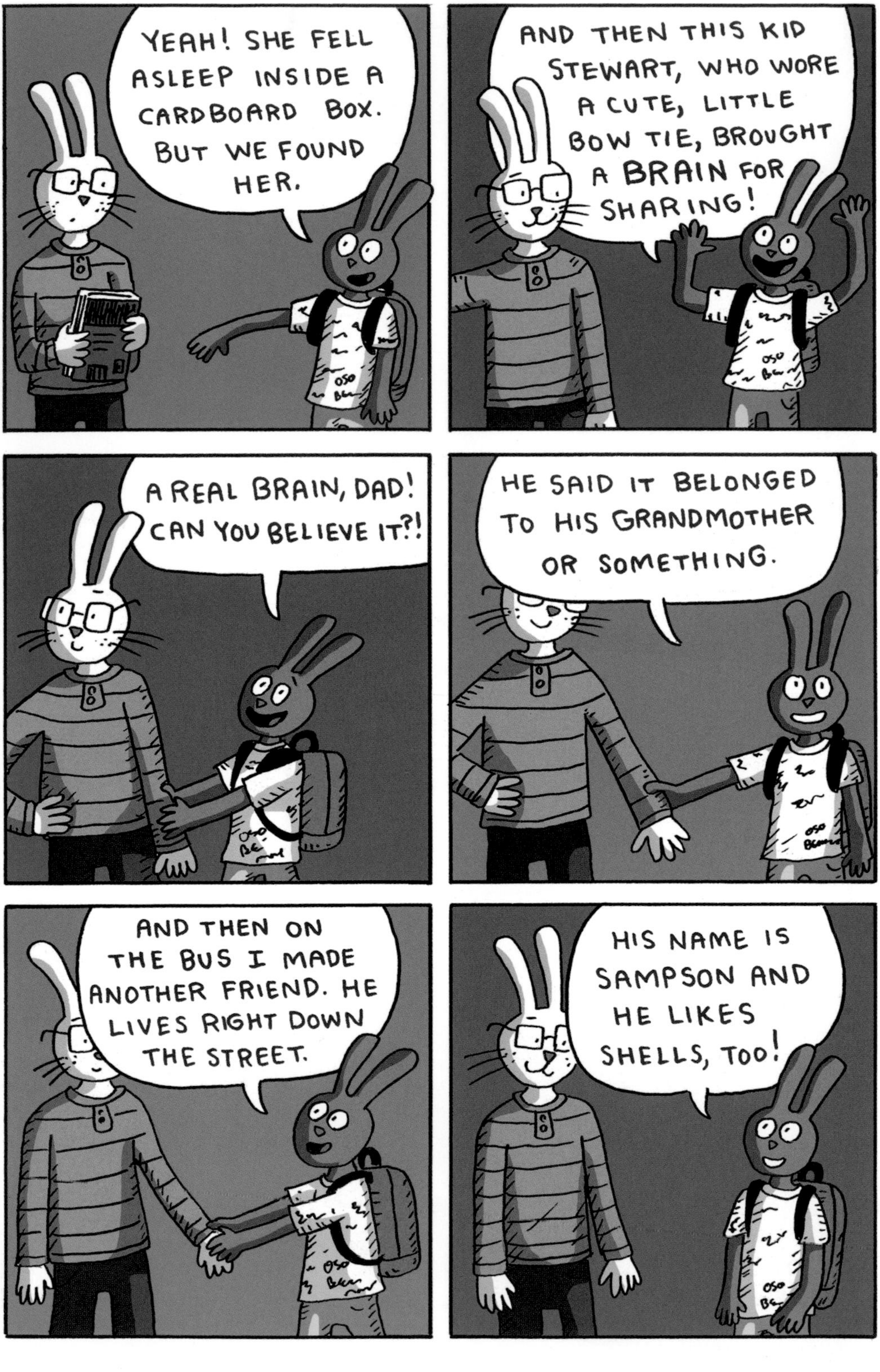
YEAH! SHE FELL ASLEEP INSIDE A CARDBOARD BOX. BUT WE FOUND HER.
AND THEN THIS KID STEWART, WHO WORE A CUTE, LITTLE BOW TIE, BROUGHT A BRAIN FOR SHARING!
A REAL BRAIN, DAD! CAN YOU BELIEVE IT?!
HE SAID IT BELONGED TO HIS GRANDMOTHER OR SOMETHING.
AND THEN ON THE BUS I MADE ANOTHER FRIEND. HE LIVES RIGHT DOWN THE STREET.
HIS NAME IS SAMPSON AND HE LIKES SHELLS, TOO!

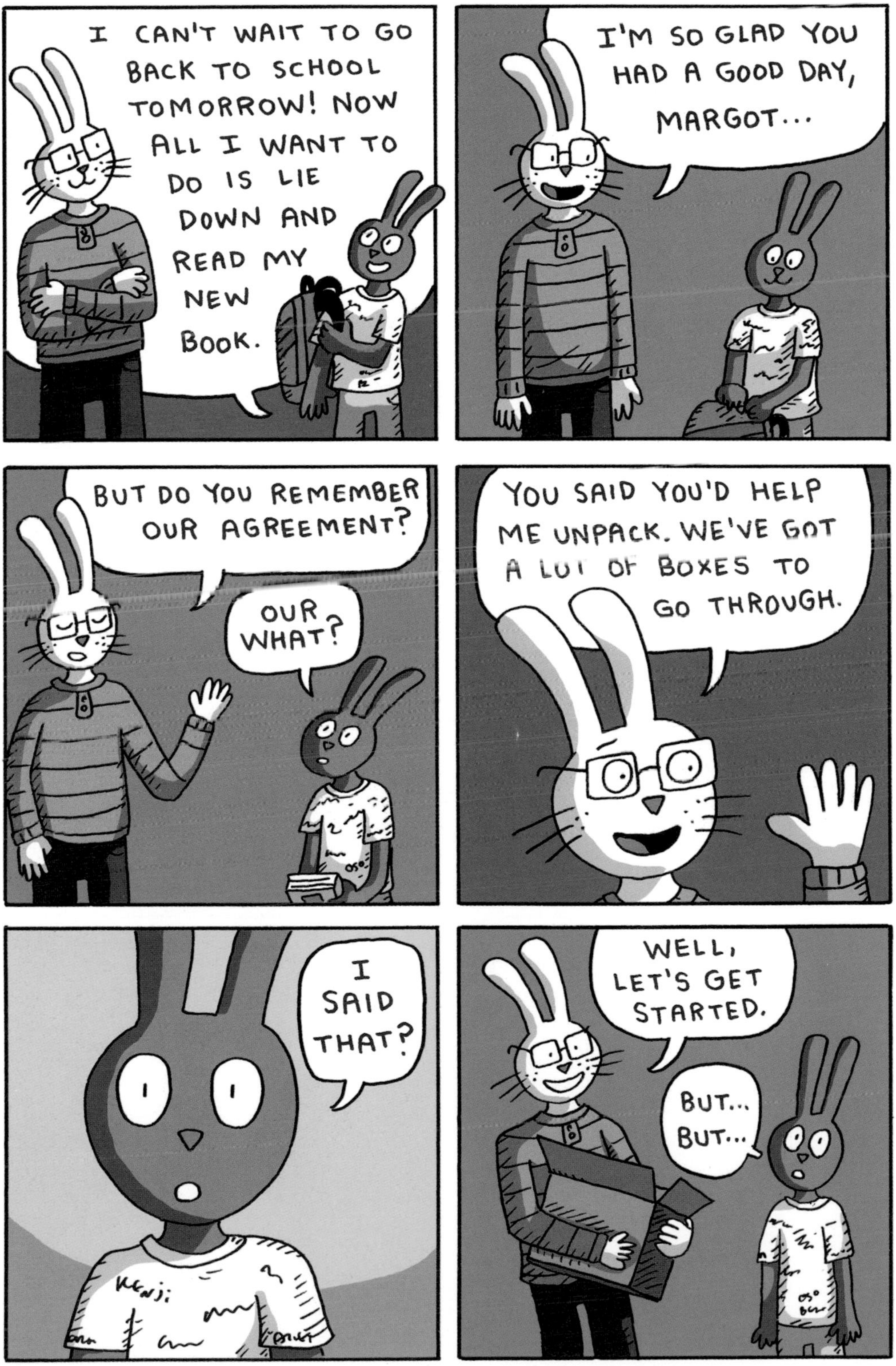
I CAN'T WAIT TO GO BACK TO SCHOOL TOMORROW! NOW ALL I WANT TO DO IS LIE DOWN AND READ MY NEW BOOK.
I'M SO GLAD YOU HAD A GOOD DAY, MARGOT...
BUT DO YOU REMEMBER OUR AGREEMENT?
OUR WHAT?
YOU SAID YOU'D HELP ME UNPACK. WE'VE GOT A LOT OF BOXES TO GO THROUGH.
I SAID THAT?
WELL, LET'S GET STARTED.
BUT... BUT...

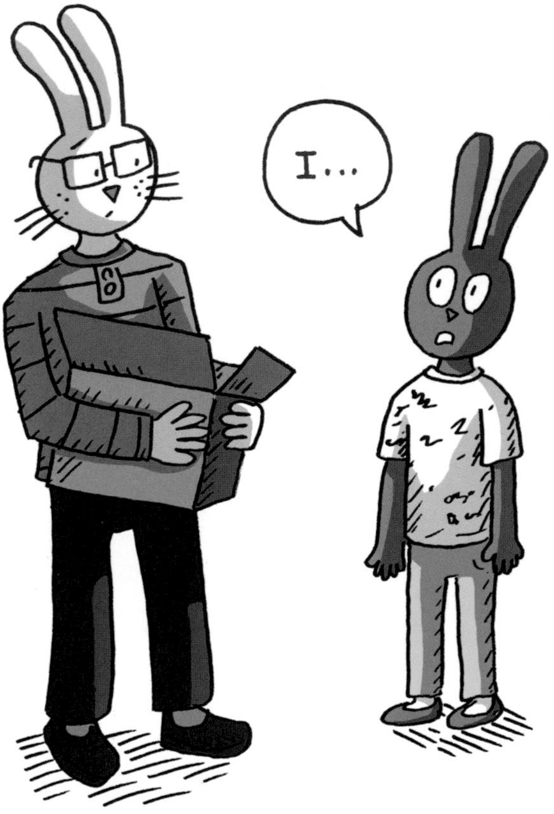
I...

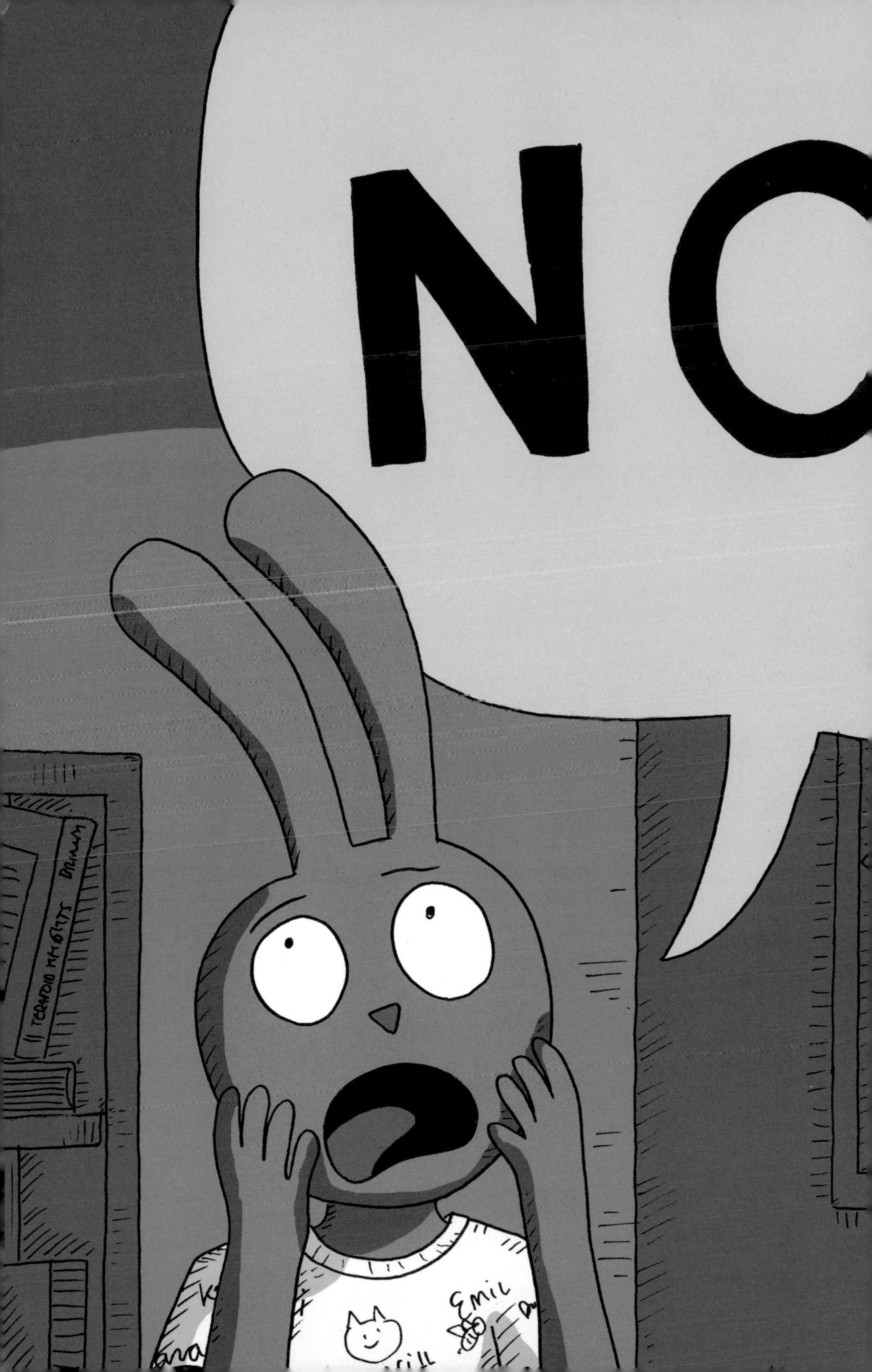
NO

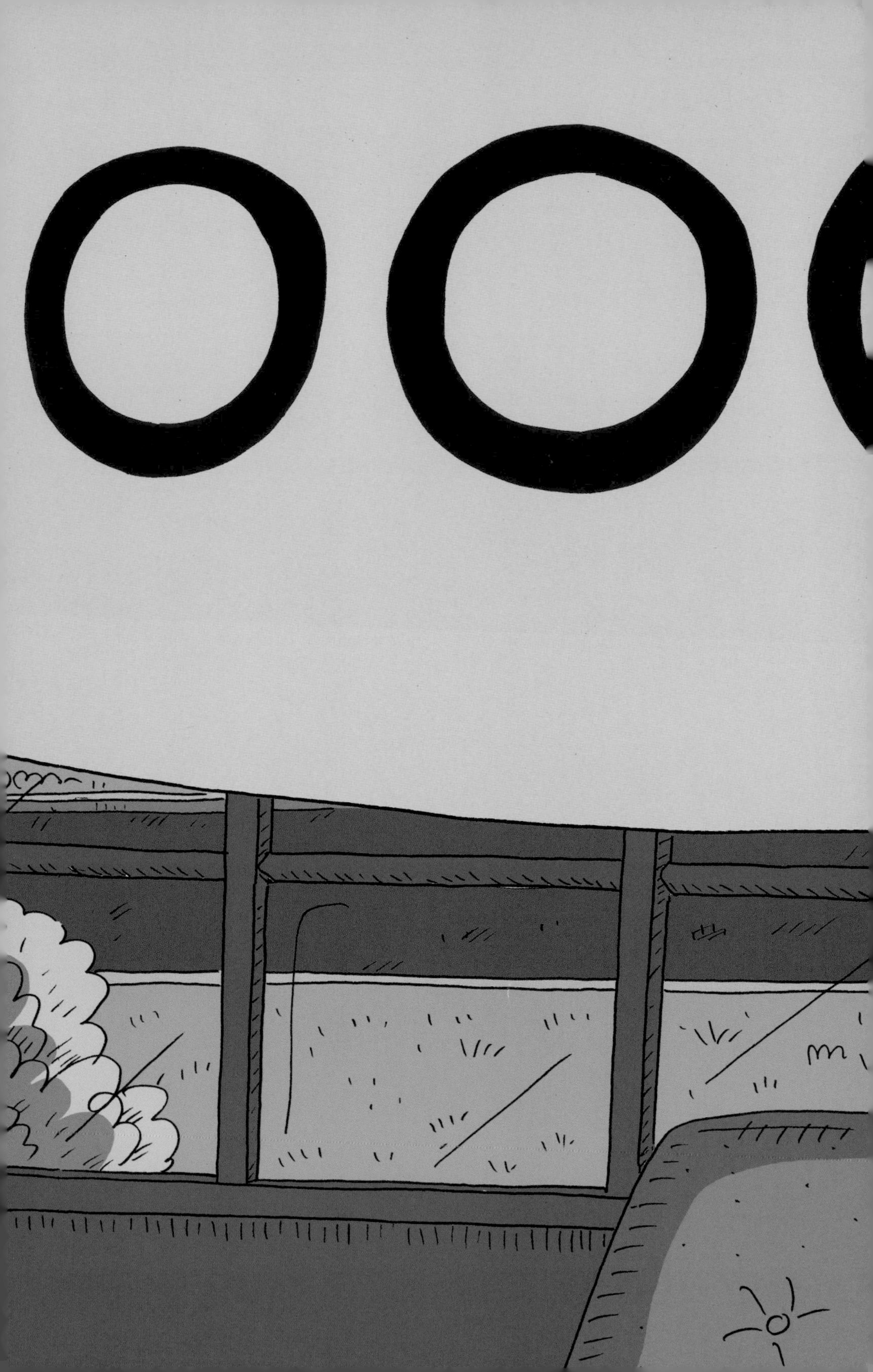
OOO

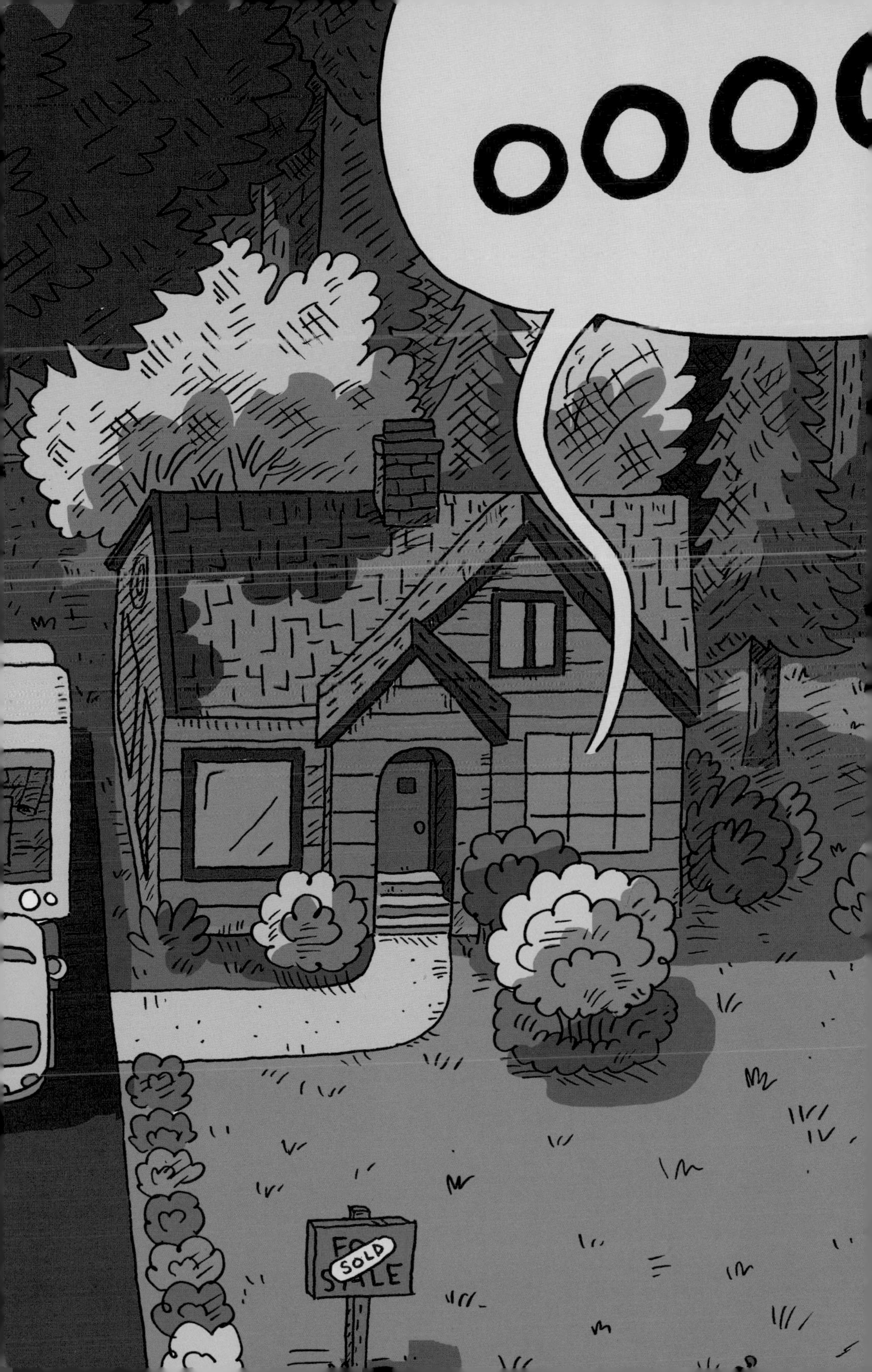
OOOO
SOLD

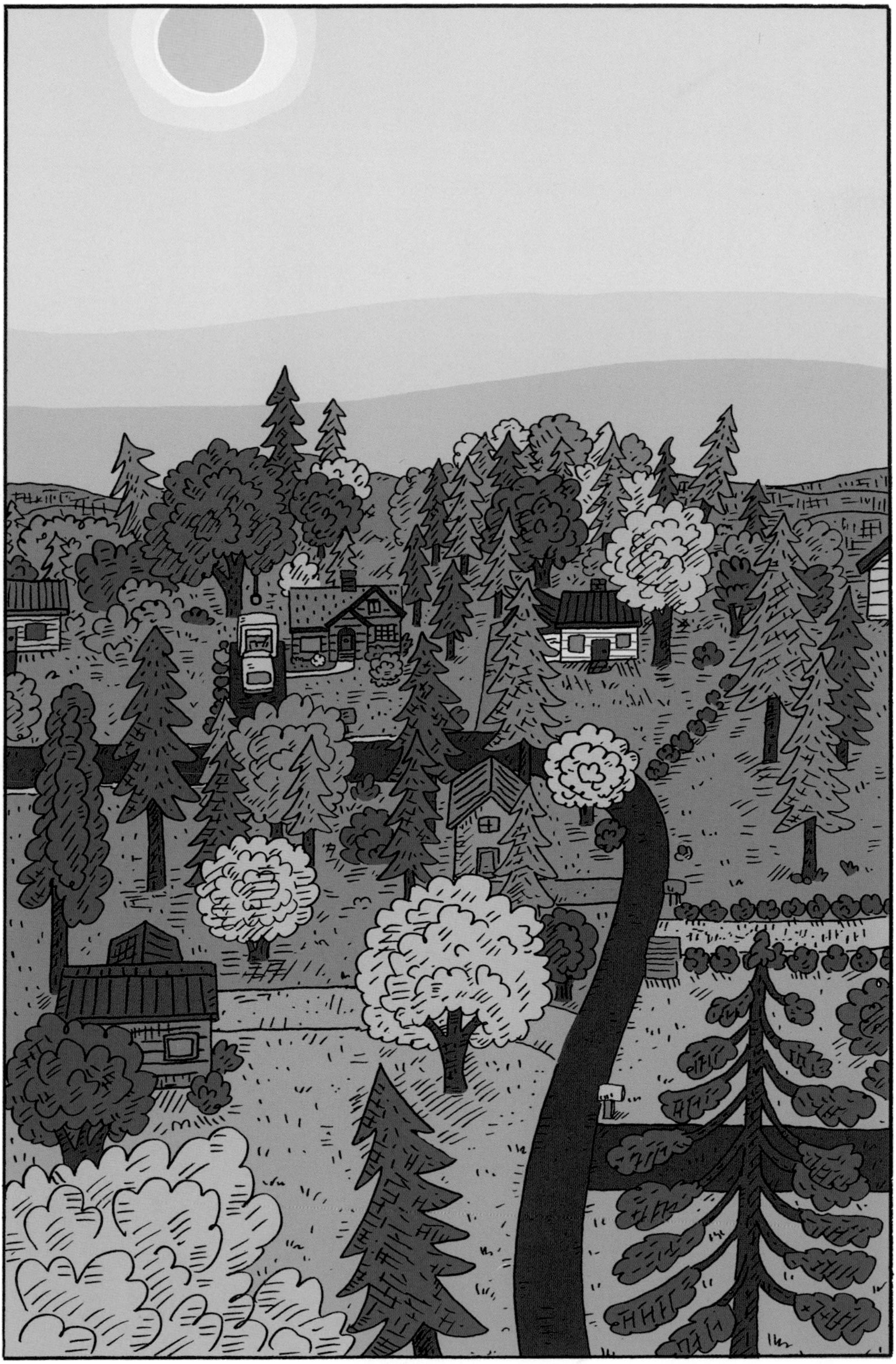

Thank you to . . .

My supportive family: My wife and son, Ariel and Marlen, for putting up with my long hours drawing comics and being the best people I could possibly spend my life with. Mom and Dad, for always encouraging me, sending me to animation school, and spending your golden years fighting climate change. My brother, Jeremy, for being my main artistic influence growing up. My in-laws Lisa and David for all that you do, which is a lot. All my other in-laws, cousins, aunts, and uncles.

My fabulous editor, Cassandra Pelham Fulton, Phil Falco, David Saylor, and everyone at Graphix. Thank you!!!

My agent, Judy Hansen, for looking out and being a boss.

Dylan Williams, Emily Nilsson, and Greg Means, for taking the risk to publish my first book. I love you all. Rest in peace, Dylan. You were a bright light for many.

All of my wonderful students that I've had over the years. I believe the key to a brighter and more peaceful future rests within the hearts, minds, and future actions of our children. I can't wait to see what you all grow up to become. I hope you are happy, healthy, and standing up for justice.

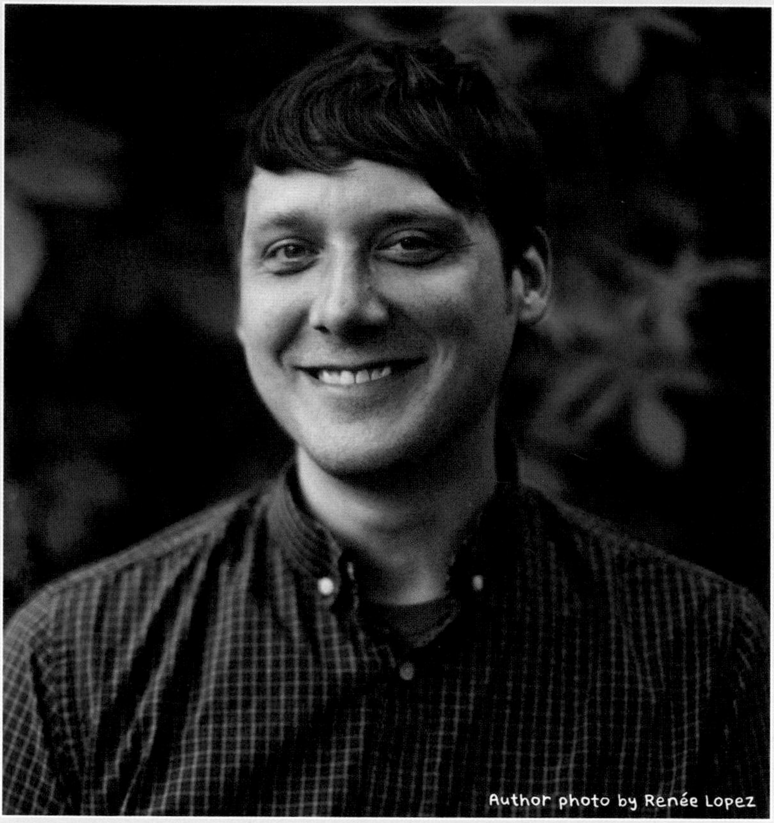
Author photo by Renée Lopez

Aron Nels Steinke is the Eisner Award-winning illustrator and coauthor, with Ariel Cohn, of *The Zoo Box*. After graduating from Vancouver Film School with a specialization in hand-drawn animation, he discovered the magic of making comics and hasn't looked back since. He teaches fifth graders by day and draws comics by night in Portland, Oregon, where he lives with his wife, Ariel, and their Robin Hood-obsessed son, Marlen. In the summer, when he's not hunched over a drawing board, you might find him swimming the frigid rivers of the Cascade Mountains or possibly hugging a tree.

Don't miss the next adventure in Mr. Wolf's class!

MYSTERY CLUB

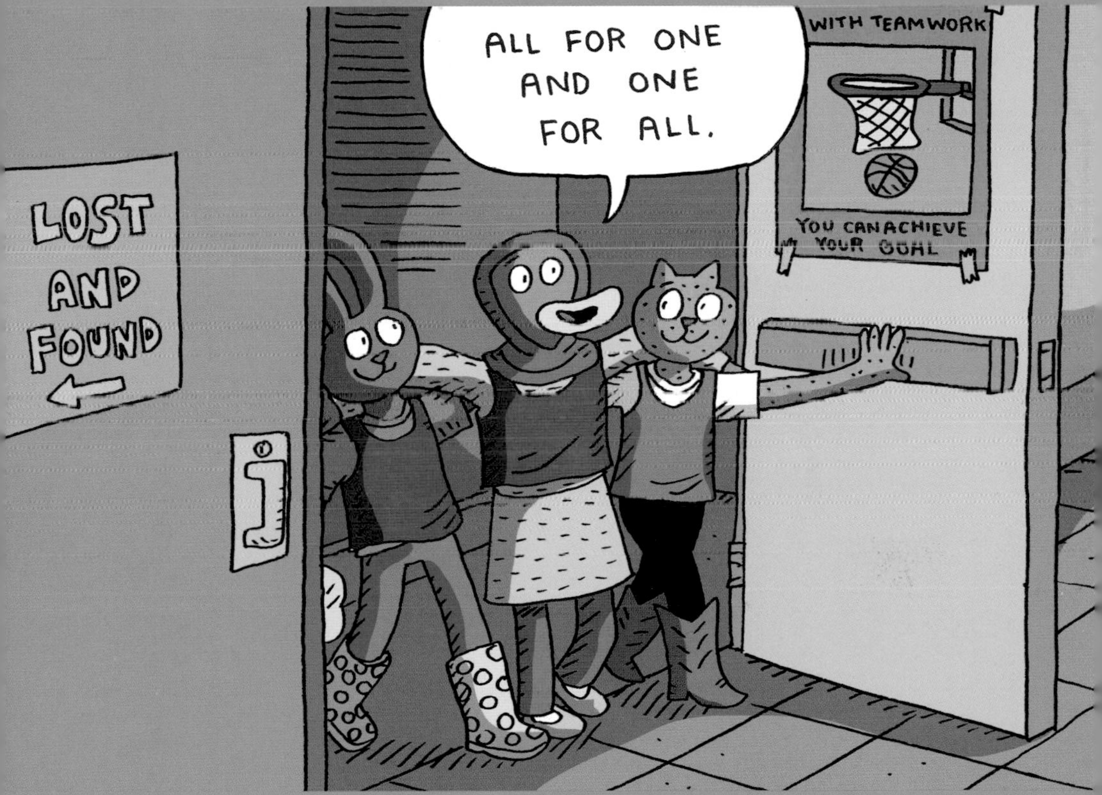
ALL FOR ONE AND ONE FOR ALL.
WITH TEAMWORK
YOU CAN ACHIEVE YOUR GOAL
LOST AND FOUND